HIGHER HOPE

HIGHER HOPE

Book Two in the Tides of Truth series

ROBERT WHITLOW

THOMAS NELSON
Since 1798

NASHVILLE   DALLAS   MEXICO CITY   RIO DE JANEIRO   BEIJING

Published in Nashville, Tennessee, by Thomas Nelson. Thomas Nelson is a registered trademark of Thomas Nelson, Inc.

Thomas Nelson, Inc. books may be purchased in bulk for educational, business, fund-raising, or sales promotional use. For information, please e-mail SpecialMarkets@ThomasNelson.com.

Scripture quotations are taken from the Holy Bible, New International Version®. © 1973, 1978, 1984 by International Bible Society. Used by permission of Zondervan Publishing House. All rights reserved; the New King James Version. © 1982 by Thomas Nelson, Inc. Used by permission. All rights reserved; and the King James Version of the Holy Bible.

Publisher's Note: This novel is a work of fiction. Names, characters, places, and incidents are either products of the author's imagination or used fictitiously. All characters are fictional, and any similarity to people living or dead is purely coincidental.

Library of Congress Cataloging-in-Publication Data

Whitlow, Robert, 1954–
   Higher hope / Robert Whitlow.
      p. cm. — (A tides of truth novel)
   ISBN 978-1-59554-449-0 (pbk.)
    1. Women lawyers—Fiction. 2. Trials (Libel)—Fiction. 3. Savannah (Ga.)—Fiction.
I. Title.
   PS3573.H49837H54 2009
   813'.54—dc22

2009003618

Printed in the United States of America

09 10 11 12 RRD 5 4 3 2

To those who believe hope is possible.
May it become substance in your life.

Against all hope, Abraham in hope believed.

—Romans 4:18

Prologue

THE AFTERNOON THUNDERSTORM THRASHED SAVANNAH WITH wet whips, the raindrops falling in waves that raced across the ground. Dark clouds spawned thin streaks of lightning that reached out with flashing fingers to bridge the gap between heaven and earth. One bolt struck the mast of a sailing yacht bobbing at anchor in a marina and destroyed the boat's electronic navigation system before blowing an exit hole in the ship's side that caused water to seep into the forward cabin. Vacationers on the beach and golfers on the greens ran for shelter. Shoppers at grocery stores backed up at the exits with their carts full. Residents of the city turned off air conditioners as the temperature dropped twenty degrees in ten minutes. Everyone sought cover to wait out the storm.

Everyone, that is, except one.

Ramona Dabney didn't budge from the blue rocker on the narrow front porch of her house. The porch was only six feet wide and completely open at the sides. No railing or screen provided decoration or protection. Three wooden steps led down to the scraggly yard. The porch roof shielded against only gentle showers and noonday sun and held no hope of protecting the small area from the approaching storm. Dabney rocked vigorously and glared at the darkening sky.

Storms made her angry.

The first large drops of rain cried out in insult and accusation as they splattered against the hot ground. Within minutes the drops merged into a waterfall that needed no river as its source. More lightning crackled. A car, its wipers vainly trying to clear the windshield, drove slowly down the street as water spilled out of the storm drains. While local gardeners gave thanks for the moisture, wet wind soaked the porch and the woman on it. Dabney rose to her feet.

It was time to confront the storm.

She moved to the top of the steps. A wave of rain ran across the ground and drenched her. She slowly maneuvered her overweight body down the steps to the ground. Her gray hair was plastered to her head, and the raindrops stung as they hit her skin. She walked to a spot about halfway between the house and the street and stopped. Tilting her head back with her eyes closed, she let the anger within build until it was stronger than the liquid bullets pounding against her. She raised her hands in the air and cried out in a voice that cracked from frequent use.

"Stop! Stop! Stop!"

Another wave of rain rushed across the yard and doused her. Distant thunder at the edge of the storm mocked her. She kept her hands in the air, refusing to budge. She cried out again.

"Stop!"

Dabney held firm, remaining in the front yard with her hands in the air. A police vehicle containing two officers slowed in front of the house. The driver, a seasoned detective, turned to his younger partner.

"Do you see that? It's been a while since I came by here during a thunderstorm."

The younger officer leaned across the seat and looked out the window.

"What is she doing? She's got to be soaked to the bone."

"Telling the storm to stop."

The younger officer grunted, "Somebody should tell her the clouds aren't listening."

1

PUTTING MY HAND ON THE BRASS DOORKNOB, I GLANCED AT MY watch before opening the door. Zach and I wouldn't get to Powell Station before dark unless we left Savannah within the hour. Mama and Daddy shouldn't see the young lawyer's light brown ponytail for the first time after sunset.

On the wall of the conference room hung a massive painting of the Savannah waterfront before the Civil War. At the end of the shiny table sat Joe Carpenter, the managing partner of Braddock, Appleby, and Carpenter. To his left was Myra Dean, a litigation paralegal. Across the table was a man I'd never met.

"Tami," Mr. Carpenter said, "this is Mr. Jason Paulding."

Paulding, a balding, stocky man in his early forties, wore an open-collared shirt with a steel beam embroidered on the front. His round head would be the perfect resting place for a hard hat.

"Any projects you have to finish before the end of the day?" Mr. Carpenter asked me.

"No, sir, but—"

"Good," the tall, gray-haired lawyer continued. "As soon as Jason started going over his problem, I knew this was a case for you. You know something about fanatic religious groups, don't you?"

"No, sir, except what I read in the paper. I've never been to the Middle East."

Mr. Carpenter smiled slightly. "I don't mean terrorists. I'm talking about the lunatic fringe of the church, fundamentalists who don't know where religion stops and tolerance begins." The lawyer turned toward Paulding. "Tami is one of the sharpest summer law clerks we've ever had at the firm. She goes to church every time the doors open, but her beliefs make her tougher, not softer. There's no 'turn the other cheek' in her version of the Bible. A week ago she stared me down in a criminal matter when I challenged her judgment."

His assessment of my conduct in *State v. Jones* made me wince.

"Mr. Carpenter, that's not quite accurate—"

"Don't argue with me, now," the senior partner said, cutting me off. "Save your ammunition for Ramona Dabney, the dime-store preacher who claims Mr. Paulding is the reincarnation of Adolf Hitler."

"It's worse than that," Paulding said, "and I want it stopped. I offered the church twice the appraised value for its property. All I got back was a bunch of harassing phone calls to people all over town."

"Jason and his staff have done some of the homework for us," Mr. Carpenter said, sliding a sheet of paper across the table. "This is a list of people contacted by Dabney."

"She even organized a protest outside our corporate office."

"Myra, copy this list for Tami, divide the names, and interview all of them. There may be more. Get affidavits or recorded statements from those willing to sign one, then provide a summary to me."

"What are we asking them?" I asked.

"Everything you can think of," Mr. Carpenter said. "Don't let anyone try to tell you what they think is important; find out for yourself. Persistence is one of your strengths. Use it."

Mr. Carpenter's mind could race ahead so fast it was difficult to see more than a cloud of dust in the distance. If patient, I hoped a fuller explanation of my task would emerge when he came back into view. I pushed my long brown hair behind my ears.

"When do you want the summaries and affidavits?" Myra asked.

My stomach turned over. A twenty-three-year-old summer clerk wasn't supposed to work overtime, but Mr. Carpenter had started treating me more and more like a junior associate.

"In the next few weeks."

I sighed in relief.

"Why wait?" Paulding asked indignantly. "With what I've told you and prepared in advance, don't you have enough to file suit?"

"Our representation is similar to your company building a shopping center. We follow a carefully laid-out plan to make sure we're thorough."

"I don't want a fancy lawsuit that takes three years," Paulding said, his voice rising. "Last week this woman wrote my wife a letter accusing me of all kinds of stuff. I know how lawyers drag things out. If you're not going to do anything, I'll find a cheaper lawyer who will. I want a court order putting a stop to this. And I want it now!"

"No you don't," Mr. Carpenter replied calmly. "It's good for you and your business if Ms. Dabney continues."

"What?" Paulding burst out, the veins in his neck bulging. "That's crazy. Are you an idiot?"

Stretching my long fingers, I put my pen on the table, certain Paulding was about to be ushered out of the office. Mr. Carpenter had plenty of business; he didn't need to put up with abuse from a prospective client.

"Who referred you to me?" Mr. Carpenter asked calmly.

Paulding rubbed the top of his head. "Frank Newsome."

"Did he accuse me of wasting time by churning his file to make a big fee?"

"No."

"What did he tell you?"

"That you saved his company when he thought he was going to lose everything."

"How is his business doing now?"

"Fine. He does a lot of subcontracting work for us. The Dabney woman went to see him with one of her crazy visions. He ordered her out of his office and told me to call you."

Mr. Carpenter pointed at me. "Ms. Taylor can work on your file for a fraction of my hourly rate. Does that sound like I'm trying to take advantage of you?"

"No, but it doesn't make sense that you want this preacher woman running her mouth all over town. If this keeps up, she's going to hurt our business. She already has."

"Good, good, that's even better," Mr. Carpenter replied, holding up his hand before Paulding could explode again. "Hear me out. How much profit did you expect to make from the development your company was going to build on the site that included the church?"

"I gave up on that deal. The church parcel was in the middle of the entire tract. Without it, the project wouldn't work."

"Was it a good opportunity?"

"Yeah, one of the best ever."

"So, what did you hope to clear?"

Paulding scratched his chin. "At least a million and a half after costs, maybe more. The anchor tenants were already lined up."

"Would you still like the deal to go through?"

"Sure. We were counting on it so much that I passed on another great opportunity. The whole thing left us losing money for the quarter, probably for the year."

Mr. Carpenter picked up a sheet of paper. "According to the copy of the deed in your file, the property is owned by Ramona Dabney, individually, not the church."

"That's what my real-estate lawyer told me."

"Tami, what do you think about that arrangement? An individual owning the property where a church is located?"

"Most church property is owned by trustees selected by the congregation or held by a denomination."

"That's the way it is at my church," Mr. Carpenter said. "Not so at the Southside Church. God's green acres on Gillespie Street are controlled by Reverend Dabney."

Mr. Carpenter's sarcastic tone made me uneasy. All ministers deserved at least token respect.

The older lawyer continued. "Jason, would you be happy if I could get an injunction ordering Dabney to stop defaming you and set her up so that if she violates the order, a judge would hold her in contempt and put her in jail?"

"Now you're talking."

Mr. Carpenter turned to me. "Tami, is obtaining an injunction difficult when there haven't been threats of physical violence?"

"Yes, sir. It would be a prior restraint against free speech."

Paulding cut in. "She's told people that I'm one of the biggest sinners in Savannah."

"Which is up to the Almighty, not her," Mr. Carpenter answered dryly. "Seeking an injunction can be part of our claim. I also recommend a civil suit against Dabney, seeking damages for libel and slander—libel for what she's written, slander for what she's said. Some of her statements are so bad there's no need to prove a negative economic impact on your business to state a claim, but it always helps to show a jury that malicious words cost dollars. When that happens, the case moves beyond hurt feelings and creates an opportunity for a significant money judgment against her."

"Which is a waste of your time and my money," Paulding grunted. "Dabney drives a beat-up car and lives beside the church in a house the fire department should burn down for practice. I want the injunction. A money judgment would be worthless."

"No, sir." Mr. Carpenter rubbed his neatly trimmed goatee. "You're wrong. A civil judgment is exactly what you need. Because Dabney owns the church property individually, it's not protected by a nonprofit denomination or board of trustees. If you have a judgment against her, you can levy on the church and house to satisfy what's owed."

"Yes," Myra muttered, her fingers flying across the keyboard.

"How much is the property worth as raw land without the buildings?" Mr. Carpenter asked Paulding.

"Standing alone or as part of our larger tract?"

"Alone."

"Not much." Paulding shrugged. "The buildings don't add value since they'd have to be torn down before something commercial could be built. Maybe fifty thousand. I offered her seventy-five thousand the day she ordered me off her front porch."

"What are the chances Dabney can afford to hire a good lawyer to stop us from getting what we want?"

"I see where you're going." Paulding nodded. "I tried to get her to talk to a lawyer. She told me she doesn't believe in them."

"Let's hope that's a conviction, not a preference." Mr. Carpenter turned to Myra and me. "Your job is to find evidence that will convince a jury to award a judgment large enough to blow up Ramona Dabney's pulpit."

"Yes, sir," Myra said.

My mouth was dry. Most American churches had wandered far from God's plan, but a broad view of religious freedom allowed my family and me to practice our beliefs. Declaration of war against a church, even one as misguided as this one, made me nervous.

"Perhaps Reverend Dabney just feels threatened and lashed out," I offered. "If we let her know someone understands her concerns, it could lead to common ground for negotiation."

"The only ground I'm interested in is the dirt where the church sits," Paulding said.

"Tami, your sympathy is misplaced," Mr. Carpenter said. "The First Amendment doesn't protect every kind of speech. This Dabney woman has crossed the line and should be held accountable. When I take her deposition, I'll throw in a few questions to uncover her latent psyche and satisfy your curiosity. In the meantime, I want you to keep your eye on the main goals—to put a cork in her mouth and find a way to pry her grip from that property."

Mr. Carpenter stood, signaling the end of the meeting. Myra joined me in the hallway. Mr. Carpenter escorted Paulding toward the reception area.

After Mr. Carpenter was out of earshot, Myra spoke in a low voice. "I've worked with Joe for fifteen years. Never criticize his theory of a case in front of a client. If he didn't like you, he would have kicked you out of the meeting. Save your questions for later after we conduct our investigation."

"How did I criticize him?"

"By suggesting negotiation when he wants to file suit."

"But what if the facts don't support his theory? Won't the client get upset?"

"No. Once a businessman like Paulding believes we're going to do everything we can for him, it's not too hard to suggest a different approach later on. Getting over the initial trust hurdle is the hard part. All Paulding cares about is finding a lawyer as passionate about his problem as he is. When you say negotiate, he hears defeat. Joe read him perfectly. You saw how he turned the meeting."

She was right, and I knew it. But it all seemed so disingenuous.

"And don't call it manipulation," Myra added, reading my thoughts. "It's simply savvy client relations. Like women's handbags, one size doesn't fit all."

We reached the law firm library that served as my temporary office for the summer.

"I'll set up a duplicate file so we have the same information," Myra said, stopping outside the door. "Then we can divide up the names and get busy on Monday."

After Myra left, I went into the library. The other female summer clerk, Julie Feldman, a Jewish law student from Emory, sat staring at one of the computer terminals we used for legal research.

"What did Mr. C want?" she asked, running her hand through her thick black hair.

I told her about the Dabney case. Her eyes widened.

"I'm stuck here sorting through IRS regulations, and you're going to bring down a televangelist."

"She's not a televangelist. More likely she has a little church in a poor area of town. And all I heard was the client's side of the story. What if Dabney is doing a lot of good? I don't want to attack someone who is faithfully serving God."

"I doubt that. She's probably on a local radio station ranting for thirty minutes on Sunday morning. Can you believe the stuff they let on the air? You should check it out. I bet she has her own show at seven thirty on Sunday mornings. If she says something defamatory about our client on the air, you could join the radio station as a defendant."

Julie had the creative energy I lacked for this fight.

"Maybe you should work on the case."

"I'd love to. I have no problem busting someone who is using religion as an excuse to harass people, and of course the very idea of a woman preacher offends me. Feminism only goes so far before stubbing its toe on the Ten Commandments."

I smiled, knowing Julie was kidding.

"I saw that," Julie said. "I'm friends with a woman rabbi in Atlanta. Does your church have women preachers?"

"Not exactly. A woman can exhort in a meeting with the pastor's permission."

"What in the world does that mean?"

Before I answered, Zach Mays stuck his head and broad shoulders into the room.

"Ready?" he asked.

"Yes."

"Give me ten minutes to talk to Mr. Appleby about a research memo I gave him yesterday."

Zach waved and left.

"Joel only looks at me like that after he's had three glasses of wine," Julie said.

Julie was in the midst of a summer romance with a young free-lance photographer.

"He always thinks you're picture-perfect."

Julie beamed. "For that, I'll help you with the Dabney case if you can convince Mr. C to go along with it. We've done that on a bunch of files already."

"But you don't know anything about religious fundamentalism. That's what seemed important to him."

"Don't be dense. I've spent countless hours in the same room with you for weeks. I'm going to be an expert on Christian fanatics by the end of the summer." She paused. "But Mr. C will be more interested in the research paper I wrote on defamation law in Georgia."

"You did a research paper on libel and slander?"

"I wouldn't lie about something like that, would I?"

THIRTY MINUTES PASSED without Zach's return, and I began to fret he'd been caught in the Friday afternoon work trap I'd escaped. An admiralty law specialist, Zach mostly worked with Mr. Appleby, one of the senior partners. For a second-year associate like Zach, the time demands of the firm were nonnegotiable. I turned on a computer and tried to pick up a thread of research from earlier in the day.

"It's a good thing Vinny went to Charleston yesterday and won't see you sneaking out of town with Zach," Julie said.

"He understands," I answered, with more confidence than I felt about the summer clerk from Yale. "We're having lunch on Monday after I get back."

"Even though he's a geek, Vinny isn't going to let you fall into the arms of another man without a struggle."

"No one is putting his arms around me."

"That's right. You have a guy on each side pulling you apart like the wishbone of a chicken."

I laughed. Julie knew I'd toiled the previous five summers in the chicken plant where my father worked as a floor supervisor.

"That got your mind off the clock for a few seconds," she said.

The door opened. It was Zach.

"Let's go," he said.

"Have fun," Julie said as I quickly grabbed my purse. "And, Zach, leave a trail of bread crumbs so you can find your way out of the mountains."

2

ZACH AND I STEPPED INTO THE THICK AFTERNOON HEAT. IT WAS easy to understand why wealthy antebellum plantation owners didn't stay in Savannah during the summer and owned second homes farther inland. The sprinkler system that watered the flowers and bushes in front of the office was spraying an invisible vapor.

"If we were in Powell Station already, I'd take off my shoes and let the mist cool my toes," I said, stepping toward the center of the walkway. "Mountain girls like me don't wear shoes before our sixteenth birthday. After that it's optional, except on Sundays."

"I packed shoes for the trip," Zach said.

"I hope they're not wingtips."

We reached Zach's car, a small white import. He opened the door for me, a habit that drove Julie nuts. She claimed no man had opened a car door for her since her father put her in a child's car seat.

The office of Braddock, Appleby, and Carpenter was at the edge of Savannah's historic district. It was several blocks to the West Hull Street home of my landlady, Mrs. Margaret Fairmont. Zach parked at the curb in front of the residence, a square two-story brick structure with tall, narrow windows on the first level and broad front steps. Two large live oaks stood between the house and the sidewalk. An iron railing extended from the steps down the street on either side, then turned toward the rear of the house. I could hear Mrs. Fairmont's pet Chihuahua, Flip, barking on the other side of the front door.

"Should I come in?" Zach asked.

"She likes talking to you, but don't be surprised if it's the same conversation you had with her last week." I put my key in the door. "I'll be ready in a few minutes."

The foyer was flanked by matching parlors, one green and the other blue. I knelt and scratched Flip behind his left ear. He gave me a thank-you lick on the tips of my fingers.

"I'll miss you," I said, "but I promise to come back with all kinds of interesting smells."

Flip gave Zach's foot a quick sniff, which was better than the animosity he showed some of Mrs. Fairmont's guests. We crossed the green parlor and entered the den. Mrs. Fairmont, wearing a stylish dress and nice shoes, sat in her favorite chair. It was a good day. She'd fixed her hair and put on makeup. The TV was tuned to a sports station. The elderly woman's eyes were closed. I gently touched her arm. Her eyelids fluttered and opened. She squinted at me for a moment, then looked past me at the TV.

"Tami, unless you really want to watch that show, I'd like to change the channel."

"You can change it, Mrs. Fairmont. I'm about to leave town," I said, motioning Zach closer. "Zach Mays, one of the lawyers at the office, is going to take me home to visit my family for the weekend."

Mrs. Fairmont turned in her chair. Zach leaned over and greeted her.

"The young man from California," Mrs. Fairmont said, her dark eyes twinkling. "I so enjoyed talking with you about your motorcycle trip down the coast. Harry and I drove that route years ago in a Ford convertible. The cliffs, the ocean, the surf on the rocks—I'll never forget it." She paused. "Until this multi-infarct dementia gets the best of me."

I left Mrs. Fairmont chatting with Zach. On her best days the elderly woman would talk specifically about her illness. It made me glad and sad: glad she was temporarily functioning at a high level; sad that it wouldn't last. My greatest fear was that she would die without believing the truth of the gospel.

I went downstairs to my apartment, a garden basement suite that opened onto a courtyard with narrow walkways and a large fountain in the middle. I'd already packed two suitcases, one with clothes and another with gifts for each member of my family. I put my hanging clothes in a dark blue bag that included the three new outfits I'd bought since coming to Savannah. I'd saved the sales receipts in case Mama didn't approve. There was a knock on the door frame. I jumped.

"Sorry," Zach said. "I thought you might want help with your bags."

He picked up the suitcases with ease. Even with his hair bound tightly into a short ponytail, there was nothing effeminate about Zach Mays. He carried himself with easy strength and was tall enough that I didn't look out of place beside him. When I went through the adolescent growth spurt that helped me on the basketball court, I began praying that God wouldn't send me a short husband. Zach and Vince Colbert were both over six feet. On that level, they were equal.

With the hanging bag draped over my shoulder, I followed Zach upstairs. Mrs. Fairmont was in the kitchen.

"Gracie already fixed supper," she said.

"And your daughter is going to come by in the morning to check on you," I said.

"Christine called earlier. She's not going to be able to make it. Something about a charity golf tournament at her club."

"Can't she skip it?"

"No, she's one of the patrons. And she drew a foursome with Peg Caldwell, who's coming in from St. Pete especially to see her. She and Christine were classmates at the Academy."

"But what if—" I stopped.

"I drop dead and no one knows about it except Flip? Do you think that's going to happen this weekend?"

"I believe the number of our days is in God's hands."

"Then pray he doesn't drop me soon. In the meantime, I'm going to brew an afternoon cup of coffee and drink it black." Mrs. Fairmont gave me a wrinkled smile. "Decaf, of course, and don't worry about me while you're gone. If I feel this good tomorrow, I may get Nancy Monroe to come by and take me out for crumpets and tea."

I shifted the hanging bag to the other shoulder.

"Have a nice weekend, and let your parents know they can come for a visit," Mrs. Fairmont continued, smoothing her dress with a diamond-bedecked hand. "Bring the whole family if you like."

I nearly laughed. I could never dump all seven members of my family in a house that was more like a museum than a home. One of my brothers might break something simply walking through a room, and the twins would want to inspect every antique.

After a good-bye pat to the top of Flip's head, I followed Zach out of the house.

"Mrs. Fairmont is having a good day, isn't she?" Zach asked.

"Yes. And the longer I stay with her, the more I like her."

"She feels the same about you."

"Are you sure? Her daughter mentioned a cousin might be coming to town before the end of the summer. If that happens, I may have to move out."

Zach put the luggage in the trunk.

"I have two extra bedrooms at my townhome. We could be roommates."

I jabbed him lightly on the arm. Even casual contact with a male was a new experience for me.

"That's not funny. And please don't make a joke like that in front of my parents."

"Who's joking?"

"You are. Or at least you'd better be."

The car rumbled across the cobblestone street. I'd spent enough time during the summer with Zach that I felt safe. His kidding didn't threaten me because he'd shown respect for me and my beliefs. That, too, was new for me, and explained why I'd invited him to visit my family. However, the butterflies in my stomach weren't totally still. Zach's respect for me didn't keep him from having strong opinions. That could create problems. My parents wanted me to meet a man with strong convictions—so long as they weren't too different from our own.

WE LEFT SAVANNAH and drove north. The flatlands of the coast gave way to the gentle swells that guarded the southern approach to Atlanta. The first time I saw the city with its skyscrapers and twelve-lane freeways it seemed like an alien world. God would have to speak to me in an audible voice before I would consider living there. It still overwhelmed me. I preferred being surrounded by millions of trees to countless people and their cars.

Zach, used to driving in Los Angeles, calmly navigated through the perpetual traffic snarl that surrounded Atlanta. Leaving the city behind, we watched the sun dip below the dark hills of the north as they rose to meet us.

"Tell me more about your basketball career," Zach said as he flipped on the car's headlights.

"I wouldn't call it a career. I played on the local high school team for four years."

"Four years on the varsity?"

"Yes."

"How many ninth graders were on the varsity besides you the first year you played?"

"None."

Zach nodded. "That's impressive. I want all your statistics: points per game for each year, rebounds, assists, and how well the team did in your conference, including any tournament games."

"I'm not sure I remember all that stuff."

Zach turned his head and encouraged me with a nod. "Yes, you do."

I'd loved playing basketball and had a knack for recalling statistics. Zach wouldn't let me leave out any details.

"There was a four-game stretch my junior year when I had more turnovers than points and missed half my free throws."

"Did the coach ever bring up your bad games after you made the game-winning shot in the play-offs?"

"No. All he cared about was how we performed in pressure situations."

"It's the same with Joe Carpenter," Zach answered. "That's why he praised you for standing up to him in the Moses Jones case. If you didn't give in when he had the power to fire you, he figures a lawyer on the other side of a lawsuit won't intimidate you either."

Even though criminal law wasn't his area of practice, Zach had mentored me in the Jones case.

"I was just trying to do the right thing."

"And believed that was more important than anything else. It's one of your strengths. The danger is confusing wrong and right."

"Such as thinking that Mr. Carpenter and Mr. Braddock were co-conspirators in covering up Lisa Prescott's murder and wanted to send Moses to prison for a crime he didn't commit?"

"Yeah," Zach answered with a grin. "That would be a glaring example. But they won't ever find out about it from me."

We passed an exit for a field that was the location of a Civil War battle during Sherman's march toward Atlanta.

"Mr. Carpenter brought me into a new client meeting this afternoon."

"Litigation?"

"Yes."

"What kind of case?"

I stared out the window. "I really don't want to talk about the office."

"Careful, don't be obstreperous. That violates the rule that summer clerks take advantage of every opportunity to talk to one of the lawyers."

"Right now, you're my driver, not my boss."

Zach laughed. "I'm good with that. Lawyers who can't leave the office behind are an unhappy lot."

We rode in silence for a few miles.

"Would you like to play some one-on-one when we get back to Savannah?" Zach asked.

"What?"

"Basketball. You'd probably beat me, but there are courts at the YMCA where I work out. I'd love to see your jump shot."

I'd never played coed sports in high school or college. Trying to guard a sweating man, or worse, having him guard me, didn't sound like a good idea.

"No, maybe we could play a game of horse."

"Or obstreperous."

"I'm not sure I can spell it."

"That will be my problem," he said. "I'll be the one missing shots."

WE PASSED A REST AREA. Trucks with running lights that looked like Christmas tree decorations were parked for the night. We turned north onto a secondary road. In about an hour I would be home. The jittery feeling in my stomach at the thought of Zach meeting my family returned.

"How do you feel?" I asked.

"Hungry. Do you want to stop at a convenience store for a snack?"

"No, I mean about meeting my parents."

Zach moved his hands to different positions on the steering wheel. "Are you trying to take away my appetite?"

"You're nervous?"

"Not enough to get a haircut."

"I didn't ask you to cut your hair—"

"Which let me know there's no Delilah in you," he answered, pulling on his ponytail. "Not that I'm claiming to be much like Samson either. I'm a bit apprehensive about meeting your family, but I believe I know a lot about them because I've spent time with you. The strength of their influence in your life makes Samson look weak."

"Is that a good thing?"

"Mostly."

"I want them to like you, especially my parents, but Mama has a lot of discernment and forms strong opinions quickly."

"Is she going to tell me all my secret sins?"

"She believes it's better to confront sin than ignore it. Anything less is insincere love."

"You've seen her do that?"

"Only with family members."

"What if the Lord lets me see her sins? Should I tell her?"

The thought of Zach confronting Mama was so bizarre that I laughed.

"No," he said, shaking his finger in my direction. "There's nothing funny about sin."

"And there's no use worrying about any serious discussions with Mama and Daddy tonight. I'll give everyone a gift, then we'll go to sleep. Saturday is a big workday about the house."

"I'm counting on you to get me a job suitable for a boy who grew up in L.A."

IT WAS ALREADY LATE when we passed through the tiny town of Powell Station. Zach slowed to the speed limit, and I talked rapidly as I tried to point out every building. Both of the town's traffic lights were green, and even going twenty-five miles an hour, we were on the other side so fast that I didn't get a chance to mention the old-fashioned ice cream offered at Jackson's Pharmacy. The chicken plant where Daddy worked wasn't on the main road.

"And Oscar Callahan is still recovering from a heart attack," I said, referring to the town's only lawyer. "He went to law school with Mr. Carpenter and gave me a good recommendation to the firm."

"Where is your church?" Zach asked.

"Not on this road. It's in the country about three miles from here. The original church was in town, but a mob burned it down."

"A mob?"

"When the revival started, a lot of people opposed it. My grandmother says the fire that destroyed the church wasn't nearly as hot as the Holy Spirit's power to burn away sin and unbelief. Some people who joined the church lost their jobs, and there were physical threats and violence. But that all happened a long time ago. Compared to the pioneers, we have it easy. The only persecution now is criticism."

"Is your grandmother alive?"

"She lives in Florida with one of my aunts. Mama is a lot like her."

We turned onto Beaver Ruin Road. Even in the dark, I pointed out landmarks that couldn't be seen.

"We'll come back in the daytime," I said, realizing what I was doing. "Putnam's Pond is a pretty place. Do you like to go fishing?"

"No, I'm a vegetarian."

I froze. I quickly tried to remember the times Zach and I had eaten together. I'd gone to lunch several times with Vince, and I'd seen Julie take big bites from a hamburger. But Zach and I had never been to a restaurant together. I tried to remember what he'd put on his plate at the firm luncheon my first day on the job.

"Is that a strong belief?" I managed.

"No, it's a lame joke."

I punched him again on the arm, hard.

"Ouch," he said.

"Good." I touched the dashboard with my hand. "There's my driveway. And remember, don't try to be funny about things like that at my house."

Zach braked and turned onto the red-dirt driveway. The car skidded slightly but stayed on the track.

"It would serve you right to eat some of that dirt," I said. "With a bug or two thrown in."

Exposed tree roots made our driveway bumpier than a cobblestone street. We passed a large tulip poplar and parked beside our family van. The lights on the front porch were turned on in welcome. The rambling white frame house was prettiest at night when its flaws weren't visible. Our two dogs came running across the yard and barked at the unfamiliar car.

"Ginger and Flip," I said, getting out and roughly rubbing the sides of their heads in quick succession. "My Flip leads a much different life from Mrs. Fairmont's Chihuahua."

The dogs left me and carefully sniffed Zach.

"Leave everything," I said. "We'll meet everyone, then distribute the gifts."

The front door opened and my twelve-year-old sisters, Ellie and Emma, ran onto the porch. Mama was behind them.

"Girls!" she called out.

"Hey, Tammy Lynn," they cried out in unison as they looked past me at Zach.

I saw Ellie put her hand over her mouth as they turned back toward the house. Zach and I climbed the front steps. I gave the porch swing a slight push as we passed. The swing was one of my favorite spots. Zach opened the screen door and held it for me.

My family was standing in a cluster in the middle of the front room used for everything from homeschool classes to church prayer meetings. Mama, wearing one of her nicer dresses, had her arms around Ellie and Emma. Daddy stood beside Mama. He'd combed his dark hair and put on his Sunday shoes. He stepped forward, kissed me in the usual spot on top of my head, and shook Zach's hand.

"Walter Taylor," he said. "Pleased to meet you."

Zach introduced himself, then shook hands with my eighteen-year-old brother, Kyle, and my sixteen-year-old brother, Bobby. My brothers weren't as tall as Zach, but Kyle, who loved working with livestock, was thicker in the shoulders and chest. Bobby, the musician in the family, was slimmer.

"Mama," I said, "this is Zach Mays, one of the lawyers I'm working with this summer."

Zach stepped close and gave her a hug. I could see the surprise in Mama's eyes and inwardly kicked myself for not giving him guidance on how to greet her. Hugging was reserved for blood relatives. No man in our church hugged a woman except his wife or daughter. As they separated, I could see Mama staring at Zach's ponytail.

"Hi, Mama," I said as we embraced, and I kissed her on the cheek.

"And this is Ellie and Emma," I said to Zach. "We've shared a bedroom since they were born."

"Tami has told me a lot about you," Zach said. "You'll have to be patient with me if I get you confused."

Seeing Zach through the twins' saucer-sized blue eyes made me realize what a chance I'd taken.

"It's okay," Ellie answered. "For you, I'll answer to Emma."

"There's pie in the kitchen," Daddy said formally. "After that, the girls need to get to bed. It's already past their bedtime, and we have a busy day tomorrow."

Mama led the way. I lagged behind. Zach put his hand on my back to guide me. I jumped.

"Don't touch me," I whispered.

Zach held up his hands in front of him. Emma turned around at the sound of my voice and gave me a puzzled look.

The kitchen was a large room added after Daddy and Mama bought the house. We ate our meals at a long wooden picnic table painted white.

"It's blackberry pie," Emma said. "We picked 'em this morning. Ellie ate some of the best ones instead of dropping them in the bucket."

"You did it, too," Ellie shot back. "And then you didn't want to roll out the piecrust—"

"If either of you wants pie, stop it," Mama said.

"And there's homemade vanilla ice cream to go on top," Daddy said. "Bobby, bring in the churn from the back steps."

Going all out for a fancy, late-night snack showed me how much trouble Mama and Daddy had gone to so I would feel special. Their kindness gave me a lump in my throat.

"I'll cut the pie," I offered. "It will be easier dividing it into eight pieces."

"And I'll dish out the ice cream," Zach said.

"No," Mama said quickly. "You're a guest. Have a seat."

"Over here." Daddy directed Zach to a place at the end of a bench.

Everyone sat in silence while Mama and I fixed dessert. Normally, we would have all been talking at once. I was used to awkward social situations beyond the borders of the house on Beaver Ruin Road when being different was normal. But having those same feelings in the sanctuary of my home was a new experience.

"This is the first time Tammy Lynn has brought a young man home to meet us," Daddy said. "You'll have to forgive us if we seem real quiet."

"Tammy Lynn's never had a date," Ellie said.

"Or been kissed," Emma added. "We don't believe in dating. We practice courtship in our church."

I felt my face flush. Zach knew I'd not had a serious boyfriend, but hearing my righteous, yet boring, life so succinctly described by the girls made me wish I were a blackberry about to be eaten and forgotten.

"I think the courtship model is very biblical," Zach said. "And many marriages in the Bible were arranged by the parents."

"We don't do that," Ellie said. "All the mama and daddy have to do is give permission."

"And a blessing," Daddy added.

"Tell us about your family," Mama said, placing the first serving of pie and ice cream in front of Zach.

"What has Tammy Lynn told you?" he asked.

"That you come from a Christian family in California and know a lot about boating law," Mama said.

"Admiralty law, Mama," I said.

"Don't make him talk," Ellie said, pointing at the pie and ice cream. "It's already melting."

"All right," Mama answered. "We'll eat, then talk."

We ate as quietly as monks under a vow of silence. I sat across the table from Zach. The sound of the tiny blackberry seeds crunching in my mouth was deafening. Zach, his head down, concentrated on his pie and ice cream.

"Delicious," Daddy announced when he finished. "Let's go back to the front room."

"Ellie and Emma, clean up," Mama said.

"But we don't want to miss—," Ellie began.

"It will only take a minute if you don't argue."

"While you work, we can get our things from the car," I said. "Where is Zach going to sleep?"

"Across from us," Mama said. "I moved the sewing machine and put our piecework in the linen closet."

Zach and I went outside. It was a new moon and except for the porch lights, totally dark.

"Sorry about the rough start," I said when we reached the car. "They're not inhospitable. It's just all so new."

"I can see that. Your sisters are cute. Do they always wear those old-fashioned dresses?"

"Yes. I do, too, when I'm around the house. We have nicer clothes when we go out in public."

Zach opened the trunk and took out two of the suitcases.

"Should I carry everything?" he asked. "I want to do what they expect."

"No, we all work around here. Grab the heavier suitcase, and I'll get the smaller one."

We went inside. Mama was in her rocking chair, and Daddy sat upright in his recliner. My brothers and the twins were squeezed together on the chenille-covered couch.

"We'll be back in a second," I said.

Zach followed me down a short hallway to the sewing room. There was a daybed against one wall. True to her word, Mama had whisked everything out of sight. I smoothed out the spread on the daybed.

"This is your place," I said. "I'll take my things upstairs. The gifts are in the small suitcase."

"Okay. Let's get back in there before they suspect something."

"They're not going to suspect anything. They trust me."

"Okay, but they don't trust me."

"How do you know that?"

"I'm not sure I'd trust me either," he answered with a smile.

I started to punch him again on the arm but stopped.

"They don't know you," I answered. "Everything is going to be fine."

3

ZACH WALKED PAST ME TOWARD THE FRONT ROOM. I TOOK MY suitcase and clothes bag upstairs, then brought the small suitcase into the living room. Bobby and Kyle were whispering to each other when I entered. No one else was talking. Zach and I sat in two straight-backed chairs facing everyone else.

"You were going to tell us about your family," Mama said.

"What about the presents?" Ellie asked.

"That can wait," Mama said, folding her hands in front of her.

Zach reached back and pulled on his ponytail. It was a nervous gesture, but here in my house it struck me as an attempt to flaunt his departure from convention.

"Our family is a lot like yours, Mrs. Taylor. We love the Lord and try to live by faith every day. I have an older sister who is a Bible translator in Tanzania. My parents have lived in the same house for about fifteen years. My father and mother taught me at home through high school; then I received a BA in English from UCLA and went to Pepperdine Law School."

"What does living by faith every day mean to you?" Mama asked in a crisp voice.

"I try to keep it simple. Loving the Lord with all my heart and putting the interests of others ahead of my own."

"That's true, but not very specific. The real proof of faith and obedience comes in the details of living. Can you tell me about that?"

"Lu," Daddy said, clearing his throat. "Zach is a lawyer, but I don't think it's fair to quiz him about his convictions when he's barely had time to swallow his last bite of blackberry pie."

The twins' eyes grew big. Daddy almost never corrected Mama in front of us, much less in the presence of a stranger. She pressed her lips together for a moment.

"You're right," she said. "This isn't a homeschool session."

I breathed a sigh of relief. Mama was an excellent teacher, and her questions relentlessly drove the educational process forward with more skill than some of my law school professors. My academic success was based on her refusal to accept mushy reasoning.

"It's all right, Mr. and Mrs. Taylor," Zach said. "If I had a daughter like Tami, I'd want to find out as much as I could about a man who was interested in her."

"Why didn't you call her Tammy Lynn?" Emma asked.

"I meant Tammy Lynn," Zach answered before I could say anything more.

"I like the sound of Tammy," Ellie said. "It's simpler."

Zach faced my parents. "Let me answer your question this way. I think it's important to be very practical and specific in walking out our faith. For example, I respect Tammy Lynn's decision not to wear pants or clothes that make her look like a man and haven't seen her dressed in anything that wasn't modest and appropriate. I know she doesn't use makeup, but even without it, she's a beautiful woman."

"Mama, I dab on a little bit of lipstick and spread it thin like we talked about," I cut in.

Being back in Powell Station multiplied my sensitivity to our strict standards of conduct.

"And I've experimented with the light shades of eye shadow, but nothing more than a hint," I added before Zach continued.

"I wouldn't be as strict with my wife or daughter," Zach said, keeping his eyes focused on my parents. "But I understand her motivation. I know Tammy Lynn honors Sunday as the Lord's Day and has the heart of a servant toward Mrs. Fairmont. At the law firm, she's quickly established a good reputation with the attorneys and staff."

"Except Ms. Patrick, the office manager," I interjected. "She scolded me for being narrow-minded."

"Tami works hard and tries to be a positive witness to her faith," Zach pressed on, talking about me as if I weren't in the room. "You would be proud of the way she relates to Julie Feldman, the Jewish law clerk. They talk all the time, and I know Tami has been a good witness to her."

"I don't know about that. I've lost my temper with her more than once. You just didn't see it."

"Why does he keep calling her Tammy?" Emma whispered loudly to Ellie.

"It's easier to use at work than Tammy Lynn. Is that okay, Daddy?"

"I guess so," he replied slowly. "No one except your grandmother and Aunt Jane calls your mother Luella."

"And I've been spelling it T-A-M-I," I blurted out.

I'd never told Mama and Daddy that I'd changed the spelling to Tami and dropped the Lynn when I applied for the job in Savannah. I didn't want the law firm to think I was a hick who'd failed as a country singer. Guilt over the unauthorized change had been bothering me for months. It was a relief to have my secret in the open.

"Why would you do that?" Kyle asked.

"I like it," Ellie said. "It's fancy. Could I spell my name E-L-L-Y-E? I wrote it on a piece of paper the other day and liked the way it looked. It reminded me of the names we were reading in *The Canterbury Tales* the other day."

"You're reading *The Canterbury Tales*?" Zach asked.

"It's a version for high schoolers with the bawdy parts taken out," I answered. "I read it, too. We do the same thing with Shakespeare."

"What does bawdy mean?" Emma asked.

"Hold it," Daddy said, raising his hand. "Ellie, your name stays the same, and bawdy is not one of your vocabulary words. Tammy Lynn, you should have told us if you were going to change the spelling of your name."

"I'll still be Tammy Lynn in Powell Station," I said hopefully.

"T-A-M-I," Bobby said, pronouncing the letters softly. "Don't people think you're misspelling it?"

"No."

He turned to Daddy. "When I go off to college, can I ask people to call me Rob or Robert?"

"Why would you want to do that?" Emma asked. "Bobby Joe Taylor is a better name for a guitar player."

"Tammy Lynn doesn't want people to think she's a hick and neither do I," Bobby replied. "I might even drop the Joe or change it to 'J.'"

"Is your name Zachary?" Emma asked Zach.

"Yes. My father was going to name me Zacharias after the father of John the Baptist, but my mother filled out the information on the birth certificate at the hospital and put down Zachary. I've always gone by Zach."

Mama cleared her throat and spoke. "I think we need to stop playing this name game and let Zach finish what he was saying before we got off track."

"If I have to call him Robert," Ellie said, sticking her elbow into Bobby's side, "I think I should be able—"

"Ellie," Mama said, raising her voice.

The younger of the twins closed her mouth and crossed her arms against her chest.

Zach finally looked me in the eye as he spoke. "Every person is unique, with different characteristics and qualities given by God. I respect Tami's uniqueness and haven't tried to change her. She is a woman of character and conviction, and I respect her very much."

I blushed.

"That's nice," Mama said, "but there's a difference between respect and agreement. In Amos 3:3 the prophet writes that two cannot walk together unless they have agreed to do so. I can respect the bravery of a soldier without agreeing with the cause he's fighting for."

"Zach is a lot like you," I offered. "He asks questions to make sure I've thought through what I believe."

"What kind of questions?"

"Mostly about the way I approach the cases I'm working on," I backpedaled.

"But we've also talked about issues of faith. When Tami visited the law firm in April, we talked about Christians sharing all things in common. Any honest Bible student has to admit that the early Christians were communists—not anti-God, of course, but fundamentally different from capitalistic, self-seeking Americans."

I winced.

"Is that what your family believes?" Mama asked, her face a mask.

"They took those verses so seriously that for years we were part of a Christian commune in Southern California. However, they gave up on group Christianity when I was about ten years old. After that, we lived in the same area as the people in our fellowship, but every family had its own checkbook. It takes a zealous group of believers to be biblical in every aspect of their lifestyle."

Zach stopped. No one spoke. Daddy looked bewildered. Mama turned pale. The twins' mouths gaped open. Kyle and Bobby fidgeted.

"Zach doesn't live like that now," I said. "He's buying a town house in a nice part of Savannah near—"

"Have you been there?" Mama asked sharply. "And gone inside?"

"No, ma'am. I've not even driven past it."

"Where have you two gone together?" she asked.

"To Tybee Island beach a couple of times on Saturday mornings," I answered, "but I agreed not to do any courting until after you met him."

"Did you buy a bathing suit?" Emma asked.

"We didn't get in the water," Zach answered. "And she wore a helmet."

"Helmet?" Daddy asked.

"I own a motorcycle, Mr. Taylor."

I could see the rest of the blood leave Mama's face. I knew she was imagining me riding on the back of a motorcycle with my arms locked around a man's waist.

"Actually, I own two motorcycles. One has a sidecar that my mother used when she and my father used to take trips up the California coast. I bought it from them a few years ago. Twice I've picked Tami up at Mrs. Fairmont's house and taken her to Tybee Island. It's a scenic drive, about fifteen miles. We walked on the pier, and I showed her a place on the marsh where I like to pray and talk to the Lord."

Everything was out in the open. Emma and Ellie were about to explode with curiosity. Kyle nudged Bobby and turned his right hand in the motion needed to rev a motorcycle.

"Well, I think it's time we all got some rest," Daddy announced.

"But what about the presents?" I asked, reaching for the little suitcase. "I thought I could give them out tonight."

"It can wait till the morning," Daddy answered, then looked at Zach. "Have a good sleep. We eat a late breakfast on Saturday mornings, usually around seven thirty."

Daddy left the room. Mama followed without looking at me. The twins, their eyes on the small suitcase, approached.

"Can you bring it upstairs to our room?" Emma asked.

"You can show us our presents, and we'll still act surprised in the morning," Ellie added.

"How can you be so selfish?" I whispered harshly. "Didn't you see what just happened to me?"

The girls, their heads drooping, left the room. Kyle and Bobby approached Zach, who stepped closer to me.

"What kind of motorcycles do you have?" Kyle asked Zach.

"My new one is a red Suzuki," Zach answered.

"Which engine?"

"A 1340cc engine."

"It must be a rocket," Bobby said with admiration in his voice.

"Yeah, it can go from zero to sixty in about two and a half blinks on an open stretch of road. The older bike with the sidecar is a Triumph 650 that's tuned so quiet you can barely hear the engine running."

I couldn't believe the boys were talking about motorcycles. No one seemed to notice that I was upset.

"You should have brought Tammy Lynn home in the sidecar," Bobby said.

"It would have been a rough ride," Zach said, looking at me. "And I don't think your parents would have appreciated it."

"We tried to talk Daddy into letting us get an off-road bike," Kyle said. "There are great places around here where you can ride for miles, especially on the power company right-of-way."

"But it would take two motorcycles to have any fun," Bobby said. "Kyle has plenty of money, but I'm barely making minimum wage this summer as a chicken catcher."

"Tami told me you were already buying and selling cattle," Zach said to Kyle.

"Yeah, I have an old pickup truck and a used hauler. I'm going to study agricultural engineering in college next year. Tammy Lynn and I are going to share an apartment."

"That hasn't been decided," I said. "Mama and I aren't sure—"

"Boys,"—Daddy stuck his head into the room—"I have a full day planned for tomorrow."

"Yes, sir," Kyle and Bobby answered simultaneously.

The boys left. Zach looked at me and raised his eyebrows. Tears suddenly stung my eyes. I quickly wiped them away with my hand.

"I'm sorry," he said.

"I'm not sure this is going to work. I know what you're like because I've been around you for weeks, but my parents will decide what kind of person you are by what you say and do this weekend. It's obvious that you're not like us, and in our world, that usually isn't a good thing."

"Then maybe you should leave this world," he said, motioning toward the front door.

"No," I said, my voice trembling. "This is who I am. My family may be different, but we have love, and I'm never going to turn my back on that."

"That's not what I meant."

"What did you mean?"

"That you need to find out who you are apart from this world."

"I've been away at college and law school for six years."

"But you've never left home in here," Zach answered pointing to his heart. "Has the change in geography really made a difference? I bet you've grown up more in the two months you've been in Savannah than any other time since leaving this house."

Zach was right, but I didn't want to admit it.

"Maybe," I said. "But I'm here now, and this is where my roots lie."

Zach started to say something else but stopped.

"Okay," he said.

"Good night," I said. "I'll see you in the morning."

I grabbed the little suitcase and left the room. When I reached the top of the stairs, I glanced down and saw Zach slowly walk into the sewing room.

THE TWINS WERE in their pajamas, waiting for me on the rug in the center of our bedroom. It was our favorite place to sit and talk.

"Have you been crying?" Ellie asked.

"Not now," I said, rubbing my eyes as I joined them.

"We're sorry for being selfish," Emma said. "We acted like little kids."

"Will you forgive us?" Ellie added.

"Of course. You are little kids."

"No, we're not," they answered in unison.

Both girls came over and hugged me from opposite sides. It was so easy to make things right between us.

"Did Mama talk to you?" Emma asked after letting me go.

"No."

"She will," Emma continued. "Probably while we're fixing breakfast in the morning. What are you going to say to her?"

"I won't know until I hear what she says."

"I like him," Ellie said. "He's smart and good-looking. And his sister is a missionary. Nobody in our family is a missionary."

"But can you see him going to church with us on Sunday?" Emma asked. "The Bible says men aren't supposed to look like women. Do his parents know he has a ponytail?"

"I'm sure his parents don't mind."

"And his boss doesn't care?" Emma asked.

"The law firm doesn't have a strict dress code for the attorneys. He keeps his hair clean and neat."

"Have you touched it?" Ellie asked.

"No."

"He probably uses conditioner," Ellie said, lowering her voice. "It was so shiny and soft-looking."

Ellie's light comment was like a pin popping a balloon. My anxiety lessened. I slipped off my shoes, and we sat in a circle on the rug.

"Do they still have the pictures of the twelve apostles on the wall in Mrs. Weaver's Sunday school class?" I asked.

"Yes, but they don't really know what they looked like," Emma said.

"Which reminds you of Zach?"

The girls thought for a moment.

"Andrew," Emma said. "His eyes are the same. It's the third picture from the left."

I remembered the image. She was right.

"And in the picture, Andrew's hair is longer than Zach's," Ellie said. "I'm going to tell Mama in the morning."

"No," I said quickly. "That will only cause an argument. She and Daddy are worried about more than the length of Zach's hair."

"What are they afraid of?" Ellie asked.

"That she'll marry the wrong person," Emma answered. "Has he proposed?"

"Of course not."

"I think you should just have some fun without worrying about marriage," Ellie said.

I eyed my little sister in surprise.

"Is that what you want to do?"

"Maybe, except I don't know how a girl could have fun with a boy. None of the boys at the church can say more than two sentences without running out of ideas. Zach seems different. He had a lot to say."

"Which can cause problems," I answered.

"Would you show us our presents now?" Emma asked.

"Yeah—we won't let you go to sleep until you do," Ellie added.

"Then we'll have to lie awake all night."

"'Hope deferred makes the heart sick,'" Emma said, quoting part of a verse from Proverbs.

"But a present opened the next day is better because you'll have time to enjoy it and not have to go to bed," I answered.

"That's not right," Ellie protested. "It says that 'a longing fulfilled is a tree of life.'"

"But sometimes you have to wait to be fulfilled."

THE TWINS SLEPT in a homemade bunk bed with Emma on the top and Ellie on the bottom. I had a single bed on the other side of the room. Between the beds was a large window where in the summer we placed a fan to draw hot air out of the house during the day and cool air in at night. We slept under thin cotton sheets.

It took only a few minutes to unpack my suitcase and hang up my clothes. The bathroom was down the hall. I put on my pajamas and brushed my teeth. When I returned from the bathroom, Emma was breathing steadily, her long dark hair strewn across her pillow. Ellie's eyes were still open.

"Tammy Lynn," she said softly. "I'm glad you're home."

"Me, too."

"Do you miss us?"

"Every day."

"We pray for you even if Mama doesn't remind us."

I knelt on the floor beside her bed and let my chin rest on her pillow.

"I can feel your love all the way to Savannah."

She turned on her side, facing me.

"Sometimes Emma and I lie in bed and pretend you're here. We take turns saying the things you would say."

"What do we talk about?"

"Everything."

"What do I say?"

"Oh, different things. Emma and I argue about stuff, but when you say something, you're always right."

"Write it down," I said. "I'd like to know what's right myself."

4

THE PHONE RANG SEVEN TIMES BEFORE SISTER DABNEY ANSWERED it. She wasn't superstitious; it just took time and energy to push herself out of the chair in the living room and walk to the kitchen where the phone hung on the wall.

"Hello," she said in a slightly nasal voice grown from mountain roots.

"Good morning! This is Bob calling from your local cable TV provider. Did you know that you can get fourteen movie channels for only $12.95 a month? Imagine, first-run premium movies without any commercial interruptions. And if you sign up for a year's subscription today, you'll get the first three months absolutely free. I'm ready to place your order for this fantastic, satisfaction-guaranteed offer! All I need is a major credit card."

"I don't own a TV or have any cable service."

"Our records show you have basic cable that gives you the option to upgrade with this special limited-time offer."

Sister Dabney closed her eyes for a moment.

"And my records show you need to ask your younger brother's forgiveness for the way you treated him when y'all were growing up."

"Are you interested in taking advantage of this fabulous movie offer for select customers?"

Sister Dabney raised her voice to preaching volume. "And will you be stiff-necked and rebellious or yield to the power of truth? What's in the past need not plague your present. Will you seek your brother's forgiveness?"

The line was silent for a moment.

"People hang up on me all the time," Bob said, dropping his telemarketing shtick. "This is what it sounds like."

The phone went dead with a loud click. Sister Dabney returned the receiver to the cradle. If she prayed, additional facts about Bob's life might be revealed to her, but he was gone, and she saw no need for unusable information.

She poured a cup of coffee. There was a knock on the front door. Visitors to the house weren't always friendly. There was another knock. She sighed and took a sip of coffee before walking down the hall. She peeked through the spy hole. It was a young man who came to the church when hungry. He was in his midthirties but looked ten years older. Sister Dabney opened the door.

"What do you want, Rusty? You walked out of the meeting the other night before it was over. Have you been drinking this morning?"

"You don't have to ask, sister. You know that for yourself." The man wiped his hands against dirty jeans and looked at her hopefully. "A hot biscuit would be nice."

"There are biscuits in the oven if you're willing to work for them, and there are a few bits of ham left in the skillet."

"If'n a man don't work, he don't eat," Rusty replied. "I know my Bible. You taught me."

"You can have two ham biscuits if you'll pick up the trash left by those heathens wanting to steal God's property from me. The men hauling off what's left of Harrison's Garage didn't bother to clean up after they ate lunch behind the church yesterday."

"Did you preach at 'em?"

"No, I wasn't home."

"Can I do my chore after I eat? I'm feeling kind of puny."

Sister Dabney pointed to the door. "There are black plastic bags in the empty planter on the porch. Fill a bag up to the brim and come back for your biscuits."

Sister Dabney closed the door after him and watched through the spy hole as Rusty picked up a plastic bag, shook it out, then dropped it back in the planter. The homeless man took a few steps, stopped, and after a glance back at the door, returned to pick up the bag and head toward the church. Sister Dabney opened the door.

"That's what repentance looks like, Rusty," she called out after him. "You decide it's better to bag up the trash of life than go off looking for something in a bottle that can't really take away how rotten you feel."

Rusty waved his hand in the air without turning around. Sister Dabney returned to the kitchen and put a fresh piece of country ham in the skillet. It would be sizzling brown by the time the trash bag was filled.

I AWOKE TO THE CALL of Chester the chicken. Our rooster needed no clock except the sun in the east. And he didn't wait for broad daylight. Chester summoned forth the day with all the volume his chicken lungs could muster.

After a few mornings at home, Chester's crowing became part of the background noise, but the first day it always wrenched me from sleep with a shock. I put my head under the pillow, but it was no use. Chester was persistent, his crowing piercing. I sat on the edge of the bed. Ellie and Emma were still asleep, as unaffected by the rooster's noise as I'd been when I was their age.

Saturdays were workdays at our house, but since Zach was here I put on a plain skirt, collared blouse, and sandals. Getting dressed at home was so different from in Savannah. I tied my hair in a ponytail and then, after inspecting it critically, decided it looked better brushed out and falling across my shoulders.

I walked softly downstairs. The door to Mama's sewing room was closed. Mama wasn't in the kitchen. Suddenly I had a sinking feeling that Zach had left in the night. Holding my breath, I rushed into the front room to look out the window. Zach's car was still there. When I turned around, he was standing in the doorway, watching me.

"Good morning," he said.

"Hi," I said, gasping slightly. "Did you hear the rooster?"

"It was hard not to. Are you okay?"

"Yes."

Zach stepped closer to me and spoke in soft voice. He was wearing blue jeans, a red T-shirt, and tan boots. He had dark eyes and chiseled features that would make attracting women simple. I glanced down at my homey skirt and wondered why he was interested in a girl like me.

"Listen, I'm sorry for creating such a stir last night," he said.

I looked past him down the hallway and reminded myself that he'd wanted to come home with me, not someone else. I really wanted the weekend to be a success.

"It's a new day," I answered. "Do you want to help me gather eggs?"

"Sure."

Zach followed me into the kitchen.

The men in our church blended into society. It fell to the women to broadcast our separation from the world. If fancy dresses were appropriate, we didn't seem too out of place. However, if pants, shorts, or a bathing suit was the norm, we stood out like the Amish at a Pennsylvania county fair.

Years before there had been a decision to require women to wear head coverings. For six months, Mama and I kept bandannas pinned to our hair except when bathing or sleeping. Then, for reasons unclear to me, the elder board reversed the requirement. A few families left the church in protest. Mama folded the bandannas and put them in a drawer. I felt relieved. Now my brothers used those bandannas as sweat rags on hot summer days.

I handed Zach the blue metal egg pail the twins and I had decorated with simple portraits of our chickens. Outside, the early morning air was fresh and cool. There weren't any clouds in the sky. The nice day lightened my mood.

"Are you afraid of chickens?" I asked as we walked across the yard.

"No," he answered, giving me a puzzled look.

Flip and Ginger trotted up to greet us. We passed the edge of our large garden. The browning tassels of the cornstalks were visible at the far end of the garden. Mama canned vegetables, and much of the food we ate year-round came from our garden. My favorite vegetable was white corn. Daddy planted thirty long rows of corn and spaced it out so we had corn on the cob every night over a four- to five-week period. Nothing tasted better than fresh-picked corn dropped into a pot of boiling water, then transferred directly to the dinner table. Our family could eat two dozen ears at a meal. Mama canned creamed corn, Mexican corn with red and green peppers, and yellow corn for use in other dishes.

"We'll have corn on the cob for supper," I said.

"It's my favorite."

"Good, we have that in common."

We reached the chicken coop.

"Do you want to wait here?" I asked, putting my hand on the latch.

"Why?"

"Have you ever been around a rooster with hens?"

"No," he answered, looking more closely into the pen.

"I'll protect you," I said, making a fist.

I lifted the latch on the gate, and we stepped onto the bare dirt area in front of the coop. Chester, who had been on the back side of the enclosure, came running around with his wings flapping and his head stretched out. He charged Zach, then jumped up in the air with his talons thrust forward. Zach jumped back and crashed into the fence. I waved my hands in front of Chester's face.

"Back off!" I yelled.

The rooster quickly retreated and began scratching the ground, completely ignoring us.

Zach brushed his hands against the front of his shirt. "So that's how you learned to hold your ground under pressure. Mr. Carpenter isn't half as intimidating as Chester. I thought he was going to slash my throat or try to put out my eyes."

I laughed. "He's the greatest bluffer in the county. At least you didn't scream like a little girl."

Keeping his eye on Chester, Zach followed me into the coop. Each hen's nesting box was marked with a carefully printed card: Juliet, Olivia, Viola, Cressida, Cleopatra, and Lady Macbeth. They clucked loudly at our approach.

"More Shakespeare?" Zach asked, touching the cards.

"Yes. Chester is the odd man out. Kyle named him. Before Chester, we had a bigger rooster named Brutus. He really was mean. I had to carry an old broomstick with me when I came into the yard."

Zach held the bucket while I reached into the nesting boxes and retrieved the morning supply of eggs. The hens protested and pecked at my hand, but as soon as the eggs were removed, they fluttered down to the ground and left the coop in search of food. The floor of the coop was covered with fresh straw. It still smelled like a chicken house but not as bad as it could have.

"One of my brothers must have cleaned in here," I said. "Did you live on a farm when your family was in the commune?"

"No, we've always been in a city neighborhood."

"How did that work? I thought you would be out in the country."

"They bought big, older houses, then put more than one family in each one. The adults worked public jobs and pooled their earnings."

We left the chicken house. Chester clucked loudly when we passed but didn't make any threatening gestures. In front of the chicken coop was a bare basketball court where I'd practiced my jump shot for many hours.

"We could play a game of one-on-one here," Zach said.

"No," I answered quickly. "Playing with the twins might be a good idea. Ellie really likes you."

"But not Emma?"

"Oh, she does, too. They pretend not to agree about anything, but when it comes down to it, they're twins through and through."

Zach rested his hand on the wooden post that held up the basketball goal.

"Should I explain to your parents what happened in the commune?" he asked.

I thought for a moment. "I'm not sure if that would be a good idea. It might be better to leave it alone."

"But I do owe you an explanation about something else I said last night. When I told you to consider leaving this world, I didn't mean you should reject your family."

"That's the way it sounded to me."

"You'll always love and honor your folks, but things have to change when you get married. The Bible commands a woman to leave her family and cleave to her husband."

"Actually, it only tells the husband to do that."

He smiled. "Yeah, but don't you think it should apply to women, too?"

"Yes, and that would be tough, especially if I married someone outside our church." I glanced toward the house. Mama might be watching and wondering. "We don't need to settle that now. Let's take the eggs inside. I need to wash them and help with breakfast."

Inside the house, Mama was placing strips of lean bacon in a skillet.

"Good morning," she said in a cheery voice that reassured me. "Tammy Lynn, will you help me with the bacon?"

"You've never tasted anything like this bacon," I said to Zach. "It has no preservatives."

"My family eats a lot of organic food."

I saw Mama cringe as she reached for another piece of bacon. Our best bacon and hams came from members of the church who raised hogs. Most hog killing was done in the fall, but Mr. Bowman would occasionally slaughter a pig after the Fourth of July. Daddy managed to keep our name at the top of the list for fresh pork by supplying the Bowmans with as much sweet corn as they could eat.

"How did you sleep?" Mama asked Zach.

"Not too well. I lay awake worrying that I came across as disrespectful last night and wanted to apologize. I didn't mean to argue with you."

Mama turned around and wiped her hands on the front of a well-worn apron.

"It's important for us to know what you believe and why."

Zach's focus was on feelings; Mama cared about facts. It was a role reversal from stereotypes of men and women. Mama poured Zach a cup of coffee while I began washing the eggs in vinegar.

"What are you going to do today?" Mama asked me.

"We can help around here," Zach answered. "Tami has already introduced me to the chicken house."

"We only collect our eggs once a day," Mama replied. "And Bobby cleaned the coop yesterday afternoon. There are always chores to do, but I don't want you to think all we do is work."

"Any suggestions?" I asked, trying to remember a time except Sundays when we didn't work.

"You could go fishing at Putnam's Pond. A mess of fried catfish would make a nice supper."

I reached up and brushed back my hair with my hand. I loved the idyllic setting of the pond.

"Maybe the twins could tag along," Mama added. "They haven't been fishing all summer."

"Is this a good time of year to catch catfish?" Zach asked.

Mama and I both laughed.

"Sorry," I said. "Catfish aren't picky about seasons. They never stop eating and bite anything on a hook, from a dough ball to a chicken liver."

"There's a tub of livers in the freezer," she said. "You'd better let them start thawing."

We had a large freezer in the cellar. Next to the sizable freezer were shelves holding rows and rows of jars of the vegetables Mama put up during the summer. Mama kept everything organized and a sheet of paper listed an inventory of the contents of the freezer. I took out the livers and marked them off the list. When I returned upstairs, Ellie and Emma, wearing their work dresses, were in the kitchen. Emma had the small suitcase in her hand.

"Now," she said, holding it up as soon as I entered.

I held up the chicken livers. "Do you want to trade what's in the suitcase for these?"

"No," Emma replied. "And I wouldn't let Ellie peek."

"Let me have it," I said. "I don't want Mama to see her present until Daddy is here."

I took out two colorful cardboard boxes and handed one to each.

"Saltwater taffy!" Ellie said.

"And different flavors," Emma said.

"From a shop where I watched them make it."

"May we have a piece?" Ellie asked Mama.

"Yes, I'm sure that's the perfect way to get your stomach ready for a good breakfast."

The twins had a brief discussion about the respective merits of different flavors. Emma chose strawberry; Ellie picked blueberry.

"That's not all," I said after they started chewing.

"What else?" Emma asked, her mouth moving slowly.

I took out two objects wrapped in tissue paper and handed them to the girls. They quickly removed the thin paper.

"Shells," Ellie said.

"A conch shell," Emma added. "Did you find them when you went on the motorcycle ride with Zach?"

"Two rides," Ellie corrected.

"No," I answered. "I bought them at a beach shop. Big ones like that come from somewhere else."

"It's a Florida pink conch," Zach said. "Hold it up to your ear."

Ellie held the shell up to her right ear. Emma did the same with hers.

"I can hear the ocean," Ellie said.

"That's neat. We've never seen it," Emma added.

"You've never been to the ocean?" Zach asked. "It's only five hours away."

I held out my hand, and Ellie handed me her shell. I listened for a few seconds to the faint roar, then returned it to her.

"Before this summer, the only time I'd been to the coast was a mission trip with the church. We helped clean up a town in Florida that had been hit by a hurricane."

"And your daddy went with you," Mama said. "There are a lot of wonderful educational opportunities along the coast, but it's an expensive place to visit."

"You could use my town house for a few days," Zach said. "It has three bedrooms. All you'd have to buy would be the gasoline to get to Savannah and groceries while you stay. I'll sleep somewhere else."

"Can we?" Emma asked excitedly.

"It's a kind offer," Mama answered in her practical tone of voice. "We'll pray about it."

"I don't have to pray about it," Emma replied. "I'd love seeing the ocean."

"Quiet," Ellie whispered.

The bacon sizzled in the skillet. I cracked open a dozen eggs into a metal bowl. The biscuits were beginning to turn golden in the oven. Kyle and Bobby came into the kitchen followed by Daddy. The breakfast aromas made a welcoming fragrance.

"Just in time." Daddy smiled.

He kissed Mama on the cheek, and the twins excitedly showed him their gifts. While I stirred the eggs, Kyle listened to Ellie's shell and pretended he couldn't hear anything. Daddy poured a cup of coffee and sat on the bench opposite Zach. I watched, trying to read Daddy's mood toward Zach—and me. He gave me a good-morning smile but didn't look at Zach.

"The weeds are getting ahead of us in the pole beans and okra," Daddy said to Bobby.

"Yes, sir, I saw that yesterday."

"Run the two-tine tiller down the rows; then use the hoe to dress them out. Kyle and I are going to finish digging the holes for the new section of the feedlot before Ed Moorefield drops off five calves."

"Do you raise calves?" Zach asked.

"No, just sell them for veal," Kyle answered. "They're males from his dairy herd. All they've eaten up to now is milk, but I'm going to add a hay-and-grain mixture for a few weeks to put more weight on them before taking them to the sale."

I loved the cute calves with their rough tongues. It always bothered me that they were so soon destined for the slaughterhouse; however, unless sold for veal, the male offspring of dairy cows were often killed at birth. Cattle culture was one society where being male was a huge negative.

"Would you like to pick up the calves?" Kyle asked Zach. "We could call Mr. Moorefield and save him a trip. His place is one of the nicest dairy farms around here."

"Tammy Lynn and I are going fishing," Zach answered. "Our job is to catch our supper."

"Unless you're good with a rod and reel, we'll be eating a vegetable plate." Kyle shook his head. "Tammy Lynn has a habit of not paying attention to what's happening at the end of her line."

I laughed. It was true. Staring at a thin line that disappeared into the dark water wasn't my idea of fun.

"And the twins are going with them," Mama said with a glance toward Daddy. "Yes!" the girls exclaimed in unison.

"After I inspect their room," she added.

The eggs were steaming when the biscuits came out of the oven. The table was set in seconds. We all looked at Daddy and waited for him to pray.

"Zach, will you offer a blessing?" he asked.

My stomach tightened. Daddy was testing Zach. We bowed our heads and held hands—except I didn't hold Zach's hand across the table. He held Ellie's hand.

"Father God," he said, "thank you for this day and the food on this table. Bless each member of the Taylor family. Guide them into the true righteousness that comes by faith."

I tensed. Zach didn't need to preach in his prayer. He hesitated. The room was deathly quiet. He continued.

"And help Tammy Lynn and me catch a lot of catfish for supper. In Jesus' name, amen."

We released our hands.

"You have a lot of faith," Bobby said, grabbing a hot biscuit. "Only Jesus could make a fisherman out of Tammy Lynn."

"Fisherwoman," Ellie said. "Get the gender of your word right."

"Gender?" Bobby asked.

"It was a vocabulary word we had in the spring, wasn't it, Mama?" she responded with her chin in the air.

"Yes, and don't use the Lord Jesus' name in a flippant manner," Mama added to Bobby. "Zach's prayer was fine. It was just another way of asking for our daily bread."

5

MAMA'S OFFHAND APPROVAL OF ZACH'S PRAYER WAS A RELIEF. Daddy didn't say anything critical. We enjoyed a breakfast more typical of life in our home than the somber dessert of the night before. Zach ate two large servings of scrambled eggs and complimented me on how fluffy they were.

"She has the touch," Daddy said. "There is skill, even in scrambling eggs."

Kyle and Bobby split the last biscuit. I took my plate to the sink, then returned to the table and picked up the small suitcase.

"Before we scatter, I want to finish handing out the gifts."

"It's odd playing Santa Claus in July," Zach said. "I worked as a shopping mall Santa over the holidays one year when I was in college."

"We don't believe in Santa Claus," Ellie said soberly.

Zach's eyes widened.

"Not even when we were little," Emma added. "He has nothing to do with the birth of Jesus."

"Zach isn't promoting Santa Claus," I said. "He's just making a comparison."

There were so many religious land mines in our household that Zach couldn't avoid stepping on one every few minutes. I caught his

51

eye and shook my head slightly, then to break the tension opened the suitcase and handed identical boxes to Kyle and Bobby.

"Is it fragile?" Bobby asked, shaking it. "Or something to eat? I wouldn't mind a box of taffy myself."

Kyle didn't try to guess. He ripped off the paper. Inside the box was a fitted ball cap with Savannah written across the front and a dark blue T-shirt decorated with a large sea turtle.

"They have concrete sea turtles all over the place at Tybee Island," I said. "The real ones come onto the beach at night to lay their eggs."

"We should go see them," Emma said to Mama.

"No, people need to leave them alone," I said.

"Did you go to the beach at night?" Ellie asked. "With him?" she added, motioning toward Zach.

"No. I read about the turtles in a book."

Bobby opened his box. I knew he expected the same gifts as Kyle, but I'd bought him a belt and a CD of folk music by coastal musicians.

"I listened to the CD," I said to Mama. "And checked all the lyrics. The songs are ballads from different historical periods along the coast."

Bobby held up the belt. It was woven leather.

"I bought the belt from a man who sold them from a pushcart. Do you like it?"

"Yes," he said with obvious appreciation.

"And for you, Mama," I said, handing her a set of two small, hand-painted planters. "I thought these could go on the windowsill over the kitchen sink."

"Violets would be nice this time of year," she said, admiring the pretty pots. "Thank you, Tammy Lynn."

Mama kept a small flower garden along the back wall of the house but didn't grow a lot of ornamental shrubs and plants. Ours was a working place, but I hoped she would enjoy a dash of color before her eyes as she scrubbed pans and casserole dishes. I handed the largest box to Daddy.

"What's this?" he asked, turning it over slowly in his weathered hands.

"Open it," Ellie said.

"I will, don't rush me."

Daddy set the box on the table and took out his pocketknife to cut the tape that held it shut. He'd carried the same knife as long as I could remember. The ivory-colored handle was worn smooth by countless hours spent in his pocket. His eyes opened wide as he lifted the lid.

"I don't quite know what to say about this," he said, pulling out a large, brightly colored ceramic rooster. "It's, uh, unusual."

I quickly checked the expressions on everyone's face.

"Where are we going to put it?" Daddy asked Mama.

"It's tacky," Emma said.

"Emma," Mama said.

"Well, it is. It's the kind of thing people put in a yard sale and try to sell for seventy-five cents. If Ellie and I tried to buy something like that, you wouldn't let us do it."

"It could go in the center of the table," Daddy said, setting it down in front of him.

"No," Mama said so quickly that we all laughed out loud.

"I bought it at a yard sale," I said, looking at Emma. "And I had to pay a lot more than seventy-five cents."

"Is it an antique?" Mama asked.

"No, ma'am. The sticker on the bottom says it was made in Thailand. I saw it one Saturday morning when I was walking Mrs. Fairmont's dog and immediately thought about Daddy working so many years at the chicken plant. I bargained with the woman having the yard sale. She wanted five dollars for it, but I got her down to three. I thought Daddy could take it to the plant and put it on the table where he checks everyone's time cards." I paused and forced my mouth not to break out in a big smile. "Or, he and the boys could use it for target practice after he takes out what is inside."

"What's inside?" Daddy asked me.

"The head comes off."

Daddy twisted off the head and extracted a thin plastic bag. He read the label.

"Jamaican Blue Coffee."

"It's supposed to be the best. And that's not all."

Daddy peered into the bird.

"Turn it upside down and shake it," I said.

Out came a piece of cloth held in place by a red ribbon. He untied the ribbon and unrolled the cloth.

"Mrs. Fairmont knows how to do embroidery," I said. "She's been teaching me."

Daddy read, "'The righteous man walks in his integrity; his children are blessed after him.' Tammy Lynn, it's beautiful."

He held it up for everyone to see. The text of the verse was in dark blue thread surrounded by a multicolored border.

"Wow," Ellie exclaimed.

"I could make a frame for it," Kyle said. "A few sticks of cherrywood would be nice."

While Kyle and Mama talked about a frame, I watched Daddy run his fingers across the delicate threads. He turned it over and looked at the back.

"It's just like the preachers say," he said and nodded. "The back of a tapestry might look like a mess, but the front is a work of art."

"Mrs. Fairmont's fingers are too stiff to hold a needle for very long, but she can still teach."

Daddy stood up. "Well, that's one of the nicest presents I've ever received."

He came around the table and kissed the top of my head.

"Can you teach me how to embroider?" Ellie asked.

"Work harder on your cross-stitch. When I know you're serious about learning, I'll give you a lesson."

The kitchen cleared. Zach and I stayed with Mama while the twins went upstairs. I watched Daddy and Kyle walk across the yard. Daddy limped slightly from an old gunshot wound he received when he was a military policeman in the army. A drunken solder shot him in the right foot. After two surgeries and months of physical therapy, the foot still hurt, especially in cold weather.

"I'd like to see the feedlot," Zach said.

"Go ahead," I said. "Mama and I can finish in here. It will take the twins awhile to clean up their part of the bedroom."

Zach jogged across the grass and caught up with Daddy and Kyle. The dogs were at their heels.

I continued to rinse and load the dishes while waiting for Mama to speak. She put her new flowerpots on the windowsill.

"Yes, that's the place," she said, scrubbing the skillet used to cook the bacon. "And violets will be the best choice."

I positioned the dirty forks and knives in the rack in the precise order preferred by our family. Utensils always stayed with their own kind, making it easier to put them away when unloading the machine.

"That's a sweet gift you made for your daddy," Mama said. "I thought he might shed a tear."

"Really? I didn't notice."

"You can sense a lot of things after twenty-six years."

Mama rinsed the skillet and started washing the one used to cook the eggs.

"I'm glad you're not spending all your free time at the law firm or riding motorcycles," she continued. "Embroidery is a gift that can honor the Lord. That's a beautiful piece of work, especially for a beginner."

"I ripped out a lot more thread than I sewed. Mrs. Fairmont usually goes to bed after supper, and I have several hours to myself. It's quiet and there's no one to distract me."

"Does Zach call you on the phone at her house?"

It was odd hearing Mama say his name.

"No, ma'am. We talk at the office, but he's always busy. The drive here was the longest time we've been alone together."

I finished loading the dishwasher. It was quiet in the house, a good sign that the twins were working, not arguing.

"Is it okay that I invited him to visit?"

"Yes."

I waited, wiping my hands several times with a dish towel. Mama reached under the sink and took out a piece of steel wool.

"These eggs can be stubborn," she said. "They're so soft to eat you wouldn't think they would stick so hard to the pan. Things don't always react to heat and pressure the way we think they will."

I waited, not sure about the connection to Zach, or me. I wiped off the container of chicken livers on a paper towel. Mama held up the skillet and inspected it.

"He seems to be an honest man, which is a lot better than a chameleon that changes to suit his surroundings. And you find out where you stand pretty quickly with Zach Mays."

"That's the way he's been with me from the beginning."

"But the question is what people are like when real difficulty comes."

"What do you mean?"

She dried the skillet, placed it on the counter, and faced me.

"What kind of trouble?"

"Tammy Lynn, you're in the boat leaving home behind. Storms will come."

"Did you see anything ahead?" I asked.

Mama sometimes had glimpses into the future. She'd known the twins were coming when they were no bigger than the period at the end of a sentence.

"That's not for me to say." Mama reached out and put her hand on my arm. "You're a spiritual woman. Stay pure and your heavenly eyesight won't get blurry."

She opened the cabinet and returned the skillet to its customary place.

"Have a good time fishing. Try to keep the girls out of the poison ivy on the west side of the pond."

"Yes, ma'am."

"And don't worry if you don't catch enough fish. There is a roast in the refrigerator that can be eaten tonight or cooked on Monday."

I walked slowly upstairs. Mama had seen more than she told me. I was sure of it. But I had no idea what it might be. God knows the past, present, and future, all at once, and sometimes he lets people like Mama have a peek. The rest of us have to walk by faith—and hope we don't stumble beyond recovery.

The twins were folding their clothes. They'd already made their beds. I opened the door of the closet we shared. Everything was neat and tidy.

"We're almost done," Emma said. "We've begged Daddy several times to take us fishing, but we haven't been all summer."

"It'll be fun going with you and Zach," Ellie said. "His hand is strong and friendly."

"We were supposed to be praying," Emma said, "but since we came upstairs, all she's been talking about is Zach's hand. I'm going to sit next to him at supper so I can feel it and find out myself."

"Have you held his hand?" Ellie asked me.

I pushed Mama's comment about storms out of my mind.

"Why would I do that if I didn't have permission from Daddy and Mama to court him?"

"Is that a 'no'?" Ellie asked.

"I haven't held his hand," I answered with a slight smile. "And you sound more like a lawyer than I do."

"I've thought about being a lawyer," Ellie said seriously. "But Emma is better at arguing than I am."

"Not," Emma retorted. "It's just that you're more stubborn."

"If you want to go fishing, stop arguing."

"Okay," Ellie said. "But maybe you should sit next to Zach at supper and hold his hand. It'll change your life forever."

"Forget about being a lawyer. You should write romance novels."

"About Christian girls who find the perfect husband and live happily ever after," Ellie sighed.

BEFORE GOING DOWNSTAIRS, I changed into an older dress and put on tennis shoes that I wouldn't mind getting dirty. However, I left my hair on my shoulders. Mama came in. The twins watched anxiously.

"I can tell when Tammy Lynn is home," she said, putting her hands on her hips.

"We did it," Ellie protested. "Even the closet."

"She's right," I said. "All I did was help fold some clothes."

"Okay," Mama said, leaning over to look under the bunk bed. "You can go to the pond as soon as someone fishes out the sock that's been hiding in the dark under there for who knows how long."

Emma wiggled under the bed on her stomach until nothing showed except her feet.

"She looks like the wicked witch of the East in *The Wizard of Oz*," Ellie said, reaching over to tickle her sister's toes.

Emma didn't flinch. She wasn't very ticklish. She threw out a wadded ball of white. Ellie picked up the sock.

"Oops, it's mine," she said, then made a perfect shot into the laundry basket.

WHEN WE RETURNED to the kitchen, the chicken livers were beginning to thaw.

"Get Zach and meet me in the toolshed," I said to the girls.

On the far side of the chicken coop was a large shed that contained anything Mama didn't want in the house. It had been freshly painted white in the past few months. I pulled open one of the heavy double doors.

Inside, multicolored gourds hung in a row from a supporting beam to the right. I'd spent many hours hollowing out gourds so Mama could transform them into works of art. Her gourds were highly prized as gifts. She'd never entered them in the county fair, but she'd be a cinch to win. I stepped around our tractor. Other farm and garden implements were lined up in neat rows on the rough floor. Small bags of chicken feed leaned against seventy-five-pound sacks of the meal Kyle used in the feedlot. I heard footsteps behind me. It was Ellie. She was standing in the door, slightly out of breath.

"Zach's coming," she said. "As soon as he finishes digging the hole he's working on."

The fishing rods hung on the back wall of the shed. I took down four poles.

"I use the green one, and Emma likes the blue one," she said. "You and Zach can have the bigger ones."

Our tackle boxes were on a bench underneath the rods. I found the one we used for catfish. Zach came into the shed. I could see he'd been working. He wiped his forehead with one of the bandannas left over from our head-covering days.

"Did you prove your manliness with the posthole diggers?"

"I hit a few licks, but your brother and father could work for hours."

I handed him the tackle box. Our fingers touched for a second. I glanced at Zach's face. It revealed nothing.

"This will be easier than digging," I said, clearing my throat.

We piled into Zach's car. The twins sat in the backseat with the fishing poles out the window. I placed the chicken livers at my feet beside a plastic jug filled with ice cubes and water. A picnic basket containing snacks and a quilt to spread on the ground were in the trunk. Putnam's Pond was just around the bend from our house, and we could have taken a shortcut through the woods, but the twins wanted to ride in Zach's car. And it was easier to drive than try to carry everything.

"I wish you'd brought your motorcycle," Ellie said. "I think it would be fun letting the wind blow against your face."

"Until a june bug flew into your mouth," Emma responded. "Motorcycles aren't safe. Mama says people don't pay attention to motorcycle riders."

"Did she tell you that since I've been home?" I asked.

"No."

Zach looked in the rearview mirror. "Emma, do you think motorcycle riding is a sin?"

"Not unless you go over the speed limit," Emma answered.

"Or don't wear a helmet," Zach added. "I always use a helmet, even in states where it isn't required by law."

"Do you always obey the speed limit?" Emma asked.

Zach looked at me. "I'm not sure if going from zero to sixty in less than four seconds is breaking the law or not, but I admit that I've gotten a few tickets."

"Daddy drives five miles faster than the speed limit signs say," Ellie said. "So does Tammy Lynn. I've watched her plenty of times from the backseat. She's a scary driver."

"I am not. I've never had a wreck or gotten a ticket."

"But you drove into a ditch on the way to choir practice at church last year."

"Trying not to hit a tortoise in the middle of the road. Turn here," I said to Zach. "And the car wasn't damaged. That means it wasn't a wreck."

The pond was surrounded by trees, but it was possible to see a glint of dark water from the highway. The gravel access road ended about twenty feet from the pond. Zach parked beneath a large oak tree. There wasn't a breeze blowing, and the water glistened like an opaque mirror. The twins hopped out and took off running.

"Stay away from the poison ivy patch," I called after them.

"We know," Emma answered over her shoulder. "Three shiny leaves grouped together most commonly found growing on the side of trees."

There was a narrow path through the grass along the southern side of the pond.

"Are there any snakes around here?" Zach asked as we unloaded the car.

"Plenty, but this time of year they're more interested in getting a suntan than bothering us. Emma and Ellie will scare them away. They come to the water to drink early in the morning and during the evening after they've eaten."

"Eaten what?"

"Motorcycle riders."

Zach laughed. I led him to a flat patch of ground between the water and a grove of pine trees.

"It will be shady here for a while," I said, shielding my eyes and looking up at the sun.

We spread out the quilt and arranged everything neatly. The girls were halfway around the pond. They'd found a flock of butterflies and were trying to lure them to land on their open palms.

"I have some swim trunks in the car," Zach said. "Would it be okay if I changed? These jeans are hot."

I looked at him in surprise. "No, we don't swim in mixed company. If a church group goes to the lake, the boys are always separated from the girls."

"Nobody sneaks through the woods to take a peek?"

"I never did," I replied, then pointed at the pond. "Anyway, this isn't a good place to swim. You'd sink down a foot in the mud."

Zach went to the car for a final load. When he returned, he pointed at my legs. "Should we move the quilt into the sun? It would help you work on your tan."

My legs were stark white, but my face flushed red.

"That isn't funny."

"I just thought you'd want to sit with part of your body in the sun."

"My biggest goal each summer isn't baking my skin to a pre-cancerous crisp," I snapped.

"I didn't—"

The twins came running over.

"We're ready to fish," Emma interrupted. "I've never seen so many yellow swallowtails in one place. It tickled when they landed on our hands."

"Zach, will you bait my hook?" Ellie asked.

I grabbed my fishing pole, scooped up a chicken liver, and took the path to the south end of the pond. I walked until I couldn't hear Zach's voice. I baited the hook and cast into the pond. There was a lead shot on the line to make sure the bait sank to the bottom where the catfish scavenged. The twins and Zach were together at the edge of the water, not far from the quilt. I heard Emma laugh. I fumed. My fishing line lay still in the water. Out of the corner of my eye I watched as the girls cast their lines into the pond. Ellie had a much better motion, and hers sailed far out over the water. Zach returned to the quilt, looked in my direction, and waved. I quickly glanced away, then felt like an immature schoolgirl. Morning silence descended on the pond. Except for my mental funk, I had to admit it was a gorgeous day.

"I have one!" Emma cried out.

She moved away from the water as she reeled in the fish. Ellie dropped her pole and came alongside her. Zach looked at me. I saw a flash of gray as the fish flopped around at the pond's edge.

"It's a keeper!" Emma screamed.

"Take the fish off the hook and put it on the stringer," I said.

Emma's rod was sharply bent, and from the angle of the pole, I could tell she'd brought the fish onto the grass. Zach reached down with his hand. A second later he jerked it back and shook it. I quickly reeled in my line and walked toward them.

"He doesn't know how to pick up a catfish," Ellie said.

"Watch out for the spines," I answered.

Keeping his eyes on the fish, Zach tried again but failed.

"Cut the line," he said.

"No, let me try."

Emma had caught a nice fish. I slid my hand over the top of the fish's head, picked it up, and took out the hook.

"The spines are on both the dorsal and pectoral fins," I said, holding the fish in front of me. "You can't let them snap back against you."

"That's the top and side," Ellie said, pointing to the correct parts of the fish's anatomy.

She handed me the stringer. I ran it through the fish's gills.

"Zach wore it out wrestling with it," Emma said.

Zach's right hand was closed in a fist. A trickle of blood seeped out from between his fingers.

"There's venom in the spines," I said. "Do you want to go back to the house?"

"Kyle says to put pond mud on it," Ellie said. "That works as good as anything."

"He's been stung by a catfish?" Zach asked.

"Yeah, when he wasn't careful," Ellie answered.

"It hurts." Zach looked at me. "Tami probably wishes it had stung me in the mouth."

I stuck the metal end of the stringer in the ground and dropped the fish in the water. It slowly swam to the end of the tether.

"No," Ellie answered, "she thinks you have nice lips."

6

"Ellie!" I blurted out. "I never said that."

"But you know it's true."

"Let me see your hand," I said to Zach, who was laughing and wincing in pain all at the same time.

I rinsed his hand with clean water from the drinking jug.

"Ellie, let's get back to fishing," Emma said. "Now!"

Zach and I could hear the girls talking as they returned to their end of the pond. Emma was doing a good imitation of Mama rebuking Ellie when she sinned.

"Ellie is cute," Zach said as soon as the twins were out of earshot. "And I totally believe she made that up."

"She did."

"And I'm sorry I said you needed to tan your legs. Mine are as white as yours." He rolled up his jeans to reveal a muscular calf much darker than mine. "Well, they were white before the summer. But even if your legs were green, they'd look a lot better than mine."

"Nice try," I said, gently patting the wound dry.

Zach touched the edge of the deepest cut and winced.

"Ouch. Your sisters are tanned from being outside all summer. I just thought"—he paused—"that I should apologize."

Ellie and Emma returned.

"I'm sorry, Tammy Lynn," Ellie said. "I made that up about Zach's lips—even if it's the truth."

"That's not what you're supposed to say," Emma retorted.

"Apology accepted," I answered.

Ellie leaned over and inspected Zach's hand.

"Is he okay?"

"It's a bad one," I said. "A nasty catfish sting can get infected and lead to amputation."

"You're kidding," he said.

"It's not likely, but it's possible," Emma said. "We've studied articles about catfish stings, snakebites, and poisonous spiders. It's part of natural science."

"Mama's a good teacher. She teaches about what's out here and doesn't put them in a plastic bubble. She says if we know about danger we're better able to avoid it."

"A fish stole my liver," Ellie said, holding up her rod.

"You can bait the hook," I said. "It's chicken liver, not an earthworm."

Ellie turned up her nose. Emma didn't share her sister's squeamishness. She put a fresh liver on Ellie's hook.

"Three more like the one you caught will give us a nice dinner," I said.

The girls returned to the part of the pond where the butterflies were congregating. I heard a sound in the grass and glanced down. Something was moving. Zach's pole was inching toward the water.

"You have a bite," I said.

He jumped up and grabbed his pole with his left hand. He put his right hand on the reel and turned it a couple of revolutions. The pole bent sharply. He winced in pain.

"Do you want me to reel it in?" I asked.

"Yeah. My hand is really hurting."

I took the pole. The fish was sitting in the water, not fighting to free itself from the hook. It felt like a rock.

"This is a huge one," I said.

I cranked the reel, but it did little more than bend the rod more sharply. I backed away from the water. The line twitched to the left. I moved past the quilt, dragging the fish to the surface. Zach approached the water.

"Can you see it?" I asked.

"Not yet."

"It's going to take off when it gets close to shore. I'll have to let out line or it will snap."

The twins dropped their poles and ran over to us.

"Here it comes," he said.

"It's a turtle!" Ellie called out.

I walked toward the water as I continued to reel in the line.

"You hooked it at the edge of its shell," Ellie said. "How did you do that?"

"Ask Zach. It's his line."

The large turtle churned up the mud in the shallow water. Its mouth opened in overt menace.

"What are you going to do with it?" Zach asked.

"I don't mess with turtles," I answered. "And we don't eat turtle soup. If you put your finger in his mouth, you wouldn't have to wait for an infection to lose it. Emma, cut the turtle loose. The hook won't hurt his shell."

Emma ran to the tackle box to get a knife. After she cut the line, the turtle snapped its jaws one more time for emphasis and returned to the depths of the pond.

"I thought we were going fishing at a peaceful pond," Zach said. "This is more like an African safari."

"It's all about knowing how to live in a world that may be hostile but doesn't have to be."

The twins continued fishing. I cast into the water. Zach left his pole by his side. We sat on the quilt. Zach's hand was beginning to get puffy. Inflamed red streaks ran across his palm.

"Are you sure you don't want to go to the house?" I asked.

"No, it's feeling better."

"It's swelling."

He opened the tackle box and handed me the pocketknife.

"You do it," he said.

"What?"

"Amputate. That way you'll know I trust you."

I chuckled. "Let's give it a few more minutes."

We sat quietly. True to Bobby's prediction, no fish showed an interest in the bait on my hook. The twins laid their rods on the ground and continued wooing the butterflies. The pond stilled.

"Sorry about your hand," I said, watching the red streaks grow longer. "I wanted this to be a nice weekend."

"It's not over yet."

"But in less than twenty-four hours you've had a run-in with my mother, shocked every member of my family, upset me twice, and taken a dose of catfish venom."

Zach shrugged. "That sums it up pretty well, but I'm having a good time."

"Why?"

"I'm with you."

I felt a streak of red run up the side of my neck. I concentrated on my fishing line.

"I can see you'd like to change the subject," Zach said, eyeing me closely. "Maybe now would be a good time to talk about the office."

"Okay." I touched my neck with my hand.

"What are you working on?"

"Not much."

"Should I give you a project?"

"No," I answered quickly. "Mr. Carpenter called me into the conference room just before we left on Friday for a meeting with a client and asked me to help with a new case. I'm going to be very busy for the next few weeks."

"A lawsuit?"

I hesitated. "Yes, it's set up as a slander case, but the real reason behind the litigation is to force a church to sell its property to a real-estate developer."

"Who does the firm represent?" Zach sat up in interest.

"The developer."

I laid out the dispute between Paulding Development Company and Ramona Dabney.

"I know the area of town but can't remember the church," Zach said. "What does Mr. Carpenter want you to do?"

"Be his rabbi. He thinks I have special insight into what motivates Sister Dabney. I'm not sure how that helps the case, but he's convinced it will give us an edge. On the practical side, I'm going to help Myra Dean with the investigation. The whole thing made me uneasy because I'm not sure Mrs. Dabney is as bad as our client claims. Who knows what he or his partners may have done to her? For all I know, they may be the bad guys."

"Did you see anything she wrote about the client?"

"Paulding says it's all verbal except for a letter to his wife."

"A letter to his wife? What did it say?"

"I'm not even sure we have a copy, which seems odd. Paulding provided a lot of background information. But most of the case will be based on phone calls, conversations, et cetera."

"Slander, no libel. That's going to be hard to prove."

"Yes."

Zach pulled a long blade of grass and put it between his teeth.

"It's good that Mr. Carpenter considers you his resident expert on religious fanatics. Every lawyer has to have a niche."

As the sun climbed higher in the sky Ellie and Emma each caught another fish. The red streaks on Zach's hand began to retreat. We stopped fishing to eat cheese, crackers, and green grapes packed in the wicker basket. The grapes were tart and juicy.

"What kind of wine would these grapes make?" Zach asked, biting into one. "A Chablis?"

"Don't go there," I warned.

"Does your family drink wine?" Ellie asked.

"Not very often," Zach said. "My mother never drinks. Her father was an alcoholic so she avoids it totally. I can live without it, especially if I have a cup of cold water like this one."

"Our water comes from a well in the backyard," Ellie said.

"It tastes great," Zach answered, holding up his paper cup.

"That's because it has trace minerals in it," Emma said. "As a science project we boiled some water and tested the residue to find out what was in it."

"There are underground rivers all around here," Ellie added. "The water in this pond comes from a spring near the spot the butterflies like. You can see the surface of the water bubbling."

"Okay, Zach's lesson is over," I said. "Back to fishing. We need to catch at least two more big fish if we're going to have enough for a decent fish fry."

The twins went to a different part of the pond. I threw my hook in the water, then returned to the quilt and shook the water jug. Almost all the ice packed in it had melted. I handed the last cluster of grapes to Zach.

"Why did you say that about wine?" I asked. "You knew it would be controversial. It's one thing to challenge me, but the twins are so young."

"And very smart, just like their sister. I'm just asking questions. Isn't that the way your mother taught you?"

"Yes."

"And one thing that makes you attractive is the strength of your convictions. Your goal in life is to be a godly woman. What Christian man in his right mind wouldn't want to get to know someone like that?"

My faith had been a turnoff to boys for so long that it was hard to imagine any other response.

"Even if your legs are a bit pale," Zach concluded.

I pulled down my dress. "Quit looking at my legs."

"It's too late," he answered with a smile. "The image is etched forever in my memory."

"I've got one!" Ellie called out.

By the time we reached the girls the fat catfish was flopping in the grass. I removed the hook and put it on a second stringer. As soon as I finished, Emma had a bite. She leaned back against the weight of the fish as she reeled it in. It looked like the other fish's twin. The sun was nearing its zenith.

"The sisters have caught sisters," I said. "Let's go home before it gets too hot."

I dipped the blue bucket in the pond and put the catfish in it. They slapped against one another. The water would keep them fresh until supper. I set the bucket on the grass and folded the quilt. Ellie peered into the bucket.

"Do you want to name them?" Zach asked her.

"They're not pets," she answered. "That's our supper."

"Don't you think we should set them free?" he said. "They were happy in the pond."

My sister looked up at him with her blue eyes. "What would we eat? Chicken livers?"

"Never mind." He laughed.

At home, Mama fixed an ice pack for Zach's hand. Daddy and the boys came inside and washed up at the large sink in the downstairs bathroom. Kyle inspected Zach's hand. The swelling had already gone down.

"Did Tammy Lynn talk to you about the possibility of an amputation?"

"Yes," he said, raising his eyebrows.

"She always brings that up when one of us gets popped by a catfish. Did she also mention the percentage of people who actually develop complications from a catfish sting?"

"No."

"The chance of a serious infection from a catfish sting is about one in one hundred thousand."

"I'm glad to know the true expert in the family," Zach replied. "Ellie said I should apply a coating of pond mud to draw out the poison."

Ellie, who was eating a banana, spoke up. "That's what you said when we were fishing with Eric Newman."

"If I said that to Eric it was a joke. He doesn't need an excuse to get muddy. He likes to fish barefoot standing knee-deep in the water."

Mama had cut up fresh fruit in a large bowl and cooled it in the freezer for lunch. I loved slightly frozen strawberries and peaches sprinkled with a hint of sugar. The mix also contained blueberries that had been picked from our bushes and stored in the freezer. The new blueberry crop would come in later in the summer. A few bites of the fruit made me feel like the day was starting over. Mama placed a loaf of homemade bread in the center of the table. The rich texture and nutty flavor of the bread went perfectly with the fruit. Three pieces of Mama's bread could fill up Kyle's stomach.

"How many fish did you catch?" Daddy asked.

"Five," Emma answered. "I caught three, and Ellie two. Zach hooked a snapping turtle under the corner of its shell."

"What did Tammy Lynn catch?" Bobby asked.

"None, but she took the fish off the hooks and put them on the stringers," Ellie said.

The twins talked all through lunch about our fishing trip. To my relief, they left out Zach's question about wine, and they'd not heard his comments about my white legs. "What are we going to do with Zach this afternoon?" Ellie asked as soon as she finished.

"Nothing," Mama answered. "You girls are going to the garden. We have rows of pole beans to pick and okra to cut."

"What about Tammy Lynn?" Emma asked.

Daddy spoke. "I talked on the phone with Oscar Callahan while you were fishing. He's at home recovering and really wants to see you. I thought you and Zach could drive over for a visit."

It was a great suggestion.

"I'd like to let him know how the job is working out. He gave me a great recommendation to Mr. Carpenter. I wouldn't have gotten the job without it."

"And there's another reason to go," Daddy added. "Take Kyle's truck and trailer. Mr. Callahan wants to sell a couple of three-year-old steers at the auction in Dawsonville. I told him we can take them down with the dairy calves from the Moorefield place."

"Who'll load the steers?" I asked.

"The man who's helping him during the week culled them from his herd and put them in the pen beside the barn. Just back the trailer up to the gate and shoo them in."

I'd never gotten involved with Kyle's cattle business. I looked at Zach.

"Are you okay with this?"

"Yeah."

I helped Mama clean up the kitchen while Zach and Kyle hooked the cattle trailer to the truck.

"Change into something nicer," Mama said when we finished. "Mr. Callahan will want you to come in the house to visit."

"What will I do if his wife starts criticizing the church?" I asked.

"Keep quiet. It's not your place to correct her."

I went upstairs and put on a blue-striped cotton dress that I'd left at home when I moved to Savannah. It was lightweight, yet nice enough for a house visit on a warm summer day. I slipped on a pair of white sandals and brushed my hair. I couldn't remember the last time I'd changed outfits so many times by the middle of the day.

When I returned downstairs Zach was washing his hands in the utility sink. I saw him splash his face and rub the back of his neck. Thinking he should have closed the door, I quickly looked away. He came into the kitchen drying his face with a hand towel. Mama had a paper grocery sack of fresh-picked corn on the counter.

"Take this corn," she said. "I don't think they've been able to keep up a garden this year."

"Should I change clothes?" Zach asked.

"No, you may have to manhandle one of the steers," Mama replied. "Black Angus can be stubborn."

I glanced at Mama in surprise.

"I'm kidding," she replied.

Mama's efforts at humor were so infrequent I didn't know how to react.

"Run along," she continued with a nervous cough. "Go straight to the Callahan place and return. No side trips."

"Yes, ma'am."

Kyle kept his truck beside the equipment shed. Zach held the door open for me. The gentlemanly gesture seemed out of place out here in the country. The door groaned and popped as it swung wide. There was a clean towel draped across the passenger seat.

"I saw something you might not want to sit on," he said.

"What?"

"Nothing alive. Just some grease and dirt."

Zach started the engine and slowly let out the clutch. The truck jumped forward, causing the trailer to jerk. The engine died.

"Do you know how to drive a straight shift?"

"Only on a motorcycle. But then, I'm a fast learner. It's the same principle."

"There's no shame in letting me drive."

"Give me another chance."

I sat back in my seat. Zach started the motor, revved the engine higher, and let out the clutch. The truck shot across the yard, veering toward the basketball goal.

"Look out!" I screamed.

Zach slammed on the brakes and slowed the truck but forgot to push in the clutch. The truck lurched several times, then died. Zach leaned forward and rested his head on the steering wheel.

"I'd do worse if I tried to drive your motorcycle," I offered.

"Okay. Your turn."

We exchanged places, and I slipped behind the wheel.

"And if we were in Los Angeles, I wouldn't be able to drive anywhere," I added, trying to assuage his male ego.

Zach didn't answer. I drove around to the front of the house. Flip and Ginger ran alongside barking.

"Are they mocking me?" Zach asked.

"No." I chuckled. "I need to run into the house and get my license."

Leaving Zach in the truck, I went inside. When I returned, he was behind the wheel.

"One more try," he begged. "I've been visualizing it in my mind."

"You don't have anything to prove to me."

"This is for me."

I got in the truck. He gingerly engaged the clutch. With a slight jerk, the truck rolled forward with the trailer bouncing along behind.

"Now we're on our way," Zach said.

He pushed in the clutch and pulled the shifter backward. Deep in the gearbox there was a collision somewhere between second and fourth gears. The grinding noise was so loud I covered my ears. Zach quickly pushed in the clutch and turned off the engine.

"End of lesson one. You take over," he said.

I drove to the end of the driveway and turned northward onto the highway. I smoothly shifted into second gear, then, for fun, slightly gunned the engine between second and third.

"Show-off," Zach said. "Pride is a sin."

7

SISTER DABNEY OWNED FOUR WOODEN ROCKING CHAIRS. SHE kept one in her bedroom, another in the living room, a third on the front porch, and the oldest on the platform in the church. Each one was painted a different color: bedroom, yellow; living room, red; front porch, blue; and church, purple.

The old woman claimed to receive revelation while rocking. Thus, when Sister Dabney sat in the blue rocker on the front porch, people in the neighborhood knew she was available for consultation. However, asking the preacher a question carried risks. Her answers could create more problems than they solved. And many considered her words nothing more than bitter imagination wrapped in judgmental opinion.

A frequent companion as she rocked was a large sweet tea in a recycled thirty-two-ounce convenience store cup. The calories didn't help her weight or her slide toward diabetes.

This afternoon three boys not yet in their teens stopped their rickety bicycles in front of the house.

"Tell our fortunes," one called out.

Sister Dabney took a sip of tea and kept rocking. The boys waited but didn't leave the sidewalk to come closer.

"She ain't no fortune-teller," another boy said. "She's a preacher."

"Aren't you Ruby Matthews's son?" Sister Dabney said in a loud voice.

"Who, me?"

"I know your mama from the thrift store. She wouldn't want you hanging out with those troublemakers. You get on home before one of them steals something and you all get into trouble."

"We ain't going to steal nothing," the third boy said.

"You already stole ten dollars from that man who paid you to cut his grass the day before yesterday," she replied.

The Matthews boy punched the speaker in the shoulder and nodded his head.

"You can't prove it," the boy said.

"I don't have to. God is watching, and he knows the hairs on your head and every sin you've committed. You'd better repent and get right before it's too late."

"Too late for what?"

"For what's going to happen when your daddy comes home tomorrow."

"My daddy's been in prison for five years."

"You wait and see. He'll be home tomorrow, and you're liable to be sleeping in the street when that happens."

The boy didn't answer.

"Is your daddy getting out of jail?" the first boy asked him.

"No, my auntie says he won't ever get out, and if he did, he wouldn't know where to find us. He got locked up when we were still living in Macon."

Sister Dabney kept rocking.

"You come back when you're ready to confess your sins and make it right. If your daddy tries to hurt you, I'll find a place for you to stay."

"Let's go," the third boy said. "She's just trying to scare me."

"When what I say comes true, you boys remember it," Sister

Dabney said, then pointed her index finger at the Matthews boy. "And you get away from those two troublemakers. Have nothing to do with deeds of darkness. Sin is crouching at the door and wants to eat you up."

IT WAS ABOUT FIVE MILES to Mr. Callahan's place. Years before, the lawyer bought one of the prettiest tracts of land in the county and built a large brick home on top of a rolling hill surrounded by a sturdy brown fence. A decorative white fence protected the yard around the house. Black Angus cattle grazed in one pasture. Another pasture was producing hay. I turned into the driveway and rumbled across a cow grate set in the pavement. To the right of the house was a hay barn with a holding pen beside it.

I drove up the hill to the barn. Everything about Mr. Callahan's place was neat and tidy, a sure sign of a second source of income. The truck rolled to a stop in front of the holding pen. Two steers were contentedly munching hay.

"There are the victims," Zach said. "Oblivious to their fate."

"The way you talk about catfish and cattle, I'd think you really were a vegetarian."

"I may be after this weekend. Life and death in the food chain is in your face in the country. I never think about a peaceful cow eating hay when I buy hamburger at the grocery store."

"That's why we only name our chickens and dogs. And those are steers, not cows. I'll get Emma to explain the difference to you later."

We got out of the truck and walked closer to the pen. The steers each weighed at least eight or nine hundred pounds. Their broad backs were covered with thick black hair. They paid no attention to us.

"They're probably twins, just like Ellie and Emma," Zach said.

"Please. You can ask Mr. Callahan."

I grabbed the bag of corn from the truck and stepped lightly to avoid a patch of mud as I led Zach toward the house. A brick walkway crossed the manicured lawn. Carefully groomed rhododendron lined the path. I pushed the button for the door chime. After a long wait, the door opened. It was Mr. Callahan.

I was shocked by the change in his appearance. The formerly robust lawyer was leaning on a walker. He'd lost weight and looked frail. Even the fire in his dark eyes had dimmed. His white hair was slightly disheveled.

"Hello, Mr. Callahan," I managed, holding out the bag of corn. "I brought this for you and Mrs. Callahan."

"Tammy Lynn, it's good to see you," the old lawyer said in a weak voice. "I thought Kyle would be coming by, but it's great to see you. Could you put the corn in the kitchen? I'm not supposed to lift anything heavier than a toothbrush."

"And this is Zach Mays. He's an attorney with Mr. Carpenter's firm in Savannah."

The two men shook hands. It was quiet, dark, and cool inside the house.

"Tell Joe Carpenter to get his ticker checked," Mr. Callahan said as he slowly led the way toward the kitchen. "My heart exploded without warning."

The house wasn't filled with antiques like Mrs. Fairmont's home, but the furniture was expensive. The living room, with its massive leather sofa and thick rug, looked like no one ever used it. The kitchen had a large island in the center. The local paper was folded on one corner of the island. I put down the corn.

"Is Mrs. Callahan here?" I asked.

"No, she went to the store." The lawyer held up a round device draped around his neck. "But I have my portable EMT with me. One push of this button and if I don't respond to a phone call, an ambulance will be here in minutes."

"My landlady in Savannah is supposed to wear one, but she never does unless her daughter is around."

"I'm not playing roulette with the few days I have left."

Seeing Mr. Callahan so sick made me sad. He'd always been full of life and anticipation for the next challenge.

"Would you like me to shuck the corn?" I asked.

"That would be nice."

"May I help?" Zach asked.

"No, you're injured. Tell Mr. Callahan about your hand. He's represented injured people for years."

I went to the sink. Mr. Callahan shuffled over to a round break-fast table and sat down. Zach joined him and told him about our fishing expedition. The older man chuckled when Zach described his efforts to pick up the fish, but the sound was so anemic compared to his usual hearty laugh that it made me even sadder.

"There's no cause of action against Tammy Lynn," Mr. Callahan said. "You clearly assumed the risk."

"And was guilty of contributory negligence," I added, pulling thin threads of corn silk from one of the ears.

I rinsed the ear of corn in cold water. The window above the sink offered a view of the rolling pastureland to the rear of the house. In the distance, the low mountains of the Appalachian foothills were shrouded with summer haze.

"Tell me about your work at the firm," Mr. Callahan said.

I opened my mouth to speak and glanced over my shoulder, then realized Mr. Callahan had directed his question to Zach.

"Mostly admiralty law. It's a strong niche for the firm, and Nelson Appleby has developed a good clientele."

"Admiralty law. Now that's an area I know nothing about," Mr. Callahan replied. "Is it mostly transactional?"

I shucked the entire bag of corn. I didn't mind being relegated to domestic duties if Mr. Callahan enjoyed talking with Zach.

"How many of these ears of corn do you want for supper?" I asked. "I'll put the rest in a plastic bag in the refrigerator."

"Leave out half a dozen. We're going to feed Barry Johnson, the fellow who is helping me take care of the place."

I knew Barry. We'd gone to high school together. He could eat six ears of corn by himself.

"How many do you and Mrs. Callahan want?"

"One or two each."

I put nine ears of corn in an empty metal pot and covered them with cool water.

"I went to a legal seminar at Pepperdine years ago," Mr. Callahan said to Zach. "It was really an excuse to write off a trip to California as a business expense."

"I graduated a few years ago from the law school and moved to Savannah."

"Why Savannah?"

"I think God wanted me to come there."

"To be a lawyer?"

Zach didn't immediately answer. He'd told me one day at Tybee Island that he believed God had directed him to Savannah but didn't reveal any details. I was very curious to hear his answer.

"Maybe," he said softly, "but in the back of my mind I think there may be something else God wants me to do."

"Careful, Tammy Lynn, he's a live one," Mr. Callahan said, his voice a bit stronger. "Anyone who talks like that can be dangerous."

"Yes, sir," I answered, then waited for Mr. Callahan to probe further.

"And how would you rate Tammy Lynn?" Mr. Callahan asked, changing the subject.

"It depends on the category. As a catfish handler, I'd give her an A."

"And as a summer associate? Or is that information you'd rather keep confidential until you prepare an evaluation for Joe Carpenter?"

"Mr. Carpenter won't put my opinion at the top of his stack. But if he did, Tami would be working at Braddock, Appleby, and Carpenter when she graduates next year."

Hearing Zach's words made me happy. Landing a permanent job was the goal of every summer associate. My future might be a long way from the hills outside the kitchen window. I joined them at the table.

"It's a good thing I didn't try to keep you here," Mr. Callahan said. "Two weeks into the summer I was in intensive care with tubes in my chest."

"Remember, you told me there would be a 'continuance' before I might come back to work for you."

"Without knowing it meant I'd come close to being dismissed from this world."

"Who's taking care of your clients?" Zach asked.

"A couple of young lawyers with plenty of energy."

"It doesn't surprise me that it took two lawyers to replace Mr. Callahan," I said. "He's a fast worker."

"Not anymore. It takes me forever to do anything. Now, Tammy Lynn is a quick thinker. Have you worked on any interesting cases or does Joe Carpenter have you stuck in front of a computer terminal doing research all day?"

I thought about the Moses Jones case, but it would take too long to unravel the watery trail through the swampy waters of the Little Ogeechee.

"Tell him about the case you brought up when we were fishing," Zach suggested.

"It's just getting started."

"But it sounds interesting. How many lawyers actually work on a slander case in their career?"

"Are you sure it's okay to mention it?" I asked. "It is pending litigation."

"Don't identify your client or reveal your trial strategy," Mr.

Callahan said, smiling. "And if you want to, we can consider this a legal consultation with independent cocounsel, which will require me to maintain confidentiality."

Glancing down at the floor in embarrassment at my reluctance to talk to the man who had been my legal inspiration, I gathered myself together and briefly outlined the issues as if giving a summary to one of the senior partners.

"Well done," Mr. Callahan said. "Have you met the woman preacher?"

"No, sir. We're going to interview the people she talked to before deposing Sister Dabney."

Mr. Callahan sat up straighter. "Did you say Dabney?"

"Yes, sir."

"Rachel Dabney?"

"No, sir. Her name is Ramona."

"Do you know her husband's name?"

"No, I'm not sure she's married."

"It's probably a coincidence, but there was a young evangelist named Russell Dabney who traveled briefly with my father in the early years. I think his wife's name was Rachel. Both of them were preachers, but the wife had a scary gift."

"What kind of gift?" Zach asked.

"She could call people out of the congregation and list their secret sins, everything from adultery to usury. She only had to do it the first night. After that, as soon as she stepped behind the pulpit, people would start running to the altar. I wondered if her information came from God or someplace else. My father never told me why they went their separate ways."

"Do you think it might be the same person?" Zach asked.

"If it is, you'll know it quick."

"I won't be having any contact with her," Zach said. "I'll leave that up to someone like Tami who doesn't ever sin."

"I don't know about Tammy Lynn being sinless," Mr. Callahan answered. "She took a fancy pen from my office one time, without permission."

I sat up in indignation. "I was ten years old. Mama brought me back that same day as soon as she found it in my purse. I confessed my sin, and you gave me the pen."

"You've always been quick to repent." Mr. Callahan smiled.

"Mr. Callahan's father was a famous preacher," I continued, turning toward Zach. "He was one of the founders of our church."

"That I don't attend anymore."

"But you're welcome to come back."

"That's nice of you, Tammy Lynn, but there are others with longer, less-forgiving memories." Mr. Callahan pointed to the refrigerator. "Speaking of forgiveness, forgive me for not being a better host. Would either of you like a glass of lemonade or iced tea?"

"Thanks, but we should be leaving," I said, glancing at my watch.

"Not on my account," Mr. Callahan said. "I've been lonely out here. People are afraid to come see me because they don't want to tire me out, but it makes me feel forgotten. Seeing your face has made this the best day of the week."

"That's nice of you to say. I just have to have Zach home in time to clean the catfish for supper. He wants to drive the nail through the head of the one that stung him."

"Drive a nail?" Zach asked.

"You'll see," I answered.

"I had a case one time that involved catfish," Mr. Callahan said. "At least stay until I can tell you about it."

I loved Mr. Callahan's stories. While Zach and I drank lemonade, the older lawyer told us about a man who slipped and fell on a muddy riverbank while fishing with his boss on company time. The men worked third shift and when everything was running fine at the mill, often slipped out and went fishing. The supervisor didn't know how to properly handle catfish and took the other fellow along as his mate. One night, they hooked a lunker and the worker injured his back trying to land the fish. The workers' compensation insurance company denied the claim, but Mr. Callahan convinced the judge that helping his boss fish was a regular part of the man's job.

"I relied on the company picnic cases where a worker is hurt playing in a softball game and gets benefits," Mr. Callahan said. "But the judge was mostly interested in finding out the size of the fish. It had grown huge eating chicken innards flushed into the river by the plant where Tammy Lynn's father works."

"They do that?" Zach asked.

I shrugged. "I think they grind them up first. It's organic."

The older lawyer rubbed his forehead with the back of his hand. I could tell he was tired.

"Thanks for everything, Mr. Callahan," I said, standing up. "But we really must be going. We'll load the steers and deliver them to Kyle. Please give my regards to Mrs. Callahan."

"Just a minute," Zach responded, staying in his chair. "I don't think we're finished yet."

I started to disagree, but then something in Zach's eyes stopped me. He leaned toward Mr. Callahan. I fidgeted.

"Would it be okay if we prayed before we left?" he asked.

Mr. Callahan gave Zach a questioning look.

"What kind of prayer did you have in mind?" he asked. "Has God been showing you all my secret sins?"

"No, sir. That wouldn't do me any good and besides, you already know them."

Mr. Callahan chuckled.

"Let's wait for a minute," Zach said.

I had no choice. I bowed my head and closed my eyes. A heaviness that could be felt settled in the room and made me think of a few prayer meetings I'd attended when no one wanted to say "Amen" because it was unclear whether to stop.

Mr. Callahan spoke. "As my father would say, 'I feel the weight of God's glory' and want to know why."

Zach didn't say anything, but I knew Mr. Callahan was right. I took a deep breath and slowly exhaled.

"I think God wants to touch you," Zach said. "Would it be okay to ask him to do that and see what happens?"

I opened my eyes and saw Mr. Callahan nod and bow his head. Zach looked past the old man at a spot on the other side of the room. I followed Zach's line of sight but saw nothing except the corner cupboard where Mrs. Callahan kept the fine china.

"Father, touch Mr. Callahan," Zach said softly.

The heaviness in the room increased. I wanted to keep my eyes open but felt that whatever God did next, I wasn't supposed to watch. I had a sudden desire to bottle the moment and open it later at Mrs. Fairmont's house.

"Hallelujah," a male voice said.

It was Oscar Callahan.

"Hallelujah," the old man repeated stronger.

I peeked and saw Mr. Callahan's faced turned upward but his eyes still closed.

"Hallelujah!" he cried out in a loud voice that sent shivers down my spine.

Mr. Callahan rose to his feet and lifted his hands in the air. He clapped his hands together so loudly that it made me jump. Zach remained seated. The old man took a few tentative steps, then began to turn around, his hands in the air.

"Hallelujah!" he repeated several times.

I wouldn't call it dancing, but Mr. Callahan began to shuffle his feet. He pushed his walker out of the way and marched across the kitchen. Zach leaned back in his chair, an amused expression on his face.

"Yes, sir," Zach said.

"Hallelujah!" Mr. Callahan said again.

The lawyer's vast vocabulary had been reduced to a single word. Over and over he said it. He marched up to Zach and slammed his hands down on the young lawyer's shoulders.

"God has touched me," Mr. Callahan said. "And I bless you for being obedient." He turned to me. "And Tammy Lynn, bless you for bringing this man of God to see me today."

"Yes, sir."

Mr. Callahan glanced around the room as if looking for someone to hit or something heavy to pick up.

"Is this going to last?" he asked Zach.

"I don't know," Zach answered.

"Hallelujah," Mr. Callahan said. "You're just the messenger."

"Yes, sir."

The side door that connected the kitchen to the garage opened, and Mrs. Callahan entered. A statuesque woman with magnificent silver hair, she'd been raised in suburban Atlanta. The lawyer's wife had rejected the fiery faith of Mr. Callahan's father as watered-down religion dispensed by a sleepy church in the center of town.

"Hello, Mrs. Callahan," I said, trying to remember my manners in the midst of a heavenly visitation. "This is Zach Mays, an associate at the firm where I'm working this summer in Savannah. We stopped by to pick up a couple of steers. My mother sent a bag of Silver Queen corn. It's already shucked and in the pot—"

"Hallelujah!" Mr. Callahan interrupted, staring at his wife, his eyes blazing with zeal. "God almighty has touched me today!"

"What the—?" she asked, her mouth dropping open.

"We'll be leaving," I said quickly. "We need to load the steers into the trailer."

Zach stood and extended his hand to Mrs. Callahan, who shook it limply without taking her eyes from her husband.

"Have a good day," Zach said, then turned to the older lawyer. "Mr. Callahan, it was an honor meeting you."

"God bless you both," Mr. Callahan boomed.

"I know the way out," I said.

As we made our way through the living room, I could hear Mr. Callahan repeating a few more "hallelujahs" accentuated with loud claps. Outside, I leaned against the front door and laughed.

"I know that was a holy moment," I said, "but it's funny to think what is going on in that kitchen right now. Mr. Callahan has been under wraps for so long, he's like a volcano about to explode. I can't wait to tell Mama what happened."

"I don't think you should."

"Not tell her?" I stepped away from the door and looked at him in surprise.

"It would be more like gossip than celebration."

"That's crazy," I protested. "Our church has prayed for Mr. Callahan for years."

"Then let him be the one to break the good news."

I started to argue, then stopped. "Okay. God used you to bring down the glory, so I guess you have the right to decide who should proclaim it."

"I don't know anything about bringing down the glory."

"Didn't you feel the presence of the Lord come into the kitchen?" My surprise returned stronger. "I thought maybe you saw an angel standing near the corner cupboard."

"I didn't see any angels. I just wanted God to touch Mr. Callahan. He's a nice gentleman."

"You didn't feel anything? That makes no sense to me."

Zach shook his head. "All I felt was a nudge to pray and had no idea if anything would happen. When it did, I watched."

"Well, let me know if God ever wants to touch me."

WE REACHED THE PEN where the steers waited. I'd left two ears of corn on the floorboards of the truck to lure them into the trailer. Zach stared at the driver's-side door.

"I'll back the trailer into position," I said. "You stick to praying, riding motorcycles, and admiralty law. Open the gate of the pen when I'm in position."

I pulled the truck forward, then backed into the holding pen. The tongue on the trailer was short, and I had lots of experience going in reverse. Zach walked beside the truck.

"Stay inside," Zach said as we passed by the gate. "It's messy in here."

I stopped the truck and handed him the two ears of corn.

"Here's the bait. Throw them in the trailer and shoo the steers in after them."

I heard the door of the trailer open and the rumble of the ramp. I looked in the side mirror but couldn't see Zach.

"Don't let them step on your foot," I said. "That would be worse than getting finned by a catfish."

"Two amputations in one day sounds bad," he said. "Come on, cows. Get in the trailer."

"Steers."

"Come on, hamburger," he said. "Move it!"

The trailer shifted as one of the steers came up the ramp. A few seconds later the second joined him.

"Make sure the latch is secure," I called out. "We don't want hamburger on the road."

Zach climbed into the truck.

"The prisoners are loaded and locked behind bars. Maybe seeing God bless Mr. Callahan can help me work through the guilt I feel about helping haul this beef to market."

8

DRIVING HOME WITH THE WINDOWS OF THE TRUCK LOWERED and the air blowing across my face, I basked in the wonder of what had happened to Mr. Callahan. I glanced across at Zach with increased respect. If he ever stopped practicing law, his future might be as a healing preacher. Zach casually picked up another long blade of grass and stuck it in the corner of his mouth.

I slowed down and turned into our driveway. The trailer bumped across the dirt ruts as I drove around the house to the feedlot. The new fence had been finished. The five dairy calves from Mr. Moorefield's farm were huddled in one corner. There was no sign of Kyle or Daddy.

"I'll park the truck and get Kyle to help us," I said.

"We can do it. Unloading should be easier than loading."

"But we don't want any of the calves to bolt."

Zach stuck his head out the window. "They look more my size, and they're off to the side. I'll get the gate."

Zach got out of the truck. I put the truck in reverse and began backing through the gate. Suddenly I saw a flash of black and white as one of Mr. Moorefield's calves ran through the opening between the fence and the trailer. Zach was standing on the opposite side of the trailer.

"One's loose!" he called out.

"Shut the gate," I said.

I drove forward, turned off the motor, and jumped out. Zach slammed the gate shut and raced after the calf. It was heading toward our garden. I grabbed a piece of rope from the bed of the truck and ran after them. The calf was zigzagging madly across the yard. After a few steps my sandals fell off, and I continued on barefoot. A runaway calf could wreak havoc in our garden and destroy a summer's work in seconds. The dry grass stung my tender feet.

"Get between the calf and the garden!" I yelled at Zach.

Zach reached the edge of the pole beans a few seconds before the calf and waved his arms. The calf spun around and headed toward the basketball goal. I ran parallel to him, then swerved in his direction. Suddenly the calf stopped. I coiled the rope into a loop and approached him.

"Easy, boy, easy," I said in a soft voice. "It's okay."

Zach came up behind the calf, whose eyes were wide with fear. The calf spun around, saw Zach, and ran toward me. Just before he reached me, Zach tackled him from behind by grabbing his rear legs. I darted forward to wrap the rope around the calf's neck, but he jumped up, pushing Zach into me. I lunged for the calf, and all three of us landed in a heap. I looped the rope over the calf, but it slid off and ended up on Zach's chest. I lunged over Zach, got the rope around the calf's neck, and pulled it tight.

The back door of the house opened, and Mama came outside. I was lying across Zach trying to control the struggling calf. Zach reached up and put his arms around me.

"Roll this way," he said, putting his hand on my left side. "Then I can hold the rope."

I shifted my weight, and we embraced. Zach got on his hands and knees. He grabbed the rope and held it close to the calf's neck.

"Do it this way," I said, putting my hands on his.

I repositioned the rope and threw in a hitch knot that I cinched down. Mama reached us.

"Tammy Lynn, get up," she scolded. "You're not dressed for calf roping."

"He was about to destroy the garden," I protested.

"And you're about to get sent to your—" Mama stopped. She grabbed the rope from Zach's hand. "Kyle and your daddy are in the front room with Mr. Moorefield. Get them."

I ran into the house. Daddy, Kyle, and Mr. Moorefield were signing some papers.

"One of the calves escaped," I said breathlessly, "but we caught it before it got into the garden. Come help."

The three men shot past me toward the rear of the house. I looked down at my dress. It was streaked with grass stains. I lifted my right foot and inspected it. The bottom was red and dirty. I rubbed it. There weren't any cuts.

I returned to the kitchen and looked out the door. Mr. Moorefield was leading the calf by the rope. Daddy, Kyle, and Zach were walking beside him. It was a tranquil scene without any hint of the drama just played out. Mama climbed the steps. I held the door open for her. She shook her head.

"Tammy Lynn, what were you thinking? Rolling around in the grass?"

"We weren't rolling around in the grass," I responded, trying to keep calm in the face of her implied accusation. "We were trying to corral the calf."

"I'm glad your daddy didn't see the way that man had his hands all over you."

Raising my voice, I said, "If by 'that man' you mean Zach Mays, there was no intent by either of us to have any improper contact. Trying not to get kicked by a spooked calf isn't my idea of a romantic encounter. We were just trying to get untangled without the calf escaping."

Mama looked sternly at me for a few seconds; then her face softened.

"I believe you were innocent, but I'm not so sure about Zach."

"You're misjudging him."

"We'll see. You'll have to soak that dress to get out the grass stains."

The door opened. It was Zach. He held my sandals in his hand. His face was streaked with dirt.

"Cinderella left her slippers in the grass," he said with a smile.

"Thanks," I said quickly.

Mama cleared her throat. "I was about to tell Tammy Lynn that you should clean the catfish before you wash up yourselves."

"Good idea," Zach said. "If one of them flops out of the bucket, it will give us another chance to roll around in the grass."

I felt all the color drain from my face. Mama didn't say anything. I jerked open the knife drawer and grabbed a filleting knife. The fish bucket was in the shade beneath the back steps. I marched past Zach, went down the steps, and grabbed the bucket. Zach followed me.

"What's wrong?" he asked in a low voice. "No one would think—"

"Then why give them a reason to? Get a piece of scrap lumber from the barn about this long." I stretched out my hands roughly a foot and a half apart. "There should be a hammer hanging on the wall near the fishing poles. Grab the hammer, the rubber gloves near the fishing poles, and a three-inch nail from one of the boxes on the shelf. Meet me by the hose connection at the corner of the house."

Zach left. I carried the bucket of fish to the corner of the house and turned on the hose. The fish had grown lethargic. They didn't respond to a splash of cold water. I considered sticking my face in the water to cool my temper. Zach returned and laid everything out on the grass.

"Where are the pliers?" I asked.

"You didn't tell me to get the pliers."

"How do you expect to skin a catfish without pliers?"

I jerked the hose and soaked the bottom of my dress.

"How do you expect me to understand what's going on if you don't tell me?"

"What were you thinking?" I replied. "Making a comment about rolling around in the grass with me? I'd just finished defending your innocence when you walked in and made catching the calf sound like a cheap setup."

"It was innocent."

"I know, but that's not how it looked to Mama."

"Then she's the one who needs to get her thinking straightened out."

"Stay here," I said. "I'll get the pliers."

I walked across the yard to the barn. The pliers weren't in their usual place, and I had to search for them. I finally found them sitting on a half-used roll of barbed wire. When I came out of the barn, Zach wasn't at the corner of the house. My heart sank. I was sure he'd gone into the house to confront Mama and accuse her of having a dirty mind. I ran to the back steps. Zach and Mama were standing beside the kitchen table. They weren't smiling. However, they weren't yelling either. Mama saw me and nodded.

"Zach was apologizing for his comment. I've accepted his apology and put it behind me." She handed me a large plastic ziplock bag. "You'll need this for the fish. Make it easy on yourself. Fillets will be fine."

Zach and I returned to the corner of the house. I turned on the water.

"What did you say to her?"

"That I'd made a thoughtless, wrong remark. I think she knew the truth."

I wasn't so sure.

"And I apologize to you, too," Zach continued. "You warned me to watch what I say. I've not done it."

I looked in his eyes. All I saw was sincerity.

"If Mama is okay, I'll let it go. Just be careful."

"Now, show me what to do with these catfish."

"Do you remember how to pick one up?"

Zach reached into the bucket. "I think so."

"Better a second lesson than another sting."

I retrieved a fish.

"Like this," I said, holding it up. "That way you avoid both the dorsal and pectoral fins. This fish doesn't have much fight left in it."

"Just like your mother when it comes to any negative opinions about me."

"No, nothing like my mama. Pour out the rest of the water. There's no reason to keep them alive."

Cleaning a whole catfish required nailing the fish's head to a board and peeling off the skin with a pair of pliers. Slicing fillets was simple. Holding the fish by the head with a gloved hand, I cut downward just behind the gills and slid the fillet knife the length of the fish, avoiding any contact with the bones. I then used the knife to separate the pale meat from the skin. I turned the fish over and handed the knife and a glove to Zach.

"Your turn."

He worked slowly but botched his first attempt.

"You give new meaning to 'mess of fish,'" I said with a smile. "Cut a little deeper behind the head and avoid gouging into the body."

I trimmed his fillet to make sure there weren't any bones hiding in it. I put another fish on the board, completed one side, and handed the knife to him.

"I get another chance?"

"Yes, there's more grace in the Taylor family than you might imagine."

He did a much better job, and his fillet was almost as large as mine. By the time we finished, Zach had mastered rudimentary filleting skills. I rinsed the final fillet in the water gushing from the hose.

"Don't tear up your med school application. You still might become a surgeon."

"That's not in my future, but every admiralty lawyer should know how to clean a fish."

"You filleted a fish, not cleaned it. We'll save the advanced course for another time."

We dumped the fish carcasses into a fifty-five-gallon drum that Daddy used to collect organic waste to mix into a compost pile on the back side of the garden. In the kitchen Mama held up the bag and weighed it in her hand.

"This should be plenty. Zach, there are fresh towels for you in the downstairs bath."

Walking up the stairs, I stopped and glanced over my shoulder in time to see Zach go into the sewing room. Several strands of light brown hair had escaped from the tight ponytail at the base of his neck. Somehow I had to let my parents know about Mr. Callahan. That would turn the tide in Zach's favor. I went into the bathroom and turned on the shower.

After I dried my hair, I spent a long time deciding which dress to wear. Everything in my closet looked the same. Finally I shut my eyes, stuck out my hand, and grabbed the first hanger I touched. It held a light blue cotton dress with faint yellow stripes, an adequate choice for a catfish supper.

When I went downstairs, the door to the sewing room was open. I cautiously peeked around the corner. Zach wasn't there, and I was pleased to see he'd neatly made the bed. There weren't any dirty clothes scattered across the floor.

"The twins took Zach outside to show him the garden," Mama said when I came into the kitchen. "I also told them to pick the corn for supper. Did you give the corn to Mrs. Callahan?"

"Yes, ma'am. She wasn't there when we arrived, but she came in just before we left."

"How's Mr. Callahan doing?"

Constrained by Zach's gag order, I didn't answer.

"Is he worse?" Mama asked, alarm in her voice.

"No, ma'am. He's better, much better after our visit."

"Good. He's always enjoyed having you around."

While we pulled the strings from the green beans, Mama reminisced about some of the times I'd spent at Mr. Callahan's office.

"I'll never forget the time he took you with him to the jail," she said. "He convinced me to wait in the car while you went into the cell block. I thought you'd be terrified, but you came out with the names and addresses of two men you wrote to faithfully for the next six months to a year."

"Bob Sellers and Renfrow Ayers," I said.

"That's right. I wasn't sure it was such a good idea and wouldn't let you put your return address on the letters. But you drew pictures, printed out Bible verses, and told them how many eggs the hens laid each week."

"And when Bob Sellers got out, Daddy got him a job at the chicken plant."

"Yes, I saw him and his wife at the grocery store a few weeks ago. They've joined a church on the east side of the county."

Zach and the twins returned from the garden with ears of corn sticking out the top of a paper sack.

"Shuck it outside at the feedlot," Mama said. "The steers and calves would probably like a snack."

"Where is Kyle?" I asked.

"In town with your daddy. They'll be back shortly. You go with Zach and the twins to shuck the corn. I'll finish in here."

We walked across the yard toward the feedlot. Zach lagged behind, and I stayed with him.

"Is your mother okay?"

"I hope so."

"Ellie gave Zach a raw peanut to eat," Emma called over her shoulder.

"Really, how did you like it?"

"It made me appreciate why they roast them."

We caught up with the twins.

"Tammy Lynn likes boiled peanuts," Ellie said. "I think they're slimy and gross."

"I've never tried a boiled peanut," Zach said.

"Most of the peanuts in Georgia are grown farther south," Emma said, "but Daddy found a variety that will grow in our soil if they break it up deep. Mama makes homemade peanut butter."

"I'm a big fan," Zach said. "Any single guy who doesn't eat peanut butter is at risk of starvation."

We reached the feedlot. The five calves from the Moorefield place looked so much alike it was hard to pick out the one that had escaped. Zach and I settled on a frisky fellow with two white blotches on its face. When we began dropping the corn husks inside the pen, Mr. Callahan's steers sauntered over. Emma and Ellie suggested a contest to determine who could remove all the corn silks from an ear of corn. I offered to serve as judge, but they insisted on Zach. He spent a lot of time inspecting each ear.

"You're spending so much time with those two ears of corn you're not cleaning any yourself," I said.

"That's the way it is with judges, Ms. Taylor. They inspect other people's work without doing any themselves."

Zach continued turning over the ears of corn. Finally he nodded his head.

"I'm ready to render a verdict."

We all stopped.

"I'm going to rule like King Solomon. Emma and Ellie have

equal claim to the cleanest ear of corn I've ever seen. Both of you are winners."

"But there was only one baby," Emma protested. "We have two ears of corn. It's not right to make the Bible fit a situation unless the facts are the same."

"Real judges do it all the time," Zach answered. "They call it judicial reasoning. If either of you doesn't like my decision, you can file an appeal with Judge Tammy Lynn Taylor."

I laughed. "And my decision is that both of you start cleaning another ear of corn before I send you to jail."

By the time we finished, the calves had come close enough to share the husks with the steers.

"I wish we could keep this one," Ellie said, rubbing the top of a calf's head. "If we did, I think I'd name you—"

"Hold it," Zach said. "You said you can't name next week's supper."

"I named the catfish that stung you," Ellie said. "I'm calling him Neptune Poseidon. He attacked you because you snatched him from the depths of the deep."

"You've studied Greek mythology?"

"Yes. The Greek god of the sea was Poseidon and the Romans named him Neptune. We have to learn about ancient religions so we can understand the books and poetry we read."

Zach turned to me. "Did you—"

"Yes. Mama teaches that kind of thing, along with the best way to can fresh tomatoes from the garden."

We took the corn to the house. Mama had a pot of boiling water waiting on the stove. After we washed our hands, we gathered in the kitchen. Daddy and my brothers had returned from town.

"Who wants cornmeal and who wants salt and pepper?" Mama asked.

"Give Zach some of both," I said. "Maybe you can cut Neptune Poseidon in two."

"What?" Mama asked.

Ellie explained while I helped Mama fry the fish. As soon as the hot fish were draining on sheets of paper towel, we gathered around the kitchen table to pray. Before I could protest, Zach grabbed my left hand.

I didn't hear a word of Daddy's prayer.

Every nerve in my body directed its attention to the places where my palm and fingers made contact with Zach Mays. Ellie was right. His hand was strong and friendly. I could feel the slightly raised places where the fish had cut him and avoided any hint of a squeeze. I didn't want to hurt him—or send a silent invitation. Still, it was one of the most intense physical experiences of my life. When contact between a man and a woman hasn't been devalued by casual use, the slightest touch can be more potent than a nuclear explosion. I took a deep breath. I didn't want the moment to end, yet wasn't sure I could stand much more if it didn't. Daddy said, "Amen." A couple of seconds passed before my hand returned to its owner.

"Which is the salt and pepper?" Zach asked Mama.

I looked at him in shock. Instead of meeting my eyes, he stepped past me toward the food on the counter, leaving me facing Ellie instead. She touched her hand and gave me a knowing smile. I tried to look serious but knew it was in vain. She stepped close.

"Was I right?" she whispered.

"Quiet," I responded under my breath. "Wait until it matters."

It was a wonderful meal. Zach was less a stranger to the family, and the conversation flowed more freely. I didn't say much.

Zach loved the salt-and-pepper catfish. Any qualms he had about eating meat he'd met in person left with the first bite. And as always, the corn was heavenly.

"Mrs. Taylor, this is one of the best meals I've ever eaten," Zach said as he deposited a third corn cob on a scrap plate at our end of the table.

"Chasing that calf gave you an appetite," Daddy said. "I heard you and Tammy Lynn ended up in a heap."

I cleared my throat.

"Yes, sir," Zach said.

"And we saved the garden," I added.

"Mrs. Taylor, I could eat this meal for Thanksgiving dinner," Zach said.

His comment prompted a discussion about the best Thanksgiving menu. Zach's mother prepared a traditional turkey. The twins liked chickens stuffed with cornbread dressing and a sweet potato casserole topped with pecans and marshmallows. Bobby kept quiet until the end.

"I'd rather have hickory-smoked barbecue than anything else," he said. "If Mr. Bowman would give us a couple of pork shoulders for Thanksgiving dinner, I'd split enough firewood to last him until Christmas."

I knew what would happen next. The subject of barbecue was more controversial in our family than the doctrine of predestination. I'd heard debates about the merits of different cuts of meat, choices of wood, and the best sauces. Mama said it gave the men something to argue about that wasn't really important. But what I'd heard over the years didn't support Mama's theory. Visible veins in a man's neck signaled the presence of a passionately held belief, and I'd heard men raise their voices over cuts of meat and sauces.

Even in our family there were sharp differences of opinion. Daddy, Kyle, and Bobby disagreed, and having Zach at the table gave each of them a chance to present his case.

"What kind do you like best?" Kyle asked Zach when he finished his argument for cooking the whole hog.

Zach didn't hesitate. "Sliced beef smoked in mesquite with a thick, sweet sauce on it. Those steers in the feedlot would be great candidates for barbecue."

The three males in my family looked at Zach in disbelief. To drop beef into the discussion of barbecue was unthinkable. In our world barbecue came only from pigs.

"Are you serious?" Bobby asked.

"Of course I am."

Zach defended the merits of smoked beef, and Mama nodded her head. She didn't like the smell of pork, which was the reason our family didn't make our own barbecue.

"That sounds good to me," she said.

"I don't know," Daddy said, "but it shows that where and how you're raised plays a big role in what you like."

"But a person can change," I said.

"Not about barbecue," Kyle and Bobby said at the same time.

"Girls, head upstairs," Mama said to the twins when we finished. "You're helping teach the first-grade class in the morning, and you need to study the lesson. I'll check with you in a little bit."

Faced with a direct order, they left without protest.

"Mr. and Mrs. Taylor, could we talk in private for a few minutes?" Zach asked after they were out of the room.

"I'll check on the livestock in the feedlot," Kyle said quickly.

"And I'll go with him," Bobby added.

The boys exited through the back door.

9

MY HEART STARTED POUNDING. MAMA WIPED HER HANDS ON A dish towel. Daddy fidgeted in the doorway and waited. Zach pulled his ponytail.

"Would anyone like a glass of ice water?" Mama asked.

"I would," I said quickly.

No one else spoke. Mama poured a glass of ice water for me. It was something she rarely did except when I was sick in bed. A healthy adult member of our family could get his or her own glass of water.

"Ready?" Daddy asked.

"Yes," Zach said.

Daddy led the way, followed by Zach, Mama, then me, in a somber parade. I commanded my heart to slow down, but it refused. Zach should have talked to me first. My mind raced through a half dozen scenarios. I hoped he wasn't going to try to force Mama and Daddy to make a decision about us courting before they had time to pray and discuss it in private. That would be a recipe for disaster. Pressure from him would be a sure sign to them that we needed to wait.

We reached the front room. I offered up a silent plea for help. Daddy and Mama sat on the sofa. Zach and I chose the same chairs we'd occupied the previous night, but I didn't want a repeat performance. No one spoke for a few seconds. I could barely stand the tension.

"Nobody asked my opinion about barbecue," I said tentatively.

"You always eat what's on your plate," Daddy replied with a nervous laugh. "I mean, not that you eat too much. But I've never considered it one of your favorite—"

"We can discuss barbecue later," Mama cut in. "Zach, we are listening."

Zach cleared his throat. "Thank you. I don't always think before I speak, and sometimes I can be blunt when I should be diplomatic, but you've been kind enough to overlook my blunders, and I appreciate the hospitality you've shown me." He turned to Mama. "Mrs. Taylor, you're an awesome teacher. What you've done with the twins is amazing. Being around the girls is an education in itself, and I look forward to telling my mom about them. It'll be neat to see what the twins are doing ten or fifteen years from now."

Mama had taught me, too, but it seemed Zach was more impressed by the twins. He turned to Daddy.

"And Mr. Taylor, you have the ability to bring out the best in each member of your family. I enjoyed working on the fence with you this morning and would like to get to know you better. Your wise words about hearing God's voice helped me gain perspective on several challenges I'm facing even now."

Zach hadn't shared his challenges with me. I wondered what they were.

"You're at peace with the path you've chosen for your family, and I don't want to do anything to disrupt that. So, to avoid any embarrassment or stress, I don't think I should go to church with you tomorrow morning. If I show up it will put pressure on you to justify why someone who looks like me is interested in your daughter. It's one thing for Tami and me to walk together on a sidewalk in Savannah; it's another for us to sit next to each other in a pew at your church. I don't want to put you or the family in an awkward situation."

Mama and Daddy looked at each other.

"We talked about that last night before going to sleep," Daddy said slowly. "If you visit the church, it will cause people who haven't met you to talk. Some of them are quick to judge."

Mama cleared her throat. "But that's not the most important consideration. Regardless of the opinions of others, the protection of biblical standards is important. You have different beliefs, which influence your conduct and appearance."

I bit my lower lip.

"If the narrow-minded people at the church could have seen what Zach did today at—"

"Tammy Lynn!" Mama said. "Watch your tongue!"

"But people should be judged by the fruit of their lives."

"And out of the overflow of the heart, the mouth speaks," Mama answered. "The way our society has blurred the differences between men and women is the cause of a lot of problems. A consistent biblical stance on this issue in clothes and relationship between the sexes is important for more reasons than I can go into right now."

"This doesn't have anything to do with appearance," I said.

Zach held up his hand.

"I'm as sure about this"—he hesitated for a second—"as your mother is about the impropriety of a man having a ponytail. I don't want to upset your family any more than I already have."

I blinked back a hot tear. Nobody noticed.

"Zach, I think it's the right decision," Daddy said.

"And I have a peace about it," he answered. "Explain to the others as you think best."

"I'm not at peace," I said.

"You know what I'm saying is the truth," Zach replied evenly.

"But I have questions." I turned to Daddy. "May Zach and I talk in private? We could sit on the porch."

Daddy looked away for a few seconds before meeting my eyes.

"No, Tammy Lynn. This isn't the time for that conversation."

"Then we may as well go back to Savannah tonight," I shot back.

Mama came over to me. "Try to calm down, dear. You can't think straight when you're upset. This is best for both—"

Pulling away from Mama, I stormed out of the house, letting the screen door slam behind me. Tears ran down my cheeks. I angrily brushed them away. I didn't slow down until I reached the poplar tree that stood as a sentinel in our front yard. Rubbing my eyes, I looked back at the house. The lights were on in the front room. Zach, Mama, and Daddy were talking. Let them say what they wanted. They could dissect me like one of the frogs from Putnam's Pond. I didn't care.

When I was eight years old, I'd run away from home. Mama, pregnant with Bobby and busy chasing Kyle all over the house, didn't have time to give me the attention I wanted. Feeling abandoned, I decided to leave and start a new life. I covertly fixed four sandwiches and threw a few apples in a bag. If Johnny Appleseed could journey across the continent with nothing more than a sackful of apples to his name, I should be able to do the same. After I'd walked a mile down the road, Mrs. Jackie Poole, a middle-aged woman from the church, stopped her car and invited me to her house for fresh lemonade. Without anything to drink, I had a burning thirst. Mrs. Poole lived in a well-kept cottage at the edge of a meadow filled with wildflowers. After I drank a tall glass of lemonade, she offered to take me home. I was too embarrassed to tell her what she, of course, already knew. Years later, we'd both laughed about it.

Now, perhaps the option to run away was real. Hadn't Mama said it was time for me to leave? I had a summer job and was on the verge of a self-sufficient career. Independence lay within my grasp. It was time to change the way I related to my parents, to end their dominance. I walked over to the poplar tree and glanced up. The branches of the ancient tree stretched upward in a leafy plea toward the darkening sky. I bowed my head and prayed, but no answer came. My heart felt numb. The threesome inside the house was still silhouetted in the window. I pulled off a piece of bark and broke it in two. Hope for happiness of any kind in my future appeared dim. Running away probably had as much chance of success now as it did when I was eight.

The front door opened, and Zach came outside. The lights went out in the front room. Zach walked over and put his hand on the tree near mine. I dropped my hand to my side.

"When you left the house you proved my point," he said.

"Don't lecture me."

"Are you afraid of the truth?"

I turned toward him, my face set. "Is that the way you talk to someone who's hurting?"

"I thought you wanted me to be honest."

"Look, I don't have the energy for another fight right now. Not with you"—I gestured toward the house—"and not with them. I've spent my entire life defending myself and my family. I've tried to see it as an opportunity to let my light shine, but often it's been a burden. I need a break from the stress. And I'm not interested in trading pressure from my parents for pressure from you. I need everyone to leave me alone, to let me be who I am."

"I don't want to leave you alone."

"But isn't that where you're heading? That was the whole point of the conversation in the house. You're separating yourself from me and my family."

"Don't blow it up bigger than it is. I don't think I should go to your church in the morning because I don't want to embarrass your family."

"But it's not just about tomorrow. Be realistic. I could try to break away from this place, but even if I want to it's not going to happen. And as long as I'm connected to the people living in that house, you can't get close to me without getting close to them. Church, home, beliefs: they're all wrapped up together. Even when we're in Savannah, the way I've been raised is the greatest influence in my life." I pulled another piece of bark from the tree.

Zach stepped closer. "I felt the energy between us when I held your hand during the prayer."

I was about to break another piece of bark in two but stopped. "You did?"

"I'm not dense. It sure felt a lot better than when Neptune Poseidon speared my hand."

Zach reached out and put his hand underneath my chin. I drew back. His hand stayed with me.

"Please," he said. "This is all I'm going to do. I want to help hold your chin up when it starts to droop. I want to encourage you, not drag you down. I can't do that unless we're together."

The breath left my body at his last words. I wanted desperately to see his eyes more clearly. But in the dark, everything was shapes and shadows.

"And I'm sure not going to church in the morning is the right decision," he said. "Don't make it bigger than it is."

I wasn't convinced. Looking toward the house, I saw a fuzzy outline of the twins' faces in the window of the second-story hallway.

"Let's go inside," I said. "Old houses have curious eyes."

MAMA AND DADDY had gone to their bedroom and shut the door. A closed door meant they were not to be disturbed. I said good night to Zach and trudged up the stairs. Ellie and Emma, wearing their pajamas, were sitting cross-legged on the rug in the center of our bedroom. I kicked off my shoes.

"Did you squeeze his hand at the end of the blessing?" Ellie asked.

"She couldn't," Emma interrupted. "That's the hand he hurt at the pond."

"I'm not thinking about his hand right now."

"It's so different from Daddy's hand or Roscoe Vick's hand," Ellie continued.

The twins had a knack for redirecting my focus. Distancing myself from them was hard to imagine.

"When have you been holding Roscoe Vick's hand?" I asked.

"Mrs. Kilgore puts the prayer requests in the center of the table, and we hold hands while she prays," Ellie said. "Roscoe always finds a way to stand next to me. His hand is kind of slippery, like he didn't get all the soap off before coming to church."

"Emma, does he ever hold your hand?"

"I wouldn't let him." She sniffed.

"Can he tell you apart?"

"I always move to the other side of the room when it's prayer time," Emma said.

I slid my legs straight out in front of me.

"Ellie, I don't want you holding Zach's hand anymore."

"Why?"

"I don't need the competition."

Both girls laughed.

"And were you spying on us when we were in the front yard?"

"Not spying," Ellie said. "Just making sure you were okay."

Emma lowered her voice. "Tammy Lynn, I thought Zach was about to kiss you. When he put his hand on your face, I thought I would faint. What was he saying? Have you decided to let a boy kiss you before your wedding?"

"It was a private conversation, and he wasn't trying to kiss me. He just wanted to encourage me."

"He could encourage me anytime he wants," Ellie sighed. "I wanted to pull his ponytail so bad at the supper table that I had trouble keeping my mind on my food."

"People are going to be talking about his hair at church tomorrow," Emma said. "It's going to be a problem."

"If anyone says anything to me, I'm going to show them a picture of Jesus in my Bible," Ellie said. "His hair was a lot longer than Zach's."

"He's not going."

"What?" both girls exclaimed.

I explained in simple terms, without my previous emotion, the conversation in the front room. I carefully avoided any criticism of Mama and Daddy.

"How did you feel?" Ellie asked when I finished. "If I heard that it would make me think he didn't like me."

My little sister's insight startled me. More than Emma, her personality mirrored mine.

"That's why Zach came outside to talk to me. I didn't try to change his mind, and Mama and Daddy agreed with him. Things like this have to go forward slowly. Remember, they haven't agreed to let me court him."

"But you want to, don't you?" Ellie asked.

I hesitated. "Yes, if for no other reason than to keep him away from you." I pushed her onto her back.

After brushing our teeth, we returned to the rug and played Scrabble. Emma won when she used a *q* and a *z* to spell *quartz* in a row that included a triple-score block. After a while, I realized I'd relaxed. When the game was over, we lay on the rug with our pillows under our heads and played a game we'd invented called "Imagination."

One of us would describe a place she'd been or read about in a book. Another would inhabit the place with a few interesting people, usually including a few from Powell Station who had as little business living in our imaginary world as Dorothy in Oz. The third person began a story with everyone taking turns to add twists and turns.

I set the scene as Oscar Callahan's farm and described it in great detail. Emma included the lawyer, Zach, and me in the opening scene. Ellie began the story and dropped in Roscoe Vick, now grown-up and working as an attorney for Mr. Callahan. Ellie's plot was a conflict between Zach and Roscoe for my affection. Romantic comedy was a new genre for us. Within a few minutes the three of us were laughing so hard my side hurt, and my heart felt better.

Sometimes it was nice not having to be an adult.

10

IT WAS A HOT, CLOUDLESS NIGHT. THE SMALL AIR CONDITIONER in the window labored to convert the humid air of the Georgia coast into a cool breeze. Sister Dabney rolled over in bed and reached across to touch her husband's shoulder. Even sleepy contact can have meaning for couples who have persevered in unity beyond the thrill of youth to maturity forged in shared experience. But Sister Dabney's right arm fell with a thud against the thin sheets. The callous emptiness of the moment brought her awake with a slight moan.

He was gone. After almost forty years of marriage. Not just for a night, but for over three years. And with a woman Sister Dabney had pulled from the pit of despair. Betrayal heaped upon infidelity.

Sister Dabney pulled a tissue from a box on the nightstand and wiped more perspiration from her forehead. It was hot; however, the night sweats were fueled more by the black fire of abandonment that burned in her heart than the heat of the night. Unseen tormentors stoked the flames, spirits of accusation she could rebuke when awake but that crept back later to shoot their arrows into her defenseless dreams.

"You lie," she muttered.

The rumblings ceased, but she knew they were there, crouching out of sight.

Sister Dabney rolled onto her back. All her life, she'd told the truth—to those who would listen and those who wouldn't. She'd seen so many secrets of people's hearts laid bare she'd grown tired of looking. There was nothing new under the sun. But the deception in her own home caught her unaware. That blindness had shaken her to the core.

She got out of bed. The floorboards popped and protested as her full weight rested on them. Sister Dabney didn't own a bathroom scale or need one to tell her what anyone could see. She left the bedroom and walked down a short hallway to the kitchen at the rear of the house. She opened the refrigerator door. She wasn't hungry, but food at any hour brought comfort.

There was a loud bang at the front door. She stopped, not sure if the sound was actual or imagined. Another bang followed. She walked toward the living room. Freedom from fear was one gift that hadn't been stolen from her. She'd laid hands on people with infectious diseases and looked into the eyes of demoniacs. If death at the end of a robber's gun barrel waited for her, it would be a welcome martyrdom. She peered through the spy hole.

It was one of the boys who had stopped in front of her house. He had a baseball bat in his hand. He lifted the bat and struck the door. Anger rose in her. After tormenting her with words, the boy had returned to assault her. She flipped on the porch light and flung open the door, prepared to deliver a proper rebuke that would send him scurrying away. The boy held up his hand to shield his eyes from the light. His shirt was torn and hanging off his back. He lowered his hand. One eye was swollen partially shut. Leaning against the steps was his bicycle.

"He came back, just like you said," the boy panted, fear and panic in his eyes.

"What happened?"

"He beat me up; then I hit him in the head with the bat and ran out of the house."

"Did you knock him out?"

"No."

"Is anyone still at the house?"

"My little sister and my auntie. They've locked the door to the big bedroom. He says he's going to burn down the house because my auntie won't tell him where my mama is staying."

"Come inside," Sister Dabney said, looking past the boy's shoulder toward the street. "I'll call 911."

The boy handed her the bat as he entered the house. There were more bruises on his back.

"You'll be safe here."

SUNDAY MORNING I rolled over and watched Emma and Ellie sleep in adolescent innocence. Every inch of the bedroom was familiar to me, down to the slight cracks in the wood floor caused by the settling of the house.

The twins didn't need to get up for a few more minutes. While I watched them sleep, I prayed their hearts would awaken to romantic love in God's perfect time. Prayer can be a long-term investment.

I slipped out of bed, threw on an old cotton dress, and tiptoed barefoot down the stairs with a pair of old sandals in my hand. I could hear the water running in the bathroom next to Mama and Daddy's bedroom. They would be in the kitchen shortly. The door to the sewing room was closed. Picturing Zach lying in bed with his eyes closed and his head resting on the pillow, I shivered slightly in imaginary intimacy and pushed the scene from my mind.

I went into the kitchen. We didn't do unnecessary work on the Lord's Day. The coffeepot was ready to go; all I had to do was press the button. I grabbed the blue egg bucket. Taking care of our animals was a seven-day-a-week responsibility. I slipped on my sandals and walked across the dew-covered yard. The wet grass tickled the ends of my toes. I knew the scientific explanation for dew, but I still considered its early-morning appearance during a hot Georgia summer a mannalike miracle. I collected six eggs and returned to the house. Mama and Daddy were sitting at the table with their coffee. I put the eggs in the sink.

"I'll finish in the bathroom, then get the twins going," I said as I walked past them.

"Thanks for the coffee," Daddy said.

"Just a minute, Tammy Lynn," Mama said.

I stopped at the door leading toward the hallway.

"I'll rinse the eggs off before we leave for church," I said.

"Will you join us?" she asked.

"You know I don't drink coffee."

"That's okay," Daddy said.

I came over to the table.

"I'll slide in next to your daddy," Mama said, moving to the other side of the table. "That way we can both see you."

"Is this a good time to apologize for how I acted last night?" I asked.

"It's always a good time to confess your sins," Mama said.

I'd confessed my sins to Mama and Daddy innumerable times. Keeping short accounts was essential to a healthy spiritual life. Forgiveness was freely granted once they determined my repentance was genuine. I folded my hands and put them on the table.

"I'm sorry that I got upset and walked out of the house last night."

"And slammed the door," Mama added.

"Yes, ma'am."

"What else?" she asked.

This type of spiritual cross-examination, although embarrassing, effectively uncovered the root causes of rebellion.

"I dishonored both of you by not allowing you to function as my parents in the way God intends. I'm supposed to submit to you cheerfully until I marry and start my own family. Even then, the commandment to honor you is a lifelong obligation."

They didn't speak.

"And I didn't set a good example for Zach," I continued. "He's watching, and we have an opportunity to influence him toward the truth. I acted out of my sinful nature and gave in to the flesh when I should have submitted to God's patience and peace."

I took a deep breath, glad to have everything out in the open.

"Anything else?" I asked.

"That's a lot better than I could do," Daddy said, rubbing his chin, "but it's not the main reason we wanted to talk to you."

"But why else would you want to—?" I began in surprise, then stopped.

"Tammy Lynn, do you still want our permission to court Zach?" Daddy asked.

I paused for a second to collect myself. "Even though he doesn't want to go to church with us?"

Mama looked at Daddy, who nodded. She spoke.

"That decision proved more about his understanding of our beliefs and ways than pretending to agree with us when he doesn't," she said. "He's the product of his family, just like you are ours. Your daddy and I aren't out of touch with reality. There may not be a man in our church for you to marry, which means you'll need to look elsewhere. Last night we saw something more important about Zach than the length of his hair. He has respect for our beliefs and consideration for our family. That's rare among outsiders. If you're going to court someone who didn't grow up in Powell Station and go to our church, that kind of attitude has to be present for us to allow a relationship to develop."

"Like Melissa Freiberger?" I asked, referring to a young woman in the church who had a good marriage to an outsider.

"And remember, permission to court isn't consent to marriage."

"Yes, ma'am."

"So, you have our blessing to get to know him better," Mama concluded.

I felt like pinching myself to make sure I wasn't dreaming.

"What potential do you see in him?" I asked, trying to uncover more of their thinking.

Daddy smiled. "The same as you."

I looked into my soul and came up empty. "Could you help me out?"

"A man after God's own heart."

"Yes, but his conduct—"

"Needs improvement. That's where the honesty comes in," Mama said.

"It took me awhile to come around," Daddy said, putting his hand on Mama's shoulder.

"But Zach may not want to adopt our ways and beliefs."

"Neither did Melissa's husband, but he's a good man who loves God," Daddy said.

"How this is going to turn out isn't clear to us," Mama continued, "but we know it's a new opportunity for all of us to exercise our faith."

Daddy took a sip of coffee. "We've placed your future in God's hands. His grace is sufficient. I think you're the greatest daughter in the world."

I was still confused, but Daddy was so sweet. I wished I could meet a man just like him.

Mama leaned forward and smiled. "And put last night behind you. I don't condone sin, but I was young once, and the fire in you isn't much different from the one that burned in me."

Daddy put his arm around Mama's shoulders. "You know, your mama could have been a lawyer."

"A better one than I'll ever be."

"No," she replied sharply. "You're the sum of our parts, and a jewel in the Lord's crown. You stand on our shoulders through your influence in the places God sends you. We believe there are great things ahead for you."

"That's right." Daddy kissed Mama on the cheek. "Very great things."

UPSTAIRS, I WENT through the steps of getting ready for church without conscious awareness of my actions. Even though my actual future was cloudy, my parents' permission to court Zach Mays transported me to a place of fantasy. By the time I finished rubbing my head with a towel after a long shower, my mind had raced through the possibilities of long walks on the beach in the moonlight, a beautiful house in Savannah, and cute, chubby babies who always smiled and never cried. When I opened the door, Emma was waiting outside.

"You take longer than you used to," she said. "I've been standing here for at least five minutes."

"You could have used that time to pray," I replied, putting my hands together in front of me.

"I did. That you would hurry up. Ellie and I have to do our hair, too."

Fixing our hair on Sunday was different. Mama always kept her long hair in a bun, but younger, unmarried women and girls only had to pin up their hair on Sundays. It wasn't necessary to wind it as tight as a tennis ball, and I usually caught mine up loosely with a few wisps hanging out the back. I selected a light blue skirt and white blouse that Mama had ironed and hung in the closet while I'd been away for the summer. Some people said our clothes looked like the 1950s; others believed the 1940s were our era. I wasn't sure. All I knew was that my clothes didn't go out of style because they'd never been in style in the first place.

I took my Bible downstairs. Kyle and Bobby were in the kitchen eating cereal. They were wearing dark pants, white shirts, and dark ties.

"Have you seen Zach?" I asked.

"He's on the front porch in jeans and a T-shirt," Bobby said. "Didn't you tell him to bring church clothes?"

"He's not going."

"Why not?" both boys asked at once.

Wondering why it usually fell to me to do all the explaining, I went through a brief version of the previous night's conversation. When I finished, Kyle turned to Bobby.

"Do you know what this means for us?"

"Yeah, we don't have to pick a girl from the church," Bobby replied.

"You're in good shape," I said to Bobby. "There's Marie, Sarah, Nancy Kate, and Sylvia."

"Sylvia? Are you kidding?"

"Sylvia Bremen is a wonderful person. She helped me last year in vacation Bible school. She's great with children."

"Have you ever heard her sing?" Bobby replied. "She sounds like a dying cat stuck in a tree."

I'd found something else for Sylvia to do during music time with the kids.

"But you shouldn't make fun of her," I said, trying to keep from laughing.

"And I don't have to court her either."

Kyle put down his spoon. "Tammy Lynn, I like Zach, but I'm not sure he'll ever fit in with our family."

I LEFT THE KITCHEN. Zach was sitting in the porch swing with a cup of coffee in his hand. I rested my hand against one of the porch posts.

"Mama and Daddy talked to me this morning," I said with what I hoped wasn't a silly smile on my face. "They've given permission for us to court."

Zach stopped rocking the swing. "Really?"

"Yes, what do you think?"

Zach rocked the swing once more before answering.

"That God answers prayer and works miracles."

The porch swing rocked back and forth several times.

"What are you thinking?" Zach asked.

"That what you just said was one of the nicest things anyone has ever told me. It's hard to believe."

"Tammy Lynn!" Mama called out. "Come here, please."

"Don't go away," I said hurriedly.

"That won't happen until we leave for Savannah."

"I know, but—" I stopped, not sure what to say. "I'll be right back."

I rushed inside. Mama was in the hallway near the sewing room.

"Sister Belmont called. She has the gout and wondered if you could teach her Sunday school class."

"What age?"

"Fourth and fifth grades."

"Sure," I said, turning back toward the porch.

"Hold on," Mama said, holding out a sheet of paper. "I took notes about her lesson for the day. The twins aren't in that class anymore and won't be there to help you."

I grabbed the sheet and quickly read it. The class was studying the miracles of Jesus.

"This will be easy," I said.

"If you spend time seeking the Lord's blessing," Mama answered firmly. "Zach will be here when we get home, and you have a long ride to Savannah later this afternoon."

I glanced at the front door with longing.

"Yes, ma'am. May I tell him?"

"I'll wait here."

I opened the screen door and told Zach about my responsibilities for the morning.

"Maybe you could tell them about our miracle," he said.

I felt my face flush. Trying to look normal, I walked quickly past Mama on my way upstairs. The twins were in the bedroom getting ready. I grabbed a chair and took it to the end of the hallway where I positioned it in front of the window the girls had used to spy on Zach and me. I could see the tree where Zach placed his hand beneath my chin and whispered that he wanted to encourage me. I melted in the memory.

"What are you doing?" Ellie asked, sneaking up on me.

I grabbed the paper with the lesson outline on it and flipped open my Bible.

"Getting ready to teach Sister Belmont's class. She's not feeling well."

"We need to leave in a few minutes."

"It won't take long to study these verses."

I made my eyes focus on the red and black letters on the page. Jesus' first miracle in the Gospel of John involved turning water into wine. It was a tricky subject, but it connected to a wedding, the celebration of the love of a man for a woman. That part sounded good.

"Please, come with us," Ellie pleaded with Zach as we left the house. "We can tell people you've taken a vow like Samson not to cut your hair."

"Which wouldn't be true. I'm not a Nazirite."

I didn't look back as we crossed the yard, but when I heard the screen door slam shut, I glanced over my shoulder. Zach had gone inside. The conversation in the van during the ten-minute drive to the church didn't penetrate my consciousness. My mind stayed home with Zach. It was strange thinking about him alone in our house.

The notion of being there with him sent shivers down my spine as I followed him through the empty rooms. I opened my lesson outline and quickly read it again.

Sister Belmont's class was filled with faces of children I'd known since they were babies. Not many newcomers joined our church—the demands of holiness raised the cost of discipleship beyond most people's spiritual budget. But the staying power of families like ours was strong. Annual revival meetings attracted a few new converts; however, there was concern in the congregation why the holy fire of the past now did little more than smolder. Daddy said Pastor Vick and the elders spent a lot of time praying for a return of the Lord's favor.

The Sunday school class was much like one I'd attended at their age. The children treated teachers, even a substitute like me, with respect. They quickly mastered the memory verse for the morning and by the end of the class could list in order the first eight miracles of Jesus recorded in John. No one asked why Jesus turned water into wine. When the bell rang at the end of the class, several of the girls politely thanked me for teaching them. I erased the chalkboard and joined my family in the sanctuary.

We were surrounded by more familiar faces. The large sanctuary could seat many more people than currently came. I'd been told that during the rising tide of our movement, the sounds of singing and shouting echoed off the brick walls of a crowded sanctuary with such vibrancy that it seemed heaven's chorus had joined those on earth. As we settled in for the start of the service, there was a buzz toward the rear of the room. I turned and saw a crowd of people gathered around someone who had entered. I couldn't tell who it was. Mama, who was sitting between Daddy and me, leaned close to Daddy, then turned to me.

"Praise the Lord," she said. "It's Oscar Callahan."

I alone knew why he'd come.

The small crowd reached our pew. Mr. Callahan glanced in my

direction and waved. Mrs. Callahan wasn't with him. The old lawyer continued to the front of the sanctuary. The ushers placed him in a seat of honor. Pastor Vick came down from the platform to personally greet him.

As the service began, I positioned myself so I could watch Mr. Callahan. He was able to stand during the long period of singing. The Lord's gift of new strength hadn't dissipated. After the offering, Pastor Vick approached the pulpit.

"Brother Callahan, would you like to say a few words to the congregation?"

Mr. Callahan walked with steady strides onto the platform. He was wearing a dark suit. From a distance, he looked more like the old photograph of his father on the wall of his office than ever before. He faced the congregation. His eyes moved across the crowd until they met mine. There was no mistaking his questioning look. He was asking my permission. I felt my face flush.

I panicked. I could sense Mama eyeing me. I nodded my head, then wished I hadn't. It was too late. Mr. Callahan spoke.

"Thank you, Pastor. I'll be brief. Yesterday Tammy Lynn Taylor and a young lawyer friend of hers from Savannah named Zach Mays came by the house to pick up a couple of steers. While sitting in my kitchen, Zach asked the Lord to touch me, and he did." Mr. Callahan raised his right hand in the air. "I'm a lawyer who gets other people to testify. But today I want to testify that Jesus Christ is the healer of my body and the restorer of my soul. Praise his name!"

He left the platform and returned to his seat. The congregation applauded. Two people shouted. My whole body felt flushed. I stared straight ahead, aware that many eyes in the congregation had turned to look at me. I didn't take a full breath until Pastor Vick approached the pulpit and opened his Bible. The rest of the service was a blur. Emma managed to slip me a note when Mama wasn't looking.

What happened? Zach?

I shook my head but knew the question would be repeated many times before I escaped the church property. At the end of the service, Pastor Vick invited anyone who needed to repent to come to the front of the sanctuary and pray. I needed to go but didn't want to attract even more attention. I bowed my head and closed my eyes until Mama touched me on the shoulder.

"Do you want to go to the front?" she whispered.

"No."

"Are you sure?"

"Zach told me not to say anything," I replied.

"You didn't."

"But I gave Mr. Callahan permission. I could see the question in his eyes and nodded my head."

"He gave glory to God," Mama answered. "There's nothing wrong with that."

I didn't answer. Something inside told me Zach Mays might not agree.

11

I stayed close to Mama as I navigated the gauntlet of people asking questions at the end of the meeting. Mr. Callahan was surrounded by a larger group and our paths didn't cross. Everyone wanted to know about Zach.

"Is he an evangelist?"

"Does he have a healing ministry?"

"Where does he go to church?"

And from several women, "Are you courting him?"

I avoided answering by shrugging noncommittally. As to courting, several women would not be put off. Mama came to my rescue.

"Yes, we've given permission for Tammy Lynn to court Zach. He's a fine young man."

That led to the inevitable follow-up question.

"Where is he this morning?"

"I'm sure you'll get to meet him if they continue to spend time together," she responded.

We reached the van. My customary place was on the rear seat between the twins. I let out a sigh of relief when the doors closed.

"What did you do at Oscar Callahan's place?" Daddy asked after he started the motor.

"You need to ask Zach. He told me not to talk about it."

"Why not?" Emma asked. "We've been praying for Mr. Callahan in Sunday school ever since he had his heart attack. I think it's a miracle. Ellie talked about holding Zach's hand when we have the blessing, but I think it's a lot more important that he has a healing gift."

"I'll put my hand on you," Ellie said, reaching across me to grab Emma.

I firmly returned Ellie's hand to her side of the seat.

"Let Tammy Lynn talk to him first," Mama said. "Don't run into the house and repeat what Mr. Callahan said in the meeting. Zach has his reasons, and I think we should respect that."

"Jesus tried to keep some of his miracles secret," I said. "We studied examples of that in Mrs. Belmont's class this morning."

"But everyone talked about it anyway," Ellie said.

She was right. I glanced out the window and watched the trees alongside the road flash by. Daddy turned into the driveway and parked in front of the house. There was no sign of Zach on the front porch.

"Where is Zach's car?" Bobby asked.

I hadn't noticed that it was gone.

"I don't know," I said. "He didn't mention going anywhere while we were gone."

"I hope he didn't go shopping," Emma said.

We didn't buy or sell on Sunday. America had abandoned Sunday closing laws but not our corner of Powell Station. None of the members of the church who owned businesses operated them on Sundays. The only exceptions to a strict day of rest were plumbers, doctors, and nurses. No doctors belonged to the church, but there were several nurses who worked at the local hospital. They tried to avoid Sunday shifts, but sometimes it wasn't possible. Plumbers answered emergency calls.

"We didn't talk about it," I said. "Maybe he went sightseeing."

"Sightseeing?" Bobby asked. "You can't make it to Rock City and back in a couple of hours."

Inside the house I looked for a note but didn't find one. I changed into casual clothes. I'd packed my suitcases before going to sleep on Saturday. Keeping the Sabbath required preplanning.

After an awkward wait of fifteen minutes, we began lunch without Zach. Halfway through the meal, I heard the dogs barking. I left the table and ran to the front door. Zach was getting out of his car with a couple of plastic bags in his hands. I met him on the porch.

"Hey," he said. "How was church? Am I late for lunch?"

"Fine, and yes," I answered. It wasn't the right time to bring up Oscar Callahan. "Where did you go?"

Zach held up the bags with the store's name clearly printed on them.

"I'd forgotten my manners and didn't bring a gift for your parents," he said. "And while I was going down the aisles, I saw something for the twins." He came closer and whispered, "I hope your mother likes expensive chocolates."

I stepped back in surprise. "Did you really buy her a box of chocolates?"

"No." He held up one of the bags. "I thought she could use some new dish towels. The ones in the kitchen looked past their prime, and these seemed pretty."

He pulled out a set of towels that perfectly matched our kitchen. On any other day, Mama would have appreciated such a practical gift.

"They're great, but, Zach, we don't shop on Sunday."

His smile evaporated. "I should have figured."

"No, I should have told you. I'll explain that it was my fault."

"Don't do that. Should I take everything back to the car?"

I shook my head. "Avoidance is my usual way of dodging problems, but it won't work on this one. And after what happened at church, I think they won't be too critical of you."

"What do you mean?"

I took a deep breath and told him about Oscar Callahan. Zach remained silent. His face didn't reveal his thoughts. I finished by describing the scene at the end of the meeting.

"Afterward the whole church was praising God for the healing and that Mr. Callahan was there for the first time in years. It would have come out eventually. I hope you're not mad."

"Mad? The whole situation was out of my control when we left Mr. Callahan's house." He stopped. "And maybe it never was mine to control in the first place. Let's go inside."

I followed him into the kitchen.

"Sorry I'm late for lunch," he said with a smile that looked forced on his face.

Everyone stared at the bags in his hands. Zach pulled out the kitchen towels and handed them to Mama.

"These are for you, Mrs. Taylor. I know you don't shop on Sunday, but you can use these any day of the week you like." He handed two bags to me. "This one is for Emma; the other is for Ellie."

I gave them to the girls. Each pulled out a beautiful sweater. Emma's was a pale yellow and Ellie's a light blue.

"It's still hot outside, but the fall clothes are on the racks," Zach said.

Emma checked the tag. "How did you know the right size?"

"One of you left a green blouse stuffed behind the bed in the room where I'm staying."

"That's yours," Ellie said to Emma. "I wanted to wear it the other day, and you couldn't find it."

"It needed a button," Emma replied.

"Both of you should thank Zach for the gifts," Mama said.

"Yes, thank you," Emma replied, stroking the sweater. "It's beautiful, a lot softer than anything I have. How did you know I'd like the yellow one?"

"And I love light blue," Ellie added. "It's my favorite color. Thanks a lot."

Zach smiled. "I can't tell you apart very well, much less know your favorite color, so as I looked at the sweaters on the rack, I said a quick prayer."

The startling notion that God would answer a prayer while Zach was shopping on Sunday wasn't lost on anyone in the room.

"The Lord is gracious," Daddy said in response to our unspoken thought, "and knew you wanted to bless us. There's a plate of food for you in the refrigerator."

Mama set Zach's food on the table.

"We already prayed," Ellie said. "You can eat."

Zach took a bite of chicken salad.

"This is great," he said.

I could see Ellie squirming in her chair.

"Did Tammy Lynn tell you what happened at church?" she asked, looking at me with a dare in her eyes. "Mr. Callahan was there. It was a miracle." Ellie spoke rapidly before Zach responded. "He's all better. There's a room in the church filled with crutches and leg braces and stuff left by people who've been healed, but most of it is old and dusty. Things like that don't happen much anymore."

"Don't forget about the Smith boy," Mama said.

"He wasn't as sick as his mama made out," Ellie answered. "But Mr. Callahan is a lawyer and everyone knows he wouldn't make something up."

"I'm glad you have such a high opinion of lawyers," Zach replied, a more natural smile on his face.

"When we saw him last week in town, he was using a walker," Emma continued. "It took him forever to go from the car to the post office. Today he jumped right up onto the platform. Miriam Smith told me he's going back to the doctor for a checkup on Tuesday to make it official."

"You should have been there," Ellie added. "People wanted to meet you and find out more about your healing gift—"

It was my turn to squirm in my seat.

"Did someone say I had a healing gift?" Zach asked, looking squarely at me.

"Not me," I answered quickly.

Zach spoke to the whole table. "Look, all I did was ask God to touch Mr. Callahan. I didn't say anything about it afterward because when God does something in private, it's often better to keep it that way. I'm just an ordinary guy, and people shouldn't have a higher opinion of me than my character deserves."

Zach ate another bite of chicken salad. The rest of us waited for more. Emma broke the silence.

"Is that the first time you've seen God make a sick person better?"

Zach wiped the corner of his mouth with a napkin. "Did you hear what I said?"

Emma opened her mouth, then shut it.

"I see your point," Daddy said thoughtfully. "If you'd been at the church this morning, people would have crowded around you like sports fans wanting a professional athlete's autograph."

"Or a lock of your hair," Ellie added.

Mama burst out laughing. We all stared at her.

"That's enough," Mama said, regaining her composure. "Let's enjoy our day of rest until Tammy Lynn and Zach have to leave."

The dirty dishes went into the sink. Mama and the twins would wash them after the sun set.

When it was time to leave, Zach came upstairs and knocked on the bedroom door frame.

I looked at the clock. "Are Mama and Daddy asleep?"

"No, we've been talking in the front room."

"What about?"

"Our favorite subject, you."

Ellie looked at Zach with puppy-dog eyes. The young lawyer was setting a standard for romance that would be hard for Roscoe Vick or anyone else to match. He reached out and took Ellie's hand in his. I thought for a second he was going to lean over and kiss it.

"I've enjoyed getting to know you," he said, shaking her hand. He turned and did the same to Emma. "I can see why your sister loves you."

I saw a hint of red in both girls' cheeks.

"Thanks again for the sweater," Emma said.

"I'll think about you every time I put it on," Ellie added with a giggle.

Zach picked up my suitcases and carried them downstairs. After hugging the twins, I followed. Kyle and Bobby were in the front room with my parents.

"Here's some homemade peanut butter," Mama said, handing Zach a small brown bag.

"And corn we picked yesterday," Daddy said, handing him a larger sack. "Cook it tomorrow and it'll still be sweet."

Daddy shook Zach's hand and then, to my shock, Mama stepped forward and hugged the young lawyer. Kyle and Bobby looked at each other and rolled their eyes.

"You can share the corn with Tammy Lynn and Mrs. Fairmont," Daddy added.

"Yes, sir."

Daddy kissed my head in the usual place, and I hugged Mama. She whispered in my ear, "Stay true."

"Yes, ma'am."

Everyone gathered in the front yard while Zach loaded the car.

Ginger and Flip came out from under the porch to get a better look. Zach opened the car door for me. I got in and rolled down the window. As we drove off, I waved.

My heart felt full of love for my family.

As THE DISTANCE from Powell Station increased, my thoughts flowed downhill toward Savannah. Sunday afternoon traffic was light in Atlanta. We zipped through the city before veering southeastward toward the coast. I stared out the window and thought about the remaining weeks at the law firm.

For every student except a handful at the top of the law school class, getting a job offer at any firm was a huge relief. I'd been a good student, but not in the rarefied air of those who could expect a judicial clerkship or an offer from a prestigious law firm. Landing the clerkship in Savannah had been a shock and happened only because another student decided to go elsewhere. Summer clerkships at law firms like Braddock, Appleby, and Carpenter were the result of three-month job interviews. The possibility of a future with the firm upon graduation raised a new set of issues.

"I know it may not happen, but if I get an offer from the firm, how long does it usually take to become a partner?" I asked.

"Already spending all that money in your mind?" Zach asked, glancing at me with a smile.

"Yes, I want to set up a foundation to help victims of catfish stings."

Zach laughed. "Put me on the list. But seriously, some lawyers like Barry Conrad never make partner. He's a permanent associate. Others don't get enough votes, so they leave. There's a small firm in town—Baker, Thurber, and Judson—made up of lawyers who put in their time at our firm and weren't invited to join."

"But Mr. Appleby relies on you so much. If he didn't have you—"

"He'd bring in someone else. No lawyer is indispensable."

"When will you know if you'll make partner?"

"The initial vote usually takes place after five years. First-ballot elections are rare. Rumor has it Mr. Carpenter never votes for someone the first time around. If the partnership door opens, it usually happens in year six or seven."

"What do you think of a woman becoming a partner?"

"None have become associates yet. That's the first hurdle." Zach pulled his ponytail. "Currently I have the longest hair of any lawyer at the firm."

IT WAS EARLY EVENING by the time we reached Savannah. The car rumbled across the cobbled streets of the historic district toward Mrs. Fairmont's house.

"This feels a little bit like home, too," I said. "Not like Powell Station, of course."

"It's part of growing up."

I smiled. "After this weekend do you think I'm grown-up?"

Zach glanced sideways at me. "You're a tall woman, but you might've added another quarter of an inch."

"Am I too tall?"

Zach laughed and shook his head. He stopped in front of Mrs. Fairmont's house. When we reached the front, I could hear Flip barking inside.

"Do you want to come in for a minute?"

"No. I need to get to bed early. I have to be at the office at 6:00 a.m. for a conference call with the solicitor of a shipping company in New Delhi."

After being with Zach the whole weekend, I didn't want him to leave.

"But I'm sure I'll see you tomorrow," he continued.

"Thanks again for taking me home."

Zach reached forward and put his hand beneath my chin. "I like it when you keep your chin up."

"It doesn't make me seem too tall?"

He looked into my eyes. "No, you're just right."

I stole a glance at Zach as he returned to his car. I hoped it wasn't a sin to seek compliments from a man, but if so, it was an exquisite vice.

As SOON AS I ENTERED the foyer, Flip became a writhing wriggle of greeting. I knelt down and scratched up and down his narrow back. He stretched to his full length. If he'd been a cat, he would have purred. Mrs. Fairmont came to the doorway. She was wearing a carefully tailored cotton dress and expensive shoes. The multiple rings on her fingers glistened. Her appearance was a dramatic contrast with that of Mama in Powell Station, but her face showed its own welcome.

"Did you have a nice weekend?" Mrs. Fairmont asked.

"Yes, ma'am."

"Flip missed you. Several times a day he ran to the basement door and sniffed to see if you were there."

The little dog was carefully inspecting my ankles with his nose.

"He smells my two dogs." I looked up. "How are you feeling?"

"A little tired. Christine felt sorry for me being alone and took me to brunch at her club this morning. I've been napping off and on all afternoon."

"Did you eat supper?"

"Just a cup of yogurt."

I pointed to the bag of corn. "Would you like fresh corn on the cob?"

We stood at the kitchen sink and cleaned the corn together. I tore off the shucks and pulled off most of the corn silks. Mrs. Fairmont enjoyed carefully removing the more stubborn strands. Her fingers, though gnarled by arthritis, retained enough dexterity to do the job, and when she finished an ear of corn, it was in pristine condition. I placed a large pot of water on the stove to boil, then opened the refrigerator.

"Gracie left you well supplied," I said, taking a quick inventory. "Let's warm up a few pieces of ham and the green beans."

"I'm not that hungry," Mrs. Fairmont answered.

"You will be after you take a bite of corn."

One of my jobs was to interest Mrs. Fairmont in food. Her daughter fought to keep the pounds off; Mrs. Fairmont needed to eat to live. I put the green beans on the stove and the ham in the oven.

"I like Vince," Mrs. Fairmont said. "He's a very nice young man."

"It was Zach Mays who took me home," I corrected her. "You've talked to him several times in the den."

"No, I mean the other young man who works with you. He came to see me yesterday."

The ear of corn I was about to drop in the pot of boiling water slipped from my fingers, spilling water over the side.

"Vince Colbert came here yesterday?"

Mrs. Fairmont blinked her eyelids behind her glasses and nodded.

"Yes. We know some of the same families in Charleston. He's not from old money; his father is a professor at the college, but his great-aunt lives south of Broad. He mentioned that his father is also an inventor. Something to do with plastics."

"Why did he come here?"

"To see you."

Vince didn't know Zach was taking me to Powell Station.

"And you invited him inside?"

"It was the polite thing to do. He left some beautiful flowers for you. They're in a vase in the blue parlor."

I put the corn in the pot, set the timer, and went into the parlor.

There was a large arrangement of fresh flowers in a clear vase resting on a small round table. I returned to the kitchen.

"Was there a card with the flowers?"

"Not that I remember."

"Did you tell him where I'd gone?"

"I mentioned that you'd gone home for a visit."

"And did you tell him about Zach?"

Mrs. Fairmont wrinkled her nose. "If they both work for Sam Braddock, I'm sure they know each other."

"Yes, ma'am. But Vince didn't know that I was spending the weekend with Zach."

Mrs. Fairmont nodded, then leaned forward and lowered her voice. "I understand. I dated two boys at the same time when I was in college. I kept one on the hook here in Savannah and the other wrapped up in Macon. It made for an interesting summer. They took turns coming to see me. I had a grand time until my father got them confused and started calling one by the other's name." She paused. "Now I can't remember either one of them."

"I'm not dating Zach and Vince," I said. "Or I guess you could say I'm dating Zach, only we call it courting."

"Courting?" Mrs. Fairmont's eyes brightened. "That's what my mother used to call dating. It's amazing how things come back in style if you wait long enough."

"It has more to do with the philosophy behind male-female relationships."

"Yes, I'm sure it does, especially for a smart girl like you. However, even the brightest girl's philosophy can get confused when a good-looking boy shows up."

It was time to take the corn out of the pot. I drained it in the sink.

"Maybe I shouldn't have called it a philosophy."

"It does sound a bit cold when describing matters of the heart."

I glanced at Mrs. Fairmont. During her lucid times, the elderly woman showed flashes of personality that made me wish I could turn back the clock and know her in her prime.

"I'll fix your plate and bring it to you in the dining room," I said.

I prepared a generous portion of steaming corn, green beans, and a thick piece of ham. Flip had followed Mrs. Fairmont into the dining room and lay curled up beneath her chair.

"Don't slip anything to Flip," I said.

She looked up at me innocently. "That's a nice rhyme."

"Table scraps aren't good for him. I'll be back with my plate and a pitcher of ice water in just a second."

When I returned Flip was licking his lips. Mrs. Fairmont was too polite to start eating without me, but her code of etiquette didn't prevent her from dropping a morsel in the little dog's eager mouth.

"I'll say the blessing," Mrs. Fairmont volunteered.

My face registered surprise.

"I'm not an expert at prayer like you," the older woman continued. "Harry always said the blessing at Thanksgiving and Christmas, but he's dead and you're stuck with me."

Mrs. Fairmont pushed back her chair and walked over to an antique sideboard. She opened one of the top drawers and took out a yellowed sheet of paper.

"Here it is," she said. Returning to the table, she positioned her glasses and read, "Almighty God, we thank thee for this bounty thou hath provided. Bless this food and all thy children throughout the earth. Amen."

Our church preferred the King James Bible, but I couldn't remember the last time I'd heard someone use old English in a prayer. Mrs. Fairmont laid the sheet on the table.

"Harry wrote that when we first married and took it to our rector so he could approve it. See, Father Pat Jenkins' signature is on the bottom."

I could barely make out a faded signature.

"What do you think?" Mrs. Fairmont asked. "Don't you think it's a perfect prayer?"

"It's, uh, traditional. Kind of like courting, I guess."

Mrs. Fairmont smiled. "Yes, it is."

Reading the prayer made Mrs. Fairmont nostalgic. While we ate, she told me how her mother staged a meeting for her with Harry Fairmont, a young architect who recently arrived in Savannah from Richmond. It sounded like the plot of a Victorian novel in which the man doesn't have a chance against a matchmaking mother seeking a spouse for her marriageable daughter.

After describing the scene down to the details of the dress she wore and the food they ate, Mrs. Fairmont asked, "Do you want to get married?"

"Of course."

"Is it more important to you than your career?"

"Yes, I want to marry and have a family."

"Some people would accuse you of being old-fashioned, but I bet a lot of girls feel the same way."

"I don't know about that," I said, thinking about my law school classmates, "but I wouldn't choose a job at a law firm over the chance to be with the right man."

"You know, Sam Braddock came to my wedding," Mrs. Fairmont said, staring across the room. "He was a little fellow in a cute outfit. I have the picture in an album upstairs. I'll have to show you sometime."

"Where was the wedding? In one of the old churches?"

"No, outdoors at the Weingarten place on a bluff overlooking the river. It's burned down now. Have you planned your wedding?"

"No, ma'am, but I'm sure it will be a simple service."

"Posh." Mrs. Fairmont sniffed. "It's a woman's day to shine brighter than all the stars in the universe. There will never be another like it.

You'll walk the aisle in a flowing white gown on your father's arm and remember the scene for the rest of your life."

I could imagine myself standing at the back of our church in a white dress. Identifying who might be waiting for me at the altar was still fuzzy. Mrs. Fairmont continued.

"After we married, Harry and I took a long trip to Italy and the Greek Islands."

Mrs. Fairmont then described a monthlong junket they had taken to the Mediterranean that dwarfed the three-day stopovers at Pigeon Forge, Tennessee, typical for newly married couples from Powell Station. The elderly woman's recollection was extraordinarily clear; however, in the midst of a detailed account of their stay on a tiny Greek island, she stopped and stared at me for a few seconds.

"Please, tell me your name again."

"Tami Taylor."

"Rambling about my honeymoon crowded out that memory." Mrs. Fairmont yawned without covering her mouth, then reached across the table and patted me on the hand. "I'm sure you'll find your true love. I bet you're already praying about it."

"Yes, ma'am."

"If your prayers are as effective as my mother's matchmaking skills, you'll get your man."

I chuckled. "I hope so."

After Mrs. Fairmont went upstairs, I let Flip scamper around the formal garden to the rear of the house for a few minutes before running upstairs to Mrs. Fairmont's bedroom, where I knew he'd sleep curled up near the elderly woman's feet. After cleaning the dinner dishes, I went downstairs and read in the quiet until my eyelids grew heavy. Following the hectic activity of the weekend, solitude wasn't a bad companion.

12

MOST CLERICAL AND ADMINISTRATIVE ASSISTANTS AT THE FIRM worked on a second floor reached by either a back stairway or a sweeping staircase in the reception area. I enjoyed the staircase, which had a plantation feel to it. Upstairs there was a large open area of cubicles. It was known in the firm as the "bull pen," even though most of the workers were women.

A few of the hourly employees had arrived. Opposite the bull pen were small offices for associate attorneys, senior paralegals, and Ms. Gerry Patrick, the office administrator. Zach's office door was closed. I knocked lightly and waited. No one answered so I peeked inside. There were papers on his desk, but he wasn't there. I went over to his desk and picked up the photograph of his older sister, Rebekah. They shared the same light brown hair, blue eyes, and square jaw.

"Tami," a female voice said.

I jumped, dropped the picture, but managed to catch it before it hit the floor. I turned around. It was Gerry Patrick.

"Do you make it a habit to snoop around in the attorneys' offices when they're not there?"

"No, ma'am. I was just going to tell Zach good morning. In the car yesterday he mentioned an early morning conference call."

"Were you at a firm social function?"

"No, we spent the weekend together."

Ms. Patrick raised her eyebrows.

"At my parents' home," I added quickly with a nervous laugh. "They were there, along with my younger brothers and twin sisters. It was an opportunity for everyone to meet."

Ms. Patrick didn't smile. "Normally, what you do outside the firm isn't any of my business. Julie has told me about the photographer she's dating. But I can tell you from experience that it's not wise for a summer clerk to become romantically involved with one of the attorneys. It's not a question of morals; it's a matter of professionalism."

"We're not romantically involved," I said, feeling my face redden.

Zach came into the room. He had a cup in his hand.

"Good morning, ladies," he said cheerily. "I just spent a couple of hours on the phone with a solicitor in New Delhi that put me in the mood for a cup of tea. The Indian lawyer sounded more British than people I've met from London."

"Tami was telling me about your weekend together," Ms. Patrick said.

"Has she gotten to the part where I was attacked by a killer catfish?" he asked, holding up his right hand.

"No, but I was informing her that it's not professional for summer clerks to become romantically involved with the attorneys. Tami reassures me that you're not dating."

"That's what she said?"

"No, I was about to explain that we're courting."

"You're what?" Ms. Patrick asked.

I looked at Zach and appealed with my eyes.

"I know it sounds like trial practice," he said, casually taking a sip from his cup. "But it's just another term for a heightened level of friendship within the proper boundaries for lawyers and summer clerks."

"Where do you draw the line in this friendship/courtship/dating?"

"So far on the side of innocence that no one should have a problem with it," Zach answered in a tone of voice that signaled an end
to the discussion.

Ms. Patrick turned to me. "Tami, your religious beliefs and termi-
nology are a mystery to me, but common sense and the power of
hormones indicate this may not be the best way to advance your future
at the firm."

"Yes, ma'am. I appreciate your concern."

"And, Zach, you know I'm just doing my job. If Mr. Carpenter
doesn't find out about personnel issues from me, he wants to know
why I didn't tell him. I'll give you a few days to address it before
I do."

"Okay."

Ms. Patrick left the room.

"Is she right?" I asked.

"About what?"

"That the firm will frown on our heightened level of friendship,
which, by the way, sounds like something a government official
would say after meeting with representatives of another country to
discuss foreign trade."

Zach laughed. "That's probably a holdover from my conference
call. But I don't think the partners would consider what we're doing
important enough to discuss."

"Will you talk to Mr. Carpenter anyway?"

"I'm not going to rush down to his office in the next half hour.
I'll get to it."

"Should I be with you?"

"No, that would keep us from being able to talk man-to-man."

"You make it seem like a joke."

"If I keep the discussion laid-back, the level of scrutiny goes
down. Mr. Carpenter has more important things to think about than
whether you and I have a heightened level of friendship."

"But Ms. Patrick said she would report it to him and—"

"Don't worry about it."

"I guess I'll have to trust you."

"I like the sound of that." Zach set his cup on the desk. "What are you working on today?"

I counted on my fingers. "Interrogatory answers in the Folsom divorce case, Bob Kettleson has given me a couple of research projects, and I should begin my investigation in *Paulding v. Dabney*. Mr. Carpenter wants to file suit quickly, but he'll want the facts nailed down so he can evaluate the chances of a counterclaim. And there could be something unexpected waiting for me from Moses Jones. I didn't go to the library before coming here."

"Has Jones been in touch with you?"

"Not since the last day in court, but I'm still praying for him."

"Meeting Moses was one of the highlights of my summer."

"Until I introduce you to Reverend Dabney. She sounds like an unusual person."

"It's an intriguing case, but at least Moses had a rickety boat he poled along the river. Ms. Dabney's property won't have anything to do with admiralty law."

"You won't help even if I get into deep water?"

"I could take you out to dinner tonight and discuss it further."

I hadn't considered how frequently Zach and I might be seeing each other away from the office. Being asked out to dinner felt nice. I smiled.

"I have to make sure Mrs. Fairmont is okay. My first obligation during the week is to take care of her."

"Sure, let me know."

DOWNSTAIRS IN THE LIBRARY, Julie was at one of the computer terminals. She spun around in her chair.

"Where have you been?" she asked.

"Upstairs talking to Zach."

"You had to see him first thing, didn't you?" Julie snickered.

"Not really."

"Don't lie to me or keep anything back that happened this weekend."

"I have nothing to hide."

"That's depressing. But I still want to know everything. It must have gone okay, or you wouldn't have been running into his arms before logging on to your computer."

"I wasn't running into his arms. Gerry Patrick was there to chaperone."

"Why?"

"She informed us that the firm frowns on fraternization between lawyers and summer clerks."

"She should know how Ned Danforth treated me on his boat. I thought I might have to throw him overboard to cool him off."

"Maybe you should tell her."

I sat down across from Julie at the worktable.

"No way." Julie tilted her head to the side. "He'll be out of my life as soon as I finish this securities law memo, and I don't want to give him the satisfaction of knowing how much he bothered me. But I've got to have every juicy detail about the weekend with your family. Did your parents freak out when they saw Zach's cute little ponytail?"

"It was an issue," I admitted.

"I'll bet it was. Were there arguments about the Bible and all the strange stuff you believe?"

"Zach believes the Bible."

Julie waved her hand in dismissal. "Nobody but my Hassidic cousins in New York takes it as seriously as you do. Don't make me drag it out of you a word at a time. Tell me all the juicy stuff."

"There wasn't any."

Julie rolled her eyes. "Not my level of juicy. Imagine I'm in your world, where a meaningful glance or the slightest touch sends shock waves to the core of your being."

"We held hands around the kitchen table when we prayed,"I said, leaning in, "and I felt shock waves to the core of my being."

"That's what I'm talking about." Julie clapped her hands. "We have twelve minutes until we have to start charging clients for our valuable legal knowledge. Cram everything you can into that time."

"With or without interruptions?"

Julie zipped her lips shut. "I'm here to listen."

I enjoyed telling Julie about the weekend. Sharing it with another person made it more real to me. I included some of the funny and embarrassing moments, but I left out what happened in Mr. Callahan's kitchen and the effect it had on my family and the church. Julie wouldn't believe a miracle unless she saw a paralyzed person get out of a wheelchair and run across the room. She made a face at my description of the different ways to clean catfish.

"I'm glad you didn't drive a nail through its head. That's a brutal way to enter the afterlife."

"Jesus hung on the cross with nails through his hands and feet. Then a Roman soldier jabbed a spear in his side."

Julie's mouth dropped open. It was the oddest way I'd ever brought up the gospel, but it was also the first time I'd seen her at a momentary loss for words.

"What happened next?" she asked.

"They took him down and put his body in a tomb. The Roman governor sent a troop of soldiers to guard the tomb, but it didn't do any good. Three days later, Jesus rose from the dead. Eventually, over five hundred people saw him alive."

"No, with you and Zach," Julie protested. "I don't want to talk about Christianity."

I didn't press the issue. I felt I'd made my point.

"That's the night Zach and I held hands during the blessing and tingles ran all over my body."

"Did he feel anything?"

"He didn't seem to at the time, but later he said something that makes me think he did."

Julie shook her head. "Men are incredibly obtuse about the subtleties of life."

"Then we ate fresh corn on the cob and salt-and-pepper catfish. When he's hungry, Zach can eat as much as my brother Kyle."

Julie brushed her hair back with her hand. "Anyone would have been starving after all that physical activity. Your home sounds like a boot camp for urbanites. You should have asked Zach to sign a waiver of liability. He could have gotten stepped on by a cow or maimed by a wild creature."

"He assumed the risk when he drove up to the house."

"Other than the hand-holding thing, what other romantic fireworks did you set off? Did he try to kiss you?"

"No."

"But you wish he had."

I started to deny her words but hesitated.

"I knew it. Don't be embarrassed. It's natural."

"I don't want to kiss anyone until my wedding."

Julie rolled her eyes. "That's insane, but it makes total sense coming from you."

"And my parents gave permission for us to court."

"What?"

The look on Julie's face was similar to Ms. Patrick's response. Even after I tried to explain, Julie remained puzzled.

"Is it like going steady? That's what my mom used to do, although her definition of steady probably lasted seven to ten days."

"Not really. There's no commitment except to spend time together to explore the relationship."

"What comes after this exploration period?"

"If we believe it's God's will, the man can ask me to marry him. After he gets my parents' permission, of course."

"Wow. Does Zach know this?"

"Which part?"

"That you're considering marriage."

"Why wouldn't he?"

"He didn't grow up in the backwoods where you're an old maid if you're not married to your third cousin by the time you turn eighteen. Have you considered a brief period of fun before settling down to a lifetime of boring monogamy?"

"I can have fun without sinning."

Julie held up her hands with her palms out. "Remind me not to touch you with my sin-stained fingers."

"That's not the point. Courting is about getting to know another person, not manipulating a relationship for selfish reasons."

"And you can share a milk shake through separate straws, but if you want to take the tingles up a notch, you'll have to graduate from holding hands while you pray. I think you should have encouraged him to kiss you, and if you need pointers on how to reel him in faster than a hungry catfish, I'm your expert."

I decided to shift the topic of conversation.

"Do you like Joel?" I asked.

Julie shrugged. "Yeah, he's a talented photographer, a nice summer diversion, and a better-than-average kisser."

"Have you thought about marrying him?"

"Not really. I'm in no rush to populate a minivan with a load of fat babies."

"Which is fine. And I'm not entirely focused on that with Zach, but at our age it would be naive to ignore the possibility that the next man we meet might be our husband."

Julie nodded thoughtfully. "You're right. The old biological time clock is ticking, and if we don't find a soul mate soon, we could end up eating dinner alone in a nursing home."

I laughed. The door to the library opened. It was Myra Dean. She pointed at me.

"I hate to break up the party, but Mr. Carpenter wants to see us about the Paulding case in the main conference room."

"Could Julie come, too?" I asked. "She wrote a research paper in school last year about libel and slander."

"Tell me more, Julie."

"I worked on it an entire semester. One of my professors is writing a book on tort law in Georgia and needed background material for the section on defamation. I think he's going to mention me in tiny print after he praises the person who typed the manuscript."

"Do you have access to your work?"

Julie opened the drawer in the middle of the table and took out a sheaf of papers.

"Here are four copies."

Myra took two of them. "Okay, both of you meet me in the conference room in five minutes. Mr. Carpenter will decide if you'll become part of the team."

Myra left.

"Go team," Julie said as she handed me a copy of the paper.

I flipped through the section headings. I could see the research was heavily annotated.

"This is impressive."

"Don't suck up to me. I'm proud of my legal analysis. But how can that compare with someone like you who has two men panting after her? I'd trade with you any day of the week."

"Two men?"

"Don't think Vinny has given up. He'll want to hold your hand while you pray and see how he registers on the tingle meter."

I blinked.

"Yeah, it's the eyes that lure them in."

JULIE AND I WALKED together to the conference room.

"Will the client be there?" she asked.

"I hope not. He's kind of creepy."

"Don't be judgmental. Remember, he's the victim."

Mr. Carpenter was sitting at the end of the shiny table with Myra to his left.

"I've looked over Julie's research paper," Mr. Carpenter said, placing the report on the table. "I know Professor Hamilton. We played golf last year at Wild Dunes near Charleston."

"How was his golf game?" Julie asked.

"Not as good as your writing. Given your recent review of the topic, it makes sense for you to work on this case."

Julie and I sat down next to each other.

"Do you still need me?" I asked.

Julie kicked me under the table.

"Of course," Mr. Carpenter replied. "You're going to give me insight into the twisted religious motivations of Reverend Dabney."

"That will be second nature for Tami," Julie said.

Mr. Carpenter stared at Julie for a second, then laughed. "I get it. That was a joke."

"Yes, sir," Julie replied with a smile.

I kicked her under the table.

"You can use Julie's paper to prepare interview questions for the witnesses," Mr. Carpenter continued. "Divide the names and find out who can provide the best testimony. It's not just about finding friendly faces but people whose testimony will support an element of the case. Someone can be hostile, yet helpful."

"Yes, sir," I said, not sure what he meant.

"If you get good information, make arrangements to record a statement or prepare an affidavit. We'll notice the best candidates for deposition as soon as the case is filed."

"When will you depose Dabney?" Myra asked.

"What do you think?" Mr. Carpenter asked, looking at Julie and me.

My mind raced in several directions at once.

"Depose Dabney first," Julie responded. "She might admit what's needed to prove the case without realizing it. From what Tami says, she seems like an arrogant person who won't consider the legal implications of her opinions and actions."

I didn't remember describing Reverend Dabney as arrogant.

"But what if the other deponents give me a lot of insight into what I should ask her?" Mr. Carpenter asked.

"Then take her deposition again based on newly discovered evidence. She might contradict her earlier testimony, which will be an added bonus."

"Do you agree?" Mr. Carpenter turned to me.

"Uh, I still think we should make an effort to resolve the dispute. All we have to go on is our client's allegations, and they might prove unfounded. If that happens, we've wasted time and money."

"So, you think I should write Dabney a letter and invite her to come into the office for a discussion about Paulding's offer to buy the house and the church?"

"Yes, sir. It might make the expense and risk of a lawsuit unnecessary."

Mr. Carpenter nodded thoughtfully. "After Jason's blood pressure returned to normal on Friday, he called me and we discussed that very thing. He considered it, but in the end insisted we go straight to litigation, the sooner the better. He doesn't have much confidence in lawyer letters, and I agree. They're usually ignored."

Myra's fingers were rapidly tapping the keys of her laptop. I'd seen her memos of meetings in files. They were court-reporter accurate.

"Who will assume my role?" Myra asked.

"One of the associate attorneys," Mr. Carpenter said. "I'm not sure who that will be."

"Why is Myra not going to help?" I asked.

"She's taking a leave of absence from the firm," Mr. Carpenter said.

I stared at the paralegal, whose face was set like stone.

"Is it a health problem?" I asked.

"It's personal," the paralegal answered curtly.

"I wasn't trying to be nosy," I said, feeling my face redden.

"What about Ned Danforth?" Mr. Carpenter asked. "He's out-going and people like him, which would help when dealing with potential witnesses."

"Could you ask someone else?" Julie said.

"Why?" Mr. Carpenter asked, raising his eyebrows. "You've worked with Ned on other projects this summer."

"It's personal," Julie answered. I could see the side of her neck turn red.

"Zach Mays could do it," I added quickly. "He and I worked well together in the Moses Jones case."

"Zach's not really a litigator," Mr. Carpenter replied with doubt in his voice.

"But he's very insightful when it comes to investigation. He steered me in the right direction when I got off track in the Jones case. He thought of issues that hadn't crossed my mind, and if the supervising attorney doesn't have to take the lead in court, he could supervise Julie and me."

Mr. Carpenter studied me for a few seconds. I held my breath.

"I'd like an opportunity to work with Zach," Julie added.

"Have either of you talked to him about the case?"

"I mentioned it briefly," I replied. "He said that it sounded interesting."

It was an incomplete truth, and I immediately felt guilty because Zach had also made it clear that he didn't want to get involved.

Mr. Carpenter turned to Myra. "Organize the file and deliver it to Zach. I'll send him an e-mail letting him know his responsibilities. I'll give these ladies what they want and see how it works out."

Julie and I left together but didn't speak until we reached the library.

"I couldn't believe I said that about Ned," Julie said as soon as the door was closed. "It just popped out. Ever since the day on the boat, I've avoided him, but I think he's mad at me, too."

"Why would he be mad at you?"

"Because I made him feel like a rejected seventh grader."

"You shouldn't have to put up with any harassment."

"Anyway, thanks for coming to my rescue with your suggestion about Zach. I don't know what I would have done if Mr. C had started to cross-examine me."

"And I don't know what I'm going to tell Zach when he finds out what I did."

"I thought he was interested in the case."

"Yes, but only in a hypothetical way. We discussed it twice over the weekend, and I can bring it up again at dinner tonight."

"That will work," Julie answered, puckering her lips and touching them with her index finger. "Wait until he finishes eating; then make him forget about anything except being close to these."

13

Sister Dabney hadn't taken a day off or vacation in five years. She didn't rest because poverty and suffering respected neither clock nor calendar, and she told people, "God rested on the seventh day, but not me."

Over the past two days, Sister Dabney had spent a lot of time with the boy beaten by his father. After the young man slept a few hours, ate a hot breakfast, and listened to her preach on Sunday morning, he cried tears of repentance at the front of the church. His aunt picked him up following the service and promised to come back in the evening. Neither of them showed up. Another member of the congregation told Sister Dabney they'd left town in the afternoon before the boy's father could post bail.

She didn't blame them. The boy might not be back, but Sister Dabney had done her part. She warned him in advance, took him in when he suffered, fed and clothed him, and pointed him in the right direction. She'd planted many spiritual seeds since leaving the mountains as the seventeen-year-old bride of a flamboyant twenty-one-year-old redheaded preacher named Russell Dabney. She didn't know whether the ground where most of her seed fell was rocky or fertile. Those questions wouldn't be answered until harvesttime.

Sister Dabney's version of the gospel didn't sound like good news to most listeners. She used fearful illustrations of judgment to warn of coming wrath. Her preaching sounded dated in twenty-first-century America. A seminary professor from Atlanta brought a class to hear her one Sunday. He sat calmly through the threats of fire and brimstone, but several of the students squirmed in their seats. Afterward, he thanked her for the opportunity to experience what he called "primitive religion." She responded with a piece of personal information about the professor's private life that caused his face to pale before he quickly left the building.

Sister Dabney had limited opportunities to rail at the rich about the judgment to come. Most of her flock worked menial jobs, collected aluminum cans, dived into Dumpsters for discarded food, panhandled at traffic lights, and did anything else they could to make a few dollars or find something to eat. They were the type of people churches helped with Thanksgiving turkeys and donations of extra clothes in winter. Sister Dabney firmly believed the poor needed more than an occasional handout; they, too, were called to repent and live a holy life. Thus, she refused to let them hide behind poverty, either as a perverted seal of approval or an irreversible sign of judgment. Sin was the problem, and Jesus the solution. The road to heaven was narrow and hard. Get on it or abandon all hope.

Monday morning at eleven o'clock, she poured a cup of sweet tea and squeezed in the juice of half a lemon. She sat in the blue rocker on the porch.

And waited to see who the Lord would send by.

JULIE HAD TO MEET a deadline on another project, so I spent most of the morning preparing interview questions for the witnesses in *Paulding v. Dabney*. One of my goals was to create a comfort level with the process. To do that, I decided Julie and I should begin each interview by telling the person a little bit about ourselves. Since we

were only summer law clerks, the environment would be less intimidating for people than talking to an experienced lawyer like Mr.
Carpenter and might give us an edge in uncovering information.
Julie's research memo was helpful in crafting questions that sounded
innocent yet had legal significance.

"Got it!" Julie said, breaking a long silence. "It's an Eleventh Circuit
case directly on point. I can't believe Ned didn't know it existed. He
should stick to legal issues simple enough for his postfraternity, keg-
party brain to process."

"Congrats."

Julie pushed her chair away from the computer screen and stretched
her arms up in the air.

"Do you think Zach has received the memo from Mr. C yet?" she
asked.

"I don't know. I hope he's not mad."

Julie touched her lips. "Don't fear. Remember your secret
weapon."

I minimized the computer screen. "I'd better call Mrs. Fairmont
and ask permission to have supper with Zach."

"Tell her it's an emergency."

I dialed the number for the house. An unfamiliar voice answered.

"Is this the Fairmont residence?" I asked.

"Yes. Tami, is that you?"

It was Mrs. Bartlett.

"Yes, ma'am."

"Mother and I were just discussing your job performance this
summer. She's very pleased with the way things are working out, and
I must say, I am, too. Your references assured me you were a responsible young woman who wouldn't shirk her duties, and you've proven
them right. I had my doubts, especially when I found out you didn't
have a cell phone. And then you got all wrapped up in that situation
with the death of the Prescott girl decades ago, but as far as I know,

you've not been sneaking out late at night and leaving Mother alone with that lifeline thing around her neck, which I doubt she'd be able to press if something happened to her."

I looked at Julie and put my hand over the receiver.

"It's Mrs. Fairmont's daughter. I wish you knew how to pray."

"Have you been practicing communicating with her through the intercom connected to the apartment in the basement?" Mrs. Bartlett continued.

"Yes, ma'am. We do it on Tuesday and Thursday nights when she goes to bed. The reception is scratchy, but I can hear her."

"Does she always respond when you call? I can't get her to answer the phone most of the time, leaving me wondering if she's lying on the floor paralyzed or watching a TV show with the sound so loud it's about to blow the speaker. If you'd been here the first time she had a bad spell and they diagnosed that multi-infarct thing, you'd be nervous about leaving her alone for ten minutes at a time. It's hard for me to get in eighteen holes without thinking something bad might be happening to her. And the only company she has here at the house all day is that miserable rat of a dog—"

Mrs. Bartlett stopped talking into the phone. I could hear her speaking to Mrs. Fairmont.

"No, Mother, it's just a figure of speech. You know I don't like dogs, and it's unfair of you to subject me to an attack from that vicious animal every time I come to visit. You'd think seeing me would be more important than keeping an oversize rodent in the house. Tami, does your family keep a dog in the house?"

"No, ma'am. All our animals stay outside."

"There you have it, Mother. Tami lives in a rural area where people have the good sense to know that God intended wildlife to stay outdoors and civilized people to live in houses, especially when they have antique rugs like the one in the blue parlor. That thing is worth a fortune, and it bothers me no end that you insist on showing it off.

Remember when Tami threw herself on the floor to keep it from getting stained by coffee when that dog scared me half to death?"

"I didn't mind," I interjected. "And frankly, I wish I'd had a dog in the house when I was growing up. The only way to get close to an animal is to share as much of your life with it as you can."

"I can tell you've been listening to Mother's animal psychology rubbish," Mrs. Bartlett said. "And it's not just the fact that he has a bad attitude. Most of the food that goes through this house is wasted because Mother drops half her meals on the floor for the dog to eat."

"Flip's stomach is about the size of a walnut," I said.

"Which Mother is trying to turn into a tree."

I wanted to be respectful, but it was hard not to defend the loyal little animal.

"Listen, I've got to be on my way," Mrs. Bartlett continued. "Ken and I are going to a benefit dinner at a new golf club down the coast near Brunswick, and I have to find an outfit to wear. What time are you going to be home for supper? Gracie brought a small roast but didn't have time to fix it before leaving. You'll need to cook it when you get here. Surely the firm will let you leave early? The last bill Ken and I received from Sam Braddock had enough padding in it to allow you to bill a few less minutes."

"I'll do what I can," I said, my heart sinking.

"Make sure you do. Mother isn't feeling well, so I want you to keep a close eye on her tonight. And don't let her propaganda about animals ruin the good upbringing you've gotten from your parents. Simplicity isn't the same thing as being simpleminded."

I wasn't exactly sure what Mrs. Bartlett meant.

"Yes, ma'am."

The phone was silent for a couple of seconds.

"Oh, yes—and if you see Sam Braddock, Mother sends her regards. Don't mention what I said about the bill. He might double the next one out of spite."

"Mr. Braddock isn't that kind of—"

"No, Mother," Mrs. Bartlett said. "Sam Braddock doesn't own the house near the pier anymore. He sold it over ten years ago to—"

The line went dead. I hung up the phone.

"Well?" Julie asked.

"Dinner with Zach isn't on the menu for the evening. I have to be with Mrs. Fairmont."

"Maybe you should ask Zach to go to lunch," she suggested.

I glanced at the clock.

"Good idea."

I picked up the phone to dial Zach's office number, then stopped. Other than my father and brothers, I'd never invited a boy or a man to do anything with me. Modern conventions of male-female behavior hadn't penetrated the social milieu of our church. Girls were always responders, never the aggressors.

For a moment I hung suspended between the propriety of a woman calling a man and the need to communicate important information. Mama wasn't in the room to ask. I knew what Julie would say. I punched the first two numbers for Zach's extension, waited, and pushed the third. I nervously listened while the phone rang. On the fifth ring, it went to Zach's voice-mail message.

"This is Zach Mays. It's Monday, and I'll be out of the office until four o'clock this afternoon. Please leave a message and I'll return your call as soon as I can, or, if you need immediate assistance—"

I hung up the phone.

"He's not there," I said.

The library door popped open. It was Vince.

"Are you free for lunch?" he asked, directing the question to me.

"Uh, Julie and I are going to grab a bite if you want to join us," I answered, nodding in Julie's direction. "And thanks for the flowers. They're beautiful. Mrs. Fairmont put them in a vase in the blue parlor."

"Flowers?" Julie asked.

I managed a weak smile. "Vince brought by a gorgeous bouquet of fresh flowers while I was out of town visiting my parents. And then he was nice enough to spend some time with Mrs. Fairmont. She loved talking to you about Charleston."

"Let's see," Julie said, putting her finger to her temple. "Was it on Saturday that you and Zach tried to catch the runaway calf and fell on top of each other in the grass?"

I cut my eyes toward Julie and wished I were close enough to kick her under the table a second time.

"That's not exactly the way it happened."

"Why don't you two go to lunch?" Julie continued. "I'm sure you have a lot to talk about without me getting in the way."

"I'd like to go," I said, trying to sound nonchalant.

Vince hesitated, his face serious.

"Okay, I'll be back in a couple of minutes."

The door closed. I turned toward Julie.

"Don't start," she said before I opened my mouth. "Did you really believe you could keep it a secret?"

"No, but I hadn't decided what to tell him. I like Vince and didn't want to hurt his feelings."

"And Vinny obviously likes you, which on TV soap operas is called a love triangle. If you're going to be so righteous and unselfish about everything, you'd better be up front with Vinny and tell him that he's not in the running before the race gets started. He'll be hurt, but it's less cruel than if you lead him on before kicking him to the curb."

"That's not the way I think."

"But it'll happen. I'm speaking from experience. I've been on the giving and the receiving ends of this type of tango."

"Then you could have talked to me when he wasn't in the room. Why bring it up like you did? It embarrassed both of us."

"Because you have to learn to face things. You would have gone to lunch and kept him in the dark."

I had to admit she was right, but I was still annoyed. She should have been more discreet.

"At least I'm honest," she added. "You could stand a dose of that."

Julie left the library. I put my head down on the table and closed my eyes. I heard the door open and looked up.

It was Zach.

"What are you doing here?" I asked.

"This is where I work."

"But you're supposed to be out of the office until four o'clock this afternoon. I just listened to the message on your voice mail."

"Mr. Appleby and I had a meeting with a client at the harbor, but our main contact is sick and had to cancel. I just got back."

"So, I have to go to lunch with Vince," I replied miserably. My woes poured out. "And I can't go to supper with you because Mrs. Fairmont's daughter won't let me have the evening off. Then you're going to be mad at me because when you check your computer, you'll find an e-mail from Mr. Carpenter ordering you to supervise Julie and me in *Paulding v. Dabney*. I only suggested it because Mr. Carpenter was going to tell Ned Danforth to do it, and Julie had a run-in with Ned. I don't want to know the details, but it happened on Ned's boat, and if it was bad enough to upset Julie, it must have been horrible."

The door opened and Vince entered.

"Hey, what's this I hear about Tami teaching you calf roping?" he asked Zach, trying to sound nonchalant.

"It wasn't calf roping," I answered. "A calf escaped from the pen and had to be caught before it got into our garden."

Zach's eyes narrowed slightly. "I wasn't teaching Tami anything. It took me a couple of days to stop calling a steer a cow."

Vince spoke. "Listen, Tami and I are going to grab a bite to eat. Would you like to come along?"

My mouth dropped open. I couldn't imagine being caught like a wishbone between the two males.

"Go ahead," Zach said. "She and I will talk later. We have a new case to discuss."

Zach left, leaving me wondering what he really thought. I picked up my purse.

"Where would you like to go?" Vince asked. "How about the place on West Oglethorpe Street?"

The first time Vince and I went to lunch he took me to a fancy French restaurant in the historic district. Since I was now courting Zach, it wouldn't be right to make him pay for an expensive lunch.

"How about the deli on the river?"

"Okay, I haven't been there in a while."

We left the office and got into Vince's car, a new BMW. He turned his head to back up. Vince had brown wavy hair and brown eyes that were both intelligent and kind. My eyes moved to a scar on the back of his right hand, the result of a severe burn caused by a careless lab mate in a high school chemistry class. At first I'd felt sorry for Vince when I saw the scar. Then when I heard the story and learned that forgiving the other boy had been a key part of Vince's spiritual journey, I considered the scar a badge of God's grace.

We parked near the river. It was a short walk across uneven cobblestones that had originally served as ballast for sailing ships coming to the New World. We ordered our sandwiches and found a table in the corner of the restaurant.

"I should tell you about my weekend," I said. "I invited Zach—"

"You don't owe me an explanation."

"But I should—"

"Try to relax. Look, I know Zach is interested in you. You're such a great person."

"I'm not a great person."

"I didn't say perfect, although you're trying hard to be that, too."

I smiled.

"That's better," he said.

A waiter brought our food. Vince took a bite of his sandwich.

"Do you know one of the main reasons I took the summer job here in Savannah?" he asked.

I didn't know how many offers Vince had received. As a top student at an Ivy League school, he could easily have had ten jobs on the table.

"It's close to your home in Charleston?"

"That's one. But I also had a sense from the Lord that I would meet someone this summer who would be an important part of the rest of my life."

I forgot to chew the bite I'd just taken. Then I was immediately thankful that a mouthful of food gave me an excuse not to say anything. One thing was clear. Vince wasn't referring to Mr. Braddock. And if Vince's unidentified person was me, Julie was right. The law clerk from Yale wasn't going to leave a bouquet of flowers at Mrs. Fairmont's house and retreat from the field of battle.

"Do you believe God draws people together?" he asked in a casual manner that made my head spin.

"That's what I've been taught," I managed as I finally swallowed my bite.

"That's amazing, isn't it?"

"Yes."

"How is your family doing?" he continued.

"Okay. I mean, things don't change much in Powell Station."

Vinny sipped his drink.

"I'd like to visit there someday."

The prospect of returning to Powell Station with a different man made my head spin again. The expression on the twins' faces when we walked through the door would be priceless; however, the look on Mama's face would be less valuable.

"I'm not sure when I'll go back," I answered lamely. "Probably not until it's time to return to school."

Vince changed the subject and began asking questions about a research project he was working on that involved competing liens against manufacturing equipment. I'd already written a couple of memos on the topic, but it was hard to find the principles in the fog he created in my brain. Somehow I made it through the rest of lunch.

While we drove back to the office, I tried to get a grip on my situation. I wasn't a foreigner to competition. I'd played four years of high school basketball, and there was rivalry among students at the law school. But I'd never been the object of romantic competition. In fact, I'd never had much hope for one romance, much less two. Vince held the door open for me at the office. I made my way back to the library. Julie was at a worktable. She glanced up when I entered.

"Are you still mad at me?" she asked.

"Not really."

"Good. I can always count on you to forgive me."

I sat down and turned on the computer. The answer to my dilemma wouldn't be found in case law.

"Well, did you let him down easy or hard?" Julie continued. "Easy takes a skill that most girls don't have. If a woman can dump a guy and make him like it, she's destined for politics. Hard gets the job done, but there's usually blood on the floor."

"There wasn't any blood on the floor. We ate at the deli down near the river."

"Vinny likes that place. He's taken me there twice."

"He has?"

I turned in my chair so I could see her.

"Yeah, but it's always to pump me for information about you. When I first met him, I thought he was a dud whose passion would be Article 9 of the Uniform Commercial Code, but he's pursued you as if he was preparing for the LSAT." Julie paused. "I have a friend in

Atlanta who might be perfect for Vinny. She's tall like you and doesn't have much experience with guys. She graduated Phi Beta Kappa from Agnes Scott and reads French novels in the original language. Vinny's brown wavy hair and brown eyes would go great with her. She's a dirty blonde. I could invite him to come home with me on a road trip and set them up on a blind date. They could jabber in French, and no one else would have a clue what they were saying."

"I don't think that's a good idea."

"Why not?"

"He's still interested in me."

Julie stared at me. "Don't tell me you led him on."

"He wants to meet my family."

"You're kidding. Is that legal in your religion? You know, to date two guys at once."

"No."

"That's reassuring." Julie rolled her eyes. "But why would Vince beat himself up like that? And don't you think Zach will put his foot down?"

"Vince doesn't seem to mind. Zach's reaction is up to him. Maybe he'll be supportive."

Julie rubbed her temples with her fingers. "Does either Zach or Vince own a gun?"

"I don't know. Why?"

"Because I need to blow my brains out. A brain is optional for someone spending the summer with you."

14

AN HOUR LATER, I PRINTED OUT FOUR PAGES OF INTERVIEW questions for the Dabney case and handed them to Julie. She quickly read them.

"This could take a couple of hours to go through with each person," she said. "How many names do we have?"

"About fifteen or twenty."

"And why is all this information in here about you and me? It sounds like a feature article on female law clerks for the human-interest section of the Savannah newspaper."

"I want the witnesses to be comfortable with us before getting into the real issues."

"That will happen when they look you in the eye and see that you've never sinned or had a wicked thought."

"What about you?"

Julie batted her eyelashes. "A couple of those will take care of the men. I'll leave the women up to you."

"How many of the questions do you want to use?"

Julie flipped through the pages again. "Here's a good one: 'Tell us what Ramona Dabney said to you about Jason Paulding or any other employees of Paulding Development Company. Get specific dates if possible.' That goes to the heart of the issue."

166 ROBERT WHITLOW

"I still think we need a way to get into the interview gradually without being so direct."

"You don't do that by talking about us. The best way to convince people to open up and trust us is to ask them to talk about themselves. Everybody loves telling their story."

"Let's call a few witnesses," I suggested. "You do it your way; I'll do it mine."

"You're on."

Julie and I divided the list. There was only one landline phone in the library, so Julie used her cell phone.

"Should we leave a message if no one answers?" I asked.

"Sure. Just don't tell them why you're calling, or we could tell them they may be prizewinners in a sweepstakes and need to call back and claim their prize."

"No way."

"I agree. I was just making sure you're still opposed to deception given the web you're weaving around Zach and Vinny."

I made a face. "Zach and Vinny are both winners."

"Very clever."

After three more unsuccessful calls, I began to wonder if we would interview any witnesses within the time deadline set by Mr. Carpenter. Julie wasn't having any success either. I punched in another number. This time someone answered. My heart immediately sped up when I heard the man's voice.

"Is this Bernard Miller?" I asked, double-checking my notes.

"I reckon so, except nobody calls me that except for my mother, and she's been dead for over ten years. My name is Sonny. Who is this, and how did you get my phone number?"

"I'm Tami Taylor." I answered the first question and ignored the second. "I'm working this summer for Braddock, Appleby, and Carpenter."

"Is that the plumbing supply company on Forsyth Avenue?"

"No, sir. It's a law firm."

"And you're a lawyer?"

"I'm a summer clerk, not a lawyer." I glanced down at my list of questions. I'd already gotten off track. "I'm investigating a case. Do you know Ramona Dabney?"

"Sister Dabney at the church over on Gillespie Street?"

"Yes, sir."

"Why do you keep calling me 'sir'? It makes me sound like you're trying to sell me something, and I don't have two nickels to rub together."

"I'm being polite. Would there be a convenient time to meet with you so I could ask some questions about Sister Dabney?"

"Meet at a convenience store?"

"No, I mean a good time to talk in person."

"We could meet at Bacon's Bargains. It's at the corner of Maxwell Street and Caldwell Road near the secondhand furniture store owned by Mr. McDonald."

I had no idea about the location, but I knew someone in the office would be able to point me in the right direction.

"That's great. What time?"

"About one thirty. Make sure you bring a twenty-dollar bill with you."

"Why do I need to bring twenty dollars?"

"That's how much I charge lawyers to talk to me."

"You charge to answer a few questions?"

"Isn't that what lawyers do?"

"Yes, sir. I'll try to bring the money. How will I recognize you?"

"Don't worry. From the sound of your pretty voice, I'll be able to pick you out of the crowd that hangs out down there."

"There will be another woman with me."

"Sounds good. Should I bring a friend?"

I felt my face flush.

"Just joking with you, sweetheart," the man continued. "But I could see if Sister Dabney wants to come along. I need a new pair of shoes, and she always keeps a pair my size at the church. It's not easy finding shoes that fit a fellow with real narrow feet."

"No, don't bother her. Let's start with you."

"Okay. Don't forget that twenty dollars. There are a couple of bottles waiting for me to rescue them from the shelf at the store."

The thought that the law firm might help fund a wino's habit made me uncomfortable.

"And you'd better bring another twenty, too," he said.

"Another twenty dollars?"

"Yeah, I need to make a payment on my cell-phone bill so you can call me anytime you want."

"We'll discuss it tomorrow. See you at one thirty."

I hung up the phone. Julie was staring at me.

"You've only talked to one witness, and you're already buying testimony?"

I told her the rest of the conversation.

"That makes perfect sense," Julie said when I finished. "But there's one thing that puzzles me. Isn't it odd that Sonny Miller has a cell phone and you don't?"

WE SPENT THE NEXT HOUR on the phone. Julie connected with three people. Two of them refused to talk as soon as she mentioned Ramona Dabney. The third, a businessman who owned an electrical supply company that had sold products to Paulding Development Corporation, agreed to meet with us on Wednesday.

"That's the kind of witness we need," Julie said as we updated our list. "It would be good if we could include a count in the complaint for tortious interference with a business relationship. That's much better than whining about hurt feelings."

There had been a section in Julie's research paper about business claims. I couldn't remember the details.

"What did the man say?"

"That after Dabney talked to him, he didn't ship a large order requested by Paulding's company."

"That doesn't make any sense."

"We'll find out when we talk to him, but it sounds like Dabney dug her nails into the guy's tender flesh until he screamed. If Paulding had to pay more for the same items from another supplier, it would prove financial injury."

I looked at the clock.

"Should we check with Zach? He ought to know what we're doing on the case."

"And about other things, too."

"I'm going upstairs to his office," I said, ignoring the dig.

"And I'll keep working the phones," Julie said. "You don't want me around making sure you're honest."

I saw Gerry Patrick at the top of the stairs. She waited for me.

"Mr. Carpenter asked Zach to supervise Julie and me in a case," I said when I reached her.

"Did Zach tell him that the two of you are spending personal time together?"

"I'm not sure they talked in person. Mr. Carpenter was going to send Zach an e-mail about the case."

"Zach isn't my responsibility, but I want you to keep me informed."

"Yes, ma'am."

Ms. Patrick descended the stairs. As I watched her, I tried to figure out why she was being so harsh. I'd made mistakes early in the summer but thought those blunders were behind me. The door to Zach's office was closed. I knocked.

"Come in," he said.

He was sitting behind his desk, facing his computer. A file folder was open on his left.

"May I interrupt?" I asked.

He swiveled in his chair. "Yes."

"Did you receive the e-mail from Mr. Carpenter about *Paulding v. Dabney?*"

"Not yet. Tell me again what he told you this morning."

I repeated the gist of the meeting, briefly mentioning Julie's aversion to Ned Danforth. Zach pushed his chair away from his desk. His face had a seriousness I'd not seen before.

"I thought I made it clear that I didn't want to be dragged into that case. I have plenty of work to do, and keeping you and Julie out of trouble was more than I needed on my plate."

"Julie and I aren't getting into trouble," I answered sheepishly.

"But you will. And if Ned Danforth harassed Julie, it should be brought to Mr. Carpenter's attention. The firm doesn't tolerate that kind of behavior, which is a lot more serious a problem than Gerry Patrick getting all worked up about you and me."

There was a ping on Zach's computer.

"Here it is," he said, spinning his chair to the side. "Mr. Carpenter has officially made me the designated driver in your case. He wants me to review your progress on a regular basis and prepare memos to keep him informed of my opinion."

"Are you really mad about it?"

"I'll do my duty. Bring me up to speed. Tell me what you and Julie have planned for Reverend Dabney."

A lump of guilt lodged in my chest. Zach made notes on his computer while I talked. He didn't approach Myra's speed, but his fingers rapidly tapped the keys.

"That's not the best part of town," he said when I mentioned the rendezvous with Sonny Miller at Bacon's Bargains.

"I've already set it up, and we're under a lot of time pressure from Mr. Carpenter."

"Let me check my schedule to see if I can come along." Zach stared at the screen for a moment, then looked at a note on his desk. "I can't go, but you should be okay at that time of the afternoon, especially if you and Julie stick together. Just don't get into any arguments with the witness. If he doesn't want to cooperate, move on."

"What about the forty dollars?"

"Get it from Gerry. She'll charge it as an expense against the file."

"Is she the only option?"

Zach's fingers hit the keys. "I've sent her a request. And I'll be available to meet with the owner of the electrical company on Wednesday. What's his name?"

"Carl McKenzie."

"Did you run a search to see if he or his company has ever been a client of the firm?"

"No, but I will."

"Do that with everyone."

"Including Sonny Miller?"

"Yes, but we'd probably have his name as Bernard. That's it. I've got to get back to work."

"Sorry about supper," I offered.

"Me, too," he answered without looking up.

I slipped out of his office and returned to the library.

"What did he say?" Julie asked.

My thoughts were on his feelings. I kept my words on the case.

"That we should be careful when we interview Sonny Miller. The convenience store is in a bad neighborhood. Zach wanted to come with us but can't do it. He's available on Wednesday for the meeting with Mr. McKenzie."

"And?"

"What?"

"Did you tell him that Vince wants to date you, too?"

"No, he didn't ask about lunch. He's mad about getting dragged into the case."

"He'll get over it."

"How do you know?"

"Men have short memories."

BY THE END OF THE DAY, Julie and I were able to make contact with several more potential witnesses. One was a woman named Betsy Garrison who'd attended Dabney's church for a number of years. Julie asked her a few questions, then handed me the phone.

"I don't know what she's talking about," Julie whispered.

"This is Tami Taylor. What can you tell me about Reverend Dabney?"

"She's going to know that I'm talking to you," Garrison replied in a slightly hoarse voice. "And she probably already knows your name, too. That's what I was telling the other girl."

"Our law firm hasn't contacted her yet."

"It don't matter. She ran me off a few months ago even though I'd been faithful to her and the preacher since they came here. They stayed for free in a rental house I owned on Morgan Street for almost a year when they decided to settle down and come off the road. I warned her about Lynnette Vinson, but no, she wouldn't listen to nobody. You can see where that got her. I think that's why she turned on me. She knew I'd been right, and it hurt her pride. Pride goes before destruction—"

"And a haughty spirit before a fall," I said, completing the verse.

"You know your Bible?" the woman asked.

"I try. Who is Lynnette Vinson?"

"The other woman. Why do you want to talk to me?"

I resisted the urge to ask about Vinson. "It has to do with a client of ours, Mr. Jason Paulding, who owns a real-estate development company. Reverend Dabney said some things about him that weren't true."

"Is he the man who wanted to buy the church?"

"Yes, ma'am."

"Sister was hot about that. She says land is like people. Once it's dedicated to the Lord's purposes, it shouldn't go back to the world."

"What did she say about Mr. Paulding?"

"A lot. I can't remember it all. She talked to the whole church about it."

"So all the members would have heard her."

"We didn't have members. Sister don't believe in that."

"Can you tell me what you heard her say about Mr. Paulding?"

"That he was going to prison and lose his marriage if he didn't repent."

I was taking notes but stopped and looked at Julie.

"She made allegations of criminal conduct by Mr. Paulding?"

"There weren't no allegations to it. She said he was a crook and a thief."

"And you heard this? She called him a crook and a thief?"

"Yeah."

"And she said this in public where a lot of people heard it?"

"We only had about forty or fifty coming to Sunday morning meetings. It was way down from when the preacher was there. Then we'd have a couple hundred every meeting along with folks who traveled in special for prayer. Those were the good times."

"Would you be willing to sign an affidavit about what you heard Reverend Dabney say?"

"You can ask her yourself. She'll tell you. Sister don't back down from nobody."

"Why do you say that?"

"You'll know what I mean when you meet her. I can give you her phone number, but don't be surprised if she calls you before you call her. She's got a knowing about what's coming down the road. But she was wrong about Lynnette and wouldn't listen to me or any of the others who warned her. Preacher, his eyes were blind, too."

"Would you be willing to meet with me and one of the attorneys from our firm?"

"I don't know. Sister hurt me bad, but she also done me a lot of good. I don't want to speak against her. Ain't nothing I'm saying that she wouldn't agree to."

"If she doesn't, could I call you back?"

"Yeah, you have a nice sound to your voice. Are you married yet?"

"No, ma'am," I answered, raising my eyebrows. "I'm still in school."

"I dropped out of school to get married. But my husband took good care of me and left me with five rental houses when he passed. The right fellow will come along for you."

"Yes, ma'am. That's what I'm praying. Good-bye."

I handed the phone back to Julie.

"Did Dabney accuse Paulding of criminal conduct in a public setting?"

"Yes," I answered cautiously.

Julie clapped her hands together. "That's slander per se. We don't have to prove anything else. Why do you look unconvinced?"

Tilting my head, I said, "I'm not sure if Sister Dabney was talking about the past, present, or future."

15

ALMOST EVERY MEAL GRACIE COOKED WAS DELICIOUS. THE ROAST was no exception. Flip scavenged a few small bites beneath Mrs. Fairmont's chair but not enough to cut into the leftovers.

"Why are you so quiet this evening?" Mrs. Fairmont asked as I picked up the plates to carry them into the kitchen.

"I have a lot on my mind."

"I wish I had more on my mind," the elderly lady replied. "I felt so sad today because, as hard as I tried, I couldn't carry on a decent conversation with Christine."

"It's difficult for me, too."

"Christine doesn't know when to be quiet, does she?" Mrs. Fairmont asked sadly. "I didn't raise her very well."

"No, ma'am, she's a good—" I paused, not wanting to lie. "Both of you have been kind, letting me stay here for the summer."

It wasn't a compliment, but at least it was the truth. Mrs. Fairmont followed me into the kitchen. I put away the leftovers and started rinsing the dishes before putting them in the washer. Mrs. Fairmont sat at a small round table in the corner of the kitchen and watched.

"Do you have to go back to school?"

"Yes, ma'am. The days are ticking off faster and faster."

"Then will you come back and work for Sam Braddock's firm?"

I'd told Mrs. Fairmont several times about my status as a summer clerk. The information never attached to a brain cell where it stuck.

"That's up to God and the partners at the firm."

"If you do come back, I hope you'll live with me."

I dried my hands on a dish towel and gave her a hug. We'd come a long way since her resistance to the idea of a "babysitter."

"That's sweet," I said. "But first I have to get a job. Then I'd have to discuss living here with Mrs. Bartlett, since she's the one who set this up in the first place."

Mrs. Fairmont sniffed. "Christine may run her mouth a lot, but she doesn't have the right to run my life. This house belongs to me until I'm gone. If I want a guest, no one can stop me. Since you've come, you've been like a granddaughter. I should call Sam Braddock and have him draw up a legal paper that gives you the right to stay here even if I have to go into the hospital or a nursing home."

"No, ma'am," I said with alarm. "Please don't do that. It would look like I'm trying to take advantage of you."

Flip, who was lying at Mrs. Fairmont's feet, got up and barked.

"Maybe Flip hears something in the garden," I said. "I'll let him outside."

Mrs. Fairmont ignored me. "I could set up a trust in my will for Flip and let you take care of him. I read about a woman in New York who did just that. It would teach Christine a lesson about being kind to animals."

I left the kitchen with Flip in my arms. Opening the door on the veranda, I whispered in his ear, "If something happens to her, I'll find a way to take care of you even if you don't have a trust fund."

When I reached the office the following day, I was surprised to see Julie's car in the parking lot. She was drinking a cup of coffee in the library.

"Thanks for taking my call," she said into her cell phone. "I look forward to receiving that information from you as soon as possible."

"What are you doing here so early?" I asked.

"Tracking down witnesses before they go to work. The lawyer has to adapt her schedule to the needs of the client."

"That's impressive."

"Not really. Joel and I stayed out so late last night that I decided it was a waste of time to go to bed."

"You haven't slept?"

Julie stretched her arms over her head. "No, and I'm hoping a strong dose of caffeine will keep me going until this afternoon. So far, my coffee and I have talked to a man who confirmed what your woman said about Dabney blasting Paulding in a church service, but he still attends the church and doesn't want to get involved. The other person I reached is a former customer of Paulding's company. Dabney left him a voice mail a few weeks ago."

"What did she say?"

"A warning that he would get in legal trouble if he did any business with our client."

"What kind of trouble?"

"Something about the IRS. I'm surprised Dabney even believes the government has the right to tax us. It's a typical sign of fanaticism. I bet your church hates the IRS."

"The Bible says to pay taxes if you owe them."

"So long as charitable deductions are allowed, I bet." Julie looked down at a sheet of paper in front of her. "Let's see, the next person on the list is a reporter at the newspaper. Her name is Brenda Abernathy. Do you want to call her?"

Julie handed me the sheet of paper. "I bet you didn't sleep last night either."

"I slept fine."

"What about your guilty conscience? I told Joel what you were doing to Zach and Vinny. He was shocked."

"No he wasn't. The only shock he had was seeing you in the morning after your makeup had worn off."

Julie's mouth dropped open. "Tami, how could you say such a catty thing?"

"Because you know I'm not serious."

I punched in the other numbers. While the phone rang, I checked the time. I doubted a newspaper reporter would be at her desk this early in the morning. A switchboard operator answered.

"Is Brenda Abernathy available?"

"Who's calling?"

"Tami Taylor, a law clerk at Braddock, Appleby, and Carpenter."

"Just a minute, please."

"That's good," Julie said while I waited. "Very professional."

"Home and Garden Department," a female voice said.

"I'm trying to reach Brenda Abernathy."

"She's not in this morning. May I take a message?"

I left my contact information and hung up the phone.

"She works in the Home and Garden Department," I said. "Why would Sister Dabney call her?"

Julie was quiet for a moment.

"I know. Dabney accused Paulding of growing marijuana in his home garden. Ms. Abernathy would be the logical person to get a tip like that."

"I doubt it," I said, shaking my head.

"Seriously, I could ask Joel about Ms. Abernathy. He's sold photographs to the paper, including some gorgeous shots of local flower gardens that he took in the spring. I bet she was his contact."

"Is he awake?"

"Probably not," Julie said with a slight pout. "For all their macho posturing, men don't have the stamina of women."

SHORTLY BEFORE NOON, I ran a search on the firm's conflict-of-interest database for all the individuals and companies we'd contacted so far. They all came up blank except Carl McKenzie, the owner of the electrical supply company.

"McKenzie hired the firm several years ago to represent him in a covenant not-to-compete case," I said to Julie. "Guess who represented him?"

"Ned?"

"Yep. Mr. Danforth filed suit, but the case was dismissed for failure to state a claim because Ned had the wrong agreement attached as an exhibit to the complaint."

"I bet the client was happy about that."

"Then Ned filed again with the proper documents, and the case was settled at mediation."

"The client probably caved in out of fear he'd get nothing."

"Mr. McKenzie didn't mention this when you talked to him?"

"I only spoke with his assistant. She's the one who set up the appointment."

"Maybe we should take Ned with us instead of Zach," I said.

Julie made a face. "That's two mean things you've said to me today, which is more than your quota for a whole week."

Julie went home at noon after promising not to go to sleep and jeopardize our interview with Sonny Bernard. I sneaked a peak into Zach's office, but he wasn't there. Left alone, I ate a yogurt in the employee break room. Then I checked with the receptionist on duty and pinned down directions to Bacon's Bargains. I didn't want to get lost in Savannah with Julie.

By 1:15 p.m., I was beginning to get nervous. It wasn't far to the convenience store, but I didn't want to be late and miss the opportunity. Finally Julie came in, slightly breathless.

"Where have you been?" I asked, grabbing my briefcase. "We need to get going. I have directions. What happened?"

"I took a shower to freshen up and keep from collapsing."

Julie had changed clothes. Her new outfit was borderline for the office and definitely not appropriate for walking the streets in a rough part of town. The receptionist rolled her eyes as we crossed the lobby. There wasn't enough time to convince Julie that we should stop by her apartment for a change of clothes. I barked out the instructions as she drove.

"Go to the third traffic light and make a left."

Julie seemed oblivious to the fact that I was upset.

"Now, drive two blocks, turn right, and go a half mile. The store should be on the right."

We entered the worst area of town I'd seen. The small houses were run-down, and at least half the brick buildings designed for businesses were vacant.

"There's Gillespie Street," Julie said as we passed an intersecting street. "Isn't that where the church is located?"

"Yes."

"I can't imagine why Paulding wants a piece of property in this part of town," she said. "This whole area should be bulldozed. Unless, of course, he wants to grow marijuana closer to his customers."

We came to the used furniture store. Mismatched chairs, cheap tables, and used mattresses were set out in front. Next door was a ramshackle building with a scuffed sign over the door that read "Bacon's Bargains—Beer, Wine, Cigarettes, Lottery Tickets."

"I guess that's the convenience store," I said.

"Yeah, it's convenient if you live down here and can't go anywhere else to buy booze, smokes, and a one-in-ten-million chance to win a lot of money."

Julie parked in front of the store. We both sat in the car.

"Aren't you going to get out?" I asked.

"This guy is your witness. Find out if he's here; then I'll back you up."

I started to argue, but a second glance at Julie's outfit made me realize it might be divine intervention that kept her in the car. I reached out to open the car door, then stopped.

"Oh, no," I said.

"What?"

"I forgot to get forty dollars from Ms. Patrick."

"Use your own money."

I opened my purse.

"I only have ten dollars."

"Likely story," Julie grunted as she opened her purse and gave me two twenty-dollar bills.

I put the money in my briefcase.

"Interest on loans in this part of town is ten percent per day," Julie said.

"Take it up with Mr. Carpenter."

Getting out of the car, I heard Julie click the door locks behind me. I looked at her through the windshield and shook my head.

The parking area was covered in cracked asphalt. A junk car was parked beside the building. No customers were in sight. I walked up three steps and opened the door. It was cool inside, and I could hear the hum of a window-unit air conditioner located behind the counter. A young man with a scruffy beard and wearing a T-shirt emblazoned with the name of a rock band was sitting on a wooden stool. He jumped up when I entered.

"I'm looking for Sonny Miller," I said, trying to sound confident and self-assured.

The young man continued to stare at me. I tried to keep my face from turning red.

"Sonny!" he called out. "Get up here!"

A door opened at the rear of the room, and a short, balding man wearing glasses entered. He was followed by a heavyset man smoking a cigarette. A third man, wearing a greasy uniform shirt and gray work pants, joined them. I suspected the rear of the store was used for illegal purposes. At the sight of the three men, I inched toward the front door.

"I'll talk to you outside," I said, not waiting to find out which of the men was Miller.

I exited the store and motioned for Julie to get out of the car. Even with the risk associated with her clothes, I didn't want to be alone. The short, balding man came outside and joined me. He was very thin, and I noticed that his feet did, in fact, look narrow. He was wearing black shoes with the laces missing in the left one.

"Are you the lawyer?" he asked.

"Law student. I'm Tami Taylor."

I gestured again at Julie, who remained in the car.

"Roddy has a place in back where we can talk in private," Miller said.

"No. Let's go outside."

Walking around to the side of the building, I could hear Miller's footsteps as he followed me.

"How tall are you?" Miller asked.

"I played basketball in high school."

"And I bet you were pretty good at it."

The car's trunk was covered with dead leaves from the previous winter.

"Do you think it's okay if I put my briefcase on it?" I asked Miller.

"I'd be more worried about getting your pretty satchel dirty. A guy traded that car to Roddy for four cases of beer and three hundred dollars just before Christmas. It didn't run past New Year's Day."

I glanced over my shoulder. The other two men were sitting on the front steps of the store. The one wearing the uniform shirt was smoking a cigarette. Julie stayed in the car. Opening the briefcase, I took out the list of questions I'd attached to a clipboard and efficiently clicked my pen.

"Please state your full name."

Miller looked at me. "I don't have a driver's license. I lost it in the river several years back and never bothered to get another one. It didn't make much sense to get another one, seeing I don't have a car to drive."

"Okay. Your name, please."

"Sonny Miller."

I didn't move my pen. "Your legal name."

Miller glanced at the other men on the steps of the store and lowered his voice. "None of those guys know my name is Bernard."

"And I won't tell them. Do you have a middle name?"

"Yeah, Gregory."

I wrote down "Bernard Gregory Miller."

"Age?"

"Fifty-seven."

"Date of birth?"

"Are you going to send me a birthday card?"

"No, sir, but I want to have accurate information."

Miller shifted on his feet. "Look, you're a pretty girl, and I want to be nice to you, but I got better things to do than stand around and answer a bunch of stupid questions. Aren't you hot out here?"

The tree above the car offered a little shade, but it was a muggy day. Julie had started the car's engine and was running the air conditioner.

"If you want to ask me anything else, we're going to have to go inside," Miller continued. "We can stand in front of the beer cooler if you want to."

The little man walked toward the store. I returned to the car. Julie lowered the window a few inches. I leaned over and spoke in an intense whisper.

"Are you going to stay in the car?"

"Yes, with the doors locked. Get in, and we'll say we couldn't convince Miller to talk to us."

"I haven't really tried. He wants to go inside the store where it's air-conditioned."

Julie shook her head. "It's air-conditioned in here, but I don't want him that close to me. He might hijack the car. Let's get out of here."

The two men were still sitting on the steps. Miller wasn't in sight. I straightened my shoulders.

"I'm going to give it one more shot. Promise you'll wait for me."

"Of course. Do you think I'd drive off and leave you stuck here?"

"No, but you look scared."

"And you're being naive."

"Give me about fifteen minutes."

Julie rolled up the window.

"I know Sister Dabney real well," the man wearing the uniform shirt said when I reached the steps. The name Earl was stitched on the shirt. "I'd be happy to talk to you for nothing."

I stopped.

"What's your last name?"

"Steele."

I wrote "Earl Steele" on the corner of my paper.

"Earl, if you can hang around, I'll be out in a few minutes after I finish with Sonny."

"My name's not Earl. It's Rusty Steele."

"Why does it say Earl on your shirt?"

The man looked down as if discovering the name for the first time.

"I got this at the thrift store."

I went inside. Miller was standing in front of a cooler filled with beer. The same man was behind the cash register. The door opened behind me, and a black woman about my age and height came inside.

"Now, she was a good basketball player," Miller said, pointing to the woman.

The young woman picked up a loaf of bread and several cans of food and took them to the cash register.

"Marie, how many points did you score your senior year?" Miller asked.

The young woman turned around, her expression flat.

"About twenty points a game, but that doesn't buy me a loaf of bread today."

"How many points did you average?" Miller asked me.

"Not that many."

The woman eyed me suspiciously.

"This is a student lawyer who's asking me questions about Sister Dabney," Miller volunteered.

The young woman didn't speak as she left.

"Does she know Reverend Dabney?"

"Oh yeah. She and her little brother have hung around the church."

"Will she tell her I'm asking questions about her?"

"It won't make any difference." Miller shrugged. "Sister ain't afraid of nothing or nobody."

I glanced again at my sheet. Questions carefully crafted in the quiet of the law firm library were unwieldy at Bacon's Bargains. I skipped to page three.

"Do you go to Reverend Dabney's church?"

"No way; that woman is too hard on sinners for me."

"Why do you say that?"

"Go to one of her meetings, and you'll find out for yourself. She'll yell her head off and point that fat finger of hers at you until you get down on your knees and start confessing your sins."

"But she gives you shoes?"

"No, she makes me work for anything."

"What do you mean?"

"If any man don't work, then he don't eat. She says that all the time."

"What has she made you do?"

"Lots of stuff—clean up around her place, pull weeds by hand. She even had me preaching on the street corner."

"You're a preacher?"

"No way," the man scoffed. "But she took a bunch of us over to stand in front of that outfit that's trying to steal her church."

"Paulding Development Corporation?"

"Yeah."

I quickly turned over to a fresh sheet.

"Tell me about that."

Miller hesitated for a moment. "Is that why you wanted to talk to me? Do you work for that company?"

"Yes," I answered, hoping a short answer would be enough.

Miller shrugged. "Then I guess it's time you showed me that forty dollars you promised me."

I took out the bills but kept them tightly in my grasp. He held out his hand.

"When we finish," I said.

"Give me one as a down payment."

I hesitated, then handed one of the twenties to him. He relaxed.

"Sister was tore up mad about the whole thing. She wrote a speech on these sheets of paper telling us what to say. I thought it would be easier to hand them out like advertisements for the county fair, but she said no."

"What did the sheets say?"

"It sounded a lot like her preaching. She said the man running that company was a big-time sinner and thief who would be hanging over hell on a rotten stick when judgment day came calling."

"Do you have a copy of what she gave you?"

"No, Sister grabbed them up when we finished. She said the spoken word has the same power as the written word. I don't know what that means, but it ain't the first time I didn't understand what she was talking about."

"What did you do at Paulding Development Corporation?"

"Like I said, we stood on the sidewalk and hollered at anybody who would listen." Miller leaned closer. "It was pretty funny. A bunch of drunks calling men in suits sinners and crooks. We stood out there for about an hour pretending to be preachers before Sister came by and picked us up."

"Reverend Dabney wasn't with you?"

"No, and you may as well call her Sister Dabney. Everybody else does. Anyway, she said we were like her twelve apostles sent out by God, except there were only five of us."

"Who were the other five?"

Miller listed four names, including Rusty Steele.

"And the police didn't do anything?"

"A patrol car came by after a few minutes and the cops watched what we were doing. They were laughing their heads off. Sister Dabney said we wouldn't be breaking no law as long as we stayed on the sidewalk and didn't get in a fistfight."

"How do you know she wrote what was on the sheet of paper? Did you see her do it? Did she sign it?"

"It didn't have nobody's name on it, but it sounded just like her, and she gave it to me with her own hands." Miller paused and leaned closer to me. His breath was stale. "Now, you answer me something. Why would a fancy law firm care about Sister Dabney?"

I backed away. "There could be lots of reasons. I'm just here to investigate."

"You're wasting your time," Miller grunted. "Sister don't have nothing worth taking. I've been inside her house plenty of times, and she don't live much better than the rest of the folks in the neighborhood. I like her and hate her at the same time. She's been on the bad side of angry since Pastor Dabney ran off with that younger woman and moved somewhere out west."

I was rapidly taking notes.

"Her husband left her?"

"Yep, several years ago."

"What was his name?"

"I only knew him as Pastor Dabney. He and Sister came to Savannah over ten years ago. They'd traveled all over the country, but Pastor got down in his back and couldn't go anymore. In the beginning, lots of people went to the church to hear him. He was different from Sister. He could make a grown man cry." Miller looked past me as if reliving one of those meetings. "I got saved at least once or twice a year when Pastor Dabney was here."

"Sister Dabney isn't as good a preacher?"

"Nah, there's an edge to the way she talks that's worse than fingernails on a chalkboard when she really gets to squawking."

"What else can you tell me about her?"

"She thinks a woman using makeup is a big sin and always goes out wearing a baggy-looking dress. There's no telling what she weighs. I don't know what made Pastor marry her in the first place. She sure ain't much to look at. I didn't go to her birthday party a few weeks ago 'cause you can't be around her if you've been drinking. She can see it on you before she gets near enough to smell your breath. It's pretty spooky."

I'd already smelled Miller's breath and didn't want another whiff whether he'd been drinking or not. And I could fill in the gaps the little man left out without meeting Sister Dabney. After a lifetime of sacrifice and zeal for ministry, she'd lost any good looks she had when she was younger. Her husband found a newer-model woman and drove off into the sunset. Left alone, Sister Dabney allowed bitterness to poison her spirit. It wasn't an excuse for her conduct toward Mr. Paulding but made it somewhat understandable. Now she was trying to hold on to the church, the only thing that remained of a past that had once been fruitful in the ministry of God.

"Yes," I said. "I can understand why you believe suing Sister Dabney might not be worth it."

I gave Miller the other twenty dollars and left the store so I wouldn't see him buying liquor with money that had recently touched my fingers. Outside, neither Steele nor the overweight man who smoked was in sight.

And Julie's car was gone.

16

I LOOKED AROUND IN PANIC. I RAN ACROSS THE PARKING AREA TO the street, frantically reminding myself that it was the middle of the afternoon, and I should be safe anywhere in Savannah. I wiped sweat from my forehead.

When I reached the street, I saw a car that looked like Julie's turn out of a side street. It came toward me, but in the sun's glare, I couldn't see the driver's face. A second wave of fear washed over me. Julie could have been abducted and now, someone else was behind the wheel. The car slowed as it approached me. As the glare dissipated, I recognized Julie. She cracked open the window.

"Get in," she said, raising the window before I could ask where she'd been.

I went around to the passenger side. The door was still locked, and I had to bang on the window before she unlocked it.

"Why didn't you wait for me?" I demanded, wiping my face with a tissue.

"After you didn't come out of the store, those other two guys came over to the car and wanted me to get out and talk to them. When one of them picked up a big rock, I took off. I've been circling the block every couple of minutes. What were you doing in there?"

"My job," I snapped. "What if Steele and the other man had been waiting for *me* with a big rock?"

"At least you know his name. All I saw were the dirty fingers of the fat one when he beat on my window, and the yellow teeth of the one named Earl as he leered at me."

"His real name is Rusty. He knows Sister Dabney and was supposed to wait for me to interview him after I finished with Miller. You probably made him mad, and he left."

"Good, and it's time we left before they come back."

Julie drove down the street. I seriously doubted her version of events was the truth. We reached Gillespie Street.

"Stop! Turn here!" I yelled.

Julie slammed on the brakes so hard that I jerked forward against the seat belt.

"What? Did I almost hit something?" she called out, moving her head from side to side.

"No, but the church is somewhere on that street. I'd like to see it before we go back to the office."

"It would be nice if you could give me a little bit of warning before yelling at me," Julie shot back, turning the steering wheel.

"And it would have been nice if you hadn't abandoned me back there," I answered. "How would you have felt if I'd driven off and left you alone?"

"I wouldn't have hung around in the first place. I told you to leave, but you had to act all self-righteous and go ahead."

"What does being self-righteous have to do with interviewing a witness?"

"It has something to do with everything you're involved in."

We rode in silence for three blocks. If my head had been a pot of water, steam would have been escaping from my ears. I turned the air-conditioning vent so it blew directly on my face. We crossed a major street, and the area changed. New construction was everywhere. We'd stumbled into the middle of urban renewal.

"There it is," Julie said, pointing to the left-hand side of the road.

In the middle of a large vacant tract was a long, white, single-story building with a crooked wooden cross in front and a hand-painted sign that read "Southside Church—R. Dabney, Overseer." The church was larger than I'd imagined. Then I remembered Sonny Miller's words that the ministry had prospered when Sister Dabney's husband was on the scene. Next to the church was a small brick house with low shrubs in front. The paint on the wooden eaves was peeling. Apparently no one had been forced to paint in return for food or shoes.

Whatever buildings had been on the surrounding property were gone, leaving a few concrete slabs and several small piles of loose bricks. The church and house formed an island in the midst of property awaiting its future. Julie pulled into an auto parts store across the street.

"She could sell and move a couple of blocks to be nearer the people she's serving," I said.

"What?" Julie asked.

"Sister Dabney could relocate. I don't know what Paulding offered to buy her out, but it wouldn't take much money to build a smaller, more modern church that's better designed for the outreach she's doing. The congregation has dwindled since her husband ran off with another woman. Sister Dabney is more interested in providing help to homeless and poor people than running a dying church."

"How do you know all this?"

"You can learn a lot if you get out of the air-conditioned car and start asking people questions," I said, turning sideways. "Did one of those guys really pick up a rock and threaten you?"

"Let me see your notes."

I opened my briefcase and handed her my legal pad.

"What happened to your checklist?" she asked.

"You would have run out of gas circling the block if I'd used it."

I waited while Julie read. Her eyes opened wider.

"She used five homeless men as street preachers to stand on the corner near Paulding's office and condemn him as a thief and sinner deserving of hell?"

"That's the way I understand it."

"That's more bizarre than the facts on a law school exam."

"Real people don't always stay within the boundaries of a law professor's imagination."

Julie returned the notes to me. "Well, this backs up what the former church member told you, only worse because Dabney took her hate outside the walls of the church. These drunks were her agents, and their actions clearly satisfy the requirements for slander—a false, malicious accusation of criminal conduct broadcast to the public at large with an intent to harm an identifiable person or persons."

"How do you know it was false?"

Julie stared at me. "Is this your attempt at sick religious humor?"

"No, I'm thinking about Sister Dabney's defense to the lawsuit. If she sincerely believes Paulding is going to be judged by God, does warning him make her conduct false or malicious? If so, hundreds of pastors could be sued for doing the exact same thing every Sunday morning."

"You're as nutty as she is. This is slander, pure and simple. My question is whether any jurors would award any damages to Paulding after they stop laughing at Sonny Miller and his band of drunken preachers. Mr. C and our client wouldn't be happy if this ended up as a big joke." Julie started the car's engine. "I wish we could get a copy of the script Dabney gave them. Not letting the guys hand out flyers was a smart move. Without something to pin them down, I'd worry the drunks wouldn't agree on what they said when they get on the witness stand. Let's get out of here."

"I think we should stay and see if she comes out of the house."

Julie tightened her grip on the steering wheel. "Tami, you're taking this investigation business too far. Mr. C didn't send us on a stakeout."

"Aren't you curious to see her?"

"I'd rather let Dabney live in my imagination than meet her in person."

"Then tell me the truth about the rock."

"There wasn't a rock," Julie answered, putting the car in drive. "But he was thinking about it. I could see it in his bloodshot eyes."

AFTER WE RETURNED to the office, I typed up a summary of my interview with Sonny Miller and the brief conversation with Rusty Steele. I threw in my impressions of the church and ideas about possible resolution of the case. Julie and I spent the rest of the afternoon working on separate projects. Close to 5:00 p.m., Zach came into the library.

"Are you ready to give an update on the Paulding case?" he asked. "Mr. Carpenter wants to meet with us in the conference room."

"I thought he was going to wait until later in the week."

"His schedule is his own. Bring your notes and come on."

The three of us walked down the hallway.

Julie tugged on my arm and mouthed, "He's still mad?"

I nodded grimly. The conference room was empty.

"I'll let him know we're ready," Zach said.

In less than a minute, Zach returned with Mr. Carpenter.

"Hello, ladies," the senior partner said.

Mr. Carpenter's slightly effeminate tone wasn't a sign of weakness; it was a velvet scabbard that concealed a sharp sword.

"I spoke with Jason Paulding about an hour ago. Dabney is aware that we're documenting her attacks. She called Paulding personally and told him he'd better back off."

"Did she threaten him?" Julie asked.

Mr. Carpenter referred to a legal pad.

"She told him that he would face God's wrath if he attacked her, and read him a Bible verse: 'Touch not my anointed, and do my prophets no harm.'"

"She can dish it out, but she can't take it," Julie said.

Mr. Carpenter looked at me. "I know the Bible is filled with allegorical references that can't be interpreted literally. What do you make of this?"

I looked at Zach, who didn't give any sign of helping.

"I'm not sure about allegory in the Bible," I answered, "but that's a passage from the Psalms warning the Jews to respect the prophets who speak on God's behalf. It could also have a secondary meaning as a messianic reference since *Christ* and *Messiah* both mean 'the anointed one.' Jesus was the ultimate anointed prophet."

"So Dabney believes she is a Messiah figure?"

My head jerked back. I hadn't considered the possibility of such a great deception.

"Maybe, but I think it's more likely she considers herself a prophet who shouldn't be criticized."

"Kind of like Judge Cannon," Mr. Carpenter said with a chuckle.

The senior partner's jokes weren't funny, but Julie and I both manufactured a smile. Zach kept a straight face.

"And if she keeps talking, it's going to make our case easier. Tell me what you've uncovered that has Dabney so stirred up."

Julie went down the list of people she'd unsuccessfully tried to contact and ended with her conversation with Mr. McKenzie.

"I think he has a lot of promise related to a tortious interference with business or contractual relation claim," she said, "especially if Paulding had to pay more for the same goods and services. That would prove financial injury."

"But you don't know," Mr. Carpenter said.

"No, sir. We're scheduled to meet with him tomorrow morning."

"He's a former client of the firm," I added. "Zach is going to go with us."

"Did you represent him?" Mr. Carpenter asked Zach.

"No, sir."

"It was Ned Danforth," I responded. "But it's been awhile ago and it was only one case."

"Anything else?" Mr. Carpenter asked Julie.

"No."

"Let's hear from you," he said to me.

I omitted the messages I'd left for people who didn't answer the phone and started with my conversation with Sonny Miller and Rusty Steele at Bacon's Bargains.

Mr. Carpenter interrupted me as I explained what the protesters did.

"Jason mentioned this in our initial interview but didn't give me details. He was out of town the day it took place, and he heard about it from his staff. Later a police officer identified a few of the men who were there."

"Miller mentioned policemen were there."

"What did the officers tell you?" Mr. Carpenter asked me.

"Nothing, yet. I tried to contact Officer Samuels, but that was before I interviewed Sonny Miller. Now I know what to ask him."

"Do that as soon as possible, even if you have to track him down in his patrol car."

"Also, I left a message for a reporter at the newspaper," I said. "She's not on a newsbeat. She writes the weekend column for the Home and Garden section. Finally a former church member verified that Dabney spoke to the congregation about Mr. Paulding and accused him of criminal conduct."

"Good." Mr. Carpenter nodded. "That should be enough to support a slander action even without any evidence of economic damage."

"But I still think Julie's witness might be the best," I replied. "Saying a businessman is a thief doesn't sound that bad. Last week I saw a man standing in front of a used-car lot holding a sign accusing the owner of 'robbing him.' Was that libel?"

Mr. Carpenter waved his hand. "The guy with the sign isn't sitting on a valuable piece of property that our client needs. Get me in a courtroom in front of a jury, and I'll convince them the value of a man's reputation is worth a lot more than Dabney can pay. That's all we need to get a judgment."

"What next?" Zach asked.

"I want a complaint with a notice to take Dabney's deposition attached to it on my desk by the end of the week. We'll serve her, take her deposition, keep looking for more evidence, and amend the complaint to increase the number of allegations." Mr. Carpenter pushed his palms together. "Winning a lawsuit is as much about maintaining pressure as it is proving facts. Attacking from multiple angles is key. Don't let your opponent have any hope of relief short of surrender. Develop that reputation, and lawyers who see your name on pleadings will either refuse to take a case because they don't want the hassle or advise their clients to settle quickly if they do."

I'd taken a trial practice course in law school, but the professor emphasized courtroom decorum, not the psychology of war. Mr. Carpenter's perspective made me doubt I'd ever be a trial lawyer. The senior partner looked at me and smiled.

"You've got that potential in you, Ms. Taylor," he said. "I know where Bacon's Bargains is located. Not many female law clerks would go there alone to interview witnesses like Miller and Steele. The absence of fear is the beginning of courage."

"Julie was—"

"You're right, Mr. Carpenter," Julie cut in. "I've been calling her Tami the Tiger."

I cut my eyes toward Julie. "No you haven't."

"Behind your back."

"There's no excuse for what this Dabney woman has done and is continuing to do," Mr. Carpenter said, ignoring us. "Make sure there are requests for admission, interrogatories, and a request for production of documents served with the complaint."

"Yes, sir," Zach answered.

Mr. Carpenter continued. "Before she left, I asked Myra to double-check the real-estate records to confirm Dabney's ownership of the property. She confirmed that Dabney's husband deeded his one-half interest to her as part of a divorce settlement three years ago."

"Did she have a lawyer in the divorce case?" Zach asked.

"No, the husband filed it pro se. She never answered the complaint, and the divorce sailed through. There's not much to go on, but it looks like he decided to give her the church without a fight when he left town. There's no security deed against the property, so she owns it free and clear."

"Good," Julie said.

"One other thing. Dabney contacted the minister at Paulding's church the other day and made some defamatory comments to him. The minister is willing to sign an affidavit, and Jason specifically wanted us to follow up with him. Nobody believes a minister in a court of law; they always support their parishioners. But it's necessary to get something from him for client relations."

"Tami and I will do that," Julie said.

"One question," I said. "What was the name of Dabney's husband? The people I've talked to simply called him Preacher."

Mr. Carpenter referred again to his legal pad.

"Fredrick Russell Dabney."

My mouth went dry. "Is Ramona Dabney's middle name Rachel?"

"No, it's Rachel Ramona Dabney."

"Anything else?" Mr. Carpenter asked.

I looked at Zach, who shook his head.

"Okay," Mr. Carpenter said. "Let's go to war."

I WAS BURSTING TO TALK with Zach as we returned to the library, but when I caught his eye a second time, he put his finger to his lips.

"I can give you a ride home today," he said.

I felt relief that maybe his anger toward me had lessened.

"Okay, thanks."

"But that's my time to bond with Tami," Julie said, jumping in. "I've been taking her home all summer."

"We definitely came unglued at Bacon's Bargains."

"Julie was there, too?" Zach asked.

"Yes and no."

"Forgive and forget," Julie answered. "That's what you're supposed to do. I can't believe you were going to make me look bad in front of Mr. C."

"I was only going to tell him that I wasn't alone. I wouldn't criticize you."

Julie grabbed her purse and left.

"What are we going to do about Reverend Dabney?" I asked as soon as I was sure Julie had gone. "It has to be the same person Mr. Callahan mentioned."

"Not here," Zach said.

We walked in silence from the office and got into Zach's car.

"Is the library bugged?" I asked. "Can we talk now?"

"No and yes. This isn't Grisham's firm in Memphis. But I need some time to figure out whether the connection between Dabney and Callahan makes a difference in our case. It's been at least forty years since Mr. Callahan was around her. Our client's problems developed within the past few months. If you'd blurted out something about Mr. Callahan in front of Mr. Carpenter, it would have taken him down a line of questioning we might not want to follow."

"What do you mean?"

Zach pulled into traffic on Montgomery Street.

"I guarantee you, Joe Carpenter would call Oscar Callahan and pick his brain about Dabney."

"What's wrong with that? I think it's a great idea. Mr. Callahan is a smart lawyer and much better qualified to be an expert about people like Reverend Dabney than I am."

"But something about Dabney bothers me," Zach responded. "I don't want to put Mr. Callahan at risk."

"How?"

"I'm not sure. Maybe that's why I didn't want to work on the case. After I received the e-mail from Mr. Carpenter, I asked myself why I've been so reluctant to help. Now that I'm involved, I'm not sure where justice lies in this dispute."

"Welcome to my world," I said with relief. "I've been uneasy about this case since the first meeting with Mr. Carpenter. Even if she's judgmental, Reverend Dabney is still a minister. You and I should be concerned that we're persecuting a Christian who is following her conscience."

"I'm in a different place," Zach said. "It's weird, but chills ran down my back when Mr. Carpenter read that verse from Psalms. It sounds like Dabney is threatening Paulding."

"Threatening him? I saw Reverend Dabney's church and the house where she lives. She's made a few phone calls and sent a group of homeless men to stand on the sidewalk in front of Mr. Paulding's business. What could she do to really hurt him?"

17

PEOPLE HAD BEEN CALLING SISTER DABNEY ON THE PHONE AND knocking on her door all afternoon. Sonny Miller came by smelling like a brewery and wanting to trade information for a new pair of shoes.

"I don't need a drunk to bring me gossip," she scoffed. "I know where you've been and what you've been doing."

"But do you know who I've been talking to?" Miller replied with slurred speech. "You don't need to spend hours rocking in that chair of yours trying to figure it out. All it's going to take is a new pair of shoes, and I'll tell all I know. Didn't you say one time that God spoke to a fellow through a donkey?"

"And you're supposed to be a man, not a donkey, which is what you turn into when you put that bottle to your lips. Get off my porch and don't come back until you're clean!"

"You shouldn't never have sent us over to that company on the east side," Miller said as he backed away unsteadily from the door. "You stirred up a hornet's nest, and you don't have to be a preacher to know that ain't smart. It was a mean thing to do, Sister. We're supposed to be loving everybody."

"Go!" she roared.

Miller kept backing up, almost falling when he reached the three steps leading down from the porch. Standing on the sidewalk waiting for him was Rusty Steele, a brown paper sack wrapped around a bottle in his right hand. The two men glanced back at the house as they walked down the street.

Miller's visit was followed by a phone call from Betsy Garrison.

"I didn't think I'd be hearing from you," Sister Dabney said. "You shouldn't be calling me if you're in trouble. Not till you repent of your backbiting and rebellion."

"I'm not in trouble, and if you knew my heart, you wouldn't be talking to me that way."

Sister Dabney closed her mouth and waited for insight that didn't come.

"I'm not your enemy," Garrison continued. "You've been mad at me ever since I saw the truth about Lynnette when you didn't see it coming. But that's not why I'm calling. That Paulding fellow who wanted to buy the church property has hired a law firm to sue you. A girl who works there called me this morning asking a bunch of questions."

"What kind of questions?"

"About you and the church meetings where you told us you wouldn't sell. She 'specially wanted to know about Paulding going to jail."

"He'll end up behind bars if he doesn't repent."

"I know, but in the meantime he's hired lawyers to come after you. It's the outfit that has the fancy office on Montgomery Street."

"I don't care who he hires. They can't make me sell. This land belongs to God."

"The whole earth is his, but I thought you ought to know so you can be praying. And if you need money to hire a lawyer—"

"Keep your money," Sister Dabney said, cutting her off. "I won't use the weapons of this world to fight God's battles."

"There's wisdom in a multitude of counselors."

"That's not speaking about lawyers and lawsuits."

"Anyway, I told the girl who called to get in touch with you

herself. She wanted me to sign an affidavit. I told her no. Her name
is Tami Taylor. She sounded awful young to be a lawyer. And she
knew a little bit about the Bible. Do you want the number?"

"No,"—Sister Dabney paused—"but I appreciate you calling.
You and I have been through a lot together, and you were right about
Lynnette. What's happened isn't an excuse for some of the things I've
said."

"Do you want to talk in person?"

"Yes, but give me time to seek the Lord."

"I need to do that, too."

Sister Dabney hung up the phone and stared across the kitchen
for a moment. She needed to begin the process of healing with Betsy
Garrison. They'd fought too many battles together to part as enemies
instead of comrades. Repentance knew no strangers. A preacher who
didn't keep short accounts would soon run out of spiritual capital.

Sister Dabney went into the living room and sat in the red rocker.
Before she could go to war about the attack from the lawyers, she
needed to let the light shine into her own darkness. After thirty minutes of personal cleansing, her thoughts turned toward the young
lawyer named Taylor. Something about her was worth hearing. Sister
Dabney closed her eyes.

And kept rocking.

ZACH DROVE AWAY after dropping me off in front of Mrs. Fairmont's
house. Even though we'd talked about the Dabney case during the
ride, the edge had been off his voice. Having a man upset with me
was a new experience. I didn't like it. Thankfully, we were back to
working on the same team.

"Christine!" Mrs. Fairmont called out when I stepped into the
foyer. "What time are Ken and the boys getting here?"

"It's Tami," I replied.

I heard the TV and went into the den. Mrs. Fairmont was watching a well-known televangelist. I'd never seen her turn to a religious program.

"Are Mrs. Bartlett and her family coming by?"

"Who knows? She'll come when she's good and ready."

"May I get you something to drink?" I asked gently.

"A cup of tea would be nice," Mrs. Fairmont said, closing her eyes. "It's cold in this house."

I went into the kitchen. It was the middle of the summer, and the air conditioner was working overtime to keep the old house tolerable. Neither the windows nor the walls provided an efficient amount of insulation. I prepared a tepid cup of tea the way Mrs. Fairmont liked it.

"Here you are," I said, handing it carefully to her.

She took a sip and placed the cup on a small table beside her. "It's good. I need something to warm my bones. Did you sleep well last night?"

"Yes, ma'am, but it's about five thirty in the afternoon. I just got home from work."

Mrs. Fairmont sat up with a look of alarm on her face. "Where's Flip?"

"Right at your feet."

I leaned over and patted the dog's head. He was curled up out of sight close to the base of the chair. Mrs. Fairmont leaned forward to check, then sat back. A choir in elaborate robes was singing on the TV show. I watched as they swayed back and forth. Mrs. Fairmont stared at the screen. She began to move her head slightly back and forth.

"What do you think of the choir?" I asked.

Mrs. Fairmont grew still and stared intently at them. "They look like a bank of spring flowers that used to grow near the fountain in Forsyth Park when I was a little girl. Have you seen them?"

"No, ma'am."

"On a hot day, the water from the drinking fountain at Forsyth Park was the best in the world."

A young minister, every hair in place, stood behind the pulpit. The camera left him and scanned an expectant crowd. The preacher read a familiar passage from the first chapter of Isaiah. He had a resonant, baritone voice. "'Come now, and let us reason together, saith the Lord: though your sins be as scarlet, they shall be as white as snow; though they be red like crimson, they shall be as wool. If ye be willing and obedient, ye shall eat the good of the land: but if ye refuse and rebel, ye shall be devoured with the sword: for the mouth of the Lord hath spoken it.'"

I kept still, watching Mrs. Fairmont and hoping she had the capacity to understand the message. Twice I'd been with older people whose resistance to the gospel diminished as their mental capacity waned, and they became more childlike. I silently prayed this might be such a moment.

Mrs. Fairmont seemed to be listening. The minister gave a simple explanation that a child could understand. It was Christianity 101. I focused all my concentration on Mrs. Fairmont, trying to will her into comprehension of the truth. Her eyes stayed open. At least she wasn't asleep. We sat together until the minister finished his sermon and extended the invitation for salvation. This was the moment of opportunity. I leaned close to Mrs. Fairmont's ear.

"Jesus loves you and died for your sins. Would you like to pray the prayer?"

Mrs. Fairmont didn't respond. I repeated the question. Her head fell forward on her chest and she slumped sideways in the chair. I jumped up in alarm and grabbed her arm.

"Mrs. Fairmont! Are you all right?"

She groggily raised her head. The choir on the TV was singing as the preacher extended the invitation. Mrs. Fairmont's eyes fluttered open. They didn't seem to focus.

"Speak to me!" I said.

She uttered a few words of gibberish. I looked around the room in panic. Flip was on his feet. He ran around the room and barked.

I rushed into the kitchen and grabbed the cordless phone. Mrs. Bartlett's number was programmed on the speed dial. I hit the number and anxiously waited while it rang. Mrs. Bartlett answered the phone.

"This is Tami! I'm afraid your mother might be having a stroke! I tried to get her to talk, but all she says is nonsense and—"

"Where is she?" Mrs. Bartlett interrupted.

"In her chair in the den. We were watching TV when she slumped over."

"Call 911. It could be a ministroke, but the doctor told us not to try to diagnose them. It will take me thirty minutes to get to the hospital from the beach. Call me on your cell and let me know what they tell you."

"I don't have a cell phone."

Mrs. Bartlett swore so loudly it hurt my ear. "Take Mother's phone! She keeps it on the bureau beside her bed. I'm on my way to town. Get an ambulance! Now!"

The phone clicked off. I dialed 911. The operator told me an ambulance would be dispatched immediately. When I returned to the den, Mrs. Fairmont was leaning to the side with her eyes closed. I could see her chest rising and falling in rhythm. At least she was breathing.

"Can you hear me?" I asked, patting her hand. "I've called an ambulance. They should be here in a few minutes. Christine is going to meet us at the hospital."

She mumbled something incomprehensible.

"You're going to be all right," I reassured her.

But even as I said the words, I wasn't convinced. My faith was weak and panic hit me. I desperately wanted to call Mama and ask her to pray. Mrs. Fairmont made a gurgling sound in her throat. The possibility that the elderly lady might slip away into hell while I watched loomed before me.

"No!" I cried out. "Not now!"

As I watched, the rising and falling of her chest stopped. I leaned over and put my ear against her chest. I couldn't hear a heartbeat. I moved my ear from place to place. No sounds came from her chest. Hot tears stung my eyes. I raised my head.

"No! Please don't die!"

I rubbed my eyes, then grabbed Mrs. Fairmont's head and held it straight to keep it from flopping to the side. She made another gurgling sound in her throat and gave a slight cough. Never had I been so glad to hear a cough. I propped her up with pillows. Out of the corner of my eye I caught sight of the televangelist holding up a copy of a book he'd written. I grabbed the remote and turned off the TV. The minister had spoken the simple truth in his sermon, but Mrs. Fairmont needed an immediate miracle, not a book to read. I began praying out loud at the top of my voice.

Although Mrs. Fairmont's face was pale, it didn't have the ashen appearance I'd seen in the hospital room when my great-grandmother died. A glimmer of hope returned. I continued praying as I hovered around her.

I heard the sound of an ambulance coming down the street and ran to the front door. The flashing red lights came into view along the curb. Two medics, one male, one female, came jogging up the steps to the house.

"She's in here," I said, leading the way into the den.

Flip launched himself at the ankles of the male medic. I scooped up the wiggling dog in my arms. It was impossible to calm him with strangers in the house surrounding his mistress.

I carried him to my apartment, set him down on the living room floor, and closed the door. I could hear him scratching and clawing as I climbed the stairs. By the time I returned to the den, the medics had brought in a stretcher and were lifting Mrs. Fairmont onto it.

"How is she?" I asked anxiously.

"Her vital signs are stable, except for her respiration, which is shallow," the woman medic answered. "What happened?"

As I talked, the medic jotted a few notes.

"And she has multi-infarct dementia," I added.

"Who are her cardiologist and neurologist?" the woman asked.

I ran into the kitchen, grabbed the cards from the refrigerator, and handed them to the woman. The two medics picked up the stretcher and began to carry Mrs. Fairmont from the house.

"Where are you taking her?"

"St. Joseph's/Candler."

"Where is that?"

"Derenne Avenue," the male medic replied over his shoulder as they reached the foyer.

The door shut. I was alone in the quiet house. I looked out one of the windows in the green parlor. Mrs. Fairmont was in the ambulance, and the male medic was closing the rear doors. The siren began to wail, and the ambulance sped down the street. I stood in the parlor, not sure what to do next. Then I remembered Mrs. Bartlett's order to get the cell phone.

I ran upstairs, taking two steps at a time. I grabbed the phone. When I opened it, a picture of Flip appeared. I hit the Menu button and found the listing for "Christine's Cell." I hit the Send button and sighed with relief as I heard it ring. Mrs. Bartlett answered.

"Are you at the hospital?" she asked.

"No, ma'am. I'm still at the house. I found the cell phone."

"Where's Mother!" Mrs. Bartlett screamed. "What's wrong with you? I told you to call 911!"

"I did," I managed in a shaky voice. "The ambulance is taking her to St. Joseph's/Candler. Her vital signs were stable except for shallow breathing. Do you want me to stay at the house or come to the hospital?"

"I thought you would be with her! I don't care what you do!"

"I didn't think to ask if I could—"

The phone clicked off. I slowly left the bedroom and walked downstairs. Partway down the stairs, I stopped, ran my fingers through my hair, and looked up at the ceiling.

I could have called Mrs. Bartlett from the phone in the kitchen. There was no need to panic over locating the cell phone. When Mrs. Bartlett calmed down enough to think straight, she would conclude I was an idiot, totally incapable of caring for her mother. I released Flip from confinement. He raced up the stairs and began searching the house for Mrs. Fairmont. In a few minutes, he returned to the den.

"She'll be back," I said with more confidence in my voice than I felt in my heart.

I held the little dog in my lap to comfort him but realized I needed it more than he did. After a few minutes, he jumped down and curled up in his dog bed. I knew I could pray for Mrs. Fairmont at her house as well as I could at the hospital, but I wanted to be closer to her. Calling Mrs. Bartlett to obtain permission to drive Mrs. Fairmont's car wasn't an option.

But I could ask Zach to take me.

Everything that happened in Mr. Callahan's kitchen flooded my mind. Zach could ask God to touch Mrs. Fairmont, and we'd watch her get up and walk out of the hospital. I grabbed the phone in the kitchen, then realized I didn't know Zach's number. I opened the Savannah phone book, but there wasn't a Zach Mays listed. Maybe Julie knew it. I ran downstairs and got my address book where I'd written Julie's cell number and called her.

"I'm sorry," she said when I told her about Mrs. Fairmont. "Do you want me to take you to the hospital?"

"Thanks, but I was trying to get in touch with Zach and don't have his number."

"It's on the law firm contact sheet Gerry Patrick gave us the first day of work."

My usually reliable memory had deserted me when Mrs. Fairmont left on the stretcher. I was acting like the person with multi-infarct dementia.

"Of course."

"Will you be at work tomorrow?"

"It depends. If she doesn't make it—" It was such a horrible thought that I didn't want to let my mind go there. "I'll let you know."

I called the number listed as Zach's residence. I didn't want to face this crisis alone, especially if Mrs. Bartlett was hysterical. The phone rang until Zach's answering message came on.

"It's Tami," I said quickly. "Mrs. Fairmont has gone to the hospital. Please call me as soon as possible."

Beneath his residence number was his cell-phone number. I called it and nervously tapped my foot while it rang five times before the away message played. I left the same message. After I hung up, I paced back and forth across the kitchen. The second hand of the old-fashioned clock on the wall crawled across the face of the dial. I didn't know where Zach might be or when he might receive my messages. I picked up the sheet and looked at the names. There were a lot of people who worked at Braddock, Appleby, and Carpenter I didn't know. Then I stopped at Vince's name. He answered on the second ring.

"It's Tami," I said.

"Hey, how are you?"

"In a panic. Mrs. Fairmont went to the hospital in an ambulance a few minutes ago, and I was hoping you could take me there. Her daughter is driving in from her house on the marsh."

"I'm on my way."

Vince lived a few minutes away from the office. While I waited,

I sat in the blue parlor with Flip in my arms and scratched the little dog in the places he loved behind his pointed ears. Flip growled before the doorbell chimed. Vince was on the front step.

"Thanks," I said when I opened the door.

While we walked hurriedly down the steps to Vince's car, I explained what had happened.

"Do you know how to get to the hospital?" I asked as I sat in the car.

"Yes. I went there with Mr. Braddock to meet a client who was recovering from surgery."

We parked near the emergency room. The ER was crowded with the poor and the rich. Sickness has a way of equalizing people. I didn't see Mrs. Bartlett. There were two staff members at the admission desk.

"Have you admitted a Mrs. Margaret Fairmont?" I asked. "She would have come in by ambulance within the past hour."

The woman checked a computer screen.

"Are you a family member?"

"No, I'm her in-home caregiver."

The phone beside the woman rang. She picked it up and started talking. It was a personal conversation about where she was going after getting off work. I had a sudden impulse to grab the phone from her hand and slam it down on the receiver. I looked at Vince, who shrugged his shoulders. Finally she hung up.

"Let's see, did you say Fairchild?" she asked.

"No, Fairmont," I said through clenched teeth.

She moved her computer mouse across a pad with the hospital's logo on it.

"I don't see her in the system," she said.

My heart sank. "Does that mean she's dead?"

18

"NOT NECESSARILY," THE WOMAN REPLIED, GIVING ME A STRANGE look. "It means she hasn't been admitted. She may be with one of the triage nurses."

"How can I find out?"

The woman continued searching.

"Here she is. It just popped up on the screen. She's being processed into ICU."

"Which floor?"

She told me and pointed down a hallway that led to the elevators. I took several steps before looking back to see if Vince was following.

"Sorry," I said. "I feel responsible."

"Responsible for what?"

"I don't know. It's just that it happened while I was at the house."

"Which is why you're there. At least you know she's alive. What would have happened if you hadn't been there to call 911?"

Vince's words always had a calming effect on me. We found the waiting room for the ICU. The atmosphere of the room was a sharp contrast to the frantic activity in the ER. About ten people were doing what the sign over the door declared—waiting. Mrs. Bartlett wasn't among them.

"Her daughter should have been here by now," I said.

As soon as the words left my lips, Mrs. Bartlett and her husband,

Ken, came into the room from the patient area. I barely recognized her without her makeup. She saw me and slightly raised her hand. I came over to her.

"How is she?" I asked anxiously.

"Stable for the moment," Mrs. Bartlett replied. "They'll have to run tests to determine the extent of the damage."

I introduced them to Vince.

"Mother mentioned you the other day," Mrs. Bartlett said to Vince. "Are you the one who brought by the flowers she put in the blue parlor?"

"Yes."

"Mother loves fresh flowers."

"I'm sorry I was so disorganized when I talked to you on the phone," I said.

"I was disappointed," Mrs. Bartlett replied, staring directly into my eyes. "I thought you had more experience dealing with medical emergencies."

I couldn't remember ever telling her that I had emergency medical experience.

"She called 911," her husband said.

"After I told her to do it," Mrs. Bartlett answered crisply. "You can spend the night at the house, but I'll review the situation tomorrow. If Mother has an extended stay in the hospital or goes to a nursing home, there won't be any need for you to be there."

My head jerked back. I thought about myself, but also Mrs. Fairmont's Chihuahua.

"Uh, what about Flip?"

"That dog has controlled Mother's life. He won't do the same to mine."

I didn't get a chance to ask about me. Mrs. Bartlett walked past and left the room. Her husband trailed after her.

"Wow," Vince said. "Did she just kick you out?"

"I think so."

"Why is she so upset with you?"

I slumped down in the nearest chair and told him. I left out some of the specific words Mrs. Bartlett used when yelling at me over the phone.

"What am I going to do?"

Vince's answer was as focused as one of his legal memos at work.

"Find another place to live," he said. "There's a vacancy in my complex. Yesterday I saw a sign on the bulletin board in the laundry room that a student at the college wants to sublease his apartment for the rest of the summer. It's the one directly below mine."

The thought of leaving Mrs. Fairmont's beautiful home and moving into a male college student's apartment for the next few weeks was depressing. I could imagine the way it was furnished.

"Do they allow pets?"

"With a five-hundred-dollar nonrefundable deposit."

That was about a hundred dollars per pound for Flip. Then I remembered Mrs. Fairmont.

"I don't need to be worrying about myself or Flip," I said. "We're here to pray for Mrs. Fairmont."

There was a phone beside the restricted entrance to the patient rooms. I walked over and picked it up.

"May I help you?" a female voice asked on the other end.

"I'd like to see Margaret Fairmont," I said.

"Are you a relative?"

"No, but I've been caring for her at her home. I was with her tonight when the ambulance came to get her."

"One of the doctors is examining her. Call back in about fifteen minutes."

I replaced the phone and told Vince. We sat down. I stared straight ahead without speaking. Vince cleared his throat a couple of times, then picked up a newspaper and began to read. Initially I closed my eyes and prayed silently. I heard Vince rustle the paper. He'd helped me see that I wasn't responsible for Mrs. Fairmont's emergency, but at the moment I needed Zach's spiritual strength. After fifteen minutes passed, I phoned the ICU.

"You can come back now," the woman said.

I motioned to Vince.

"Me, too?" he asked.

"Yes."

We entered an ICU area that consisted of a row of rooms on either side of a central nursing station. Mrs. Fairmont was lying motionless on her back with an oxygen tube in her nose, a blood pressure cuff on her arm, and an IV bag on a rack beside her bed. I gently touched her hand that no longer glistened with the diamond rings she usually wore. She didn't stir. Vince stood at my shoulder. Not trusting myself to say anything without bursting into tears, I glanced back at him.

"Will you pray for her?"

Vince nodded. I closed my eyes and waited. After a few moments of silence, Vince began quoting the Twenty-third Psalm. He had a deep, clear voice, and the words filled the room. When he finished, I opened my eyes. But before I could say anything he continued, this time quoting Psalm 91. When he reached the concluding verse about God's promise of long life and salvation, chill bumps raced across my arms. I opened my eyes again, half hoping, half expecting to find Mrs. Fairmont alert and asking for something to eat. The elderly woman remained in dignified unconsciousness. I carefully searched her face for change but saw nothing.

"That was beautiful," I said to Vince, hiding my disappointment.

"I hope God touched her."

"What did you say?" I asked sharply.

"That I hope God touched her."

I glanced back at Mrs. Fairmont again. Unlike Oscar Callahan, she showed no signs of shouting hallelujah and clapping her hands.

"We should probably leave," I said.

We didn't encounter Mr. and Mrs. Bartlett on the way out of the hospital. I wasn't surprised. I doubted she would spend the night in the ICU waiting area just so she could see her mother for a few minutes every hour. I stared out the window as Vince drove me home.

"Thanks again," I said as the car came to a stop in front of Mrs. Fairmont's house. "It meant a lot for me to see her."

"I'm sorry for the way her daughter is acting. Maybe she'll cool down in the morning and let you stay. I don't think her husband agreed with her."

"Unfortunately he's not the boss in the family, and when it comes to her mother, Mrs. Bartlett's only competition comes from Mrs. Fairmont."

FLIP SLEPT IN BED with me. He whimpered and refused to settle down until I went upstairs and got one of Mrs. Fairmont's sweaters. Then he nestled against the sweater and dozed off. Once in the night he barked. I sat bolt upright in bed but saw nothing through the faint light coming in from the garden. It was only a dog dream.

I left a note in the morning for Gracie, letting her know what had happened to Mrs. Fairmont. Mrs. Bartlett would surely call her, but I didn't want to take a chance. Gracie had worked for Mrs. Fairmont for over twenty years. The house would need cleaning and dusting, even if no one lived there.

Flip was a more troubling dilemma. He could fend for himself if I left dry dog food in a dish and water in a bowl. But the idea that Mrs. Bartlett might take him away while I was at work was more than I could bear. Mrs. Fairmont would want me to stand up for the little dog. He had no other champion. I skipped my morning run and took Flip out for a walk instead. As we approached the house, I was startled by a car horn blaring beside me. It was Zach. He stopped and I got in.

"Sorry about Mrs. Fairmont," he said. "I tried to call, but I guess you were at the hospital."

"Yes, Vince took me."

"How is she?"

"I don't know. There's no news since last night and I didn't find out much then."

We stopped in front of the house. I explained what had happened with Mrs. Bartlett.

"Do you have any plans?" he asked.

"There may be a place to sublease in the complex where Vince lives, but I haven't seen it and don't know what to do about Flip."

"That dog means a lot to you, doesn't he?"

"Yes, but Mrs. Fairmont really loves him. He's the one thing I can take care of that will honor her wishes. I'm worried Mrs. Bartlett will take him to the pound."

"He could move in with me," Zach offered. "I'd have to install a doggie door for him to use during the day."

"You'd do that?" I asked, a wave of gratitude washing over me.

"Yes, but I'm not going to let him sleep in bed with me. It will just be two boys hanging out together."

I had a sudden urge to lean over and kiss Zach on the cheek. I scratched Flip on the head instead.

"But that doesn't take care of you."

"I could rent a room by the week at a motel if I have to. There's less than a month left before the job ends."

"That doesn't sound good."

"It's not the primary thing," I said, turning toward him. "I'm really worried about Mrs. Fairmont. I wish you could have been with me at the hospital last night. Vince and I were able to see her. He prayed a beautiful prayer quoting verses from the Psalms, but it wasn't like Mr. Callahan's kitchen. Nothing happened."

"And you think it would have been different with me?"

"Maybe."

Zach shook his head. "Tami, I can be kind to a dog any day of the week, but I can't promise an immediate answer to prayer every time I open my mouth."

"I know, but—" I stopped, not sure what to say.

I opened the car door. Flip hopped out. I held the leash tight.

"I'll see you at work," I said.

"Don't forget the meeting with Mr. McKenzie at ten thirty. And make sure you or Julie follows up with the reporter at the newspaper. It's odd that Dabney contacted the Home and Garden editor. I doubt that's a full-time job."

"It might be in a city like Savannah. There are a lot of homes and gardens to write about."

JULIE WASN'T IN THE LIBRARY. When she arrived at nine thirty, she immediately wanted to know about Mrs. Fairmont. For once, she remained serious.

"I hope she's going to be okay. And if you give me her daughter's phone number I'll straighten her out. How incredibly rude."

I wondered if Julie might invite me to stay with her at her apartment for a few days, but no offer came. We worked on separate projects until time to leave for our interview with Carl McKenzie.

"Are you ready to talk to Mr. McKenzie?" Julie asked as I put the file in my briefcase.

"I thought you would take the lead," I answered in surprise.

"We'll let Zach decide."

IT WAS ONLY a five-minute drive to the electrical supply business. Julie and I rode with Zach. Julie insisted I sit in the front seat.

"Your legs are so much longer than mine," she said.

Zach didn't try to hide his smile.

McKenzie Electrical Supply Company was in a modern building that stretched half a city block. We entered a showroom devoted to hundreds of different light fixtures, everything from ornate crystal chandeliers to burnished steel crafted to look like a piece of modern art. A salesman directed us to a nicely furnished office suite. We sat in burgundy leather chairs for a couple of minutes until a young woman escorted us to a conference room. Oil portraits of three men hung on the wall.

"The brothers McKenzie," Julie observed when the woman left.

"No, two generations," a middle-aged man said from the doorway. "My grandfather, father, and uncle."

The family resemblance was obvious. All four men had the same broad face, slightly flat nose, and bushy eyebrows over dark eyes. The dark suits in the paintings were so similar that it was impossible to date the portraits.

"When will yours be unveiled?" Julie asked, flashing a slightly embarrassed smile.

"Not until I'm dead, and it will be up to my son and nephew to make that decision. They'll probably want to put up a picture of the race car we sponsor. Have a seat."

Mr. McKenzie had a thin folder in his hand. He sat on one side of the table with Zach, and Julie and I sat on the other side. Zach introduced us.

"Thanks for agreeing to meet with us," he said.

"Jason Paulding was a longtime customer," McKenzie said. "This has been a very awkward situation."

"He's no longer a customer?" Zach asked.

"That's under review."

"You're not going to do business with him in the future?" Julie asked.

"I'm not going to answer that question. As I said, it's under review."

I agreed to meet with you this morning in an effort to work this out amicably. If you want to cross-examine me, we'll need to do that in my lawyer's office."

Julie's face fell. I could see red on the side of her neck.

"Who's your lawyer?" Zach asked.

"Brad Mix."

"Does he know you're talking to us this morning?"

"Yes, and he supports what I'm trying to do. I met with him after receiving the call from the secretary at your office."

"That was me," Julie said.

"I'd like to ask a few questions. Just let me know if I get out of line. Could you start with your first contact with Ramona Dabney?"

McKenzie opened the folder. I could see it contained loose pieces of paper with handwriting on them and computer printouts of numbers.

"I received a phone call a couple of months ago from a woman claiming to have information about a commercial project north of the city. The developer was an outfit from Atlanta, and Jason's company won the bid to handle part of the construction. He was also in line to manage rental of the spaces after completion. We provided all the electrical materials at a significant discount in return for a small percentage of Jason's cut of the rental revenue for a period of time after the project opened. Our discount was the main reason he was able to bid his part of the construction phase low enough to get the business. We saw the deal as an opportunity to make a significantly better profit if we were patient."

I was taking notes as fast as I could write.

"So, you were a silent partner in the management of the development," Zach said.

"Yes, we look for opportunities outside our core business."

"What happened?"

"I thought everything was fine. Construction progressed nicely, the spaces leased out within a couple of months, and Jason began sending us checks. The payments weren't as much as we'd projected, but he told me competition in the market had increased and the developer in Atlanta lowered the rents in order to fill up the spaces quickly. Jason provided all the documentation our financial people requested. Then one morning I get a call from this Dabney woman claiming to have inside information about the project. I thought she was a nut until she told me how much we'd discounted our rate to get involved."

"A percentage or a dollar amount?" Zach asked.

"Dollars."

"And she told you the exact amount?"

"Close enough that it got my attention. Only a couple of people in our company would have access to that kind of data. She claimed Jason was cheating us. When I asked how, she went into a Bible story, then hung up." McKenzie glanced down at a sheet of paper. "It's Luke 16:1–10."

"The story of the unrighteous steward," I said.

"That's right," McKenzie replied, giving me a puzzled look. "I read the story, but it didn't make sense because Jesus praised a man who cheated the guy he worked for. I called the minister at my church for an explanation. After he talked about Roman culture for a few minutes, I realized he didn't know either." He looked at me. "Maybe this young woman can shed some light on it."

"It's a controversial passage," I replied.

"And we're lawyers, not theologians," Zach said.

"Anyway, I called Jason and told him about the phone call from Ms. Dabney. He told me she was slandering him because he wanted to buy her property on Gillespie Street, and she didn't want to sell. He mentioned what he'd offered and it sounded reasonable for a transitional neighborhood. Then I told him that even if Dabney was a nut, I'd like to audit our project and see if the numbers added up correctly. He agreed."

"Have you completed the audit?"

"Yes."McKenzie slid four sheets of paper across the table. "My accountants and attorney have reviewed this information. I'm providing it to you as Jason's counsel. I'm willing to work this out with him."

I leaned over to get a closer look but couldn't decipher the meaning of the figures. Zach scanned the sheets.

"You're claiming these administrative charges should have been included in Paulding Development's revenue for purposes of calculating the money paid to your company?"

"You don't have to be a theologian to figure that out. The shortage is around two hundred thousand dollars."

"Our firm hasn't been hired in this matter," Zach replied, turning over the pages, "but I'll make sure this information reaches Mr. Paulding. If he wants us to represent him, should we communicate with you or Brad Mix?"

"Try me first. I've had enough experience with lawyers to know they have a place, but I don't need someone to hold my hand. I hope this is an oversight that Jason will correct as soon as he's presented with the facts. He knows how important our relationship is for his business."

"Okay. Anything else you can tell us about Reverend Dabney? Did she call again about Mr. Paulding or send anything to you in writing?"

"No, that's it. She left her number, but I didn't keep it. She sounded like my mother when she wasn't on her medicine, cranky and mad at the world. But I can't argue with the accuracy of the financial information she gave me. How she guessed or found it out is a mystery."

"She didn't tell you?"

"No."

WE DIDN'T SPEAK until we were out of the building.

"What did you make of that?" Zach asked once we were seated in the car.

I looked at Julie in the backseat.

"Don't look at me," she said. "I was humiliated."

"That sort of thing happens," Zach said. "Forget it."

"But will you forget it?"

Zach looked in the rearview mirror. "If you're asking me not to include it in my evaluation of you for the firm, the answer is yes. My only suggestion is that you practice keeping quiet when you don't know who might be listening."

"Yes, sir."

"With that out of the way, what do you think about the case?" he asked us.

"Which one?" Julie answered. "*Paulding v. Dabney* or *McKenzie v. Paulding*? Any evidence for a business tort against Dabney with Mr. McKenzie as our star witness was buried by the figures uncovered by his auditor. But the good news is there might be another case for our firm if Paulding hires Mr. C to represent him in the new dispute."

"Lawyers always float to the top," Zach said.

"What could you tell from the auditor's summary?" I asked him.

"That we'll have to see the contract to sort it out. If McKenzie is right, Paulding will owe him a substantial sum of money." He paused. "And Reverend Dabney will have scored a direct hit with her prophetic gun."

"Huh?" Julie asked.

19

Zach went upstairs to his office to prepare a memo about McKenzie's claim against Jason Paulding. Julie tried unsuccessfully to reach Brenda Abernathy at the newspaper.

"I wonder why Paulding listed her as a possible witness," I said after she left another message. "He didn't do a very thorough job investigating his witnesses or he would have found out there was a problem with McKenzie."

"All it says on the sheet is that McKenzie and Abernathy called him and told him they'd been contacted by Dabney. There may not be any slanderous allegations involved."

"That leaves Officer Samuels," I said.

"He's your bookend to Sonny Miller," Julie replied. "Why don't you try to track him down while I start preparing the complaint? The police officer's testimony would be valuable at trial, but it's not necessary to initiate a lawsuit."

I phoned the police station. When the dispatcher on duty learned where I worked, she insisted on radioing Officer Samuels in his car. I put my hand over the phone and told Julie what the woman was doing.

"She's either a satisfied client of the firm, or she wants a better-paying job if one opens up."

The dispatcher came back on the line.

"Samuels is coming off his break in about half an hour. He can meet you in the administrative offices at the jail."

"I'll be there."

The law firm had a compact car used by runners and employees temporarily without transportation. I'd been nervous the first couple of times I drove it. But it was a lot easier to operate than Kyle's truck with a cattle trailer hooked onto the hitch. Twenty-five minutes later, I parked in front of the Chatham County Correctional Center. I'd been there several times while representing Moses Jones.

The lobby was a large open room. It wasn't visiting hours, and it was empty. The modern facility smelled as clean as a hospital. A sign on the wall directed me toward the administrative wing. My shoes tapped against the shiny waxed floor. I felt much more confident than when I'd arrived for my initial interview with Moses. It was much less intimidating meeting a man who enforced the law than one accused of breaking it. I gave my name and reason for being there to a male officer on duty.

"I think Samuels is in the break room," the officer replied. "Have a seat while I check."

I sat on a hard plastic chair and reviewed the notes of my interview with Sonny Miller. After about fifteen minutes, a black officer in his forties came into the waiting area.

"Ms. Taylor?" he asked.

"Yes, sir."

"We can meet in one of our conference rooms," the officer replied in a mellow baritone voice.

I followed him into a plain room with a table and six chairs. There was a white grease board on the wall. We sat on opposite sides of the table. Officer Samuels had stripes and bars on his uniform that I suspected had significance.

"Officer Samuels, your name was on a list—"

"I'm not a patrol officer, Ms. Taylor. I'm a lieutenant."

"I'm sorry. I don't know much about uniforms. My father was in the military but that was before I was born."

"Which branch?"

"He was an MP in the army."

"Really?" Samuels smiled. "Me, too. When was he on duty?"

I gave him the dates.

"He was about ten years ahead of me," Samuels replied. "If he served as an MP, he knows what it's like to be an unpopular man."

"Yes, sir. He was shot in the foot by a drunken soldier while making an arrest. He still has a lot of problems with it."

Samuels' face became sympathetic.

"What can I do for you?"

I explained my purpose, then said, "I've already interviewed a man named Sonny Miller who was involved, and I'd like to confirm what he told me."

"Was Sonny sober when he talked to you?"

"Yes, sir."

"Then he's probably not far off the mark. Sonny likes to pretend he's a big shot, but he's harmless."

"Could I go over his statement?"

"Sure."

Samuels listened without interruption as I read my summary.

"That sounds like Sonny," he said when I finished. "Officer Daniels and I were there within a few minutes of the men showing up outside Paulding Development. It was a spectacle, but not a violation of any ordinance. The group stayed on the sidewalk and didn't cause a disturbance. I knew all of them."

"Do you recall what they said?"

"Not specifically, but the intent was clear. Jason Paulding should repent or face divine judgment for trying to buy the church property on Gillespie Street. I don't recall anything about Paulding dangling over hell on a rotten stick. That may be something extra Sonny came up with from a sermon he heard. I have to admit that Officer Daniels and I chuckled a time or two. You can imagine the scene."

"Yes, sir. I also met Rusty Steele."

"Be careful there. He can turn mean when he's intoxicated."

"Yes, sir."

Samuels leaned back in his seat. "Overall, it wasn't much different from messages I heard in church as a boy."

"But in a public place, naming a particular individual."

"True."

"Were there allegations of criminal conduct by Mr. Paulding?"

"It's possible, but nothing more specific than calling him a crook. I'll leave it up to the lawyers and judges to decide if that's slander."

"Wouldn't you consider a statement like that serious if made about you?"

"I've been called worse, especially by a bunch of drunks." Samuels paused and shook his head. "For all her weird ways and ideas, Sister Dabney has helped a lot of people most folks don't care about."

I swallowed.

"What kind of help?"

"Well, the other night she took in a boy whose father beat him up. The young fellow hid out at her house while we tracked down the father and apprehended him. The man had just gotten out of jail and went on a rampage that will land him behind bars for another long stretch. I think Sister Dabney reported the problem. If she hadn't contacted us, other members of the family might have been seriously hurt or worse."

"Have you ever been to her church?"

"Not on Sunday, but I've been by at other times. She also runs a food pantry and clothes closet. Have you met her yet?"

"No."

Samuels looked at me for a moment, then laughed.

"I won't ruin that moment by trying to prepare you. It wouldn't do much good anyway. Sister Dabney can be sweet as sugar one moment and screaming at the top of her lungs the next. Did you know she likes to stand out in the rain and tell it to stop?"

"No."

"Stands in her front yard without an umbrella, yelling at the sky. I asked her about it one time, and she quoted some verse from the Bible about opposing spiritual evil in heavenly places. I worry she might catch pneumonia." The officer paused with a faraway look in his eyes, as if remembering a time he'd watched Sister Dabney do something weird. "With her, you never know what you're going to get. Maybe a psychiatrist could shrink her head and tell you what's in it. But I'm just a cop. From where I sit, for all her odd ways, she does more good for this city than harm."

"I'll pass that along, but we have a client to represent."

"Everyone has a job to do," Samuels said, then leaned in closer, much as I suspected he would if questioning a criminal suspect. "But it makes no sense why a big developer like Jason Paulding would be interested in suing Ramona Dabney. I doubt she has any money. Lawsuits filed for spite are a waste of everyone's time. Can you help me understand what's going on?"

I couldn't reveal Mr. Carpenter's theory.

"No, sir." I swallowed nervously. "If we subpoena you to court, would you be willing to testify?"

Samuels relaxed and smiled. "Unless they're teaching something different in law school, I don't think I'll have a choice."

"Yes, sir, but I want to treat you with respect."

"Is that what they taught you in law school?"

"No, sir. That's what my father taught me."

WHEN I RETURNED TO THE OFFICE, Julie wasn't in the library. There was a Post-it note from Gerry Patrick beside my stack of work. The office administrator wanted to see me as soon as I returned. I walked upstairs with apprehension. Her door was open. She motioned for me to enter.

"I just heard that Margaret Fairmont is in the hospital."

Ms. Patrick had introduced me to Christine Bartlett and her mother. I explained as simply as possible what had taken place at the elderly woman's house. But I couldn't keep the tears from my eyes.

"I guess I've been in a little bit of shock," I said, taking a tissue from a box on the corner of Ms. Patrick's desk. "Thinking about it again upsets me more now than it did last night."

"I've received rave reviews from Christine about your care."

"You have?" I asked in surprise.

"Yes."

"That's nice to hear, but it looks like I'll need to find another place to stay."

"Why?"

I chose my words carefully. "Mrs. Bartlett told me she wouldn't need me to stay at the house if her mother is in the hospital or a nursing home."

Ms. Patrick frowned. "I hadn't considered that. Christine ought to have someone in the house to watch over all her mother's valuables. An empty house is an invitation to thieves. Is the antique silver still there?"

Mrs. Fairmont had a collection of eighteenth-century teapots, forks, and knives worthy of a museum.

"Yes, ma'am."

"She should have put that in a safe long ago. I'm going to call Christine and suggest she let you stay on until—"

"Please don't," I interrupted. "Mrs. Bartlett has so much on her mind; I don't want to add to it."

"That's unselfish, but Christine should exercise common sense in the midst of a crisis. She's been impulsive ever since our school days."

"You went to school together?"

"Yes, she's a few years older than I am. I won't tell you how many, but we've known each other a long time."

I stood up to leave.

"One other thing," Ms. Patrick said. "Has Zach talked to Mr. Carpenter about the two of you?"

"I don't think so."

"Make sure he does."

"Yes, ma'am."

"And it should be obvious that the firm would frown on your moving in with him."

My face flushed red.

"I'd never do that in a thousand years," I managed.

"No need to be dramatic. A simple 'no' would suffice."

I WENT DOWNSTAIRS TO THE LIBRARY. Julie was at the worktable sipping tea from a Styrofoam cup.

"What happened to your face?" she asked.

"Is something wrong with it?"

"You look like you just got some bad news."

"I'm upset about Mrs. Fairmont."

"Vinny told me about going back to see Mrs. Fairmont in ICU. He said he prayed for her. I told him I'm sure it made you feel better even if Mrs. Fairmont couldn't hear him. Prayer has as much to do with us as it does God."

I wasn't in the mood for a theology lesson from Julie.

"I'd better type the notes of my meeting with Lieutenant Samuels while it's still fresh. I'll print a copy for you as soon as I'm finished."

I BURIED MY MIND IN WORK. Toward the middle of the afternoon the door opened. Zach came into the library.

"I've finished the first draft of the complaint," Julie said.

"How long is it?" Zach asked, eyeing the thick stack of papers. "This isn't a class-action lawsuit against Microsoft."

"It's thorough," Julie responded with her nose upturned. "I'm sure Mr. C wants Dabney to realize the seriousness of her actions."

"And the discovery?" Zach asked.

"The requests for admission are done. I'm about to start on the interrogatories and requests for production of documents. Mr. C wants to notice Dabney's deposition before she has time to respond to the lawsuit, so I'll attach one of those to the complaint, too."

"Let me read what you've done so far."

Julie handed the complaint to Zach, who sat down at the table next to her. Julie watched him read. I continued with the research I was doing on another project. Several minutes passed before Zach turned over the final sheet.

"This is good," he said. "You organized it very well."

"So I've redeemed myself after the disaster with McKenzie?"

"I told you not to worry about that. Learn from a mistake and go on."

Julie spoke in a syrupy voice. "How come I like it when you teach me a lesson, but it makes my skin crawl when Tami corrects me?"

"I'll leave that to the complexities of women beyond the understanding of men."

The office intercom came on.

"Call for Tami Taylor on line 801. It's a Mrs. Bartlett."

I looked at Zach and Julie.

"I'm about to find out when I'll be sleeping on the street."

I hit the numbers.

"Where are you?" Mrs. Bartlett asked.

"At work."

"What time are you coming to the hospital?"

"I'm not sure."

"Mother is doing much better, but of course you know that. They are going to move her to a regular room as soon as it's ready. Dr. Dixon left a few minutes ago. He confirmed she had another stroke, but it's not as serious as they first thought. Naturally, the first thing she asked about this morning was that dog of hers. I would have thought she'd want to ask how I was holding up under the strain. Anyway, I assume you took care of the animal before leaving the house. Gracie has enough sense to let him out so he doesn't soil one of the carpets. That would be the end of him at my house, but Mother will tolerate anything if he's involved. They're not sure how long she'll be here. You can help keep the house in order until they discharge her. She asked about you and remembered your name, which the doctor said was a good sign, since it required use of recent memory. Then she ran on about some of my escapades when I was a teenager while one of the nurses was in the room. I had to interrupt to keep her quiet. Mother's blood pressure was fine; mine was about to pop through the roof."

I looked at the others and put my hand over the receiver.

"Mrs. Fairmont is better. I'm not kicked out."

Zach pointed skyward. Julie gave me a thumbs-up. I listened for another three or four minutes.

"Make sure you stop by the hospital on your way home," Mrs. Bartlett concluded. "They can tell you the room number at the information desk. Mother insisted I leave the room to get in touch with you."

"Yes, ma'am."

She hung up the phone. I told Zach and Julie what Mrs. Bartlett said.

"God heard Vince's prayer, Julie. It wasn't just for our benefit. It helped Mrs. Fairmont."

Julie didn't turn away from the computer screen. "I'm hearing fingernails on a chalkboard."

"I need to let Vince know."

"Go ahead," Zach said. "I'll help Julie with the discovery that will be served with the complaint."

Julie scooted her chair closer to Zach as I left the room.

BECAUSE VINCE WORKED so closely with Mr. Braddock, the senior partner had carved out a workstation for the summer clerk near his office. Within the short time span of the summer, Vince, and his ever-present laptop, had become invaluable to the older lawyer.

"Can I interrupt?" I asked. "It's about Mrs. Fairmont."

Vince pushed back his chair and listened as I told him about the phone call.

"So we're not going to be neighbors," he said. "I'm not sure you would have liked the apartment below mine anyway. I smelled an odd odor outside the door when I walked by last night."

I held my nose for a second. "I'm supposed to be with Mrs. Fairmont. She wants me to come by the hospital after work."

Vince hit a few keys on his keyboard and stared at his screen.

"Mr. Braddock has bombarded me with questions for a meeting he has in the morning. He's gotten used to a fast turnaround."

"So you won't be able to come with me?"

"Not until nine o'clock."

"Is the research something I could help you with?"

"No, it would take as long for me to explain the issues as it will to unravel the problem. But I want to see Mrs. Fairmont and spend time with you outside the office as soon as possible."

20

SISTER DABNEY HAD SPENT SO MUCH TIME IN THE RED ROCKER
reserved for war that she hadn't been on the front porch all week. Some
people tired in a fight; spiritual warfare energized her. One of the verses
she fired in a shower of arrows was "Let God arise, and his enemies be
scattered." Over and over she proclaimed the words, knowing her
cause just, her right to triumph indisputable. Where the arrows landed
depended on Providence. Her job was to bend the bow in faith and let
them fly. And woe to those who abandoned heaven's protection. She
knew their blood, and the blood of those close to them, would be upon
their own heads.

On Wednesday evenings at seven o'clock the congregation came
together for a prayer meeting. Sister Dabney walked slowly over to the
church to unlock the building. Only a handful would probably attend,
but the power of two or three in unity could shake heaven and earth.

She stepped inside and turned on the lights. Bare bulbs illumi-
nated cement-block walls painted a pale yellow. Rows of simple
wooden pews stretched from the rear to the front platform. A thin
gray carpet covered the floor. On the platform stood a rickety book
stand with her purple rocker behind it. The blandness of the interior
made the explosive color of the rocker stand out.

Sister Dabney walked up the aisle, following a path taken by multitudes in repentance. Familiar faces, forgotten names, unknown futures. She climbed the three steps to the platform and took her seat in the rocker. She didn't mix with the congregation until the conclusion of the service. The back door opened, and a few people came shuffling in. Many were there for the sack of groceries offered at the end of the meeting. Others came because they believed praying mattered.

At seven, two women Sister Dabney had plucked from the gutter several years before joined the small cluster of people. The women now had good jobs and would leave enough cash in the offering box to pay for the food.

The prayer meeting started. Anyone prayed who wanted to. After about thirty minutes, the back door opened, and a teenage girl hesitantly peeked inside. Sister Dabney recognized a young woman whose father and mother had long resisted the demands of the gospel and forbidden their daughter to have any contact with the church or its leader. The girl's countenance told a tale of sadness that could be read without prophetic revelation. Sister Dabney's militancy melted. Before her stood the need of the moment. Tomorrow's battles gave way to today's troubles. She motioned to a woman and pointed to the girl. The woman got up, went to the child, and guided her to a pew. Seconds later, the young woman dissolved in a pool of tears.

Sister Dabney cried out in a loud voice, "That's it! He's here! Let us pray!"

"I CAN SEE WHY YOU LIKE ZACH," Julie said as she slid a complete set of the pleadings in *Paulding v. Dabney* across the table. "He inspires me, too."

"What do you mean?"

"The way he looks at me, his tone of voice, the little smile when he's teasing, and the pull on his ponytail for emphasis. It's all darling. It made me want to work extra hard to do a good job."

"Are you trying to steal him away?"

"Could you stop me?"

I didn't know what to say. I was better equipped to land a catfish than catch a man. Julie must have seen the bewilderment on my face.

"Don't worry, if I wanted to bewitch Zach I'd sneak around behind your back and lure him away while you were reading your Bible. But I can appreciate him even if I can't have him. At first I was rooting for Vince to be your bachelor number one, but now I'm leaning toward Zach."

"I'm not sure I've chosen. I'm exploring my options."

"Please. Don't make your love life sound like you're a commodities trader discussing pork bellies. Zach is perfect for you. He believes enough of the weird stuff that's important to you, yet he thinks for himself."

"And, unlike me, it doesn't sound like fingernails on the chalkboard when he corrects you?"

"Careful, I'm rubbing off on you."

We went to work. From Julie's law school memo on defamation law I knew she was a good writer. But the complaint and discovery material put together in less than a day was equally impressive. The pleadings came across as a serious lawsuit, not a claim based on the ranting of a handful of derelict street preachers. If I'd received the stack of papers from the hand of a deputy sheriff, I would have considered myself in serious trouble. I made a couple of minor corrections and suggestions.

"This is good," I said when I finished. "But I still wish Mr. Carpenter would try to negotiate a settlement."

"You wouldn't think that way if it didn't involve a church."

"Maybe, but wouldn't it feel weird if this case involved a rabbi and a synagogue?"

"No. Intolerance and slander shouldn't be part of any religion."

"That's your opinion."

"You disagree?"

I could tell Julie was in debate mode, poised on the edge of her seat. I pressed my lips together in frustration for a moment.

"It's all in the way you categorize it," I answered. "Just because the truth sounds harsh doesn't mean it's any less true."

"And who decides what's true in a defamation lawsuit?"

"The jury."

"Right. And our job is to give them the opportunity to decide. Isn't that better than a gunfight at noon between Paulding and Dabney in the middle of Bay Street?"

There was no use arguing. Paulding and Dabney wouldn't shoot it out, but the preacher was in the law firm's gunsight, and Mr. Carpenter wanted to pull the trigger.

WHEN I ARRIVED AT HOME, the note to Gracie was gone and she'd left a fancy salad with fresh tomatoes, cucumbers, lettuce, and celery for me in the refrigerator. There was no sign that Mrs. Bartlett had been in the house. Flip hadn't chewed the edge of the antique rug, and the silver was still in its place. I ate on the dining room table. Flip curled up in his usual place beneath Mrs. Fairmont's chair.

After supper, the phone rang. It was Mrs. Bartlett.

"Where are you?"

"In the kitchen."

"Mother is in a regular room, number 3426. She asked again about you before I left. Get over to the hospital before they sedate her for the night."

"How? Vince Colbert, who took me last night, has to work late."

"Drive Mother's car." I could hear the exasperation in Mrs. Bartlett's voice. "Do you know where she keeps the keys?"

"Yes, ma'am. They're on a hook in the kitchen cabinet where she keeps the Wedgwood china cups."

"That's right. You do know how to drive a car, don't you?"

"Yes, ma'am."

"Good. I thought for a minute you'd never been on anything except a tractor."

I bit my lip, not sure why Mrs. Bartlett was lashing out at me again.

"I'll be leaving in a few minutes."

"Don't get her excited."

I hung up the phone and tried to remember when Mrs. Fairmont acted excited. The elderly woman had seen much of life. From my observation, what now passed by the window of her soul no longer had the capacity to swing her very far in either direction.

I grabbed the car keys. As an afterthought, I picked up a small photo of Flip that Mrs. Fairmont kept in a silver frame. The car was in a single garage attached to the house. Vernon, the man who maintained the yard and garden, kept the inside of the building neat and started the car for a few minutes every week to make sure it would be available in case of an emergency. Feeling like a Savannah dowager, I backed the enormous vehicle slowly down the driveway. The twins would have loved the cavernous backseat. At the hospital, I parked at the far end of the lot to avoid exposing the car to a ding or a dent.

Instead of entering through the emergency room, I went into the main lobby. There was a bank of elevators to the left of the information station. Before going up, I went into the gift shop and bought the best-looking flower arrangement available. It didn't rival Vince's flowers, but it would add color to the room. Mrs. Fairmont's room was on the third floor. I knocked on the door and waited. When there wasn't an answer, I slowly entered the room.

The elderly woman was in bed with her eyes closed and her head elevated. She was still in a hospital gown, and I made a note to bring some outfits from home on my next visit. The tubes, except for an IV, were gone. I set my flowers beside a nice arrangement from one of her friends, then sat in a chair beside the bed and quietly placed the photo of Flip on the tray table used for her food.

I'd spent many hours taking care of older women. It was the main way I earned money while attending college. Often there wouldn't be much to do but sit; however, if the woman in my care needed attention, I tried to treat her like my grandmother. Honoring my elders was a response ingrained in me by my mama, not an option to be applied at my whim.

When she was at home, Mrs. Fairmont asked me to wake her if I found her napping in the den. She considered it rude to sleep in the presence of another person. To illustrate her point, she told me a long story about an aunt who would nod off at family gatherings and snore. But tonight, rest was a remedy. I closed my eyes and leaned my head against the back of the chair. I needed to unwind, too. I dozed off.

I woke to sounds coming from the bed and quickly sat up. Mrs. Fairmont was trying to clear her throat. When she saw me, she motioned toward a plastic pitcher of water on the tray table. I poured a cup of water.

"Are you thirsty?"

She nodded, so I carefully held the cup to her lips, letting a tiny bit run into her mouth. She took several sips.

"Thank you," she said in a clearer voice. "Have you been here long?"

"No, ma'am. You were resting so peacefully that I grabbed a short nap, too. How are you feeling?"

"I've been on a long journey."

"As long as your honeymoon trip to the Mediterranean?" I asked, wondering if I'd caught her in a lucid moment.

"And I wasn't sure I was going to be coming back. You were with me at the beginning."

"Me?"

"Yes."

"Do you know my name?"

Mrs. Fairmont gave me an exasperated look that increased my hope.

"You're Tami Taylor, the young woman who's staying with me this summer. Why would you ask me such a ridiculous question? You sound like Christine."

"I'm sorry. When you mentioned a long journey, I thought you might be confused."

"I've been confused my whole life. And it started a long time before I had the first stroke." Mrs. Fairmont closed her eyes and licked her lips for a moment. "Did you know I almost died the other night in my den?"

"I was afraid."

"I saw the whole thing, or at least enough to know that the EMTs couldn't do anything for me if it was my time to go. Then, when I saw you praying, I realized that you and the others knew something I didn't."

My skin crawled. I'd read about near-death experiences but had never talked to someone who'd gone past the edge and returned.

"What others?"

"Those who were praying. I couldn't see their faces, but I'm sure Gracie was one of them. You know how she's always pestering me about what's going on at her church. I've always seen right through it. It's her way of trying to convince me to believe like she does. And then you came into my life thinking the same things. I know you've been praying, too."

Tears touched the corners of my eyes.

"Yes, ma'am."

Mrs. Fairmont lifted her hands a few inches from the bed. "The sound of voices filled the air. Yours was the only one I recognized. Maybe that's because I could see you. Anyway, the next thing I knew, I heard the young man who brought the flowers to the house reading the Bible in my hospital room. By the time I got my eyes open he was gone."

"You heard Vince?"

"Yes, I wasn't sure he'd really been here until Christine told me he'd been with you. Gracie came by to see me today. When I told her what happened she got so excited she shouted. One of the nurses came in to see if I was all right. Christine thinks I was hallucinating."

"Do you remember anything Vince said?"

"Yes, he read the Twenty-third Psalm, and then some beautiful poetry about the wings of God."

"You weren't hallucinating. That's exactly what happened."

Mrs. Fairmont closed her eyes and smiled. "I was hoping you'd say that. God has never seemed more real to me. I've even been praying for Christine and pretending there are voices surrounding her, too."

That night I went to sleep in silence. My heart shared Mrs. Fairmont's hope that we live life surrounded by the prayers of the saints.

By MID-MORNING all the pleading prepared in *Paulding v. Dabney* had been delivered to Mr. Carpenter for comment.

"Do you think he'll change anything?" Julie asked.

"I'd be shocked if he didn't."

"But you thought it was good. So did Zach."

"None of us have worked enough with Mr. Carpenter to predict what he'll do. He might want a six-paragraph complaint that contains barely enough information for the clerk of court to assign a file number. You told Sister Dabney everything we've uncovered in our investigation, and what you didn't reveal can be guessed from the discovery questions. The only thing left hidden is that Paulding is really filing suit so he can levy on the church property and take it away from her."

"Don't be shy about your opinion."

"I'm in an analytical mood this morning, practicing for the day when I'm a partner in a law firm and a young summer clerk hands me a pleading that she's slaved over for a couple of days. It will be my job to let her know how the practice of law really works."

"Remind me not to be around you when that happens."

"Oh, you'll be sitting in a corner office on the thirtieth floor of an office tower in Atlanta getting ready to attend a power lunch with one of your rich clients."

Julie laughed. "I like that picture, but can I have my old, syrupy-sweet Tami back?"

The intercom came on. It was Mr. Carpenter's secretary.

"Julie or Tami, please pick up."

We looked at each other, but neither moved.

"You're feeling tough," Julie said.

I put the phone on speaker mode.

"This is Tami."

"Mr. Carpenter has reviewed the pleadings and said you did a good job. He's made a few corrections and will provide a copy to Mr. Paulding at a meeting tomorrow morning. In the meantime, he wants you to follow up with interviews of the minister at Mr. Paulding's church, the newspaper reporter, and Mr. Paulding's wife."

"Yes, ma'am. What's our deadline?"

"First of next week. He's setting the defendant's deposition a week after she's served with the complaint."

She hung up the phone.

"Did you hear that?" I asked with a broad grin. "Mr. Carpenter liked my complaint."

Julie threw her pen at me. I knocked it away.

"You have the partner thing down already. Let someone else do the work and you take the credit."

I called the minister at Paulding's church. As soon as I let him know why I wanted to talk to him, he found an opening in his schedule. We arranged to meet in the afternoon.

"Paulding must give a lot of money to his church," I said to Julie when I hung up the phone. "His minister is dropping everything to meet with me."

"No," Julie said, smiling, "he's heard about you and wants to meet someone who can tell him what he's doing wrong."

I RESERVED THE FIRM CAR for the afternoon, then went looking for Vince to give him an update on Mrs. Fairmont's condition. Mr. Braddock's secretary didn't know where he'd gone, but instead of returning to the library, I went upstairs to Zach's office. His door was cracked open, and I peeked inside.

"Busy?" I asked.

He looked up and pulled on his ponytail.

"Yes. I don't have time for lunch."

"That's okay, I wasn't looking for an invitation." I felt my face redden.

"But I'd like to take you for a motorcycle trip on Saturday."

"Where to?" I regained my composure.

"I'm still working out the details, but it would take most of the day."

I hesitated. It was odd not having to call Mama or Daddy to ask permission. I had to remind myself that I had the authority to make up my own mind.

"Okay. Unless I need to do something for Mrs. Fairmont."

I quickly told him about her condition, leaving out details about her out-of-body experience. Vince had the right to hear it first.

"That's good news," he said. "Just let me know about Saturday."

I didn't want to leave. Zach returned his attention to the papers on his desk; when I didn't move, he looked up.

"Tami, I really need to finish reviewing these documents for Mr. Appleby within the next thirty minutes."

"Of course. Things will be a lot more relaxed when the air is rushing past your face on Saturday."

I backed out of the office, stumbling slightly over my feet, which mirrored how I felt on the inside.

THE CHURCH Jason Paulding attended was in a newer area of town. I made a couple of wrong turns before the large, modern structure came into view. There were several reserved parking spaces near the entrance to the church office. I parked next to an expensive car. It was cool inside the building, and there was thick blue carpet on the floor. While I waited, I picked up a glitzy magazine published by the denomination and flipped through it.

"Good afternoon," a smooth male voice announced. "I'm Jim Fletchall."

The minister, a physically fit man in his forties, had blond hair and was wearing a red golf shirt and khaki pants.

"I hope I'm not keeping you from a golf game," I said.

"My tee time isn't for another hour. Come into my office."

I followed him into a room almost as large as Mr. Carpenter's office. Diplomas hung on the walls, along with photographs I recognized as scenes in Israel. Some were black and white, others in color.

"Thanks for agreeing to meet with me," I said as I took out a legal pad and a pen. "Mr. Paulding told us that Ramona Dabney called you."

"Actually she came by the church."

"You met with her?" I asked, as if it was surprising to see him alive after the encounter.

Reverend Fletchall smiled. "We talked for a moment in the reception area, then came in here. It was an unusual conversation."

"What did she tell you?"

"She was interested in the photos of Israel and made a few observations."

"What kind of observations?"

"Comments about why it was right for me to be interested in the land and its people. She even mentioned I should consider studying conversational Hebrew. She had no idea that I've been studying the language for over a year through a correspondence course. Then her voice got loud, and she told me someday I'd live in Israel on a part-time basis. No one except my wife knows I'd considered that as a possibility for the future."

I wanted to ask more questions, but a quick glance at my legal pad reminded me why I'd come.

"What did she tell you about Mr. Paulding?"

"She laid out her version of Jason's attempt to buy her property on Gillespie Street. I wasn't familiar with the deal, but I knew there had to be two sides to the story. When she finished, she wanted to know if I would warn Jason that the property had been dedicated to God and couldn't be used for a secular purpose. She thought that as his pastor, I could dictate his conduct."

"What did you say?"

"First, I told her I don't have that level of control over the members of our congregation. Second, I informed her I didn't agree with her theory about irrevocable dedication of property for religious use."

"How did she react?"

Reverend Fletchall gestured toward a panoramic photo of Jerusalem.

"She took that picture off the wall and told me Jerusalem belonged to God, and no man or human government could take it from him. She believes the same applies to Jason Paulding's efforts to buy her church for a mixed-use commercial/retail development. It was an exegetical stretch, but Reverend Dabney seemed one hundred percent convinced."

"Did she make any personal accusations against Mr. Paulding? Call him a crook or a thief?"

"Yes, those words were used."

"Did she allege any specific criminal conduct?"

"I asked for details. At that point she told me I wouldn't believe the truth. Jason says she's been slandering him all over town."

"What did you think about her?"

The minister paused for a moment. "She's psychotic, psychic, or a prophet. Take your pick."

"Which would you choose?"

Reverend Fletchall shook his head and smiled. "I don't want to repeat her mistake and make a judgment about another person I can't back up. That's irresponsible. She could be any one of those or a mix of all."

"Did she tell you about her personal life or background?"

"No, and I didn't ask. She wasn't here for a counseling session. What have you found out about her?"

"We're still checking it out," I replied, dodging the question. "Would you be willing to sign an affidavit?"

"It depends on what it says."

"A summary of her comments about Mr. Paulding, not what she said to you personally."

"Okay, but I'm not sure what's going to be gained by dragging this woman into court. I can't tell Jason what to do, but I may suggest that in this situation it would make sense to overlook an offense and go on with life. There's a proverb that states, 'Where there is no wood—'"

"'The fire goes out.' Proverbs 26:20."

"You know the verse?"

"Oh yes. I have two brothers and two sisters. We all had to memorize that one."

I left the church more confused than when I'd arrived. Since deciding to go to law school, I'd role-played hypothetical scenarios that might challenge my convictions and worked out a response in advance. I was prepared for a divorce case without the presence of adultery, a guilty client facing criminal charges, and a witness who refused to tell the truth. But there was no file in my mind for an out-of-control preacher like Sister Dabney.

BACK AT THE OFFICE, I pushed *Paulding v. Dabney* to the side and dived into research about a secured transaction question for a bank trying to repossess equipment from a manufacturing company in financial trouble. Application of the complex rules of priority had an elegant simplicity. It was much simpler than unraveling human motivations. Julie walked in.

"Did you talk to Paulding's minister?" she asked.

"Yes, more of the same. General characterization of our client as a crook and a thief accompanied by a twist or two about Dabney's ministry."

"What does that mean?"

"Nothing worth explaining."

"Well, I had a very nontheological discussion with Paulding's wife."

"Did Dabney accuse Paulding of cheating on his wife?"

"How did you know?"

"The longer I work on this case, the more I'm beginning to think like Sister Dabney."

Julie nodded. "That makes perfect sense. Fifty years down the road, and you could be the defendant in a case like this."

"That's not funny."

"Because it's true. Have you considered this is your chance to look in the mirror and see where your religious fanaticism ends up?"

I started to snap back, then stopped. There might be more similarity between Ramona Dabney and me than I wanted to admit. People with a high level of zeal for God could get off track and into major error in a short amount of time.

"What else did the wife say?" I changed the subject.

"That she cried for three days after receiving the letter. It contained enough known information to make it seem credible. Mary Paulding wasn't able to discuss it in person with Jason until he returned from a business trip. Fortunately, Dabney's accusations were all false. Jason had the hotel and phone records to prove it."

"Hotel and phone records?"

"Yes, to show where he was and who he called on the dates Dabney accused him of coloring outside the lines. We need to throw a count in the complaint for malicious interference with the marital relationship. I know it's an archaic cause of action, but Mary will make a great witness. She's a nice lady who would bring a boatload of sincerity into the courtroom. Have a look."

Julie laid her folder on the table. I didn't touch it. I'd been around enough of Sister Dabney's work to avoid summarily dismissing what she'd written.

"And maybe we should verify the alibi, too," I suggested.

"That's not our job."

"Then how do you know the records are legit?"

Julie opened the folder and slid several sheets of paper across the table. There were copies of phone bills and hotel check-in/checkout data.

"Jason Paulding and his cell phone were in Phoenix when Dabney claims he was in Atlanta with his paramour. And the name Dabney gave for the other woman is one of Mary Paulding's best friends. The friend is happily married with two children and a third on the way. Mary told the woman about the letter, and she was able to prove the impossibility of the accusations."

The idea of this type of sin, even if it wasn't true, made me feel sick.

"Okay, Mr. Carpenter can let us know if there's anything else we should do. Did you hear anything from Brenda Abernathy at the paper?"

"No. If I'd grown the biggest rose in the history of Savannah, it would have died and fallen off the bush before she called me back." Julie paused. "That gives me an idea. We could contact the paper under pretense and see if we can reach her."

"What do you mean?"

"It's an old trick used by the investigators who worked for the divorce firm where I clerked during the school year. The investigator would pretend to be someone else in order to find out information."

"They would lie?"

Julie rolled her eyes. "Just on the surface. Is it wrong to create a diversion in order to find out the truth?"

"Yes."

"Then cover your ears for a few minutes."

Julie picked up the phone. I bolted from the library, thinking perhaps my future in the practice of law should be limited to sitting in front of a computer terminal performing research on esoteric issues. Dealing with real people and their problems created too many moral land mines.

21

I RAN INTO VINCE IN THE HALLWAY AND KNOCKED HIM BACKWARD.

"What's going on?" he asked, putting out his hands to steady both of us. "Why the hurry?"

"Running away from sin."

"What?"

I told him about Julie.

"If she thinks that's allowed under the rules of professional conduct, Julie won't keep her license very long if she ever becomes a lawyer."

He stepped toward the library.

"What are you going to do?" I asked.

"Warn her. If this gets back to Mr. Carpenter, she could be fired on the spot. You could get into trouble for not turning her in."

I'd become so used to sparring with Julie that I'd lost touch with the actual implications of her ideas. Vince brushed past me and opened the library door.

"Hi, Vinny," Julie said perkily as she returned the phone receiver to its cradle.

"Tami told me you made a call to a newspaper reporter under pretense—"

"Of course not." Julie sniffed, cutting her eyes toward me. "That would violate more ethical rules than I could cite, including the Ten Commandments. I was kidding."

"I didn't think it was funny. Neither did Vince."

"Tami,"—Vince touched me on the arm—"could I talk to you for a minute?"

As soon as we were alone in the hall, I burst out, "Sometimes she makes me furious. If you hadn't jerked me out of there, I would have exploded."

"I know. The steam from your ears was burning the side of my neck."

"There's a time and a place for righteous indignation."

"And this was one of those times?"

"Please, you sound like Zach. He's always analyzing my feelings and treating me like an insect under a microscope."

Vince took a step back. "Sorry. I wasn't trying to tell you what to think or feel."

"No," I sighed. "I guess it takes two men to keep me from running off a cliff. I'd wanted to see you anyway. And tell you about Mrs. Fairmont."

"That's what Mr. Braddock's secretary told me." Vince glanced down the hall. "Let's go to a conference room."

There were two small conference rooms on the main floor. One was occupied by a group of lawyers taking a deposition; the other was empty. We went inside and sat down.

"How is she?"

"Better than I'd hoped for, but she had an unusual experience."

I told him about Mrs. Fairmont's "journey" and hearing the voices of those who prayed for her.

"Before the ambulance arrived, I was praying and crying out so loudly you'd think I believed volume was important to receiving an answer. Maybe that penetrated her consciousness."

"It all sounds positive to me," Vince said thoughtfully, "but you'll have to see how it affects her over time."

Talking with Vince made me wish I'd been sharing the library all summer with him instead of being imprisoned with Julie.

"And I'll be praying for you and Julie," he added. "I don't think she realizes the impact her words have on you."

I suspected Julie knew exactly what she was doing.

"How will you pray?" I asked.

He smiled. "Loud enough to be heard."

I RETURNED TO THE LIBRARY. To be with Zach, and now Vince, when God touched a sick person was a tremendous blessing. People could go years without a hint of a miracle. I'd seen two in two weeks. That was a lot more important than my frustration with Julie.

"Did you have a nice chat with Vinny?" Julie asked.

"Yes," I answered curtly.

Julie pushed her chair away from the computer terminal.

"Hey, what I did was over-the-top. It was a random thought and I ran with it. I pushed it too far. I'm sorry."

I searched her eyes for a hint of mockery.

"Okay," I replied.

"Do you think I should say something to Vinny?"

"Probably."

"Vinny is a prince. If he could see anyone but you when he opens his eyes, I'd plant myself in the center of his vision. Could you see us as a couple?"

I couldn't stifle a smile.

"Why is that funny?"

"I can't figure out whether I'm supposed to be a couple with Zach or Vince. Trying to fit you in the picture makes it really crowded."

AFTER WORK, I spent a half hour playing with Flip in the garden. As I was coming inside, the phone rang. I ran into the kitchen and checked the caller ID. It was Mrs. Bartlett.

"Tami?"

"Yes, ma'am."

"Mother needs to finish her supper. She's having trouble swallowing, so they have her on a thick liquid diet that requires supervision. I've got to be at a reception for a friend who returned from six weeks in France. I'm going to be late as it is. What time are you going to be here?"

"I haven't eaten, but I can come anytime."

"Make it now. I've been waiting for a nurse's aide to help. It doesn't look like anyone is going to show. You can be here in five or ten minutes and get Mother through mealtime. She's not talking to me because I won't put up with her foolishness. I knew it would come to this eventually, but that doesn't make it any easier." Mrs. Bartlett lowered her voice. "You almost wish the stroke had taken her to avoid all this."

The "you" referred to by Mrs. Bartlett didn't include me. I'd seen pathetic situations of failed health. Mrs. Fairmont's condition wasn't one of them. Not yet.

"I'm on my way," I said and hung up the phone. I didn't want to listen to anything else Mrs. Bartlett might have to say.

Mrs. Bartlett's attitude toward her mother, me, and life in general had deteriorated since I first met her. If she'd been so negative then, I might not have agreed to stay with Mrs. Fairmont. That thought brought me up short. Both my parents and I agreed living with Mrs. Fairmont was probably one of the main reasons God had brought me to Savannah. Compassion for the elderly woman flooded my heart. When I entered Mrs. Fairmont's room, a nurse's aide was, in fact, helping her eat.

"Thanks so much," I said to the aide. "I'll take over from here."

"Are you her granddaughter?" the aide asked.

"No, but I wish I was."

"That's nice," Mrs. Fairmont said as soon as she swallowed a bite. "I went to sleep on you last night while you were here. I'm afraid I wasn't a very good hostess."

"No, ma'am, I'm just so glad you're better."

I'd fed patients who needed to use a thickening agent to help them swallow. Mrs. Fairmont had almost finished, and I helped her with the final bites. To my untrained eye, she seemed to be doing well.

"A sip of apple juice would be nice," the elderly woman said. "Even if it's not as good as an after-dinner port wine."

The apple juice hadn't been thickened. I started to stir in the powdery substance.

"No, let me try it straight. I've been able to handle a few sips of water."

I held the cup close to her mouth so she could use the straw. She took a sip and coughed slightly.

"I'll be cutting into a rare steak before you know it," she said.

"I hope so. What's the doctor telling you?"

"That I have a choice to make."

A hollow feeling hit me in my stomach. I knew what was coming before she said it.

"They can only keep me here a few more days. You know how hospitals are about kicking you out as soon as possible. After that, he recommends either a nursing home or an assisted-living facility."

Mrs. Fairmont reached up with a hand that trembled slightly and picked up the photo of Flip I'd brought the night before.

"After the doctor left, I stared at that picture and wondered what to do. I really want to go home and sleep in my own bed with Flip curled up at my feet. I could have a stair elevator installed and promise to wear my lifeline all the time. I even considered turning the den into a bedroom and using the guest bath on the main floor. That would be totally against the decor of the house, but—" She stopped.

"It's your house," I finished.

"Tell that to Christine."

"What does she want you to do?" I asked, trying to keep my voice level.

"Move out so the house can be sold and the furnishings distributed. Christine has her own things, but there are a few items that would fit in her house. Some of the antiques are museum quality and can be donated before my death. The rest would be placed with dealers on consignment. Is there anything you'd like to have?"

Mrs. Fairmont's question caught me so off guard that I couldn't stem my emotions. It was impossible to keep two tears from racing down my cheeks. I quickly rubbed them away, but she'd seen them. She reached out her hand and touched my arm.

"Tami, you're a good girl, as sweet as anyone I've met in a long time. I didn't think young people like you were still being made in this day and age."

Her words weren't helping me calm down. I sniffed loudly and wiped my eyes with the back of my hand.

"There's tissue on the windowsill behind you."

I reached back and grabbed a couple, then blew my nose.

"Would you be able to go home if you had a sitter who could stay with you twenty-four hours a day?" I asked through my sniffles.

"I don't know if it's worth the trouble to try and put that together. Friends who've used agencies to staff that sort of thing have had lots of problems. That's why I was reluctant to let you stay with me when Christine brought it up."

"I'm glad you did."

"Me, too."

Mrs. Fairmont closed her eyes. "If I shut my eyes, I can pretend that I'm sitting in my chair in the den with Flip at my feet and the TV tuned to a station I don't really care about watching."

"I wish I could take care of you."

"You already have, but you have your own life to live. It's going to take more than you can offer to keep me going."

"Would Gracie know someone?"

"We've talked about it before. She has a great-niece who needs work, but she's not reliable." Mrs. Fairmont looked at me. "You know, I can't talk to you like this when my brain short-circuits."

"Yes, ma'am. But even when you're confused you have a good attitude. You just ask a lot of questions and have an active imagination."

"Like what?"

I remembered the time she was convinced a bird had flown into the house.

"I'd rather not bring that up."

"All right." She nodded, closing her eyes again. "Tell me how Flip's doing."

She listened with a smile on her face as I told her what she already knew about the little dog's routine. When I finished, Mrs. Fairmont turned her head slightly and made better eye contact with me.

"May I tell you something?"

"Yes, ma'am."

She put her hand on her chest. "Something has happened in here. I think I'm more like you and Gracie."

"How?"

"I've been thinking about my life. I've made plenty of mistakes, but I know God has forgiven me and loves me anyway. Isn't that why Jesus came?"

"Yes, ma'am." I could hardly believe my ears.

"I knew there was something different about you and Gracie. But I couldn't put my finger on it until now. I tried to explain all this to Christine. She wouldn't sit still to hear me out."

"She'll think about it even if she walks away."

"I hope so. She believes it's an old woman's crutch. I told her it's better to go into heaven limping than not at all."

"There won't be any limping in that place." I smiled as my eyes watered again.

"For a few seconds when I was watching myself in the den, I felt so healthy, so alive—and I wasn't even dead."

I beheld the elderly woman, her body failing, yet God's mercy coming to her before it was too late. And believed.

"You're right," I said as tears flowed again. "And there won't be any crying either."

All the way to Mrs. Fairmont's house from the hospital, I repeated, "Thank you," softly under my breath.

Each time I said the words, another wave of gratitude swept over me. When I got home, I called Mama and Daddy.

"We're proud of you, Tammy Lynn," Daddy said when I finished. "Proud in the right way."

When I awoke in the morning, I didn't hear Chester crowing, but my heart cried out in greeting to the new day. The more I thought about my conversation with Mrs. Fairmont, the more amazed I was at God's grace. During my morning run, my feet sprouted wings and I almost flew down the street as I circled Chippewa Square.

I DIDN'T TELL JULIE what had happened to Mrs. Fairmont. She couldn't have shaken my faith, but she might have tried to undermine my joy. God's ability to reach Mrs. Fairmont, after a lifetime of her indifference, gave me hope that the same could happen to Julie. Vince was right. More prayer was needed.

With the complaint in *Paulding v. Dabney* on its way to the courthouse, Julie and I scrambled to complete other projects that had been pushed aside. Late in the morning I quietly hummed as I scrolled through a court of appeals decision to determine if I should print out a hard copy of the opinion for a research memo.

"I can't name that tune," Julie cut in.

"You don't know it. It's a Christian praise chorus."

"Is God in a good mood today?"

"Probably. I know I am."

"What happened? Did you figure out which bachelor is going to receive a rose?"

"What?"

Julie rolled her eyes and looked up at the ceiling. "It's from a TV show. I'm sure you've never watched it."

"I don't own a TV."

Julie held up her hand. "Okay, don't start in on the evils of TV. I know there's a lot of trashy stuff, but there are shows that help numb my brain cells worn out from staring at case law all day."

Julie glanced at the clock on the wall. "I'm going to have lunch with Maggie Smith. Do you want to join us?"

I'd met Maggie when I worked on the Moses Jones case. Several years before she'd been a summer clerk at Braddock, Appleby, and Carpenter but hadn't received a permanent job offer. Now she was one of the chief assistants in the Chatham County District Attorney's Office.

"Why are you having lunch with her? You're not working on any criminal cases."

"Girls have to stick together. We've met for drinks a couple of times. It's been helpful hearing her perspectives on life and the law."

"You're not going to drink at lunch, are you?"

"No," Julie sighed. "Unless you can get a buzz from water with a twist of lemon. This isn't an invitation to debate. I'm just offering you a chance to spend an hour with a woman who's been practicing law for five years. In case you haven't noticed, there aren't any female attorneys at this firm. The last time I saw Maggie, she asked me about you."

"I only saw her when we appeared in front of Judge Cannon. I'm surprised she remembers me."

"Who knows, you might be under criminal investigation, and it's a way for her to check you out before serving you with a grand jury subpoena."

I smiled. "Okay, at least I'll have my lawyer with me."

"It would be fun representing you. Then you'd have to take my advice."

Julie drove to a small restaurant that catered to a female lunch crowd. The only men in the place were with women who'd probably dragged them along. The decor was feminine, with lacy tablecloths, small chairs, and real china with a flowery design around the edges. Maggie Smith arrived a minute behind us. The assistant DA was about Julie's height with short brown hair and dark eyes. Smith had the confident demeanor of a lawyer who spent a lot of time in the courtroom. I remembered she'd not tried to hide her interest in Zach when the three of us talked for a few minutes before the judge called the Jones case.

"How's your boat man doing?" Maggie asked in a soft Southern drawl after we exchanged greetings.

"I haven't heard from him, so I hope he's only tying up at Mr. Fussleman's dock."

"Probably, or a new case would have come across my desk. You did a good job representing him."

We sat at a table near a window. A few rays of sun penetrated the leaves of a large birch tree next to the building. I felt very grown-up. In another era we might have been three young women discussing what dresses to wear at the summer ball. In the twenty-first century, we were professionals crafting a career.

"I recommend the quiche of the day," Maggie said. "It's the best in Savannah."

"Tami loves anything to do with chickens," Julie said, "especially fried chicken livers."

"I haven't had any good chicken livers since I left Montgomery," Maggie answered with a grin. "My great-aunt knows how to fry them crisp and light. There's nothing like a fresh chicken liver with a touch of hot sauce on it."

Julie's mouth dropped open.

"I've handled a few hundred thousand livers," I said.

Maggie shot me a curious look. The waitress came. We all ordered quiche with fresh fruit on the side. I described my summers working at the chicken plant with my father. I left out the more graphic anatomical details of how a chicken is processed for the human food chain.

"My daddy worked as a plant manager in a sock factory," Maggie said when I reached a stopping point. "He was there almost forty years. He started out as a sorter and worked his way up."

"My father is an ophthalmologist," Julie said. "He wears socks except when he's at the beach, and he eats chicken at least twice a week."

"Everyone has their role to fill in society," Maggie answered with a sweet laugh, then looked at me. "Tell me about your summer at the firm."

So much had happened. I was momentarily stymied.

"It's been a growing experience, both legally and personally," I answered slowly.

"Sounds like something you'd put on an evaluation form," Maggie replied. "What have you learned about yourself?"

Something in the lawyer's face told me she really wanted to know the answer to her question. I glanced at Julie.

"If you don't tell her, I will. I've psychoanalyzed you enough I could recognize your brain if someone put it in a jar."

"You wouldn't say that if you'd seen the evidence in some of the cases I've worked on," Maggie said. "I've had to put pictures of body parts into evidence that looked a lot worse than a plate of chicken livers."

"I've gained a lot of confidence that I can really be a lawyer."

The words popped out of my mouth, but as soon as I spoke, I knew it was the truth. I quickly searched my heart for the dark glint of pride.

"That's good," Maggie answered. "A summer job at a firm like Braddock, Appleby, and Carpenter will either overwhelm you with what you don't know or remove any doubt that you've chosen the right profession."

"How was it for you?" I asked.

"Probably not much different than for you. I tell people I'm from Montgomery, but my hometown is really a slow spot in the road about twenty miles from the city. I came to Savannah wondering if I could survive in such a different social and professional strata. Not only did I survive, I thrived."

"But you didn't get a job offer from Braddock, Appleby, and Carpenter."

"No, but neither did the other clerk. That's the year they hired Ned Danforth. He'd spent the summer with a firm in Richmond."

"Giving Ned a job was a huge mistake," Julie added.

"You shouldn't say that in public," I said. "It might get back—"

"Don't worry. Maggie knows all about Ned."

"And I'm not here to bash him or the firm. Even though I didn't receive a job offer, I made the contacts at the DA's office that led to my present position. Like you, I received special permission to work on an indigent defense case. The district attorney saw me in court a couple of times and told me to call him if I had an interest in becoming a prosecutor. That side of things suited me a lot better than defending the guilty. When I didn't get an offer from the firm, I contacted him. He offered me a position over the phone, and I took it."

"Maggie has tried over seventy-five felony cases," Julie said.

"And a lot more misdemeanors. This job is a great teacher because there's nothing like actual trial experience to hone your skills."

I suddenly realized the assistant DA was getting ready to ask me if I had an interest in becoming a prosecutor.

"Where do you think you want to work after you graduate?"

"I don't know. I'm just trying to do a good job this summer." Then, wanting to divert attention from myself, I turned to Julie. "Are you thinking about becoming a prosecutor?"

Julie laughed. "No way. I don't have enough self-righteous chromosomes to do a good job."

"It doesn't take that," Maggie replied. "But you have to be tough enough to deal with difficult people and unpleasant issues."

"Then spending the summer with Tami qualifies me," Julie said. "And we're working on a case against a woman who is as crazy as some of the psychopaths you put behind bars."

"Who is that?" Maggie asked.

"No," I said to Julie. "It's pending litigation."

"There's no harm. The complaint will be public record within a couple of days, and didn't you tell me it lays out all the facts of the case? Maggie can hear it from me or read it at the clerk's office."

The waitress brought our food. Between bites, Julie plowed ahead with a summary of *Paulding v. Dabney*. The whole conversation made me uncomfortable. I made a mental note to ask Zach about the ethical propriety of discussing the facts of a case with a lawyer not involved in the litigation. Maggie listened closely and laughed at Julie's description of Sonny Miller and the gang of derelict street preachers.

"I think I've seen that guy. Nothing serious, but he gets in trouble enough to appear in court. He's a nonstop talker who refuses to let the judge appoint a lawyer to represent him."

"That sounds right," Julie said.

I was tempted to add that Julie kept the windows of the car so tightly shut, she never actually talked to Miller.

"Paulding's company was one of the developers for the townhome community where I live," Maggie continued. "Other than being aggravated by Reverend Dabney, why would Paulding go to all the trouble and expense to sue this woman? I know what Joe Carpenter charges per hour."

"That part isn't in the complaint," I cut in before Julie could answer.

"No problem," Maggie said, giving me a knowing look. "I see so many real crooks, I forget a respectable person could get really upset about being called one, even if it comes from a nut like Reverend Dabney."

When the waitress brought the check, Maggie grabbed it as soon as it touched the table.

"We can pay our way," Julie said.

"I know, but you've entertained me enough to earn a free lunch."

After the waitress left with Maggie's credit card, the lawyer turned to me.

"What's Zach Mays up to? He never handles any criminal cases, so it was a treat to see him in court helping you with the Jones case."

"He's busy," I said, glancing at Julie and pleading with my eyes not to make a snide comment.

"He's overseeing our work in the case I just told you about," Julie said.

"Really? I wouldn't think that was his area of expertise either."

"He's broadened his interests a lot," Julie said with a teasing glance toward me. "There's more to Zach than that ponytail. But wouldn't you love to grab it and give it a tug? I know Tami and I would."

"Don't let Mr. Carpenter see you do it," Maggie replied. "I dated one of the young lawyers a few times when I was a clerk. It was a mess."

"Which one?" Julie asked.

"He's no longer there. They really frown on romance within the firm, especially involving summer clerks. Braddock, Appleby, and Carpenter is a mix of old and new. Sometimes it's hard to know where you stand."

"They fired him?" I managed, struggling to absorb all the information.

"Before the summer was over. I wasn't in the partner meeting, of course, and the guy wouldn't talk to me about it because he signed a confidentiality agreement as part of his severance package. I think he's with a firm in Dallas. We never stayed in touch."

"Why would they make such a big deal about it?" I asked.

"Oh, I don't think that was the only thing he'd done wrong, but it played a big part. To survive and get ahead, you have to know every law firm's culture."

"What advice would you give us?" Julie asked.

Maggie looked at both of us before responding.

"I'll use an old chicken cliché—don't put all your eggs in one basket."

JULIE AND I WERE SILENT in the car as we returned to the office. She pulled into a parking space but didn't turn off the engine.

"What do you think?" she asked me.

"About Zach?"

"No, that's your deal. I'm thinking about us at the firm and putting all our eggs in one basket. I've never been in a henhouse."

"When you visit me in Powell Station, I can correct that flaw in your life experience. We use a blue metal bucket and put all the eggs in it each morning."

Julie ran her hands around the steering wheel. "Be careful with Zach and Vince," she said in a conspiratorial voice. "I know it's none of my business, but I don't want any of you to end up like the lawyer who was fired."

VINCE CAME BY THE LIBRARY toward the end of the day. We made arrangements to visit Mrs. Fairmont in the hospital. When we arrived, Mrs. Fairmont was asleep, looking like she'd aged five years in five days. I left Vince in the room and checked with one of the nurses on duty.

"Would it be okay to wake her?" I asked.

"She's tired. Her daughter was here late this afternoon along with the family lawyer. They had a long discussion, and I think it wore her out. Are you the young woman who lives with her?"

"Yes."

"She showed me the picture of her dog and told me how much the dog loves you, too. I've owned a couple of Chihuahuas. It made me want to get another puppy."

"Did you meet the lawyer?" I asked closely. "I work for the firm that represents Mrs. Fairmont. I didn't know someone was coming to see her."

"He mentioned his name, but I don't remember. I left the room to give them privacy."

"Was he an older gentleman in his sixties with thinning white hair and blue eyes?" I asked, describing Mr. Braddock.

"No, he was in his mid-forties."

I pressed my lips together in concern. "Okay, I'll sit with her for a few minutes and see if she wakes up."

I pulled Vince into the hall and told him about the visit from the lawyer.

"It definitely wasn't Mr. Braddock," I said. "Doesn't he do all Mrs. Fairmont's legal work?"

"You'd know more about that than I do. I can check her name through his billing records and see if there's been any recent activity."

"No, I don't want you to get into trouble."

"It's not against the rules. He sees my time sheets and gave me access to his information so we can coordinate our billing reports to keep them consistent. What's the problem?"

I thought about Maggie Smith's trouble dating a lawyer at the firm but mentioned Mrs. Fairmont.

"Mrs. Fairmont's daughter is pressuring her into decisions. It's none of my business, but I can't help being concerned."

"Then let me check it out. I can ask Mr. Braddock first if you want me to."

We returned to the room and sat quietly for almost thirty minutes. Mrs. Fairmont didn't twitch. She was resting so peacefully, I didn't have the heart to wake her. On the way out of the hospital I turned to Vince.

"Don't bother Mr. Braddock. I can talk to him myself if I have a question."

"Okay, but let me know if I can help."

We reached Vince's car. I told him about Maggie Smith and the associate attorney who was fired.

"I thought we should be careful," I said.

"Why? If the firm gets upset because we visited Mrs. Fairmont together in the hospital, I wouldn't want to work there anyway. And who knows what really went on with Maggie Smith and the lawyer? Ask Zach. He might know the whole story."

I did a quick calculation in my head.

"She was a summer clerk six years ago. Zach's only been an associate for two years."

"Check with him anyway."

"I will."

Vince stopped in front of Mrs. Fairmont's house.

"Thanks again," I said as I opened the door to get out.

"You're welcome. Let me know if you ever need me."

Vince drove away. For such a smart guy, he was simple and uncomplicated. I felt so relaxed and secure with him. Before entering the house, I looked up at the stars, not for guidance, but assurance that the God who created them and held their light, and my life, in his hands would direct my steps according to his will.

22

FRIDAY NIGHTS WERE SPECIAL FOR SISTER DABNEY. WHILE MOST of the world looked forward to celebrating the weekend, Sister Dabney closed the blinds and kept her eye on the kitchen clock with the newspaper opened to the page that gave the time for sunset. As the sun went down, she lit a single candle and placed it on the scuffed-up coffee table in the living room. Sitting in the red rocker, she opened her Bible to a book she reserved for herself.

And read about the bride and the bridegroom.

The ritual had started years before when she was a young woman. She and Russell were holding tent meetings in southern Illinois. People started coming to the services, and the Dabneys checked out of a cheap motel to move into a duplex owned by a Jewish woman. The woman, a widow, lived in the other half of the house and believed Jesus was her Messiah. As part of the rent she allowed Sister Dabney to wash and dry clothes in her unit. The woman listened to Sister Dabney but politely refused an invitation to attend the meetings.

One Friday evening Sister Dabney went next door and found the woman dressed in nice clothes, lighting candles, and singing in a language Sister Dabney didn't recognize.

"What are you singing about?" she asked.

"It's a song my mother sang when I was a girl. I'm welcoming the Sabbath. Shabbat Shalom."

"You don't have to do that anymore."

"I know; I get to. It means so much more to me now than before."

"That's the bondage of the law."

"It might be bondage for you or someone else, but to me, it's a celebration."

The shining look in the woman's eyes stopped Sister Dabney's rebuke.

"Tell me," she said.

And for the next hour, the woman took Sister Dabney through Jewish history. The session ended when Russell came looking for her. It was time to leave because they were holding an all-night prayer meeting at the revival tent.

Sister Dabney wept through the night. Never had she considered the Bible as a whole. Story after story, verse after verse, rose up in her heart and revealed themselves in greater glory. Toward dawn, she faced with a trembling heart the book she would have cut from the Scriptures if it had been up to her—the Song of Solomon.

And fell in love with Jesus.

From then till now Sister Dabney never preached in public from the Song of Solomon, not because it embarrassed her, but because its intimacy was reserved for her time alone with the lover of her soul. Countless hardships, some deserved, some not, had battered her heart in the years since that night in Illinois. Hope can take long vacations. Russell's betrayal had been the worst. But in the midst of abandonment and sorrow, she still held on to what some might label a dead tradition.

She read a passage, closed her eyes, and rocked. Old and ugly, she knew no earthly bridegroom would knock on her door. But resurrection follows death, and undying love drawn from a purer reservoir might still be hers. This night, a few drops of healing balm touched her wounded soul.

AFTER MY MORNING RUN, I spent extra time with Flip. The little dog loved chasing a ball in the courtyard. The only problem with the game was that once he caught the ball, the second part of the game began. That part required me to chase Flip until I caught him. If he'd not been weighed down by the ball in his mouth, he could have eluded me forever. But carrying the extra weight, he couldn't zigzag as fast between the brick walkways. Laughing and out of breath, I would scoop him up with one hand, dislodge the ball from his mouth, and throw it across the courtyard to start another cycle.

After my shower, I waited for Zach. I didn't know where we were going but suspected it might be near the ocean. I put on a long skirt that looked like a beach cover-up and a loose-fitting blouse. I stuffed a floppy hat Zach had bought me earlier in the summer in a canvas bag. Zach arrived wearing jeans and a T-shirt. I could see the black motorcycle with sidecar attached parked at the curb in front of the house. One of Mrs. Fairmont's neighbors was walking down the sidewalk. She slowed to stare.

"Good morning, Mrs. Kaufman," I called out. "Mrs. Fairmont is doing better. This is Zach Mays, one of the attorneys at the firm."

The woman waved her hand and kept walking.

"I'm not sure Mrs. Kaufman heard you," Zach said.

"It doesn't matter. She'll tell her friends whatever she wants to."

Zach leaned over and scratched Flip behind the ears.

"What's he going to do all day?"

"He'll be fine. He goes out his doggie door, and I'll leave him plenty of food and water."

"Do you want to bring him with us?"

If the little animal was confined with me in the sidecar, he might scratch my legs to pieces.

"No, that's not a good idea. Wait here while I get my bag."

I didn't want Zach inside the house with Mrs. Fairmont gone. My personal morality was a much better moral guardian than Mrs. Kaufman's gossipy imagination.

The sidecar was black with orange flames painted on the sides. There was a matching helmet with smaller flames, which I slipped over my head. A microphone embedded near my mouth allowed us to communicate helmet-to-helmet.

"Ready?" Zach asked.

Hearing his voice in the confined space made it seem like he was inside my head.

"Roger and 10-4."

He laughed. "That's a mixed metaphor of signals."

There was no graceful way to get into the sidecar, but I slipped my legs in as fast as I could and let the rest of my body follow. Zach swung his leg over the motorcycle and started the engine. It was fairly quiet. I wouldn't have enjoyed the roar of a motorcycle that rattled the plate-glass windows of stores when it passed by.

When we pulled away from the curb, the sidecar, with its small tires and no shock absorbers, bumped sharply over the cobblestone streets. My teeth rattled together.

"This will be over soon," Zach said.

"I know," I replied in a voice that shook.

We left the bumps of the historic district and crossed the Savannah River. Riding in the sidecar was a cross between riding in a convertible and a go-kart. As we came across the bridge, I looked back over my left shoulder at the riverfront. We continued north on Highway 17, the road that skirted the coast of Georgia and South Carolina like the hem of a garment. We seemed to fly down the road.

"How fast are we going?" I yelled into the microphone.

"You don't have to shout," Zach replied in a normal tone of voice. "It might cause me to swerve off the road. We're going fifty-three miles an hour."

The speed limit was fifty-five. Lots of cars were passing us in the left lane. It was the sensation of speed in an exposed position that made it seem so much faster.

"Are we going to Hilton Head?" I asked.

"Yes. Have you ever been there?"

"Countless times," I joked. "My family owns a time-share at one of the resorts, and we spend a week every summer."

Though I couldn't see his face, I knew Zach was smiling. It was a beautiful day, not too hot, and the air rushing past kept me cool. I snuggled into the sidecar and ignored the constant stares of drivers and passengers of cars. It took less than an hour to reach the bridge that connected Hilton Head to the mainland. As soon as we reached the island, we were surrounded by signs of conspicuous wealth. We stopped at the welcome center to stretch. Sitting in the sidecar had been a little like being in a body cast from the waist down, so it was fabulous to stretch my legs. We took our time walking through the coastal discovery museum on the second floor.

"Mama could turn this place into a week's worth of lessons," I said as we stood in front of a display about local history.

"We can come back when they visit," Zach replied. "Have you talked to them about it?"

"No," I admitted, pointing to information about the struggles of early settlers who grew indigo. "And my family would be as foreign to this world as they were to theirs."

We left the welcome center. Traffic on the island was heavy as we rode to the south end of the island and the Harbour Town Lighthouse where we squeezed into a tiny parking space next to a pair of bicycles. The lighthouse wasn't built to guide eighteenth-century sailors past treacherous shoals; it was constructed in 1970 by Charles Fraser, the man with a vision for commercial development of the island, to attract golfers, not merchant ships. Zach and I walked through the gift shop and climbed to the top of the lighthouse.

We stood shoulder-to-shoulder and looked south toward Sea Pines Plantation. The sand traps glistened white on a golf course. When Zach's arm brushed against mine, the thrill that shot through me when we held hands during the prayer in Powell Station returned. Not wanting to send the wrong message, I moved away an inch or two, then leaned on the railing. We watched people walking in and out of stores below and the sailboats coming up the channel. My heart, which had sped up a few beats, returned to normal.

"How well do you know Maggie Smith?" I asked.

"Barely. She clerked for the firm a few years before I came but either didn't get an offer or turned one down. Since I don't handle criminal cases, our paths don't cross."

I told him about our lunch. When I mentioned Maggie's questions about the firm, he interrupted me.

"Why would she be so interested in your experience at the firm? Did she ask Julie the same things?"

"Not when I was there, but they've gotten together several times already. This was more about me."

"Does she want you to work at the district attorney's office?"

"That's what I thought, but she didn't bring it up."

"Did she criticize the firm?"

I paused for a moment before answering.

"Not really, except for the reason she wasn't hired."

I told him about Maggie and the associate attorney. The words spilled out faster and faster.

"And what Ms. Patrick said to us the other day now makes a lot more sense. I don't want you to get into trouble because of me."

Zach stared out at the scene below us. "I bet there was a lot more going on with Maggie Smith and Rick Donaldson than a motorcycle trip to Hilton Head."

"You knew him?"

"No, but I've seen his name on files. Like me, he worked with Mr. Appleby."

My stomach tightened. "Are you going to talk to Mr. Carpenter?"

"Eventually; I just didn't think it was important enough to schedule a meeting for that reason alone. Firm business that doesn't involve a client, a case, or a fee is pushed to the bottom of the pile. Maybe I can bring it up when we talk about the claim McKenzie Electrical Supply has against Jason Paulding."

"Has anything else happened on that?"

"After he read my memo, Mr. Carpenter contacted Paulding, who claims McKenzie is relying on a preliminary, verbal discussion that was modified by the subsequent written agreements. If that's the case, there may not be a discrepancy. It'll probably end up as an accounting dispute that will be cheaper to resolve than litigate in court, especially if Paulding wants to continue to do business with McKenzie's company."

We left the lighthouse. Hilton Head has a few thru roads and countless winding culs-de-sac. From the low-riding sidecar, I saw the island from a child's view. Twice we stopped and walked a short distance to the white sand beach.

"Are you going to comment on my lack of a tan?" I asked, digging my toes into the sand.

"No, except to ask if you put on enough sunscreen."

"Gobs," I answered from beneath a floppy sun hat.

We ate a late lunch at a seafood café. Zach smiled a lot, and for the first time since I'd dragged Zach into the *Paulding v. Dabney* case, I felt we were back on track. While we waited for the waiter to bring the bill, Zach's cell phone rang. He listened for a moment.

"No, sir. I wasn't planning on coming into the office today." He paused, then said, "I'm at Hilton Head with Tami Taylor."

I set my glass of tea on the table.

"Just for the day," he said. "We'll be back later this afternoon. If you want me to take—" He stopped and listened again.

"Are you sure that's a good idea?" he asked with a puzzled expression on his face. The waiter returned with the bill. Zach took it in his free hand.

"Yes, sir. I understand. Of course, it's billable time. And Tami?"

The person on the other end of the call spoke for a long time. The air-conditioning in the café kept the restaurant as cool as fall in the mountains, but my hands were perspiring.

"I'm sure she won't have a problem. I'll meet with you Monday morning."

He hung up the phone.

"Mr. Carpenter."

"Do you still have a job?"

"Oh, yes. We both do."

"He's not mad that we're together?"

"Not yet. He had something besides fraternization between associates and summer clerks on his mind. He wants us to visit Reverend Dabney's church in the morning."

"To go to the Sunday morning service?"

"That's right."

My hands decided to keep panicking.

"Why?"

Zach leaned forward. "To secretly record the service in case she says something about Jason Paulding. Dabney found out about the lawsuit, and Mr. Carpenter thinks she'll say something to the congregation that might help the case."

"How did she find out? It hasn't been served."

"Who knows, but she left a message last night on the answering machine at Paulding Development. Paulding heard it this morning and called Mr. Carpenter."

"What was the message?"

"Mr. Carpenter didn't say."

"Zach, this isn't going to work. Sister Dabney will spot us within five seconds after we come into the sanctuary, tell everyone who we are and why we're there, then harangue us until we leave."

Zach flipped open his phone and handed it to me. "You're right. It's a waste of time. Call Mr. Carpenter and straighten him out. Just hit the Send button."

I stared at the phone, trying to summon my jaguar courage. I pushed the button and saw the screen light up with Mr. Carpenter's name and number. As I raised the phone to my ear, I pushed the End button with a sweaty finger and handed the phone back to Zach.

"Nice bluff. For a second, I thought you were going to give a repeat performance of your courtroom confrontation with Mr. Carpenter in the Moses Jones case."

"That was different," I sighed. "I believed in my client."

He laid his cell phone on the table. "Don't take your hunches too far. Dabney may be the leader of a church, but that doesn't give her the right to slander Jason Paulding. If her church won't discipline her, it may be necessary for a court to do so. There's a place in the system for accountability."

"Zach, this lawsuit isn't about getting her to do right. It's a setup to grab a piece of property for a real-estate developer. What if Dabney was accurate about the McKenzie transaction? What if she's right about Paulding being a crook and a thief? What if Paulding has been cheating on his wife? The last time I checked, truth was a defense to a defamation action."

"But is it up to you to decide who's right in each and every detail of a case?"

"It is if someone wants me to be their lawyer."

Zach shook his head. "That's asking a lot. Most people are a mix of good, bad, and something in the middle. Motivations and actions have a way of tripping over each other to create a confused mess. Both Paulding and Dabney may have a measure of justice on their sides. That's the reason each side should have an attorney."

ROBERT WHITLOW

"Sister Dabney doesn't believe in lawyers."

"Then she'll represent herself or change her belief. If there's a verse in the Bible that condemns all lawyers, show it to me, and I'll surrender my law license and find work coaching high school soccer."

I pounced. "Is that why God sent you to Savannah? To coach high school soccer?"

Zach shook his head. "No, and I'm waiting on that verse."

"'Woe to the lawyers.' That's what one of the men at my church said to me when he found out I was going to law school."

"That's directed toward Pharisaic Jewish leaders who spent all their time burdening ordinary people with religious obligations that didn't produce true righteousness."

"Don't get so theological on me."

Zach stopped and smiled. "Look, I don't want to spy on Reverend Dabney any more than you do, but given the circumstances of the case and our obligation to our client and the law firm, I can't think of a compelling reason not to."

I paused. "And I'll go. But you'd better drive your car."

"I agree. The motorcycle with you in the sidecar would definitely attract the wrong kind of attention."

23

In spite of the liberal dousing with sunscreen, my skin felt prickly when Zach dropped me off at Mrs. Fairmont's house. I would be glowing when we visited Sister Dabney's church, but unfortunately, not with the glory of God. There was a message on the answering machine from Mrs. Bartlett.

"Tami, where are you? I hope you haven't left that dog alone all day. If he chews a hole in the rug, it won't be covered by the home-owner's insurance. Call me as soon as possible. Mother isn't cooperating about the move to a nursing home. I need you to talk some sense into her."

I punched the button and listened again. The short message raised several issues. First, I'd never considered whether pet damage might be an insured event in a home-owner's policy. Second, I had to decide whether or not to return Mrs. Bartlett's call. However, so long as I lived in the house, I had to call her even if it was a hard thing to do. Third, and the most troubling problem—how to respond to Mrs. Bartlett's demand that I help shove her mother out of the house into a nursing home. I stepped into the blue parlor to check on the antique rug. It was a few hours older but no different from when I'd left in the morning.

"Good dog," I said to Flip, who'd followed me into the room. "Keep guarding all the valuable antiques. And remember, there aren't any bones buried beneath that carpet."

I walked back to the kitchen and returned the call to Mrs. Bartlett.

"I'm sorry I missed your call," I said before Mrs. Bartlett could start an interrogation. "The rug in the parlor is in great shape for a two-hundred-year-old fabric."

"Is that supposed to be a joke?" Mrs. Bartlett retorted.

"No, ma'am," I replied, realizing with embarrassment that I'd sounded like Julie Feldman. "I knew you wanted me to make sure it was okay, so I checked before calling. Flip uses the doggie door and knows his chew toys."

"You and Mother give that dog credit for a higher IQ than most college freshmen."

"Yes, ma'am. I mean, that would be incorrect, not that I'm disagreeing with you, it's just—"

"Mother is physically better, but her mind is going haywire," Mrs. Bartlett said, interrupting me. "Dr. Dixon can't keep her in the hospital beyond the weekend. I've called all over town and found an opening at a nice place. Mother refuses to consider it. She claims you're encouraging her to return home. That's none of your business, but now that you've stuck your nose into it, I expect you to straighten it out."

I tried to keep my voice calm in the face of her groundless accusation.

"Mrs. Bartlett, all I did was listen to your mother. I didn't suggest that she come home. That's a decision your family should make."

"You told her Gracie could help find a live-in sitter."

Mrs. Bartlett was partially right.

"That was part of the discussion, but I didn't make a recommendation, and I didn't mention it to Gracie."

"I spoke to her. She won't be looking for anyone to move in with Mother."

I thought for a moment. "I'll talk to Mrs. Fairmont, but I'd like you to be there to make sure I don't get out of line."

"Let me ask Ken what he thinks about that idea."

She muffled the phone so I couldn't hear. In a few seconds, she came back on the line.

"That's acceptable. I'm not coming back into town this evening. I'll see you at the hospital in the morning around ten."

"I can't do that. I have to go to a church for the law firm."

"You what?" she asked, raising her voice.

"It has to do with a case," I answered in my best professional voice. "I'm sorry, but I can't give the details. I'd be happy to meet with you in the afternoon."

"I was going to play golf, but this is more important. Be there at three thirty."

ALL EVENING my thoughts went back and forth between Mr. Callahan and Mrs. Fairmont. I knew it had been decades since the older lawyer had any contact with Ramona Dabney or her husband, but I wanted his advice about the lawsuit against her. I phoned Mama and Daddy to tell them about my week and give them an update on Mrs. Fairmont.

"And I'll be praying that she keeps improving," Mama said. "Do you know when she'll be released from the hospital?"

"That's one of the problems I'm facing," I replied, then explained the situation.

"If she can function at home and wants to be there, that's where she should be," Mama said emphatically. "Her daughter ought to honor her mother's wishes."

"Yes, ma'am, but Mrs. Bartlett has a different idea."

"Your mama's right," Daddy said. "And I'm glad the Lord has used you to give Mrs. Fairmont hope. Ever since the day I met her when you moved into the house, I've believed there was a reason for you being there beyond watching after her in the evenings and at night. Now she's in his hands."

"Thanks, Daddy."

"And don't neglect the opportunity to speak a timely word," Mama added.

"Yes, ma'am," I replied, hoping my role would be one of prayer instead of confrontation. "But I have something else I need to ask you about. It has to do with Oscar Callahan."

There was a moment of silence before Daddy spoke.

"We were going to tell you about that in a minute. Mr. Callahan is back in the hospital."

"No!"

"He was in a car wreck on Friday while driving Mrs. Callahan to town," Daddy continued. "I think he took too much blood pressure medicine, passed out, and ran off the road. They hit a tree and totaled his car. Both of them were wearing seat belts, and she's okay, but he had some kind of neck injury. The doctors are running tests to find out what's wrong."

"Is his heart okay?"

"I think so."

"Why would that happen so soon after God touched him?"

"We live in a fallen world," Mama answered.

I knew that was true, but I didn't have to like it.

"Please let me know how he does," I said as we ended the call.

THE FOLLOWING MORNING I prepared for church as if I were home on Beaver Ruin Road. I washed my hair and put it in a bun. Although slightly sunburned, I didn't use any makeup except for a single swipe of lipstick. I selected a yellow-and-white dress that reached well below my knees and closed-toe shoes. I stood in front of the full-length mirror on the door to my bathroom with my biggest Bible in my hand. It would take a heavenly revelation for Sister Dabney to discern that I was a law student. Zach's occupation would be equally hard to guess, although for different reasons.

Zach arrived wearing a white shirt, dark sport coat, gray slacks, and a conservative tie closely knotted at his neck. With his hair pulled back tight, it wasn't obvious he had a ponytail until he turned to the side.

As we walked down the steps, I told him about Oscar Callahan's wreck.

"I mean, he has a miracle, then a couple of weeks later he's hurt in a car wreck," I said. "It doesn't make sense."

We left the historic district and followed the same roads Julie and I traversed when we went to Bacon's Bargains.

"Did you bring a recorder?" I asked as we waited for a streetlight to turn green.

Zach patted his jacket. "It's in here with a microphone on my lapel that you haven't even noticed."

I glanced closer and made out a tiny black dot peeking out of his lapel.

"That's a microphone?"

Zach reached inside his coat, took out the recorder, and pressed a button. In a few seconds I heard my voice saying, "That's a microphone?"

"Have you been recording all our conversation?"

"To test it out. It's very sensitive. Mr. Carpenter sent it by courier to my house last night. I don't know if it's owned by the firm or borrowed from a private investigator."

I thought about Julie threatening to obtain information by pretense from Brenda Abernathy at the newspaper.

"Is this legal?"

"I didn't have time to research it. Does Reverend Dabney have a reasonable expectation of privacy in what she says during a public meeting of her church congregation?"

"Probably not," I admitted. "And she's not been shy about expressing her opinion outside the church. Do you want to know the real question?"

Zach turned his head toward me. "Yes."

"How are you going to react when Sister Dabney calls you out in the meeting and wants to know if you're going to repent for secretly recording the service?"

The closer we got to the church, the more nervous I became. Zach quit talking, too. I was busy running down imaginary rabbit trails regarding what might happen to us. Zach timed our arrival for exactly when the service was scheduled to start so we could avoid questions from members of the congregation. I hoped Sister Dabney was punctual.

"Can I wait in the car?" I asked as he parked the car beside an older van with one of its side mirrors missing.

"Yes," he replied without hesitation. "I've been thinking about that for the past few minutes. It's a good idea for you to stay. There's really nothing for you to do. I have the recorder in my pocket, and if your prediction of Dabney's ability to spot an intruder is accurate, there could be a negative reaction from the crowd. Alone, I have a better chance of getting out without an ugly incident." He pointed across the street where Julie and I stopped the first time I saw the church. "Take the car over there and wait for me. As soon as I come out, pick me up."

I'd not been serious. Zach's carefully thought-out answer surprised and blessed me. I reached over and touched him on the arm.

"I'm not used to someone shielding me from controversy."

"It makes sense. There's no reason for you to be here." He turned off the car's engine and handed me the keys. "Just don't be like Julie and abandon me to explore the neighborhood."

I got out of the car and walked quickly around to the driver's side. As soon as I reached Zach, who was straightening his tie, I slipped the keys in his coat pocket.

"What?" he asked.

"I appreciate your concern for me, but I know a lot more about what might happen in that meeting than you do. As Mr. Carpenter and Julie like to say, 'I'm the local expert on religious fanatics.' You may need my expertise before this morning is over."

My confidence surprised me. There were about twenty cars in the parking lot. No one was standing at the door waiting to greet people. Even before we entered the sanctuary I could hear voices singing.

"How close to the front do we have to sit?" I asked in a soft voice.

"Anywhere in the room should work. Just avoid crying babies or whiny children."

Zach held the door for me. I quickly surveyed the room. The sanctuary could hold at least two hundred people, but only about fifty or sixty were present. A skinny woman was playing the piano. Seated in a garish purple rocker on the platform was an obese woman in her mid- to late sixties rocking back and forth. Her gray hair was wound in a bun. She was wearing a blue cotton dress that could have come from my mama's closet. Sister Dabney, her eyes closed, was listening, not singing. Zach and I quickly slid into one of the rear pews.

"There she is," I whispered.

"Are you sure?" he asked.

"Of course; who else would be sitting alone on the platform?"

Zach leaned over and spoke into the microphone. "Let the record reflect that Tami Taylor has made a positive identification of Reverend Ramona Dabney, a large older woman sitting in a purple rocking chair."

"Don't make jokes." I raised my finger to my lips.

A woman on our pew picked up a hymnbook, opened it to the correct page, and handed it to Zach with a smile.

"It's our anthem," she said happily with a smile that revealed a few missing teeth.

I didn't recognize the words or tune, but it had the exuberant melody similar to some of the older songs we sang at my church. My grandmother would have enjoyed it. The message was simple—the sinner's desperate need and the Savior's sufficient grace. The woman beside us clapped her hands and sang in a loud voice. There was sincerity in her gap-toothed rejoicing. Everyone in the room seemed to share her enthusiasm.

And in that instant I ceased being an observer and became a participant.

I just couldn't help it. I was in the midst of primitive mountain religion sprouting in the sandy soil of the coast. Within half a verse I was singing along with the rest of the congregation. Zach gave me a puzzled look. I let him hold the hymnbook and began clapping my hands, not worrying that my singing would be the featured music on his recording of the service.

The congregation was a mixture of black, white, and brown with one thing in common—these people seemed glad to be in church. The piano player transitioned into another song. It was one I recognized. Taking the hymnbook from Zach, I found the correct page number and handed it back to him. I didn't need to see the words or music.

Sister Dabney continued to rock with her eyes closed. The congregation didn't pay any attention to her. They kept singing and clapping, with an occasional shout thrown in for good measure. They sang five or six songs before circling back for another run through their anthem, a signal that apparently ended that part of the service. The piano player ran her fingers along the keyboard in a final flourish, and everyone sat down. Sister Dabney remained seated in the rocker with her eyes closed. I waited for someone to step onto the platform and announce the next part of the service, but no one moved. Zach gave me a questioning look. I shrugged.

After a couple of minutes of awkward silence, a man sitting toward the front stood up and began to pray. Immediately almost everyone in the room joined in. It was chaotic. I saw Zach touch the microphone with his finger. I couldn't imagine what Mr. Carpenter would think when he listened to the recording of the meeting. The woman on our pew didn't try to hide the burden of her heart. She cried out for her daughter, who had moved to Jacksonville and left God behind in the process. Zach leaned over to me.

"Wow," he said. "Is this what happens at your church?"

"Not on Sunday morning," I answered somewhat defensively.

The commotion continued without abating, then suddenly died down. When I looked toward the platform, I knew why. Sister Dabney had gotten out of the rocking chair. She had the broad, heavily creased face of a woman who had seen much in life and been scarred in the process. It was not the visage of a person who spent her time baking cookies for squealing grandchildren. She walked slowly to the podium. I slid down in the pew and tried to make myself invisible.

"Does anybody want to hear the Word of the Lord?" Sister Dabney asked in a voice that would have been at home any place within fifty miles of Powell Station.

"Yes, yes," called out people across the congregation.

Sister Dabney stood silently and waited for anticipation to build.

"You can run," she said slowly, "but you can't hide. Know this, all who can hear my voice. Your sins will find you out!"

She stopped and closed her eyes. Dread crawled up my throat. I knew this must be the part of the meeting where Sister Dabney listed the secret sins of everyone in the congregation who looked guilty. I glanced at the woman beside me on the pew. She seemed as relaxed as someone waiting for a table in a restaurant.

"Do I need to tell your sins or will you repent without shame?" Sister Dabney continued.

As if on cue, almost everyone in the congregation streamed toward the front. In a few seconds Zach and I, along with a man to our left and a woman on the right, would be the only people left in the pews.

"Let's go up front," I said rapidly. "We need to repent."

"What did we do wrong?"

"I don't know, but if you don't move, we're going to attract a bunch of attention."

I pushed past Zach and made my way out of the pew and down the aisle. Zach didn't follow, which both embarrassed and infuriated me. I'd learned early in life that it was better to keep short accounts with God than try to convince him of my righteousness. Zach's refusal to humble himself was the fruit of pride, and an invitation for Sister Dabney to fillet him like the catfish that had stung his hand. I didn't look back.

There was an open space in front of the platform. As soon as people reached the area they knelt down. Many put their faces against the carpet. Sister Dabney remained behind the podium. I avoided her eyes. People prayed quietly for several minutes. I tried to blend in.

"You there," she said.

I looked over my shoulder and saw Zach sitting impassively at the rear of the sanctuary.

"Young woman," Sister Dabney continued, "the one wearing the yellow dress. Stand up."

I glanced down at my dress. It had not miraculously turned green.

"That's right, you," Sister Dabney said. "With the brown hair."

An older man next to me on the floor nudged me in the arm. There was no escape. I'd left the safety of the pew to be surrounded by a mob that would offer me as a human sacrifice upon Sister Dabney's command. I had no choice but to look up and meet Sister Dabney's gaze. She had startling blue eyes beneath bushy eyebrows. I touched my chest with my index finger.

"Yes," the old woman answered impatiently. "I don't want to spend the whole service playing hide-and-seek with you. Get up."

I rose to my feet. Everyone else stayed on their knees. I heard nothing from Zach in the rear of the room.

"I know what's in your heart," Sister Dabney said.

I swallowed. I was found out. I could either stand there and be blasted or take the initiative. Like a soldier who knows how to respond in combat because of countless repetitions in training, I knew what to do.

"I'm sorry," I began in a voice that surprised me with its strength. "I came here today—"

"Quiet!" Sister Dabney cut me off.

I shut my mouth.

"You came here today burdened for a man I haven't thought about in many years. Does the name Callahan mean anything to you?"

I swallowed again. This time in shock.

"Yes, ma'am."

"Many years ago I knew a great preacher named Callahan. He had a son who wandered from the fold of God, but I see that son coming back to the faith of his father. Continue to pray for him, and this time he will not backslide."

"Yes, ma'am."

Sister Dabney paused. "And he will recover fully. The enemy wanted to take him out, but the angels of God didn't let his foot strike a stone."

I nodded. "Thank you."

"Don't thank me, child. Thank the one who doesn't want any to perish but all to come to the knowledge of the truth. How many prodigals are in God's house this morning?"

Hands all across the front shot up. Sister Dabney turned away from me and commanded a man on the opposite side of the room to stand up. She told him some things about his childhood that caused him to weep.

I returned to my place on the floor and prayed for Oscar Callahan.

24

By THE END OF THE SERVICE, I'd decided Sonny Miller's negative description of Sister Dabney's meetings was the product of his own rebellion. The congregation returned to the pews, and Sister Dabney preached a message not unlike hundreds of others I'd heard during my lifetime. She knew the Bible and quoted verses from memory. There was a sharp edge to her presentation, but I knew from experience sometimes that's what people need to hear. The service ended with an altar call for anyone who needed prayer. Zach nudged me.

"Let's go," he said.

"You want to go down front and pray together?"

"No, leave."

The woman next to me waved good-bye as I slipped from the pew and followed Zach outside. When we were seated in the car, he took out the recorder and turned it off.

"We didn't get anything for Mr. Carpenter," he said. "Jason Paulding wasn't on the program for the day."

I hadn't thought about the developer after the meeting started. Zach turned onto Gillespie Street.

"But what did you think?" I asked.

"About the service?"

"Yes, that would make sense considering where we've been the past hour and a half."

Zach reached back and gave his ponytail a slight tug.

"You enjoyed it more than I did."

"How could you not be blown away by what she said to me about Oscar Callahan?"

"Mr. Carpenter might say she did her homework."

"What do you mean?" I asked with surprise.

"She knows the law firm has filed a lawsuit against her and could have found out about you and your connection to Powell Station. Didn't you say that for years Mr. Callahan was the only lawyer in Powell Station?"

"Yes, but why would she go to all that trouble? Researching me doesn't make any sense. Sister Dabney didn't know we were going to be in the congregation this morning. And what she said about Mr. Callahan was positive, not negative."

Zach took a deep breath. "Look, you jumped into Reverend Dabney's little pond this morning and felt right at home. If God showed her something about Mr. Callahan, I think that's great. However, that doesn't change how she's treated our client, which looks more like harassment than the conduct of a sincere minister."

Of course, Zach had a point about Sister Dabney. I also sensed he was more negative about the meeting than he let on. It had been different from my home church, but similar enough that I liked it. Sister Dabney and most of the people in attendance were serious about their faith.

"What are you going to say to Mr. Carpenter?" I asked.

Zach shrugged. "It would be entertaining to play the recording, or at least the part where Dabney talks about Mr. Callahan, but Mr. Carpenter isn't interested in a sociological study of religion. I'll prepare a brief memo that will disappear into the file."

We turned along the riverfront.

"Where would you like to eat?" Zach asked. "There are a couple of good restaurants ahead on the left."

"Thanks, but I have something at Mrs. Fairmont's house."

Zach slowed to a stop at a light.

"No eating out on Sunday," he said. "I forgot."

I knew we were thinking similar thoughts. Two many jagged edges of belief could rip compatibility to shreds.

"The firm will expect you to bill the time spent in church to the case," he said.

I'd been so caught up in the drama of the morning I hadn't thought about time and billing for work on Sunday. Would it be wrong to bill a client for attending a church service?

"He'll notice if I don't?"

Zach nodded. "Absolutely. He's meticulous about that sort of thing."

"What do you think?"

"I'm not your conscience. Because I was there on law firm business, I'll bill the time."

"Maybe I could work extra tomorrow and make up for it."

"He'll want you to bill that, too."

Zach stopped in front of Mrs. Fairmont's house.

"Are you enjoying my predicament?" I asked in frustration.

"No, but if this is a conviction for you, it could become an issue at the firm later. Situations arise with clients or cases that force all of us to go into the office on Sunday. It doesn't happen a lot, but you can't entirely rule it out."

I thought for a moment.

"Okay, bill my time since we were there mostly for work reasons, especially to hear what Sister Dabney had to say about Mr. Callahan."

Zach drove off, leaving me with frustration at him and lingering guilt about Sunday morning billing.

When I called home, my family hadn't returned from church. I

wanted to let Daddy know what Sister Dabney told me about Oscar
Callahan. Sitting in the kitchen, I ate a salad I'd fixed the night before.
It wasn't that hard honoring the Sabbath; it just took a little prepara-
tion and planning. After I ate, I phoned home again. Still no answer.
Either the morning service had lasted longer than usual or my family
was spending the afternoon away from home.

I left a few minutes early for my meeting with Mrs. Bartlett. I'd
gotten used to driving the big car. I knocked quietly on the door of
Mrs. Fairmont's hospital room. No one answered so I peeked inside.

The room was empty, the bed ready for a new patient. Mrs.
Fairmont's flowers, clothes, and the photo of Flip were gone. I hur-
ried to the nurse's station.

"I'm looking for Margaret Fairmont."

"She was discharged this morning," the nurse on duty answered.

"Where did she go?"

The nurse turned to another woman sitting at a different station.

"Louise, do you know where they took Mrs. Fairmont? She was
in 3426."

"A spot opened up at Surfside Manor," the woman answered.

"What's that?"

"A brand-new nursing facility south of town."

I was stunned.

"Do you have the address?"

The nurse pulled a folder from a small cabinet and handed me a
brochure.

"This has the contact information and a map to locate it."

In the elevator, I speed-read the brochure. The pictures made it look
like a resort, but there weren't any patients in the photos. From experience I knew the rooms wouldn't look so inviting if occupied by someone
with severe dementia or end-stage cancer. Mrs. Bartlett had obviously
been able to coerce her mother into doing what she wanted.

I backed out of the parking space, intending to return to Mrs.

Fairmont's house, but after paying the parking fee, I turned south instead. The nursing home, even though it was named Surfside Manor, was on the Abercorn Expressway, closer to the Little Ogeechee River than the Atlantic Ocean. Sure enough, the only surf in sight was a cresting wave painted on the sign at the entrance. I entered a sparkling clean lobby exactly like the picture in the brochure. I asked about Mrs. Fairmont.

"She checked in earlier today," a woman at the information desk told me after checking a computer screen. "Your name, please?"

"Tami Taylor, Mrs. Fairmont's caregiver before she was hospitalized a few days ago."

The woman took out a diagram of the complex and drew a line showing me the location of Mrs. Fairmont's room. As I walked down a long hallway, I glanced from side to side. Most of the rooms were empty. Mrs. Fairmont's room was at the end of a short hall, which meant she probably had an extra window. The thought of such a tiny bonus made me sad when I considered the beauty of the elderly woman's home. The door was closed. I knocked.

"Come in," a familiar voice responded.

Mrs. Fairmont was sitting up in bed, watching TV in a large private room with a separate sitting area and a shiny coffee table. I recognized several items from her house. The photo of Flip was prominently displayed on a shelf near the bed. I took it all in with a glance. Sure enough, she had an extra window.

"This is nice," I said, trying to sound appropriately enthusiastic.

"Don't be silly," Mrs. Fairmont replied, turning off the television. "It's a gilded cage. Better than one with iron bars, but still a prison."

She was wearing a nightgown with an IV still attached to her hand.

"Sit down," Mrs. Fairmont said, pointing to the chair closest to her bed. "You weren't around to represent me so I had to do it myself."

"What do you mean?"

"Christine brought in a lawyer to talk to me. I listened for a few minutes, then pretended to go to sleep. They didn't leave, so I told them I needed to call Sam Braddock about any legal matters. That took care of the lawyer."

"What did he want you to do?"

"Sign a paper so Christine could take care of all my business."

"A power of attorney?"

"Probably, I didn't even read it. She already has one that gives her the right to make decisions about my medical care if I turn into a vegetable, but as long as I have a few lucid moments, I want to handle my own affairs."

I was so relieved that Mrs. Fairmont seemed to be doing better. It made me feel happy even though we weren't sitting in the blue parlor at her home.

"This really isn't a bad place," I said. "It smells nice, and looks more like an apartment than a hospital room."

Mrs. Fairmont sniffed. "This is a compromise Christine and I agreed to after listening to Dr. Dixon. He says I need to be monitored closely for a few weeks and then I may be able to go home. I didn't want to hear the part about being monitored. Christine didn't want to hear the part about me going home. This place agreed to let me pay a month's rent. The sales agent who showed us around hopes I'll want to come back when I really can't look after myself."

"And Christine brought some things from your house?" I said, pointing to a familiar vase.

"No, Gracie stopped by the house this morning before coming to see me. She said you weren't there."

"I went to church with Zach."

"Which one is he?"

"The one with the ponytail and the motorcycle."

Mrs. Fairmont nodded. "He's all right, but I like the boy from Charleston better. What's his name?"

"Vince."

It was the first time Mrs. Fairmont had expressed a preference between the two men.

"And a little competition is good for their egos," she added. "There are too many girls chasing boys these days. I think the flower should attract the bee."

I smiled at the old-fashioned image.

"Yes, ma'am."

Mrs. Fairmont closed her eyes for a moment. I sat quietly, not sure if she was dozing off or not. After a couple of minutes she opened her eyes.

"Will you bring Flip to see me? I miss him."

"Yes. There are benches near the entrance where we could sit outside."

"Bring him to my room. I asked Dr. Dixon if spending time with Flip could be part of my therapy, and he put it in my chart."

"You're better at getting your way than your daughter."

Mrs. Fairmont smiled. "Even though Christine can be hard to deal with, I see her differently now. And it's not that I'm getting senile. It has to do with how I feel about life."

Mrs. Fairmont reached out and took my hand. We'd never had contact like that.

"Promise me one thing," she said, looking directly into my eyes.

"Yes, ma'am."

"That you'll bring Flip to see me tomorrow."

I laughed and released her hand.

"We'll both look forward to it."

I left Surfside in a much lighter mood. Back at Mrs. Fairmont's house, I called home. One of the twins answered the phone. When I wasn't around the girls every day, it was hard to distinguish their voices until I heard more than a simple greeting.

"Tell me who," the girl on the phone replied when she knew I was on the line.

"I can't in three words. What was your memory verse last week?"

"'For You are my hope, O Lord God; You are my trust from my youth. By You I have been upheld from birth; You are He who took me out of my mother's womb. My praise shall be continually of You.'"

The words washed over me. No poetry could be more beautiful.

"That's wonderful, Ellie. Where is that?"

"Psalm 71:5–6. Emma and I liked it, too. We used it to practice our calligraphy. It made it so easy to remember."

"Are Mama and Daddy there?"

"No."

"How's Mr. Callahan doing?"

"He's going to be okay. Daddy said he was stiff, but should get better."

"Amen," I said with relief.

"You sound like a preacher."

THE FOLLOWING MORNING I was working alone in the library. The door opened and Gerry Patrick entered. I immediately sat up straighter in my chair.

"Mr. Carpenter wants to see you in his office. Zach is already waiting there."

I swallowed.

As a homeschooler I'd never been summoned to the principal's office, of course, but I suspected this was how it felt. I walked a step behind Ms. Patrick, too numb with apprehension to ask her a question. I brushed my hair behind my ears, knowing it would immediately fall back into place. Mr. Carpenter's secretary didn't look up as I passed—the reaction of a bystander not wanting to have eye contact with the condemned.

Zach was sitting across from Mr. Carpenter's desk. Both the senior partner and the young lawyer had serious expressions on their faces. Ms. Patrick sat in a chair behind me in the corner.

"Sit down," Mr. Carpenter said to me. "I asked Gerry to be here since she has administrative responsibility for you as a summer clerk."

I scooted my chair away from Zach's before settling in.

"Primary responsibility for this problem lies with Zach," the older lawyer began. "But you also played a part."

"Yes, sir," I managed weakly. "But the whole thing has been completely innocent. There hasn't been anything improper—"

"Would you call not following my instructions proper conduct?" Mr. Carpenter asked, his voice rising.

"No, sir."

"And you have to learn to take responsibility for your mistakes."

"Yes, sir. I'm sorry and apologize. I should have come to you before now."

"You knew?"

"Yes, sir."

"Why didn't you contact me yesterday or first thing this morning? Did you think I wouldn't learn about this?"

"No, sir. I knew you would eventually find out."

Zach turned to me. "How?"

"You knew, too," I responded with a puzzled expression. "We were together."

Mr. Carpenter, his eyes blazing, turned toward Zach. "This is making me wonder if we have a more serious problem than failure to follow instructions. Explain yourself."

Zach pulled his ponytail before he spoke. "Mr. Carpenter, I've told you everything. I don't know how Tami found out about anything else."

I kept my voice as level as possible. If nothing else, I could try to divert the attack away from Zach. I was expendable. I looked directly at Mr. Carpenter.

"I understand that you're upset because Zach and I visited my parents for the weekend and went to Hilton Head together for a few hours this past Saturday. But it isn't as it appears. We're different. Both of us."

"What?" Mr. Carpenter asked.

I motioned over my shoulder at Ms. Patrick.

"Ms. Patrick said the firm frowned on dating between lawyers and summer clerks. Only we're not dating. It's just a way to get acquainted that has my parents' approval. The closest we sat to each other was at Sister Dabney's church."

I heard an explosion of laughter and turned to see Ms. Patrick with her hand over her mouth.

"I'm sorry, Mr. Carpenter," she said.

I glanced quickly at Zach and Mr. Carpenter. Zach was trying to suppress a grin. Mr. Carpenter appeared bewildered.

"Why are we here?" I asked.

Zach spoke. "Because we left Reverend Dabney's church before she held a congregational meeting to discuss the Paulding lawsuit."

"She was praying for people," I said. "That's usually the last thing to happen."

"I know," Zach said, "but not this Sunday. A new employee of Paulding's company was also visiting the church. He's a laborer who didn't know anything about the lawsuit but stayed and reported what happened to Paulding when he came to work this morning. Apparently Reverend Dabney made some inflammatory remarks that would have helped us if we'd gotten them on the recorder."

"Oh," I replied, looking at Mr. Carpenter. "So Zach and I aren't in trouble for fraternizing?"

"That's a fancy word choice for whatever you're doing in your personal lives. But right now I'm upset because you missed an opportunity to obtain valuable information in pending litigation. One of the mistakes lawyers often make is giving up just before they uncover a key piece of evidence."

"I wanted to stay—," I started, then stopped. "But only because I was interested in seeing what happened to the people receiving ministry. I wasn't thinking about the case."

"Which is another lesson," Mr. Carpenter said. "Don't get side-tracked. I've attended sporting events with clients or other lawyers and had to block out the game so I could concentrate on business. It's the same principle."

"Yes, sir. I'm sure it's the same on the golf course."

"Yes." Mr. Carpenter raised his eyebrows. "Do you play golf?"

"No, sir, but it seemed analogous."

"Right." Mr. Carpenter put his fingers together in front of his face. "And while you're both here, I don't think it's a good idea for associates to date summer clerks. You should get to know all the lawyers in the firm, not pair off like two kids at summer camp."

"Yes, sir."

"So, are you and Zach dating?"

I took a deep breath.

"No, sir. We're courting."

Mr. Carpenter shook his head. "That's an archaic word to go with your fraternizing."

"Yes, sir, but the important thing is that we're not violating any firm policies. Wherever I am, I always try to obey the rules."

Mr. Carpenter turned to Zach.

"What do you have to say?"

"Tami is right. We're spending time together but not dating. I intended to talk to you about it. We've been so busy I hadn't gotten around to it. I encourage her to take advantage of every opportunity to interact with the other attorneys for the reasons you mentioned."

Mr. Carpenter looked past me. "Gerry, do you want to wade into this conversation?"

I didn't turn around but felt the skin on the back of my neck tingle.

"Tami has some unusual ideas," the office manager replied crisply. "I've been taking a wait-and-see approach. This needed to be mentioned. I accept Zach's explanation."

"Okay," Mr. Carpenter said to Zach. "Keep it casual and don't monopolize her time."

"Yes, sir."

"And at some point you'll need to interview Jason Paulding's employee. Do it before we take Dabney's deposition." Mr. Carpenter sat back in his chair. "That's it. At least Gerry got a good laugh out of this meeting."

Once we were away from Mr. Carpenter's office, Ms. Patrick chuckled.

"I know that wasn't an act," she said to me, "but it was probably the best thing you could have done. Mr. Carpenter couldn't chew you out after I lost it."

"I was worried, especially after I heard about the problems Maggie Smith had when she clerked for the firm."

Ms. Patrick's eyes widened. "You know about that?"

"Yes, ma'am."

"I don't blame Maggie for that problem. She's a fine woman and, from what I've heard, is doing a good job at the district attorney's office."

Ms. Patrick left Zach and me.

"Whew," I said. "Was he really mad?"

"He wasn't happy. I've not worked much with him, and this case hasn't made me want to volunteer for more assignments. Mr. Appleby is more even-tempered, even when we're under pressure to put together a big deal. I'm going to stick to admiralty work."

"I'm sorry I dragged you into this."

Instead of reassuring me, Zach merely shrugged and left me standing outside the library door.

I WORKED ALONE through lunch, worried the whole time that Zach was upset with me about the Dabney case, again. Julie returned in the middle of the afternoon.

"Did you elope over the weekend?" she asked as she dropped a file folder on the table.

"No," I responded more lightly than I felt, "but we went for a motorcycle ride to Hilton Head on Saturday."

"Scouting out the honeymoon suite, I'm sure. I'd expect the two of you to plan everything down to the last detail."

"Then we went to church together."

"That sounds romantic. Bernie Loebsack and I used to hold hands in synagogue until our mothers found out and wouldn't let us sit next to each other."

"I don't think hand-holding would have gone over very well at Sister Dabney's church."

"You went there?" Julie's jaw dropped open. "That's like walking into the lion's den."

"We had no choice. Mr. Carpenter ordered us to go."

Julie sat down at the table and listened. She winced when I told her about the morning meeting with Mr. Carpenter.

"It's hard enough for one of us to beat Vinny out of a job without getting a demerit on our record."

"I'm not competing with Vince."

Julie rolled her eyes and snapped her fingers in my face. "I'm out of your life for three days, and you're in a fantasy world."

"I'm not sure I want to work here even if they offer me a job," I said, then quickly added, "but please don't say that to anyone."

"I already knew that. It's why I invited you to lunch with Maggie Smith."

"But I don't think I want to be an assistant district attorney either. If you'd asked me about it before the summer, it would have made sense. However, after representing Moses Jones, my thinking about that type of work is confused, too. I'd never want to represent a guilty person, but it would be terrible to prosecute someone who was innocent."

"I'm not talking about being a prosecutor," Julie answered, lowering her voice. "Maggie is thinking about leaving the district attorney's office and starting her own firm."

I stared at Julie for a second.

"What would that mean to you and me?"

"She's looking for someone who can invest the start-up capital in return for an instant partnership share."

"I don't have any money."

"But I do, or at least my father does. He would pony up the coin. I think it would be neat having my name on the letterhead of a Savannah law firm the day I pass the bar exam. Maggie would make the switch to private practice, and I could specialize in divorces. There's always room for a woman attorney willing to represent other women in domestic cases."

"Have you talked to your father about this?"

"Enough to know that he doesn't think it's a good idea, but I haven't really gone to work on him. He hasn't turned me down for anything I really wanted since the eighth grade."

"Where would I fit in?"

"You'd be our associate."

I chuckled for a few seconds, then burst out laughing. As I laughed, the tension flowed out of my body. I ended up close to tears and wiped my eyes.

"What's so funny?" Julie asked. "Are you too good to be an associate?"

"No, just not that desperate. I'd rather work in a chicken plant than try to get guilty people off or help break up marriages. If you and Maggie Smith want to start that kind of a law firm, I won't try to talk you out of it, but I'm holding on to my belief that being a lawyer will hold a higher goal for me."

"That's arrogant," Julie said, her jaw set.

I knew I'd hurt her feelings.

"It's nice of you to even consider me," I added.

"Don't go there. It's condescending," Julie said curtly. "But please keep this conversation between us. I'll do the same for you."

We spent the rest of the afternoon in icy silence. I regretted laughing, but the idea of a three-woman law firm with me as the third wheel seemed so funny at the time. Now, both Zach and Julie were upset with me. Later in the day I thought about Sister Dabney, who had probably been served with the complaint. She wasn't aware of my involvement in the lawsuit, but once she was, she would be mad at me, too. I shut down my feelings and focused on brain talks.

I spent the rest of the week on a tight schedule, balancing work during the day and taking Flip to see Mrs. Fairmont in the evenings. The barrier between Julie and me lowered but didn't disappear. Zach took seriously his promise to Mr. Carpenter that I should interact with other lawyers in the firm and set up two lunches for me with mid-level partners I'd seen only in passing. Zach didn't come to the lunches, which were all business—my studies, interests, goals, and the future opportunities at the firm.

On Thursday I contacted the Paulding Development Corporation employee who had been at Sister Dabney's church. His name was Jorge Rivera. I didn't let him know Zach and I had been there, too.

"How did you choose the church?" I asked.

"My parents went to a tent meeting years ago when Sister Dabney and her husband were in Texas. Sister Dabney called my mother out by name and gave her a message that changed her life."

Several weeks before I would have been instantly curious. Now it didn't surprise me at all.

"How did you find out she was in Savannah?"

"I was with a demolition crew working not far from the church and saw her name on the sign out front. I had to find out if it was the same person. Is her husband dead?"

"I'm not sure, but I know they're divorced. Tell me about the congregational meeting this past Sunday."

"I was about to leave when she said they had church business to discuss. She said Mr. Paulding had hired some crooked lawyers to sue her and that God's judgment was going to fall on all of them."

"Okay." I shifted uncomfortably in my chair. "Did she describe the type of judgment?"

"No, but she quoted some verses about God's wrath against the wicked."

"Anything else?"

"She said Mr. Paulding was a crook, and the lawsuit was his way of trying to steal the church property."

"Did she explain what she meant by stealing the property?"

"No, but it bothered me a lot. I've only been in Savannah for three months, but Mr. Paulding has been a great boss. When I had to be off work for a couple of days for a family emergency in Texas, he let me go home even though I hadn't accrued enough vacation or sick days."

"Did Sister Dabney find out you worked for Mr. Paulding?"

"We didn't talk, but she's the kind of preacher who knows stuff even if no one tells her. I know that sounds weird, but it's the truth."

"I believe you."

"It's none of my business, but I think this should be worked out without a big lawsuit."

"Most lawsuits are settled before they get to court," I said. "Pray that's what will happen here."

"Are you a Christian lawyer?"

"I'm a law student working here for the summer. One of the senior partners is handling the case."

"But are you a Christian?"

The man's bold persistence impressed me.

"Yes, I am."

"There's a boss over your boss and Mr. Paulding. That's who we need to talk to."

"I will."

"Me, too."

As soon as I hung up the phone, I knew that in addition to praying there was someone else I had to talk to. I took a slip of paper from my purse and dialed the number for Oscar Callahan.

25

THE PHONE RANG SO MANY TIMES WITHOUT THE ANSWERING machine picking up that I thought I'd dialed a wrong number. I was about to end the call when a slightly out-of-breath male voice answered.

"Hello," he said.

"Mr. Callahan?"

"Yes."

"It's Tami Taylor, I mean Tammy Lynn Taylor."

"Hey, I just walked in the door. I was checking on a new calf. And don't worry. Your name change is safe with me."

"My parents know. It came out when Zach Mays and I were in Powell Station a few weeks ago."

"How is the ponytail preacher doing?"

"He's not a preacher."

"Not yet. When will I get to see him again?"

"We don't have another trip planned."

"You'd better get on it," Mr. Callahan answered emphatically. "It takes a unique man for a woman like you. He might fit the bill. Not that I'm trying to play matchmaker."

I smiled. I'd never considered Oscar Callahan the matchmaker type.

"Yes, sir, but he's upset with me because I got him involved in the slander case I mentioned when we came to see you. The defendant is Rachel Dabney, only now she goes by Ramona."

"You're kidding. After all these years."

"It's her."

"Is her husband, Russell, a defendant?"

"No, he left town with another woman a few years ago. Zach and I went to her church this past Sunday to see if she was going to slander our client. While we were there, she talked about you."

"Me?"

The lawyer listened as I told him everything Sister Dabney said about him.

"And she didn't know before the meeting that you knew me?"

"No, sir."

"Did you mention it later?"

"No, we left before the service ended."

"Well, it sounds like she hasn't lost a step. I'm a little stiff from the car wreck but thankful to be alive without any serious injury. My heart is ticking along fine. I still take blood pressure medicine and a cholesterol pill, but it's more to keep my doctor's blood pressure normal than my own. And as old as I am, I feel like the prodigal son."

"How is Mrs. Callahan?"

"Trying to figure out what happened to her cynical husband. She's warming up to the new man and starting to like me better than ever."

"You weren't cynical."

"Behind my mask. Seriously, tell Zach how much I appreciate his obedience to pray that day in the kitchen."

"Yes, sir. I'm glad you're doing so well."

"And thanks for calling to check on me."

I realized he was about to hang up.

"Wait, there's one more thing. I need your advice about the lawsuit. Isn't it wrong to sue a preacher like Sister Dabney?"

Mr. Callahan was silent for a moment.

"Is there evidence she slandered your client?"

"Yes, unless what she said was true."

"Do you know the answer to that?"

"No, sir, but you can see how accurate she is about people."

"That doesn't make her perfect. There's accountability that comes with a gifting. This lawsuit could be God's way of humbling her."

Mr. Callahan's answer surprised me. "Is that what you believe?"

"I have no idea, but it's clear you're not considering all sides of the issue. So long as you represent your client with integrity and don't misrepresent the evidence, it may be necessary for the legal process to sort out the truth."

Mr. Callahan could see the different facets of a lawsuit from across a courtroom or hundreds of miles away.

"You trust the legal process that much?"

"It's not perfect, but I don't have illusions about my personal omniscience either."

I took a deep breath and exhaled.

"It can be a tough call," Mr. Callahan said. "There were times when I withdrew from a case or sent a client on his way, but I'm not sure it was always the right thing to do. And remember, you're not working for yourself. At Joe Carpenter's firm those types of decisions will be made for you until your name moves to the partner side of the letterhead. That's one reason I hung out my own shingle in Powell Station. I always wanted to have the last word on the work I took in."

"Have you ever regretted it?"

"Sure. No matter the path you take in life, there will always be challenges."

I paused for a moment. "Do you think I could do that? I mean, come back to Powell Station. The two lawyers who took over your practice probably don't need me, but I know a lot of people and—"

"Tammy Lynn, you could come home and make a go of it. But you have a big advantage over me at your age."

"What's that?"

"You're trusting God to direct your steps. My decision was my own."

AFTER I HUNG UP, Vince buzzed me and we made arrangements to see Mrs. Fairmont that evening. I worked alone for a couple of hours until Mr. Carpenter's secretary paged me on the office intercom.

"Julie and Tami, please come to Mr. Carpenter's office."

I pressed the button.

"Julie is out of the office at a hearing in federal court in Brunswick."

"Then he'll see you alone."

"If it's about the Paulding case, Zach Mays should probably be included."

"He only asked for the two of you. Do you want me to put you through to him?"

"No," I said quickly. "I'm on my way."

Grabbing a legal pad, I walked down the familiar hallway. The interior of the law firm had been so intimidating and mysterious the first few days at the office. Although infinitely fancier than the inside of the chicken plant in Powell Station, there were similarities. One place handled birds; the other processed people with problems. I entered the waiting area for Mr. Carpenter's office.

"Go on in," his secretary said. "He's talking to Judge Cannon about the Paulding case."

I knocked lightly on his door and entered.

"That's right, Judge. I've served her with a notice to take her deposition next week. I suspected she wouldn't hire a lawyer. Her conversation with you confirms it."

Mr. Carpenter listened for a few moments.

"Yes, I know you don't like pro se cases. None of us do, but we had to take action. I confirmed service of the notice of deposition about half an hour ago, but I have no idea if she'll show up."

He was silent again.

"No, given what's transpired between the parties, I consider the possibility of settlement remote. However, I would agree to a bench trial, which would be quicker and less messy than steering the case through a jury proceeding. Do you want me to mention it to the defendant?"

Mr. Carpenter listened.

"Yes, sir, it would be better if you took the initiative. I appreciate the call and will keep you informed."

Mr. Carpenter hung up the phone.

"Your friend Judge Cannon has been assigned to the case."

"He only saw me long enough to reject our first plea agreement in the Moses Jones case."

"He'll see more of you before the summer is over. I was talking to him about *Paulding v. Dabney*."

"What did she say to the judge?"

"Not what she should have. She warned him that he would be judged by God if he let the case go forward. Judge Cannon has been threatened by the best; she won't faze him. He mentioned the possibility of a bench trial. What do you think about agreeing to that from our side?"

"Usually, that's not the best for the plaintiff."

Mr. Carpenter raised his index finger. "Except when the defendant is going out of her way to antagonize the judge. Then it might be the fastest way to a judgment that will enable us to levy against that property."

At that moment, Oscar Callahan's confidence in the judicial process sounded hollow.

"Your job is to help me prep for the deposition. You know more about how this woman thinks than I do. Julie can prepare questions that cover the legal requirements for libel and slander, but I need you to get me behind her personal defenses. Everyone has buttons that when pushed reveal weakness. When weak, a party is more likely to give up valuable information. It sounds esoteric, but it's practical. And since it's a deposition, we can take risks I wouldn't hazard at trial."

I wasn't exactly sure what Mr. Carpenter wanted me to do, but I suspected that was all the explanation I would get.

"When do you want the questions?"

"By the end of the day on Monday. The deposition starts Wednesday morning at nine. Put it on your calendar."

"You want me to be there?"

"Of course."

"And Julie?"

"No, I promised Jason I would try to keep costs down. It will be you and me." Mr. Carpenter gave me a toothy smile. "The Reverend Dabney won't intimidate either of us."

I left Mr. Carpenter's office and returned to the library. Julie was there.

"Sorry I missed the party," she said. "I ran into Mr. Carpenter's secretary in the reception area and found out you didn't wait for me."

"You could have crashed the party," I answered glumly.

"What was it about?"

I told her about the assignment.

"That will be easy for me," she said lightly. "I've already done the research and can plug in the information we've obtained from the witnesses. You have the fun part."

"Why is it fun?"

"For the same reasons I've had fun goading you all summer. Only this time, it's for the cause of justice."

IT WAS A WARM EVENING, but Mrs. Fairmont insisted on sitting outside with Flip. Vince pushed her in a wheelchair to avoid the possibility of a fall on the uneven ground. In one corner of the property there was a bench shaded by a live oak tree that had escaped the blades of the bulldozers. Mrs. Fairmont sat in the middle of the bench with Vince and me on either side. She held one end of Flip's retractable leash in her hand as he ran around sampling new smells before scampering back for reassurance that they were still attached to each other.

"Dr. Dysart came by to see me today," Mrs. Fairmont said.

"You mean Dr. Dixon, the cardiologist?" I asked.

"That's right. Anyway, he's pleased with my progress and placed me on a regular diet. I called Gracie as soon as he left. She brought me the best meal I've had since I went to the hospital."

"What did she fix?"

"Baked salmon, broccoli, and a small tossed salad."

"Any idea when you may be able to go home?" Vince asked.

Mrs. Fairmont didn't immediately answer. Vince looked past her toward me and repeated the question. Mrs. Fairmont wrinkled her brow. She paused before answering.

"I need to know if you're working for Christine or me."

Vince stood so Mrs. Fairmont could see his face. "I'm Vince Colbert, a summer law clerk at Sam Braddock's law firm. Mr. Braddock has been your lawyer for years."

Mrs. Fairmont looked peeved. "Then why didn't he come himself? Is he trying to avoid being around old people? He's not that far behind me, you know. I've always paid his bills as soon as they came in the mail."

"Mrs. Fairmont," I said softly, "Vince and I brought Flip for a visit. This isn't about business."

Flip trotted up to me. I lowered my right hand and let him lick my fingers. Mrs. Fairmont watched.

"He knows you," Mrs. Fairmont said.

"Yes, ma'am."

"You're the young woman who's staying at my house."

"Yes, I'm Tami Taylor. Do you want to go inside? It's so hot out here."

"Maybe we should," Mrs. Fairmont replied with a sigh. "I'm getting a headache and don't feel too well."

I helped her into the wheelchair. Vince pushed her across the mix of dirt and new grass. Flip ran ahead, glancing back to see if we were still following. Inside, I took a deep breath of the cool air and noticed that Mrs. Fairmont's head was tilted to the side. I touched the wheelchair. Vince stopped.

"Mrs. Fairmont," I said, coming alongside her. "Are you all right?"

The elderly woman's eyes were closed. They slowly opened but didn't communicate any sign of recognition.

"Let's take her to the nurse's station," I said, pointing down the long hall.

I took Flip's leash. The nurse on duty came out from behind the nurse's station.

"We went outside for a few minutes, and she's not feeling well," I said quickly to the middle-aged black woman on duty.

The nurse took Mrs. Fairmont's hand. "How are you, sweetie?"

"Tired," Mrs. Fairmont mumbled.

"Let's get you into bed," the woman answered, then turned to me. "I'll take her from here. The dog needs to go outside."

"Her doctor prescribed—," I began.

"I'll do it," Vince said, cutting me off. "You stay with her."

Vince took the leash from me. I could hear Flip's claws scratching against the tile floor as Vince dragged him away. The nurse and I went to Mrs. Fairmont's room. Together we helped her from the wheelchair into bed.

"Is she okay?" I asked.

"Now that she's in bed, I'll check her vitals. Are you the granddaughter who lives with her?"

"I'm her in-home caregiver, but we're not related."

The woman retrieved a blood pressure cuff from a hook near the head of the bed.

"She thinks you're her granddaughter."

"Only when she's confused. I thought she was doing better."

"She is, but that doesn't mean she won't have her spells."

Mrs. Fairmont slept while the nurse took her blood pressure and checked her pulse and respiration.

"Were you here when Dr. Dixon met with her this afternoon?" I asked after the nurse made a notation in the chart.

"Dr. Dixon didn't come today. That was yesterday."

"Are you sure?"

"Yes. I reviewed her status when I came on duty at three o'clock."

"Did he put her on a regular diet?"

"No, she's still on soft foods."

I bit my lip. "So, her housekeeper didn't bring her salmon, broccoli, and a salad for dinner?"

"No, I helped feed her myself." The nurse chuckled. "She ate all her applesauce."

It wasn't funny to me. The nurse took off Mrs. Fairmont's shoes and placed a sheet over the elderly woman's thin legs.

"Stay as long as you like."

I sat on the edge of the bed and prayed. It was difficult riding the ebb and flow of declining health. One day's optimism could be crushed by the following day's negative report only to be replaced by the hope of a new day. I lightly touched Mrs. Fairmont's hand and remembered when she'd reached out to me in the hospital. I might not be her granddaughter, but I loved her.

THE PERSPIRATION WAS ROLLING off Vince's face when I found him in a large open area behind the building. Flip was tugging on the end of the leash like a fish caught on a hook.

"What happened?" I asked.

"He slipped his head out of the collar and took off."

I could catch him in the small courtyard behind Mrs. Fairmont's house, but corralling the little dog out in the open if he didn't want to be caught would be next to impossible.

"How did you get him back?"

"I called, which did no good. Then I ran after him. I cut him off before he darted into the highway and chased him behind the building. He paused to catch his breath, and I scooped him up."

Vince held out his left hand. There were red marks on it but no blood.

"He nipped me a few times. That kept him busy long enough for me to get the collar around his neck and tighten it down."

"Here, Flip," I said.

The little dog trotted over to me. Vince shook his head. I reached over and scratched behind Flip's ears.

"You're like the horse whisperer," Vince said.

"Did Vince hurt your teeth with his rough, tough hand?"

Vince laughed. "It's always the man's fault."

"He'll tell you how sorry he is later," I reassured the little dog, whose eyes closed in contentment as he enjoyed the scratch.

I held Flip in my lap in the car. He laid his head on my knee.

"Thanks for not letting him get away," I said as Vince and I drove away from the nursing home.

"I panicked. Seeing how much Mrs. Fairmont loves that dog, it would be terrible if he wasn't waiting for her at the house when she comes home."

"That may be a long time."

"Why?"

I told Vince about my conversation with the nurse.

"She was convincing, especially when she talked about Gracie bringing her supper."

"It was all a delusion. She may be slipping deeper into dementia." I paused. "But you believe what happened to her in the hospital was real, don't you?"

"Do you?"

Mama had trained me not to yield to sentimental fantasies, especially in vital matters of religion. I looked within my heart and saw a grain of faith. It might be as small as a mustard seed, but I knew it had the power to move a mountain.

"Yes," I answered confidently. "Because God wants her to be saved, and it's what I prayed for."

26

Sister Dabney didn't say a word when the middle-aged sheriff's deputy handed her the thick packet of papers. As soon as she inspected him through the peephole in the door, she knew his sister was in the hospital about to undergo major surgery. The woman would survive the operation, but Sister Dabney couldn't see the effect of the illness down the road. She'd learned from past mistakes it was usually better not to reveal half the future because people tended to finish the story the way they wanted to. A tragedy on earth might ultimately be revealed as a triumph in heaven.

The cover sheet declared it was a "Complaint for Injunctive Relief and Money Damages." Sister Dabney read the allegations and then scribbled what she thought about each one in the margin beside it. There was also a thick set of questions and statements called "Interrogatories, Requests for Admission, and Request for Production of Documents." As she read, Sister Dabney felt vindicated. It was obvious someone had been paying attention to what she was saying. The greatest insult to a preacher is to be ignored. An angry person has heard the message and can repent; an indifferent one has no chance of change. Her warning about Paulding Development Corporation and Jason Paulding, its owner, had found the mark.

The clerk's office made a notation of the judge assigned to the case, so Sister Dabney had called Judge Cannon. His arrogance flowed through the phone line. She doubted he would heed her warning, but his blood wasn't on her hands. The Bible contained specific promises and punishments for unjust judges. They either reaped the benefits or suffered the consequences. Her conscience was clear.

The "Notice to Take Deposition" puzzled her. She looked up the word *deposition* in the dictionary and learned it was the testimony of a witness taken before trial. The notice contained the phrase "day by day," which indicated it might last several days and would take place at the office of Paulding's lawyer. Sister Dabney didn't consider hiring an attorney of her own. She'd rather pray than pay.

She knelt awkwardly on the rug and placed her hands on the legal papers. King Hezekiah spread out a written threat from a pagan general before the Lord God and was delivered from his enemies.

Sister Dabney expected nothing less.

JULIE BREEZED THROUGH TEN PAGES of deposition questions for Sister Dabney.

"I don't think she'll show up," Julie said, putting the finishing touches on her work. "But if she does, Mr. Carpenter will be able to work on her from five angles to get what we want."

I was on page three of my questions, none being very good. Julie's tidy summation sounded so lawyerly and confident.

"We can't count on a nonappearance, and I still don't know what Mr. Carpenter wants me to do."

"Pretend I'm questioning you. That's the point I made the other day. You've been on the receiving end of harassment for your nutty beliefs. Now it's your turn to dish it out."

"Maybe you should do this."

"No, I'm not going to bail you out this time."

"I've helped you at least as much as you have me," I protested.

"Yeah, but I have a bunch of other work to do."

I had other work as well, but I didn't want to go into the weekend with this particular assignment hanging over my head. The phone buzzed in the library. The receptionist's voice came through the speaker.

"Brenda Abernathy from the newspaper on line 802 for Julie."

Julie stared at me. I pushed the button to respond.

"She'll take it."

"Put it on speakerphone," Julie said.

I connected the call and pointed at Julie.

"Ms. Abernathy, thanks for returning my call. I have you on speakerphone with Tami Taylor. We're summer law clerks working on a case for Jason Paulding and Paulding Development Corporation against a woman minister named Ramona Dabney."

"I already know about the lawsuit. I have a copy of the pleadings on my desk."

Julie and I stared at each other again.

"Okay," Julie said. "Why would the Home and Garden writer be interested in a defamation claim?"

The reporter laughed. She sounded young—nothing like an old woman who'd found a niche writing about old houses and pretty flowers.

"Savannah is proud of its homes and gardens, but that's not my only job. I also have investigative assignments and special long-term projects. I've been working on this story for several weeks."

"What story is that?"

"About religious frauds. Ramona Dabney's harassment of your client after she accused him of criminal activity puts a broader spin on the topic."

"What have you found out about Dabney?" Julie asked.

"You have this backward," the reporter responded. "I'm calling to ask you some questions."

"Anything like that would have to come from Mr. Carpenter, the supervising attorney on the file," I said.

"Then why did you contact me?"

"We understood Dabney may have slandered our client to you and wanted to find out what she said."

"I can't help you if you won't help me."

Julie looked at me and shook her head. "We'll have to take that to Mr. Carpenter."

"You should do that"—Abernathy paused—"soon."

Julie ended the call.

"What was that about?" she asked.

"Can't you see?" I responded excitedly. "She's not interested in Dabney; she's going after Paulding. Based on information Sister Dabney gave her, Abernathy uncovered dirt on Jason Paulding and is going to write a big exposé in the paper. Paulding will have to leave Savannah in disgrace or, worse, face criminal charges. Something like racketeering would be my guess."

"That's crazy."

"Maybe, but we need to let Mr. Carpenter and Zach know what she said."

"Absolutely," Julie answered. "Zach's been gone a lot this week, but see if you can find him while I prepare a memo for Mr. Carpenter."

"How do you know he's been gone?"

Julie glanced up at the ceiling. "Because he hasn't been hanging around here waiting for you to notice him."

"He's never been like that."

Julie waved her hand and motioned toward the door. "Right; you're always right, especially about men. Go, track him down."

I left the library and went upstairs. The door to Zach's office was closed. I knocked softly. No answer. I knocked more loudly.

"Come in."

I opened the door. Zach, at least a day's growth of stubble on his face, was sitting behind his desk. There were four empty coffee cups and several disorganized stacks of papers strewn about.

"What's going on?" I asked in surprise.

"One of the biggest deals of Mr. Appleby's career. We've been retained by a Brazilian steel manufacturer to handle a huge contract to ship coal from the U.S. to South America. I've been dealing with lawyers and businessmen all over the western hemisphere. Last night it looked like it was going to fall through, but I was able to locate a new supplier in West Virginia who can send the right product by rail to Savannah for transport."

"That sounds like business, not law."

Zach gave me a tired smile. "One rule shared by summer clerks and junior associates is 'Don't give an excuse; find a way.'"

"You haven't told me that one."

"I just made it up. And sorry if it's seemed like I've been ignoring you. I've been swamped and working long hours. How is Mrs. Fairmont?"

"Shaky. Vince and I saw her last night."

"Vince? I want to go with you to the hospital as soon as I can catch my breath."

"She's not in the hospital. They've moved her to a nursing home for follow-up therapy."

"Okay." Zach nodded. "And the Paulding case?"

I explained why I'd come to see him. His expression didn't change.

"But Julie and I can take care of it," I hastily added.

"Great. I'm waiting now for a conference call being set up in São Paulo."

"Sure."

"And after this marathon is over, I'm going to put in a good word for you with Mr. Appleby," Zach said. "Your name came up the other day. He mentioned there have been a lot of positive comments among the partners."

"Really?"

"He didn't give any details, but I've worked with him long enough to tell what he's thinking. There's an empty office near the end of the hall. It doesn't have the greatest view, but it's reserved for an associate attorney. Check it out before you go downstairs."

"And you get some rest," I said.

"That will have to wait."

I gently closed the door and walked down the hall. There were two empty spaces, both about the same size as Zach's office, across from each other. I peeked into each one. The one on the right overlooked the firm parking lot and Montgomery Street; however, in the distance was the historic district. The one on the left offered a view of some older buildings that looked like warehouses and the new bridge over the river. I debated the merits of each space. The Montgomery Street side would have morning sun but shade in the afternoon. That would probably be my preference.

Then I shook my head.

Whether I would have a choice of offices at Braddock, Appleby, and Carpenter was as speculative as the likelihood I would work as an associate for Maggie Smith and Julie Feldman. I returned to the library. Julie printed out her memo while I told her about Zach.

"I bet the beard makes him look rugged."

"Not really. Scruffy would be a better word."

"Did he let you touch it?"

I took the memo from the printer. "If he did, I wouldn't tell you."

"You didn't," Julie said confidently. "Let's go see Mr. C."

"How old do you think Brenda Abernathy is?" Julie asked as we walked down the hall.

"She sounded young."

"Yeah, but with an old-fashioned name."

"Julie is an old-fashioned name, too. It's solid, if unexciting."

"I admit it's not as hip as Tami; however, that's not your real name, Tammy Lynn."

We reached the waiting area for Mr. Carpenter's office.

"Go in," Sharon said. "He's expecting you."

Mr. Carpenter, wearing a light gray suit, white shirt, and yellow-striped tie, looked as neat as Zach did disheveled.

He glanced up from his desk. "Give me the deposition questions."

Julie turned to me. Delivery of unexpected news was going to fall on me.

"They're not finished," I said. "We're here because a few minutes ago we talked to a reporter from the newspaper."

"Brenda Abernathy? The one Jason wanted us to interview?" Mr. Carpenter asked.

"Yes, sir," I answered, impressed that he'd remembered her name.

"Is she trying to take up Dabney's cause against the evil corporation and its CEO?"

"I'm not sure," I said. "She's investigating Reverend Dabney's allegations for the newspaper and wanted to ask us some questions."

"We said we'd have to get permission from you," Julie added. "Here's a memo of the conversation."

Mr. Carpenter took the memo from her hand but did not look at it.

"Anyone with a few years' experience at the paper knows I won't comment on pending litigation. It's easy to commit an ethical violation. The judges don't like lawyers who try their cases in the media. I'd rather offend Ms. Abernathy by keeping my mouth shut and make Judge Cannon happy."

"But aren't you concerned about what she might write?" I asked.

Mr. Carpenter shrugged. "Pretrial publicity might taint the jury pool. And I'm sure Jason wouldn't want his name dragged through the mud. If Ms. Abernathy hasn't been with the paper very long, she might get excited and cross the line."

"What do you mean?" I asked.

"Suing Dabney is easy. Would Jason Paulding be considered a public figure under the *New York Times v. Sullivan* test?"

"No," Julie answered. "It wouldn't be necessary to prove malice or reckless disregard for the truth to support a defamation claim."

"Then the paper might open the door to a libel suit if it prints information about him that isn't accurate."

"But they'd only report Dabney's statements," Julie said.

"That's not what an investigative journalist does," Mr. Carpenter replied. "Nothing's happened yet. Your job is to finish the deposition questions."

"Yes, sir."

Julie didn't say anything until we were in the library. "Okay, let me see your questions."

"Why?"

"Because I want to help. Haven't I proven how unselfish I am by now? Your problem is my problem, and if I can be part of the solution, I'm here for you."

Julie took the sheets and went to work. By the end of the day she had a matching set to the questions she'd prepared on the legal issues. I had to admit she had a flare for ferreting out information. There was an edge to her inquiries without sounding petty.

"This is good. I'll make sure Mr. Carpenter knows that you did most of the work."

"Don't. He never knew how we divided the research on the Article 9 question you helped me with a couple of weeks ago."

"That was easy; this was—"

"Easier for me than you. Mr. Carpenter knows we've collaborated. Our work product is so jumbled up the partners couldn't figure out where you started and I ended."

It was true.

"Which is why they're going to offer Vinny a job instead of you or me," Julie said. "Get used to the idea and enjoy the rest of the summer."

I didn't say anything about the upstairs offices.

FRIDAY EVENING Mrs. Fairmont greeted me with a big smile.

"I'm going home tomorrow," she said, beaming. "Dr. Dixon signed the discharge papers when he was here this afternoon. Christine wants you to help move my things."

"Are you sure?"

"Why wouldn't I be? I didn't make it up! Christine was here, and he talked to both of us. She asked a lot of questions, but I kept quiet. I didn't want to say something that might change his mind."

"That's great," I said, then, noticing the empty plastic ice bucket in the corner of the room, I asked, "Could I get you some ice?"

Mrs. Fairmont nodded. I immediately went to the nurse's station and introduced myself to the woman in charge.

"If she's going home tomorrow, I need to get the house ready," I said. "Can you check her chart to make sure?"

"I don't have to. Her cardiologist signed the discharge papers before he left this afternoon."

"Do you think she's capable of caring for herself?"

"That's for the doctor to decide. Sometimes she hides her problems so that it's hard to sort out when she's not thinking clearly."

"I know."

"But I don't think she's a danger to herself so long as she stays out of the kitchen, doesn't climb ladders, or drive a car. Things like that."

"Okay. If I'm going to help her check out, what time should I be here?"

"Around eleven. We like to handle it in the middle of the shift."

I returned to Mrs. Fairmont's room. She was sitting up in bed with Flip curled at her feet.

"Where's the ice?" she asked.

I glanced down at the empty bucket.

"I forgot."

Mrs. Fairmont shook her head. "Remember, I'm the one with multi-infarct dementia."

TRANSPORTING MRS. FAIRMONT from Surfside to home took longer than I'd thought. Signing all the paperwork at the nursing facility was tedious, and quite a few of the items Mrs. Bartlett, Gracie, and I had brought from the house had to be carefully wrapped. After we finished, Mrs. Bartlett pulled me aside into the kitchen.

"I'm relying on you to make sure nothing happens to her."

"What do you mean?"

"Don't play lawyer with me. You supported her in this crazy idea to live at home. I don't want you leaving her for hours at a time on the weekends while you—" Mrs. Bartlett paused. "What do you do on Saturday and Sunday? You can't go to church all the time, and you don't golf or go out for a drink with your friends."

"I play with Flip," I answered with a straight face. "We spend hours chasing each other in the courtyard."

"Whatever." Mrs. Bartlett shrugged. "Be here for all meals. I don't want Mother to choke. She's still having trouble swallowing. Gracie is going to start coming more often while you're at work. Once your job ends in a few weeks, I'll have to find another person for the weekends. Gracie's niece is unacceptable. She can't walk through a room without breaking something. Things would be a lot simpler if Mother had agreed to buy a life-estate unit at Surfside."

"That time may come, but she seems happier here for now."

Mrs. Bartlett looked past me toward the den where Mrs. Fairmont was watching a TV show about baby tigers.

"I know," Mrs. Bartlett said, "but worrying about her puts a lot of stress on me."

A wave of compassion for Mrs. Bartlett washed over me.

"Which is why you're kind enough to let me stay here. I'll do everything I can for her."

"Okay, I'm gone. I'm keeping my cell phone with me all the time now. Call me. Not if Mother has a little spell of confusion, of course, but if anything major happens. You should enter the twenty-first century and get a cell phone yourself."

A couple of minutes later the phone in the kitchen rang. I answered, sure it was Mrs. Bartlett. She was like a lawyer who had to get in the last question at a deposition.

"Hello," I said.

"It's Zach. I slept ten hours, shaved, and took a bath."

That was a bit more personal information than I wanted.

"Did the big deal go through?"

"As far as we could push it for now. Things still have to go to the top of the corporate ladders for a couple of the companies, but there's nothing else I can do, so I wanted to invite you out for a round of golf. It's cloudy and won't be terribly hot."

"I can't. I need to stay close to Mrs. Fairmont."

"She's home?"

"As of yesterday. Her daughter warned me five minutes ago not to be gone too long."

"Then could we have dinner? There's a place on the south side I think you would enjoy."

"Uh, I have to be here for Mrs. Fairmont's supper to make sure she doesn't choke."

There was a brief silence on the other end of the line.

"Is this your way of avoiding me?" Zach asked.

I could hear the hurt feelings in his voice.

"No," I responded quickly. "It's the truth."

"Okay, I guess I'll see you next week."

"We could go to Sister Dabney's church tomorrow. Mr. Carpenter is going to take her deposition next week. After that, I'll need to avoid Gillespie Street."

"I'll pass. One dose of Dabney was enough to last me for a while. She's wrapped so tightly in her religious straitjacket I don't see how she can breathe."

My head jerked back as if I'd been punched.

"Do you think I'm wrapped up in a religious straitjacket?"

"That's a loaded question. I doubt you'll be anything like Sister Dabney when you're her age."

"But you think I might?"

"Please, Tami, forget it. It was a stupid thing to say."

It was an excuse, not an apology.

"I'll see you on Monday," Zach continued. "Oh, and do you know if Mr. Carpenter wants me at the deposition?"

"No, from now on you're not going to be tied to this case as tightly as you feared. Mr. Carpenter has taken over."

"That's good." I could hear the relief in his voice. "Except for the chance to spend time with you, of course."

"Okay."

We ended the awkward call. I took Flip down to the courtyard and threw his ball into the far corner. He bounded after it. The little dog didn't know how different I was from other women. Or care.

THE FOLLOWING MORNING I spent time praying and trying to make up my mind whether to attend Sister Dabney's church alone. There had been a sense of home in the service that touched a familiar place in my heart, but also a potential for disaster.

"Would it be okay if I went out for a couple of hours?" I asked Mrs. Fairmont when I brought her a cup of coffee.

"Yes."

"Are you sure you'll be all right?"

"What's wrong with me?" She looked up with slightly clouded eyes.

"Nothing. I just wondered if I should stay with you in the house."

"Not if you have someplace to go. You should be at work by now."

"It's Sunday. I'm going to church."

Mrs. Fairmont picked up the remote. "Then I should be watching a service on TV. What is the name of the minister I enjoy listening to so much?"

"I don't know. But let's avoid the one you had on when the ambulance came."

"I don't remember him."

"There wasn't anything wrong with him, but I would feel strange leaving you alone in the house with the same program on the TV. Let's look together."

I glanced down at my watch. Mrs. Fairmont handed me the remote. I quickly settled on an older, white-haired minister with an open Bible on the pulpit and a choir wearing burgundy-and-gold robes standing behind him. He was talking about Jesus' parables of the kingdom in Matthew 13. I listened long enough to be sure he was sticking to the text.

"Try this one," I said, handing the remote back to the elderly lady. "He seems like a good speaker."

"And the people behind him, what are they called?"

"The choir."

"Yes, they have nice robes."

I stood to the side and watched Mrs. Fairmont for several seconds. A mild level of confusion wasn't uncommon, but so soon after her hospitalization, I was extra cautious. She saw me and waved her hand.

"Go on," she said.

As I left the room, she called after me, "Get the spinach salad!"

I returned to the doorway.

"Why?"

"Because it's the best thing on the menu."

I hesitated again but made a quick decision that Mrs. Fairmont's behavior hadn't risen to the level of danger described by the nurse at Surfside. And I certainly didn't want the devil to use fear to keep me from going to church.

I pulled into the church parking lot a few minutes late and found a seat on the same pew Zach and I had occupied. The gap-toothed woman who had shared it with us wasn't there, but the same piano player was belting out the anthem, and the congregation was singing with gusto. Sister Dabney rocked in her purple chair with her eyes closed. Without Zach there to squelch me, I joined enthusiastically in the song.

Every church has its own DNA, and the service followed the pattern of the previous week. There was a lull in the music and everyone prayed out loud. I expressed my thankfulness for the ways God had touched Mrs. Fairmont and my concerns about her future. When everyone streamed down to the front of the room, I joined the crowd and found a spot on the floor. This morning I could have been invisible. The preacher called out several people, but even when I opened my eyes and tried to catch her gaze, she passed by me without acknowledging my presence. The second time that I tried to pull her attention in my direction, I caught myself up short.

What was I trying to do? Sister Dabney was more likely to rake me over the coals for compromising my faith by participating in a godless inquisition against her ministry than assure me that God was going to extend Mrs. Fairmont's life. I was relieved when it was time to return to our seats. Sister Dabney opened her Bible. My relief was short-lived.

"'Why do the heathen rage, and the people imagine a vain thing? The kings of the earth set themselves, and the rulers take counsel together, against the Lord, and against his anointed.'"

Her eyes ranged across the congregation like the probing beam of a coastal lighthouse. When she reached me, I involuntarily ducked my head. Fortunately, she kept going. Then, taking a deep breath, the preacher launched into a diatribe of judgment and doom against those who dared lift a finger against God and those called to serve him. Even though she didn't name anyone, it took no imagination for me to know the objects of her wrath. Oscar Callahan's statement that preachers should be held accountable for what they said was dry toast to the raw meat of Sister Dabney's onslaught against her accusers. I felt myself shrivel up on the inside. I pressed my arms against my sides and slid down in the pew to make myself smaller.

"And if you find yourself in the midst of this rebellion, there is one, and only one, way to escape judgment," she thundered. "As the apostle Paul wrote to the Corinthians, 'Wherefore come out from among them, and be ye separate, saith the Lord, and touch not the unclean thing; and I will receive you.'"

I bit my lower lip. I'd heard enough. While the preacher's attention was focused toward another part of the room, I fled the building.

I entered Mrs. Fairmont's house with a heavy heart. She was watching a game show on TV.

"Did you have a nice time in church?" she asked.

"Yes, ma'am," I answered, then realized my answer wasn't accurate. "Actually, no, but I think it was necessary for me to be there."

"I listened to the show you found for me. The minister made me feel really good."

THE UNSETTLING INFLUENCE of Sister Dabney's message had lessened some by the next morning, but I was still wrestling with the issue during my walk to work. There had been a thunderstorm in the night, and green leaves were scattered on the sidewalk and into the street. The leaves had been plucked prematurely from the branches by the violence of the storm and would never fulfill summer's purpose or reveal fall's glory. Whatever happened, I didn't want my storm to rob me or allow a worldly outlook to direct my steps. When I arrived at the library, there was a handwritten note on the worktable I shared with Julie. It was from Mr. Carpenter.

"Call me."

Beneath the words was the senior partner's cell-phone number. Mr. Carpenter answered on the second ring.

"This is Tami Taylor. I received your note."

"Yes, I left it yesterday afternoon. I'm in the car on my way to Atlanta for an argument in the court of appeals this afternoon. There have been some recent developments in the Paulding case that have to do with Brenda Abernathy at the newspaper."

I stiffened. I was about to be delivered. Once Jason Paulding's criminal activity was exposed by the newspaper, the last thing he'd be interested in pursuing would be a libel suit against Sister Dabney. In a few weeks I would be out of Savannah, leaving the Dabney case behind and happily burying my nose in casebooks.

"I ran into Abernathy's boss at a restaurant over the weekend," Mr. Carpenter continued. "As you know, I avoid the press, but he wouldn't leave me alone, and I'm glad I heard him out. I know what they're up to. The newspaper wants to run a series of exposés on charlatan preachers. It's a risky topic in a religious town like Savannah, but they think it'll sell papers. The leadoff article is going to feature our defendant. The editor asked if Abernathy could be present at the deposition on Wednesday. I told him no, but if it goes well and Paulding gives his permission, we could release excerpts of the testimony after the fact. In the meantime, I agreed to allow Abernathy a chance to review portions of the statements we've obtained. Since you're more familiar with that evidence, I want you to screen the information and delete anything that might hurt our client."

"Uh, I'm not sure if there's anything like that. I'll have to review them."

"Do it first thing. You can expect a call from Abernathy later today. I know she didn't want to tell you anything the other day, but her editor is going to instruct her to pass along information that may help at the deposition. Now is the time to strike, and strike hard."

My mouth was bone-dry. I tried to moisten it.

"Mr. Carpenter, I'm not sure—"

"If you have any doubts, don't give the information to the reporter," Mr. Carpenter interrupted. "Like I said, it may be best to pass along a summary with contact information so she can follow up with the witnesses on her own. The paper has promised not to mention our firm. I won't be available to talk until I leave the judicial building in Atlanta. Zach can handle any questions that can't wait. I spoke to him yesterday afternoon. He said you weren't available."

"Yes, sir, I was—"

"Don't apologize. Summer clerks aren't expected to be at my beck and call all the time. That will come next year"—Mr. Carpenter paused—"if you come to work for the firm. I'll talk to you later."

The phone clicked off. I stared off into space, then closed my eyes. I wondered if I had the courage to quit my job and, as the apostle Paul said, "come out from among them and be ye separate."

27

I WENT UPSTAIRS TO FIND ZACH. SEVERAL OF THE SECRETARIES and clerical workers passed me with cups of coffee in their hands. For them, this was just another day at the office. The door to Zach's office was cracked open. He was on the phone but motioned for me to come inside. I slumped down in the chair. It was a long phone conversation with someone in another country. I started to get up, but Zach pointed at the chair, so I stayed put. Finally he ended the call.

"I can see you went to hear Reverend Dabney yesterday," Zach said as he lowered the receiver.

"How can you tell?"

"Because you look like a condemned criminal."

I didn't feel like backing down. "It's not right what the firm is doing to her. And now the newspaper, with our help, is going to drag her name through the mud. If that doesn't bother you, I think you've got a problem."

"It bothers me, but it also makes me face the fact that I can't control what other people do. Jason Paulding and Joe Carpenter are going forward with a lawsuit, and Brenda Abernathy is going to write her article even if I go on vacation for the next two weeks."

"But I can control what I do," I shot back.

"What does that mean? You can't talk to Dabney."

"No, but I can tell Mr. Carpenter I'm quitting. I'd rather work on the chicken line for my father and have a clear conscience than become a partner in this law firm and know I compromised my beliefs."

"Okay, quit."

My jaw dropped.

"Is that what you think I should do?"

"Look, I'm not going to try to talk you into or out of anything. If nothing else, the news that you've resigned will shake things up around here for a few days. More people than you realize are aware of your convictions and will decide you were too weak to make it in the real world, so you ran back to the hills where you can live in a pretend world."

"That's not true."

"It isn't?"

"No."

"Then why don't you try to influence the situation. If you're willing to quit, you shouldn't have a problem getting fired. There might be a measure of honor in that. You can make your case to Mr. Carpenter, who will listen for at least a few minutes before he tells you to pack your things and leave."

"I tried to talk to him on the phone a few minutes ago, but he kept cutting me off before I could say anything. He's on his way to an oral argument at the court of appeals."

"Then wait until he comes back from Atlanta. Or better yet, put off the confrontation until after he takes Dabney's deposition and gets a chance to hear her himself. Then, if she makes any sense, you can use her words to argue on her behalf. If you leave today, you won't have a chance to affect anything that may happen down the road."

"But I don't know what she may say."

"You think she'll admit to slandering Jason Paulding?"

"No, because I believe what she said about him is the truth."

"How do you know that?"

"Because she was right about Mr. Callahan."

Zach leaned forward in his chair and put his hands on his desk.

"Repeat yourself; then tell me what's wrong with what you're saying."

"She was right about Mr. Callahan"—I hesitated—"which doesn't make her infallible about everything. But she was also right about Mr. Paulding trying to defraud Mr. McKenzie. And some of the people I talked to that know her think she does a lot of good for the community."

Zach pointed to a thick file on his desk. "I've not had a chance to analyze all the financial records in the McKenzie deal, but Paulding has given us the data to find out. Maybe he tried to cheat, maybe not, but there's nothing in the Dabney file that you can base a decision on."

"So you don't want me to quit."

Zach smiled slightly. "No, it's amazing that you would consider it. But you're also impulsive."

"This isn't a quick decision. I've been upset about this case since the first day I met with Mr. Paulding."

Zach started to say something else, then stopped.

"What is it?" I asked.

He shook his head. "You've got to decide for yourself. I pray you'll make the right choice."

I returned to the library. Julie was sitting at one of the computer terminals.

"It's about time you got here," she said, glancing over her shoulder.

"I've been here long enough to talk to Mr. Carpenter and Zach."

"That combo has never worked well for you. Talking to men about romance problems is as helpful as interviewing a rock about the weather."

"I don't have romance problems."

"Fortunately I know that's not true." Julie turned her chair so that she faced me. "What's really going on?"

"It has to do with the Dabney case."

"That doesn't surprise me. Every time it comes up, a dark cloud appears over your head."

"Are you going to mock me?"

"No."

And for once, I believed Julie was sincere. I laid out my dilemma. She listened without interruption.

"I can understand loyalty to your people," she said when I finished. "It hurts me when a Jewish girl is mistreated, even if I don't really know her. And as weird as she is, Sister Dabney is like one of your family."

"Not that close, but the connection is real."

Julie rubbed her hands together. "Do you want my opinion?"

"Yes."

"Zach is right. You can't help a situation by running away from it. But I also think it's good you've made up your mind to quit before compromising your beliefs. If that's decided and you find yourself in a situation you can't go along with, you won't have to agonize as much about pulling the plug. I just have one request."

"What?"

"I want to be there and see the expression on Mr. Carpenter's face when you tell him to flush the job down the toilet. I already have tons of stories about our summer, but that would take the prize."

I was quiet. Julie brushed her hair back with her hand.

"You're not going to quit," she said.

"How can you be so sure?"

"How many times do I have to remind you that I have the gift of psychoanalysis? You're an interesting case study, but fairly predictable in your responses."

"Shut up," I said with a grin.

"I knew you were going to say that." Julie leaned forward. "You're a fighter, not a quitter."

I spent the rest of the morning reviewing the witness statements and crafting summaries designed to provide Brenda Abernathy with as little ammunition as possible. When a phone call was routed to the library, my heart raced in anticipation that it might be the reporter. But all the calls were for Julie.

Finally the receptionist said, "Brenda Abernathy on line 804 for Tami."

"This is Tami Taylor," I said in my most professional voice. "I have you on speakerphone with Julie Feldman."

"I heard from my boss; did you talk to yours?"

"Yes. I've been working on the file all morning."

"Go ahead. I'm going to record what you tell me."

Mr. Carpenter hadn't said anything about a recorded interview.

"It's my understanding our firm isn't going to be mentioned as a source of information," I said.

"Correct. That's the first thing on the tape."

Julie picked up a digital dictation unit, turned it on, and placed it beside the phone.

"Is it okay if we make a recording on our end?" she asked.

"Sure, but I thought we were on the same side. Both of us would like to see this woman run out of town."

"We're representing our client," Julie answered. "It's not personal."

"Whatever you say. I'm listening."

I took a deep breath and went as rapidly through the summary as I could. To my surprise the reporter didn't interrupt me once.

"That's it," I said. "I'm surprised you didn't have any questions."

"I do, but I've learned it's better to turn people loose and let them talk rather than interrupt the free flow of information."

Julie nodded her head in appreciation. And for the next hour Abernathy peppered me with questions. I used my summary as a script, but revealed more than I intended because several times it would have sounded worse to dodge a question than answer it. Twice Julie came to the rescue.

"We're ready to hear from you," Julie said. "Dabney's deposition is scheduled on Wednesday, and we need time to revise our questions."

"I don't have much to add to what you've found," the reporter answered. "You're way ahead of me."

"That's ridiculous," Julie responded abruptly. "Mr. Carpenter said if we opened our file to you that you would reciprocate. Do I need to set up a conference call with him and your editor?"

There was brief silence. I wondered what the reporter was doing. For the first time, I considered she might not be alone.

"No, but I don't think my investigation is going to be relevant to your case."

"We're the lawyers," Julie answered. "Let us decide."

"Law students," I corrected.

Julie rolled her eyes at me. And for the next thirty minutes Abernathy unloaded a litany of Dabney's alleged heavy-handed requests for money, the absence of accountability, exaggerated accounts of miracles, and personal prophecies that made the preacher sound like a second-rate fortune-teller at a country fair. Some of it was probably true, but parts didn't fit with what I'd seen and heard. Any church and its minister have a backlog of disgruntled ex-members whose perceptions are skewed by bitterness. Abernathy had found a few malcontents. The reporter's obvious intent to transform an occasional problem into the norm turned my stomach.

"You can see why your information takes the article to another level," the reporter said when she finished.

"How?" I asked.

"My stuff is typical for this type of story. What she did to Paulding and his response to her stand out. They're unique."

"If it's—," I started, then stopped.

"True or false?" Abernathy quickly inserted. "Is there any doubt Dabney's allegations against Paulding are false?"

"That's not what she meant," Julie interjected. "We have to

determine if Dabney's conduct is slander or libel under Georgia law. Just because something is false doesn't mean all the legal requirements are satisfied."

"What are the legal requirements?"

I sat back while Julie rehashed the chapter she'd written for her professor's book. The reporter was very interested in getting a free seminar on a topic relevant to her job.

"That's helpful," Abernathy said when Julie finished. "I'd like to get together with you some other time and talk some more about this. I was with Maggie Smith last week and your name came up."

"Are you friends with Maggie?"

"Yeah, she gives me bits of information from time to time. I think she's a great lawyer. Any other questions about Dabney?"

"Not from me," Julie replied.

I thought for a moment.

"One," I said. "Have you talked to Maggie Smith about Dabney?"

There was a brief pause.

"Only off the record."

Julie looked at me and raised her eyebrows.

"We're off the record," Julie said. "Go ahead."

There was another period of silence.

"Turn off your recorder."

Julie pushed the button to stop the machine.

"Done," she said.

"Dabney is being investigated by the police and district attorney's office. I've been told there's an informant involved."

"A member of the congregation?" I asked in dismay.

"I don't know, but Maggie says it's someone on the inside."

Images of the simple people I'd seen at the church flashed through my mind. It was hard to imagine who would be cooperating with a criminal investigation.

"Lieutenant Samuels didn't mention anything about that to me," I said.

"He may not know."

"And neither did Maggie when we had lunch with her," I added, glancing accusingly at Julie. "She listened to Julie talk about the case as if she'd never heard of Sister Dabney."

"Something about the state racketeering statute, but I'm not a lawyer," Abernathy answered evasively. "I don't think Maggie will be bringing any criminal charges until after my article is published."

The reporter and the prosecutor were working together for maximum publicity. My mouth went dry. We ended the call. I turned to Julie.

"Don't blame me for picking on Dabney," Julie said before I could say anything. "She's making plenty of enemies all by herself."

"I wish you hadn't talked so much to Maggie Smith."

"Do you think it really made a difference?"

"I don't know. But a criminal investigation may not be good news to our client."

"Why not?"

"If there are fines levied by the state against Sister Dabney as part of a criminal proceeding, they could take priority over a civil judgment and would have to be paid before the property could be seized by Mr. Paulding."

"Ouch," Julie said, her face falling. "You're the one thinking like a lawyer; I'm the law student rushing to conclusions."

SHORTLY BEFORE TIME TO GO HOME, the library door opened and Mr. Carpenter entered wearing an expensive-looking suit.

"Atlanta bullies the rest of the state," he said. "There were lawyers from the Florida line to south of Chattanooga, all wasting an entire day for a twenty-minute argument. I think they should bring back the days when the court of appeals traveled across the state to serve the needs of the people."

"How long ago were the good-old days?" Julie asked. "I'm not sure our books go back that far."

"A good idea never goes out of style," Mr. Carpenter responded with a smile. "Did you talk to the reporter?"

"Yes," Julie replied.

"Give me the five-minute version."

I was content to let Julie give a report. One of her strengths was succinct verbal organization.

"Not much gained," Mr. Carpenter grunted. "That criminal stuff is hot air. Abernathy has her goal; we have ours."

"Yes, sir," Julie answered. "But I went ahead and added more questions based on the conversation."

"Show me."

Julie handed him a stack of papers.

"The new questions are in blue."

"I haven't seen color-coded sentences since I read a book to my granddaughter," Mr. Carpenter said. "Not that there's anything wrong with it."

He quickly scanned the sheets.

"Does this contain your questions?" he asked me.

"Yes, sir, but they're mixed in with the ones Julie prepared."

"That doesn't help me evaluate your respective work product."

I glanced at Julie.

"Sorry," I said.

"Keep it in mind. I've allowed you to cooperate, but from now to the end of the summer, keep things separate."

"Yes, sir," I replied.

"And, Tami, I don't want you slinking into the deposition on Wednesday looking like you're at the dentist's office for a root canal. You've been holding back on me, and I can tell it. You set a high bar for aggressiveness in the Jones matter, but in this business you're only as good as the last case you handled. We have a job to do, and our conduct is governed by the Rules of Professional Responsibility, not the book of Revelation. Unless there's something in the rules that applies, I expect zealous, wholehearted advocacy for our client. Is that clear?"

It was my moment of truth.

"Yes, sir," I answered weakly.

Mr. Carpenter left. Julie turned to me.

"It wasn't very dramatic, but you made the right choice."

"I just couldn't quit. At least not yet."

28

ON TUESDAY SEVERAL PEOPLE CAME BY SISTER DABNEY'S HOUSE to let her know a reporter was asking questions about her and the church.

"I thought she was another woman lawyer," Sonny Miller said as he stood on the front porch.

"Another woman lawyer?"

Sonny rubbed his hand across his eyes. "Oh yeah. I forgot to tell you about the tall girl who asked me a bunch of questions a few weeks ago outside Bacon's Bargains. She claimed she wasn't a real lawyer, but she sure acted like one. She had one of those yellow pads and wrote down notes of what I said."

"What did she ask you about?"

"That day you sent Rusty and me and the other boys to preach on the street in front of that building on Second Avenue. I mean, everybody knows what we did. It weren't a secret."

"And that's what the lawyer was interested in?"

"No, she wanted to know how you got people to do what you want them to do by hitting them over the head with what it says in the Bible. I told her you believed no one should eat unless they work. Hey, could I pick up around the church and get paid a few bucks? I ain't eaten anything since a bologna sandwich about this time yesterday. Walking over here I saw where someone dumped out an ashtray right next to the driveway. It's a mess."

Sister Dabney pressed her lips together. Attacks weren't new, but it was getting harder and harder for her to view persecution as a chance to counterpunch for the gospel and land a few licks for the truth. Fighting on multiple fronts caused fatigue. Martyrdom had its appeal.

"Wait here," she said.

She went to the kitchen, got a black plastic bag, and returned to the porch.

"Don't come back until this is full," she said to Sonny. "And while you're picking up trash, think about asking the Lord to put your sins in a dark bag where no one can see them and throw them away."

Sonny took the bag. "And what can I be thinking about to eat?"

"I'll fry an extra pork chop."

Sonny turned around and took off for the church at a slow trot.

"Don't just look for something big to put in that bag," Sister Dabney called after him. "The Lord hates little sins as much as big ones."

WEDNESDAY MORNING I couldn't get the Dabney deposition out of my mind during my morning run. Over the past two days I'd considered countless scenarios—everything from Sister Dabney rebuking Mr. Carpenter like an Old Testament prophet to the woman preacher leaving the room in triumph after the senior partner sheepishly agreed to drop the case. In my most realistic version, Sister Dabney stared at me without saying a word until I broke down in tears, vowed never to practice law, and quit my job. Of course, there was also a good chance Mr. Carpenter would do nothing more than make Sister Dabney look like a bigoted idiot.

All my clothes were conservative and modest, but I selected a dress I knew Mama liked and left off the faint swipe of lipstick and hint of makeup I'd started using since working at the law firm. I wrapped my hair in a bun and checked my appearance from several angles. Then I debated: I'd never worn my hair in a bun to work, but it would send a strong signal of respect to Sister Dabney and might divert her wrath into another direction. The hairdo would be lost on Mr. Carpenter. Julie, on the other hand, would attack me mercilessly. I opened my fingers and let my hair fall past my shoulders. Wearing my hair in a bun today would be an act of cowardice, not conviction. I brushed it out.

When I walked into the library, Julie was staring at a computer screen.

"What are you doing here so early?" I asked in surprise.

"Trying to do my job."

"You usually begin that later in the day."

Julie pushed her chair away from the computer.

"I had trouble sleeping last night and decided I may as well do something productive besides tossing and turning in bed."

"Is there a problem with Joel?"

"No, he wasn't there."

I felt my face flush. "That's not what—"

"Actually, my mind was spinning in circles about your preacher woman's deposition. Have you thought how she might react to being questioned? Mr. Carpenter will be aggressive."

"I know."

"What if she stands up and starts screaming at the top of her lungs or goes postal and pulls out a gun?"

"She might yell, but I don't think she's violent."

"How do you know? Haven't you ever taken a religious history course? People do more crazy, violent things in the name of religion than anything else. And most of them believed they were obeying God the whole time."

"No." I shook my head. "That's not going to happen."

"Are you going to guarantee the safety of everyone in the room?" Julie persisted.

"You sound hysterical."

Julie looked at me, her eyes wide. "I've had premonitions like this before and they've been pretty accurate. I'm warning you to be on the lookout for anything threatening. Dabney might be willing to hurt herself if she can get vengeance against her enemies. Is Mr. Paulding going to be here?"

"I don't think so."

"Good."

Muttering, Julie turned back to the computer terminal. I opened the file and stared unseeing at the deposition questions. The minutes dragged by. Julie left for a meeting with one of the other lawyers. At ten o'clock the intercom buzzed. I jumped. It was Mr. Carpenter's secretary.

"This is Tami," I said, pressing the button.

"Come into the main conference room. Mr. Carpenter wants to meet with you and the client. Bring your investigation files."

As I walked down the hall, all I could think about was why Jason Paulding had decided to attend the deposition. I knocked softly on the door to the conference room and entered.

"Tami, you remember Jason Paulding from our initial interview. While we wait to see if Dabney shows up, I thought it would be helpful for Jason to hear what you've uncovered in your investigation."

"What part?"

Mr. Carpenter gave me a forced smile. "The relevant parts would be a good starting place."

I sat at the table and read excerpts from the witness statements in a monotone voice. Mr. Carpenter interjected comments about the connection between the information and the legal requirements for libel and slander.

"As you can see, we have her both ways," the senior partner said at one point.

There was a knock on the door. Mr. Carpenter's secretary came in.

"Ramona Dabney and the court reporter are in the reception area."

"Thanks, Sharon."

The secretary left. Mr. Carpenter turned to Paulding.

"I owe you that bottle of wine," the lawyer said with a smile, then turned toward me. "I'd bet Jason a liter of good cabernet that the defendant wouldn't show up."

"She's never backed down in any of my attempts to deal with her," Paulding answered with a shrug. "I didn't think she'd start now."

"Are you staying?" I asked, trying to hide my apprehension.

"Of course not," Mr. Carpenter answered. "Jason, I'll give you a call when we finish and give you my initial take on what we get from the witness. Don't expect to hear from me for several hours."

"I just wanted to claim that bottle of wine," the developer replied. "Spending five seconds in the same room with Dabney would spoil it."

"I'm glad he won't be here," I said as soon as the door closed behind him. "I think his presence would have needlessly antagonized the witness."

"You're right," Mr. Carpenter answered grimly. "That's my job."

He pressed the button on the phone for the intercom. "Send in the court reporter, wait two minutes, and send in Ms. Dabney."

The court reporter, an efficient-looking middle-aged woman, arrived and set up her machine at one end of the table. I sat with my sweaty hands resting on the conference table. I could see that Mr. Carpenter had marked up the questions Julie and I had prepared.

"You should be taking this deposition," Mr. Carpenter said.

"Why?"

"Because you don't want to. It'd make you a stronger lawyer. But don't worry, you'll have plenty of opportunities to push your limits. Believe it or not, it still happens to me every now and then. There was a case in federal court in Jacksonville six months ago—"

The conference room door opened, and Sister Dabney came into the room. She was wearing a light blue dress that looked like it had come from a thrift store. Her hair was in a tight gray bun; however, a few strands had escaped and were plastered to her forehead. It must be a hot day outside. The wrinkles in her face were more pronounced up close. Like me, she'd not put on any makeup. Her eyes went to mine and stopped.

"This is Ms. Taylor, one of our summer law clerks," Mr. Carpenter said affably. "And I'm Joe Carpenter, the attorney representing Jason Paulding in this case. Please sit beside our court reporter so she can do her job more efficiently."

Sister Dabney paid no attention to Mr. Carpenter. She kept her gaze fixed on me. I felt myself slipping into one of my imaginary scenarios. But no tears came to my eyes.

They came to hers.

Mr. Carpenter cleared his throat. "Would you like a glass of water or a cup of coffee?"

Two tears raced down the woman's wrinkled face. The one on her left cheek beat the one on the right and fell from her face onto the shiny table. Barely breathing, I looked into the old woman's eyes and saw deep pain entombed in an indomitable will. Anxiety about a job, my future as a lawyer, or what others might think about me shriveled to microscopic insignificance. I was in the room and not in the room; the veil between heaven and earth thinned. Mr. Carpenter became as irrelevant as a poorly worded question. All that mattered was Rachel Ramona Dabney, a person in need, a woman for whom God's compassion had not yet found its limit. But I didn't know what to do or say.

"You need to speak it," the old woman said in a creaky voice.

And in that instant I knew the meaning of the moment.

"'Lazarus, come forth,'" I said in a calm voice.

Sister Dabney lifted her hands and let out a shriek that made the hair stand up on the back of my neck.

"Ma'am, if you're not feeling well, we can reschedule the deposition for another day," Mr. Carpenter said in alarm.

I continued, "'And he that was dead came forth, bound hand and foot with grave clothes; and his face was bound about with a napkin. Jesus saith unto them, "Loose him, and let him go."'"

Sister Dabney cried out again, bent over, and began to sob. Her body shook violently. Mr. Carpenter looked at me.

"I don't know what's going on here, but you need to put a stop to it!"

"I can't."

He redirected his attention to the witness. "Ms. Dabney, it won't be possible to go forward with your deposition if you aren't able to control yourself."

Sister Dabney shook her head from side to side and continued to wail. Mr. Carpenter turned to me in dismay.

"Should we call an ambulance?"

"No, sir," I replied with surprising calm. "I think we should wait a few minutes and see how she feels. Could we let her sit in here by herself for a while?"

"No," the senior partner replied.

"Then I'll stay," I volunteered. "You and the court reporter could take a break. I'll find out if we can go forward with the deposition or not and let you know."

Mr. Carpenter stared at me for a second, then looked at his watch. "I'll wait ten minutes. If she's emotionally unable to answer questions, we'll reschedule the deposition."

Sister Dabney let out a loud sob. Mr. Carpenter spoke to her.

"Madam, this outburst won't change anything that we're going to do to represent our client's interests." As he left the room, he said to me in a low voice, "Remember why we're here."

"Yes, sir."

The court reporter followed him from the conference room.

Sister Dabney, her head bowed, continued to sob. She neither paid attention to Mr. Carpenter's departure nor seemed to care that I remained. I sat quietly and waited. Sobs turned to softer crying that dissolved into a few sniffles. I slid a box of tissues across the table. She grabbed a handful but didn't look at me. I checked my watch. Five minutes passed before the crying subsided. Sister Dabney raised her head. Her eyes and nose were red, which made her appear more bizarre than ever.

"I didn't see this coming until I stepped into this room. It's the last place I would have expected to find the word of life. But that's what a tomb is all about. No one expects life to come forth out of a grave."

"Yes, ma'am."

"Who are you?"

"I'm the young woman who knows Oscar Callahan."

"You've visited the church a couple of times. And I was led into prayer for you one day at my house." Her face clouded over. "You were spying on me?"

"Yes, ma'am. But the first time I came to the church, I felt like I'd come home."

Sister Dabney glanced around the conference room as if seeing it for the first time.

"There is much wickedness in this place. Overweening pride lives here. What fellowship does light have with darkness?"

"None, but I think I was supposed to be here for you this morning."

"Yes, you were." She nodded, then stared at me for a couple of seconds. "Do you want me to tell you what I see?"

"Only if you're supposed to."

Sister Dabney grunted. "Not many people give me that answer. I'll hold on to the message and ask the Lord to make it grow."

"I'm young and want to—" I stopped.

"You don't know what you want," she said brusquely. "But you've been obedient today. That's the place to start. I heard the sound of resurrection in your voice calling me out of the cave of despair. I've been laboring for others without hope for myself. A few strips of my grave clothes are gone, and now I have faith more will fall."

"Yes, ma'am. God's Word never loses its power."

Sister Dabney cried out again. I jumped. It wasn't a shriek or a wail; it was a shout that sounded vaguely familiar, like the occasional cries from older members of my church when they felt moved by the Spirit. Sister Dabney clapped her hands together.

"This has been a good meeting," she said, her face cracking into a smile that made her wrinkles run uphill. "It's about time for your boss to return."

As if on cue, the door opened and Mr. Carpenter stuck his head in the door.

"Is she ready to proceed?" he asked me.

I turned to Sister Dabney and raised my eyebrows.

"Let's get to it," she said, turning in her chair so she could face Mr. Carpenter. "It doesn't matter what you ask, all you'll get from me is the truth."

29

Mr. Carpenter cleared his throat. "Tami, please get the court reporter. She's in the reception area."

I left the conference room and found the court reporter reading a women's magazine and sipping a cup of coffee.

"We're ready," I said.

"Could I borrow this for a couple of days?" she asked, holding up the magazine. "I'd like to finish this article about the best beaches on the East Coast. I can bring it back when I'm here on Friday for a deposition with one of the other lawyers."

I nodded, not sure if I had the authority to authorize removal of magazines from the office, but feeling bold enough to risk it. The court reporter gathered up her equipment.

"That was a different way to start a deposition," I said.

"I do a lot of domestic cases. Hysterical women aren't all that uncommon."

We returned to the conference room. Sister Dabney, her eyes closed, was sitting in a chair with a bottle of water in front of her. Mr. Carpenter had his head down, reviewing his notes. The court reporter took her place.

"Ready," she announced.

"This will be the deposition of Rachel Ramona Dabney taken

pursuant to notice for purposes of discovery under the provisions of the Georgia Civil Practice Act . . ."

I listened to Mr. Carpenter recite the lawyer's litany before the start of a deposition. I'd read several depositions, and he tracked the customary language without a slip. It was like watching an experienced driver buckle a seat belt, turn on a car's engine, and scan the gauges to make sure nothing appeared amiss. He finished and turned to the court reporter.

"Will you swear in the witness?"

I watched as Sister Dabney raised her right hand and said, "I do."

"Please state your name," Mr. Carpenter said.

"Rachel Ramona Dabney."

"Have you ever gone by any other names?"

"I was a Miller before I married."

"How long ago was that?"

"Forty-one years."

Sister Dabney's voice was level. Except for redness around her eyes, she showed no signs of the emotion that had racked her body a few minutes earlier. I knew Mr. Carpenter would ask a lot of background questions without any direct relevancy to the case. A discovery deposition is an unrestricted opportunity to find out as much as possible about a person. Few objections are allowed, and since no lawyer was representing Sister Dabney, the only limit to Mr. Carpenter's questions would be the witness's willingness to answer. Soon it was apparent that Sister Dabney didn't intend to frustrate the process. She came across as very open and forthright. Her grammar was good, and it didn't surprise me to learn that she'd finished college at a small school in central Alabama. When the questions started exploring her life in ministry, the answers grew longer. I listened with interest as she described the places she'd been and what she and her husband did. She rarely glanced in my direction. After an hour, she asked if we could take a bathroom break.

"I'll show her where it is," the court reporter volunteered.

The two women left Mr. Carpenter and me in the conference room.

"Whatever you did worked," the senior partner said when the door closed. "This is going much more smoothly than I'd hoped. I thought she would be refusing to respond or try to ask me questions. Was that a Bible verse you cited?"

"Yes, sir. It's from John chapter eleven."

"The code these fanatics use is beyond me. Not that I'm lumping you into the same pot as Dabney," he added quickly, "but you understand religious lingo, which is like a foreign language to me."

"Sister Dabney and I may not be in the same pot, but we're cooking on the same stove."

Mr. Carpenter gave me a puzzled look. "I won't unpack that with you now, but at some point I need to know how that might affect your ability to function in this law firm." He paused. "So long as we don't violate any of the antidiscrimination laws, of course. I trust you're interested in a job when you get out of law school, not a lawsuit because you don't get an offer."

His concern almost made me smile.

"Mr. Carpenter, I can assure you I'm not posturing for a discrimination suit. I appreciate the opportunity to work here. It's been hard, but as you told me the other day, that's how I can grow."

"Good," Mr. Carpenter grunted. "You're honest, more blunt than I'm used to from a summer clerk who is so polite most of the time, but that's not necessarily a bad thing."

Mr. Carpenter stood. "I'll be back in a minute. Don't start without me."

Sister Dabney and the court reporter returned together.

"My sister and I only see each other at Christmas," the court reporter was saying. "I'm not sure what she'll think if I call her out of the blue and tell her what you told me. She might think I'm nuts."

"That's a chance anyone takes who speaks for God," Sister Dabney replied. "If you don't say anything, what would the consequences be?"

"Should I just blurt it out?"

"That's better than keeping silent and having her blood on your hands. You can bring the peace."

The court reporter was preoccupied as she sat down. Mr. Carpenter returned.

"Ready to continue?" he asked lightly.

The court reporter stood up. "Mr. Carpenter, could we wait a few more minutes? I need to make a quick phone call."

Mr. Carpenter looked at his watch. "Can't you take care of it later?"

"No, sir," she answered emphatically.

The court reporter left her machine and exited the room.

"Why didn't she make the call during the break?" Mr. Carpenter asked the rest of us.

I didn't know. Sister Dabney sat as still as a stone. While we waited, Mr. Carpenter reviewed his notes and Sister Dabney closed her eyes. The court reporter returned.

"Thanks," she said with obvious relief in her voice. "I had an unexpected family emergency."

"Is everything okay?" Mr. Carpenter asked.

The woman looked at Sister Dabney as she answered.

"Yes. I think there's hope."

"Good," Mr. Carpenter replied. "Let's get back to business."

The next round of questioning left no stone unturned about Sister Dabney's past involvement with the law. She and her husband had been arrested several times for trespassing, disturbing the peace, and creating a public nuisance. All the arrests sounded like examples of religious persecution.

"Whenever we were locked up we tried to be like Paul and Silas," Sister Dabney said at one point.

"Were they part of your denomination?" Mr. Carpenter asked.

Sister Dabney looked at me when she answered. "Yes, they were respected leaders who spent a lot of time in jail and found ways to make it count for good. When Brother Russell and I were in that Arkansas jail, we started a Bible study for the inmates."

"How long were you incarcerated?"

"About twenty days, but we redeemed the time."

"Do you know the disposition of the case?"

"The judge let us out and told us to leave town."

"Did you comply with the court's order?"

"Yes, we'd already heard from the Lord that it was time to move on. We shook the dust from our feet in judgment against them and left."

It took over two hours of questioning before Mr. Carpenter reached the period of time when Sister Dabney and her husband came to Savannah. They'd planned on staying for a couple of months that turned into years.

"Being on the road is hard," Sister Dabney said, "but we probably should have kept moving."

"Why?"

"Because of what happened. Brother Russell got lazy and fell into sin with a woman we were helping."

To my surprise, Mr. Carpenter didn't dig up all the lurid details about the disintegration of Sister Dabney's marriage. I was taking notes and wrote myself a reminder to ask him why. Instead, he moved to the legal structure of the church, which I knew had a lot more importance to the endgame of the lawsuit.

"And the church property and the house where you live were placed solely in your name after the divorce?"

"Yes."

"Do you have any debt secured by either piece of property?"

"No, he who borrows is slave to the lender."

"Do you have any personal debt?"

"If I don't have the money, I don't buy. God supplies what I need to do the work he calls me to do."

That prompted a long series of questions about the amount of money given to the church and how it was spent. I was surprised at Sister Dabney's specific answers. She either had a good memory for figures or had reviewed the financial information shortly before the deposition. One thing was clear: there wasn't much surplus for Sister Dabney's personal needs. I could see Mr. Carpenter making quick calculations on his notes. If Brenda Abernathy wanted to accurately criticize Sister Dabney's use of money, she'd better document it. The preacher owned a ten-year-old car, purchased used furniture, and lived on not much more than the women who worked on the chicken line in Powell Station.

"Do you have records substantiating this information?" Mr. Carpenter asked.

"Yes."

"Do you file tax returns?"

"Yes, the Bible commands us to pay taxes to the government."

Mr. Carpenter glanced at me. I nodded.

"Do you own any other real estate?"

"No."

"When did you first meet Jason Paulding?"

The sudden mention of our client's name jarred me. I sat up straighter and gripped my pen.

"About this time last year. He came by my house one evening after I told a man who worked for him that I didn't want to sell the church."

"Tell me everything you remember about that meeting."

The first encounter between the two antagonists didn't set off any fireworks. Paulding asked her to sell the property. She told him no.

"I explained that once I'd dedicated the property to the Lord it shouldn't be used for worldly purposes."

"Why is that?"

"It's holy."

Mr. Carpenter wrinkled his brow.

"Can you explain?"

"It's no longer in the world system. It belongs to God, so he controls what should be done with it."

"Is it your belief that no property on which a church is built should ever be used for anything except religious purposes?"

"For the church on Gillespie Street that's right. I can't say about apostate churches, but I know what's true about this particular plot of ground."

"What kind of churches? I'm not familiar with that term."

Sister Dabney turned to me. "She is."

"But I'm asking you the questions," Mr. Carpenter answered.

"It's a church that isn't walking in the truth."

"What's the 'truth' about your church's property?"

"God told me not to sell."

Mr. Carpenter wrote something on his notes. I readied myself for a lengthy interrogation that established Sister Dabney as delusional. His next question surprised me.

"Ms. Dabney, your beliefs about God aren't my main concern. Let's stick to your interaction with Mr. Paulding. Do you recall your next conversation with him?"

"I think it was a phone call about a week later."

Mr. Carpenter painstakingly went through the communication between the parties. I realized his strategy was to remove any possibility that Sister Dabney could later claim something was said or done that hadn't been covered in the deposition. Over and over he asked her, "Is that all? Do you remember anything else? Are you sure?"

He then pulled out a copy of the requests for admission served with the complaint. The artfully worded statements closely tracked what we knew about Sister Dabney's allegations that Jason Paulding was a criminal. Mr. Carpenter asked the court reporter to mark the document as an exhibit and handed it to the witness.

"Did the sheriff's deputy who served the legal papers at your house also give you these requests for admission?"

"Yes."

"Did you review them at the time?"

"Yes, I read them."

"Did you read them again when I handed the exhibit to you?"

"No."

"Would you take the time to do that?"

We waited while Sister Dabney read.

"I'm done," she said after a few minutes.

"Having read the requests for admission at least twice since they were served to you, do you agree the information contained in them is correct?"

"Yes."

My mouth dropped open. Agreeing with the information in the requests for admission proved our case. Mr. Carpenter cleared his throat.

"All of them?"

"Yes, and this man still hasn't repented."

Mr. Carpenter's eyes were wide open. "I understand. Let me go over each one to make sure about your answers. Number one: admit that within the past year you personally made public statements that Jason Paulding has been involved in criminal activity. Is that true?"

"Yes."

"What was your source of information that Mr. Paulding has been involved in criminal activity?"

"God told me."

This time I knew he would have to dissect Sister Dabney's claim. I could already hear the sarcasm dripping from the senior partner's lips as he asked whether the Almighty spoke King James English or sounded like Charlton Heston in the old movie about the Ten Commandments. But to my surprise, he continued his review of the requests for admission.

"Number two: admit that within the past year you solicited the aid of third parties to make public statements that Jason Paulding has been involved in criminal activity. Is that true?"

"Yes."

"Number three: Do you admit that within the past year you told Rev. Jim Fletchall that Jason Paulding has been involved in criminal activity?"

"Yes. I went to his preacher and talked with him. He needed to know a thief was in his sheepfold."

There were twenty-five requests, all worded in a way that Sister Dabney obviously thought was nothing more than a summary of her belief that Jason Paulding should be confronted with his sin. However, the requests contained no alleged *evidence* of wrongdoing by our client, only conclusory statements. I saw the brilliance of Mr. Carpenter's plan. It sounded like he agreed with the witness, and Sister Dabney didn't understand the legal significance of her testimony. When coupled with an affidavit from Paulding that the allegations were false, the requests for admissions would prove all the essential elements of a slander-and-libel claim. The judge would simply determine the amount of damages. I sharply let out my breath. Sister Dabney looked at me. I quickly put my hand over my mouth. Mr. Carpenter methodically worked his way through all the requests for admission. Sister Dabney only quibbled with one of them.

"Number twenty-five: Do you admit that within the past year you told Mary Paulding that her husband, Jason Paulding, had committed adultery?"

"Yes, but the unfaithfulness has been there longer than a year."

"That's not what I asked. The year relates to the period of time for your conversation with Mary Paulding. Did you talk to her within the past year and accuse her husband of adultery?"

"Yes, back during the winter. She cried and told me she knew something was wrong."

"What was your source of information about Mr. Paulding's personal life?"

"God told me. He certainly loves this man."

"What did you say?" Mr. Carpenter looked up from his notes.

Sister Dabney leaned forward.

"God loves Jason Paulding even though he's a wicked man who has broken the law, cheated on his wife, and tried to bully me into selling my church. I've done everything I could to confront him with his sin so he could repent. Now he's hired you to sue me for telling him the truth. The Bible calls a man like him a fool. I've washed my hands of him. Maybe he will listen to you where he's ignored me, but he should know that God's Spirit won't always strive with a man. At some point, judgment comes."

"You claim you've done these things to try to help Mr. Paulding?" Mr. Carpenter asked incredulously.

"Why else would I go to all this trouble?"

Mr. Carpenter shook his head.

"No further questions."

30

I WASN'T SURE WHETHER TO STAND AND APPLAUD SISTER DABNEY'S courage or get down on my knees and beg her to apologize for what she'd done. Her claim that her actions were motivated by God's love for Jason Paulding caught me completely off guard. She might be right that our client was a crook and an adulterer, but why she thought her tactics would produce the desired repentance stretched my system of belief.

I leaned over to Mr. Carpenter and whispered in his ear, "Shouldn't we find out if she has any evidence supporting her allegations?"

The older lawyer shook his head.

"Mr. Paulding will want to know," I pressed him.

"No."

"Are you finished?" Sister Dabney asked.

"Yes," Mr. Carpenter replied, avoiding my eyes. "If you want a copy of the deposition, you'll need to contact our court reporter. Ms. Johnson, please expedite delivery of the transcript."

"It will be in your office by Friday at three o'clock."

Mr. Carpenter stood. Sister Dabney remained seated.

"That's all for today, Ms. Dabney," the lawyer said. "You may leave."

Sister Dabney ignored Mr. Carpenter and spoke to me in a soft voice. "Thank you for your word, child. The voice of freedom lives in you. The smell of smoke isn't on you yet. Maybe you're called to walk in the fire and not get burned."

I didn't know what to say. Sister Dabney looked up at Mr. Carpenter.

"And whatever you and Jason Paulding are planning to do to me will come to ruin. 'Lift not your hand against the Lord's anointed and do his prophets no harm.'"

"We're finished here, ma'am," Mr. Carpenter said. "You'll be notified of the next step in the legal process."

Sister Dabney continued. "You can turn your back on my words, but they have power beyond anything you know."

"I'm asking you to leave—now," the senior partner said firmly.

The court reporter, her equipment packed up, spoke. "Ms. Dabney, I'll be happy to show you the way out."

Using her hands to brace herself, Sister Dabney pushed herself up from the chair and slowly followed the court reporter out of the conference room. I waited, expecting the older woman to turn and deliver a parting word. None came. Mr. Carpenter waited until the door closed, then clapped his hands together.

"Could you believe that?" he exclaimed. "Dabney admitted every essential element of our claim. Any lawyer would have told her to deny the requests for admission as stated and provide an explanation, but she had no idea what I was doing. And her only justification for defaming Jason Paulding all over Savannah is that God told her to do it. I didn't want to give her a chance to explain what she meant or raise an issue that might be hard for us to disprove. That's why I didn't want to ask your question. Keep it clean and simple."

"But it's a discovery deposition, a time to find out everything we can."

"You're wrong. As soon as she didn't try to wiggle out of the requests for admission, I changed my strategy. This deposition will be the basis for a summary judgment against her. When Judge Cannon hears this foolishness, he'll give us anything we want. Prepare a motion for summary judgment. Nothing fancy, just enough to get the case before the judge. We'll supplement the record with the deposition and an affidavit from Jason denying her claims. I may get affidavits from some of the other witnesses stating that Dabney's allegations are false. In the meantime, I'll call Jason and let him know how well everything went."

I nodded forlornly.

"And there's no reason for you to feel bad about anything you did. You got her to vent, and she didn't build up a head of steam until we finished. In the middle, we got everything we needed. Now it doesn't matter if she hires a lawyer or not. This case is buttoned down tight. Get the motion along with a draft affidavit for Jason to me in the morning."

"Yes, sir."

"Oh, and stay away from Dabney. I don't want you to have any contact that would give her a chance to accuse us of anything. She's off-limits, period—no exceptions."

"Yes, sir."

"Good. You helped make this a success."

Mr. Carpenter left the conference room. I checked my watch. The deposition had lasted almost four hours. I'd not eaten lunch, but I had no appetite. As I walked down the long hallway, I had my notes in my hand, but the words spoken by Sister Dabney that wouldn't be part of the transcript burned in my memory. I pushed open the library door. Julie, Zach, and Vince were sitting at our worktable.

"Surprise!" Julie cried out. "It's your birthday!"

"No, it's not," I said, giving her a crooked smile. "My birthday is November 14."

"It seemed like the best thing to say since we were all here at the same time."

"I'm not in a birthday mood."

"Mr. C's secretary told me Dabney had some kind of emotional outburst before the deposition started. You could hear her halfway down the hall."

"Do you want to talk about it?" Vince asked.

I sat down at the only vacant chair at the table.

"I may as well tell all of you at once," I said, then pointed at Julie. "But I don't want to be interrupted."

"Relax." Julie held up her hands. "Don't have an emotional outburst all over me."

I laid my notes on the table but didn't need them. When I quoted the verse about the raising of Lazarus from the dead and the removal of the grave clothes, Zach spoke.

"How did that come to your mind?"

"Don't interrupt," Julie shushed him.

"I'm not sure. It was so spontaneous. I've assumed Sister Dabney was a wounded animal striking out against a larger predator threatening her space. Maybe that influenced me; perhaps it was simply God's Spirit. But my perspective was only partly right. She's been wounded by life, especially the betrayal of her husband, but that's not the main reason she lashed out at Jason Paulding. Her motivation for that was sincere, even if the method may have been misguided."

"Huh?" Julie and Vince both said at once.

"Let me go through the whole thing."

I gave a summary of the deposition testimony. Julie's mouth dropped open when I told them about Sister Dabney's wholesale agreement with the requests for admission.

"She was clueless. No one agrees with those things," Julie said.

"She doesn't have any guile," Vince said.

"Exactly," I said. "The subtleties of verbal booby traps laid by lawyers are lost on her. She considered the requests for admission statements of fact and didn't realize their legal significance. But even if she'd known, I don't think she would have cared."

I'd written down verbatim Sister Dabney's claim that she'd attacked Jason Paulding because God loved him and wanted him to repent.

"When she said that, Mr. Carpenter decided he'd heard enough."

"Me, too," Julie said. "I can understand some of this woman's rants, but that's psychotic."

"Not necessarily from her point of view," Zach answered thoughtfully. "As Tami said, it could be misguided but sincere."

"So were a lot of mass murderers," Julie shot back. "This woman has put herself in a place God keeps for himself. She needs to be muzzled."

"I still think you have to respect her motives," I said.

Julie threw her hands up in the air. "Will someone beam me up and out of this planet?"

"Don't get so worked up," Vince said. "You love every minute of this. Didn't you tell me boredom was your greatest enemy?"

"That was before Tami and Dabney cross-pollinated to produce an alien life-form. Now I'm scared."

"What is it Mr. Carpenter is always saying?" Vince replied with a grin. "Step into your fear. It will make you a stronger person."

"I'm stepping into the break room for an afternoon cup of coffee," Julie said. "A shot of caffeine will jar me back to reality."

After Julie left, I turned to the two men. "Mr. Carpenter is going to do his part to silence her. At least at the Gillespie Street address. He's going to file a motion for summary judgment within the next few days."

"Did he tell her?" Vince asked.

"No, he told me. I have to prepare the motion and an affidavit for Mr. Paulding to sign stating that Sister Dabney's allegations are false."

"Are you going to do it?" Zach asked.

I thought about Sister Dabney's words. The law firm was a wicked place where I'd been walking in the fire without being burned.

"I didn't quit when he gave the order."

Zach and Vince looked at each other, then me.

"What are you thinking?" I asked them.

"Now?" Zach asked Vince.

Vince nodded.

"We've been talking about you," Zach began.

"Behind my back?"

"Yes. We think you've been under too much pressure."

Vince held up four fingers. "There's Mrs. Fairmont's stroke, the turmoil of the Dabney case, trying to figure out where you stand at the firm, and not knowing if you had a place to live."

"And interacting with us," Zach added, touching his thumb. "We want to make things easier for you, not harder, and thought maybe we should give you some space."

A wave of rejection hit me. Hot tears stung the corners of my eyes.

"Why bring this up now? I just spent four hours with Mr. Carpenter and Sister Dabney."

Vince looked at Zach. "I wasn't sure this would work."

"Work?" I asked. "I'm not interested in how you two have planned out my life. But you're right about one thing. I need some space, and I need it now!"

I stood, my eyes flashing. The two men left the room. I collapsed in a chair. The door opened. Julie came in with a cup of coffee in her hand.

"Vinny and Zach looked shell-shocked," she said, then stopped. "What happened? Did you pull a Dabney on them?"

It was my turn to cry. It was hard to get out a cohesive sentence, but Julie quickly picked up on the gist of the conversation. She came around the table and put her arm around me.

"I'm sorry. I know it hurts."

I blubbered for a few more seconds, then blew my nose on a tissue.

"They're ganging up on me."

Julie patted me on the shoulder. "Two hardly qualifies as a gang. Did they say anything besides wanting to give you some space?"

"No." I sniffled. "Supposedly it's because of all the pressure I've been under in other areas."

Julie gave my shoulder a final squeeze and released me. "It's a typical male response. A damsel in physical danger is a welcome challenge; a woman who needs emotional support is a liability."

I nodded. "That's right."

"The separation is probably more for them than you. Vinny and Zach are feeling insecure themselves trying to compete for your attention and decided to call a truce, which pushes you to the side."

I wiped my eyes.

"What should I do?"

"You don't drink, so picking up a guy at a bar isn't an option. You and I are around each other so much during the day that it would stress our friendship to hang out after work." Julie patted the Dabney file. "That leaves you with nothing to do but pour yourself into your work. Men have been doing it for generations, so there must be something therapeutic about it. And I think you could probably hold your breath for as long as Zach and Vinny will stay away. Both of them are crazy about you, so this 'giving you space thing' is temporary."

"I'm not so sure you're right," I replied with a final sniffle.

I TOOK JULIE'S ADVICE to get my mind focused on work and started preparing the motion for summary judgment against Sister Dabney. True to Mr. Carpenter's instructions, I kept it simple. The affidavit

for Jason Paulding was more troublesome. Every time I typed his
denial of Sister Dabney's allegations of criminal conduct, I felt as if
I were committing perjury. If Mr. Paulding swore to the truthfulness
of the statements in the affidavit, and they ultimately proved false,
he would have more to worry about than a perjury charge. When it
was close to time to leave the office, I asked Julie to give me a ride
home.

"You don't want to wait and see if Zach comes by?"

"No."

Julie nodded. "Good strategy. Make the man realize he's expendable, a plaything you can discard at your whim."

"That's not what I'm thinking. I just don't want to walk home in
the heat."

"A boring reason, but I'll still give you a ride."

GRACIE HAD PREPARED a supper of salmon, asparagus, and scalloped
potatoes. Mrs. Fairmont was wearing a nice dress, and we ate in the
dining room, much like we did the first day I arrived. I couldn't tell
Mrs. Fairmont anything about the Dabney case, but when she asked
how Vince was doing, I told her about my conversation with him
and Zach. Thankfully, I was able to leave out the tears.

"I don't know," she replied with skepticism. "They should be
competing for your affection, not agreeing to retreat from the field
of battle."

Mrs. Fairmont ate a small bite of salmon and dropped a piece on
the floor for Flip.

"I'll be curious to see how long this truce lasts," she said.

Partway through the meal, I asked, "Is there anything you'd like
to do tonight?"

Mrs. Fairmont paused for a moment. "Yes, I'd like to take a ride
in the car. You drive, of course, and I'll tell you where to go."

Mrs. Fairmont sat in the den and listened to the evening news while I cleaned the dishes after dinner. Normally she didn't have much interest in national or international events unless they had a connection with Savannah.

"I'm finished," I called out as soon as I'd put the last item in the dishwasher and turned it on.

Mrs. Fairmont didn't answer, and when I went into the den, she was asleep with Flip curled up on the chair beside her. I gently shook her shoulder.

"Mrs. Fairmont, it's Tami. Do you still want to take a ride in the car?"

The elderly woman stirred and opened her eyes. "A car ride?"

"Yes, ma'am."

"No, let's do it another night."

THE NEXT DAY I dutifully delivered the motion for summary judgment and affidavit for Jason Paulding to Mr. Carpenter's office. The senior partner wasn't in so I gave the documents to his secretary.

"I'll let him know," she replied. "He's already talked to Judge Cannon's office, and we're getting several dates for a hearing."

"That's too soon. Sister Dabney, I mean the defendant, can object. She hasn't even answered the complaint."

"Mr. Carpenter seems to think there's a chance she won't file an objection."

He could be right. Sister Dabney hadn't shown any interest in trying to protect her rights under the rules for civil procedure. Unlike criminal cases that had mandatory safeguards, due process in civil matters could move speedily if one side pressed the issue and the other side didn't do anything to slow the case down.

"He wants you there," the secretary continued. "That means we need to squeeze it in before the end of the month."

I wasn't surprised. I'd been bound to the Dabney case with a thousand ropes and didn't possess the strength of Samson to break them off.

"Just let me know."

JULIE WAS OUT of the office on Friday, and I spent the whole day waiting for Zach and Vince to come by the library. By early afternoon neither of them had peeked in to check on me, and I began to doubt Julie's assessment of their ardor. Finally curiosity got the best of me. I called Mr. Braddock's secretary.

"I'm trying to get in touch with Vince," I said.

"He's been out for the day and won't return until Monday."

I hung up. Finding out about Zach would be trickier. He didn't have a full-time secretary but used a number of people in the secretarial pool. Knocking on his office door wasn't an option. I went into the reception area.

"Is Zach Mays here?" I asked the receptionist.

"No, he called early this morning and said he'd be in Brunswick all day. I don't expect him back."

The whereabouts of my erstwhile suitors settled, I was less distracted for the remainder of the day and completed a lot of work. With no one to give me a ride home, I walked home in the heat.

JUST BEFORE NOON on Saturday, the phone rang. I went into the kitchen and answered it.

"I'm surprised you're there," Julie said. "I thought you might be rolling down the aisle of a church."

"I only do that on Sunday."

"I'm sorry I wasn't at the office yesterday to see Zach and Vinny come groveling to the library. How are you doing?"

"They were out of town."

"Thinking about you the whole time. Listen, Maggie and I are going to grab a bite to eat and wanted to invite you."

"Why?"

"Tami, don't talk me out of it. It took an act of my will to punch in the phone number."

I glanced into the den.

"Let me check with Mrs. Fairmont. She's having a good day, but I need to make sure she's okay if I leave."

I placed the phone on the counter and told Mrs. Fairmont about the invitation.

"Go ahead," she replied. "There's enough in the refrigerator for me to fix a snack."

"We'll be by in a few minutes," Julie said when I told her.

JULIE AND MAGGIE were wearing shorts and skimpy tops. I had on a lightweight skirt and short-sleeved shirt.

"Some things haven't changed this summer," Julie said, pointing to my outfit as I got in the backseat.

"And I trust never will."

We drove to the sandwich place Vince liked near the river and found a table in the corner. While we waited for the food, I expected Maggie and Julie to talk about their plans to start their own law firm, but Maggie was more interested in talking about Braddock, Appleby, and Carpenter.

"Can you tell if Mr. Carpenter's litigation practice is growing?" she asked me.

"I don't know. He's busy but always seems to get things done."

"And doesn't have a problem delegating," Julie added. "He doesn't hesitate to ask Tami and me to do things normally reserved for associates."

"Is Ned working with him?" Maggie asked.

"Not really," Julie answered. "Fred Godwin is on his team, but he's overwhelmed with his own projects. Tami and I haven't worked much with him. Myra Dean serves as his paralegal, but she's on a leave of absence."

"Do you know why?"

"I do," Julie responded, "but I'm not supposed to."

"That's okay," Maggie said. "Then it looks like Joe Carpenter needs a litigation associate."

"That would be Tami," Julie answered. "If she wants the job."

"Is that what you want to do?"

Our food came before I answered.

"Tami prays before she eats," Julie said. "I told her if she stayed away from pork and shellfish, the blessing is automatic."

"Is the pastrami on your sandwich pork-free?" I asked.

"Go ahead and pray," Julie said.

When I finished, Maggie said, "I don't have a problem with praying. My mother wishes I did it more myself."

"My mother would freak out," Julie said.

We each ate a bite of our sandwiches.

"Has Julie talked to you about the firm we're setting up when she graduates from law school next spring?" Maggie asked.

"Yes."

"And she laughed in my face," Julie inserted.

Maggie didn't smile. "I want you to consider being a part of it."

I returned my sandwich to the plate without taking another bite.

"You're offering me a job?"

"We'd have to discuss the details, but if you decide not to take a position at Braddock, Appleby, and Carpenter, it might be a good arrangement for all of us."

"How would you have enough business to support three lawyers?"

"We wouldn't start out with big salaries. It's not what you make the first year that's important; it's the potential for growth that's the key."

"Wouldn't your cases primarily be criminal defense? Isn't that what most prosecutors do when they go out into private practice?"

"There would be some of that, but I've developed other business relationships that would have more stability."

"Maggie worked on a white-collar crime case against a bank executive," Julie said. "A top guy in the legal department for the bank's home office was so impressed that he told her to let him know as soon as she's available to represent them in this part of the state."

"And I have other strong contacts. Law firms today are all about finding niches. A group of women would stand out in this town and attract business just because of our gender. Of course, it would take quality work to keep the clients and generate referrals."

"Girl power," Julie said gleefully.

"And I'd be an associate?"

"Yes, just like you would be for any other firm."

"And Julie?"

"Is going to bring the start-up capital needed in return for immediate partnership."

"Maggie and I went to Atlanta and met with my father," Julie said. "He's given us the green light."

"It's an interesting thought," I said cautiously. "I'll have to pray about it."

Julie turned to Maggie. "I told you that's what she'd say, but it's like me and my dad. God always goes along with what she wants."

"And you can wait to see what happens at Braddock, Appleby, and Carpenter," Maggie said. "There's no need to decide before you go back to school."

ON MONDAY MORNING there was a memo to my firm e-mail address that the motion for summary judgment in *Paulding v. Dabney* was set for the following week.

"Mr. Carpenter isn't wasting any time," Julie said when I told her. "But if Dabney shows up and asks for a continuance, the judge is going to give it to her."

"I hope so."

"Which means it won't be on a motion calendar until we're finished for the summer," Julie said, reading my thoughts. "We can go back to law school and live in the pretend world again."

"Yes."

LATER MONDAY MORNING Zach and Vince came into the library.

Julie glanced up and said, "That's my cue to get a third cup of coffee. I won't be able to hear any yelling and screaming in the break room, so if things get out of hand, someone else will have to call the police."

Julie left. The two men looked like schoolboys waiting for the next word in a spelling bee.

"How are you doing?" Zach asked, his hands folded in front of him.

"Okay."

"Good," Vince said a little too quickly.

"There's no use beating around the bush," Zach continued. "We want to apologize for what happened last week. It was bad timing."

"We meant well, but we blew it," Vince added.

"It hurt, a lot," I said, keeping my voice steady. "I was already a mess after Sister Dabney's deposition and felt totally rejected."

"Yeah," both men said.

There was an awkward silence. I wasn't about to let them off the hook so easily.

"Are you still getting together to talk about me?"

"And pray for you," Zach said. "We've met at Vince's place several times."

The sharp words on the tip of my tongue evaporated.

"Pray?"

"Yeah." Zach nodded.

"But both of you—" I stopped, not sure if I should openly label them as rivals.

"Are Christian brothers," Vince replied. "And that's what we want to be to each other and toward you."

I wasn't sure exactly what either of them meant or thought about me, but I couldn't criticize them for praying.

"Uh, thanks."

"You're welcome," Vince replied with obvious relief.

"Ditto for me," Zach added, pulling his ponytail.

They left satisfied and me in confusion. Julie returned.

"Well?" she asked.

"They apologized for hurting my feelings."

"That's a good start."

"And said they've been meeting together to pray for me."

Julie's face registered shock. "You're kidding! They ought to be challenging each other to a sword fight or a duel, not kneeling on the floor."

I tilted my head to the side. "And I have no idea what they're praying."

I HAD A VERY BUSY WEEK. It seemed as though lawyers who hadn't asked me to help them all summer suddenly had to have my assistance on a variety of projects. Friday I went to lunch with Zach. During the drive, he didn't say anything about Vince and him continuing to pray. He drove us to a beach sort of place where we sat at a table under a large white fan that slowly stirred the air above us. I couldn't keep quiet.

"Are you and Vince still getting together to pray?"

"Yeah."

"When I'm the subject, what do you pray?"

"Different things."

I pressed my lips tightly together for a moment. "Come on, Zach, don't tease me."

He smiled. "Okay. We pray about the past, present, and future."

"Explain. In detail."

"Do you know what you want to eat?" he asked.

I glanced down at the menu and picked the first item I saw.

"The shrimp salad croissant with fresh fruit on the side."

"Sounds good to me."

Zach called over a waiter and placed our order.

After the waiter left, I motioned with my hand for Zach to continue. "I'm listening."

He leaned forward with his hands on the table. "No one can change the past, or necessarily want to, but Vince and I've prayed that you will become the person God intends—holding on to the good from your family and leaving the not-so-good behind."

"What isn't good?"

Zach shook his head. "That's not our call. When we pray, we're not examining your background with a critical eye under a spiritual microscope, and I'm not going to start now. But if you believe you're perfect and don't have room to grow, you're already off the mark."

"I'm not perfect," I answered quickly.

"And neither am I. Deciding exactly how you're supposed to build on the past and how to leave it behind takes wisdom that only comes from above."

"What about the present?"

Zach smiled. "That's when we get specific. For example, we know what a strain the Dabney case has been for you, so we've asked God to help you every step of the way. It's not enough just to get through a tough situation; there's usually a purpose hidden within the challenge. Neither of us wants you to miss it."

Sister Dabney's reaction to my words at the beginning of the deposition was an obvious example of an answer to their prayers. Appreciation for the two men welled up in me.

"Thanks. I don't want to miss an opportunity either, at least most of the time."

"And we've prayed for your relationship with Mrs. Fairmont. When I was in Powell Station, your father said God may have sent you to Savannah solely for her benefit."

The mention of the gracious old woman made my heart ache with appreciation.

"It's been a time I'll never forget."

"And then there's Julie." Zach smiled.

I shook my head. "She's a very present part of my present."

"You may not see it, but Julie's respect for you has blossomed over the summer. Who knows where that will lead in the future?"

I couldn't mention the job offer from Maggie and Julie, but it immediately came to mind.

"And we've prayed that each of us would relate to you as we should. That's one reason we felt bad for hurting your feelings. It was the opposite of what we wanted to do."

"Do you and Vince want to relate to me in the same way?"

"No."

"What's the difference?" I persisted.

"I'm not going to speak for Vince. You'll have to ask him that question. But nothing's changed from my side. I want to spend time with you and get to know you better."

"You've been mad at me ever since I dragged you into the Dabney case."

The look on Zach's face was one of honest surprise.

"I've not been mad. Just busy, and the added responsibility made me busier."

"That's not how it's felt to me. You've been short with me, ignored me, and tried to make me feel guilty about asking for help."

"Chalk it up to the difference between women and men," he said with a rueful expression. "In the future, let me know when you feel that way about something. I don't want it to linger."

The waiter brought our food. We ate in silence for a few minutes as the increasing realization of the two men's unselfishness grew within me. It was almost beyond comprehension.

"What about the future?" I asked after most of my sandwich was eaten.

"That's more vague," Zach answered, taking a sip of water. "And personal."

Suddenly I realized Zach and Vince might be praying I would find the right man to marry, a scenario that didn't follow the pattern of the mild romance novels Mama let me read as a teenager. In those stories strong women of faith ultimately married for the right reasons, but the men vying for their affection never got along, much less prayed together.

"Of course we pray you'll get a good job with the right firm," Zach continued. "Did you know there's a reason why you've been so busy recently?"

I'd noticed an increase in requests for help, but had no idea it was based on anything except an abundance of work that needed to be done before my inexpensive labor ended for the summer.

"I just thought the lawyers had a lot of overflow."

"True, but that's not all. A decision is about to be made about job offers for the summer clerks, and the partners want to check you out. It's a good sign that everyone is dumping work on you. Is the same thing happening to Julie?"

"No. She's finishing her projects. I've asked if she can help on a couple of things and been told no."

"That tells you something about her prospects."

"What about Vince? He's been busy."

Zach smiled. "Someday I may be calling him boss."

I tapped my spoon lightly against the table. "What are you hearing about my prospects?"

"Nothing specific, because I'm not in the loop. Everyone has to prepare a memo making a recommendation about the summer clerks by the end of next week. The partners will meet after that and decide who receives a job offer."

"What goes in the memo?"

"Personal and professional stuff."

"What are you going to write?"

Zach smiled and shook his head. "If I told you, it would violate firm policy, but I'm sure my opinion won't carry much weight. Everyone knows I want to lure you back to Savannah."

The waiter took away our plates.

"Have you thought any more about going back to Powell Station after law school?" Zach asked after the waiter left.

"Working for Mr. Callahan would have been my first choice until he had his heart attack. Now I'd love being close to my family, but—" I stopped. "That wouldn't allow me to break from the past in the way I need to."

"Yeah." Zach nodded. "Do you have any other job possibilities?"

Faced with a direct question, I wasn't sure what to say. I spoke slowly. "Kind of, but I can't talk about it."

"Does it involve Maggie Smith?"

I looked at Zach in shock. He laughed.

"Gossip in the Savannah legal community isn't governed by the rules of confidentiality. People know Maggie has been trolling for business. Most lawyers who work for the district attorney's office eventually branch out. I think she has a chance to do well. She's aggressive, but likable."

"Hypothetically, what would you think about me working with her?" I asked cautiously.

"Are you asking me for advice against the best interests of my employer?"

"No, and you don't have to answer."

"I will anyway. You need to take into consideration that not every new firm succeeds. Often the lawyers muddle on for years and go through a lot of agony because their pride won't let them admit failure. Leaving a bankrupt practice isn't the best way to find another job."

"But there would be more freedom to take the kind of cases I want to handle."

"Unless economic pressure dictates otherwise. A lot of attorneys handling low-budget divorce cases would rather be doing something else, but they have overhead to pay. But I'm not worried. Vince and I have been praying you'll make the right choice—about that and everything else. Do you want any dessert?"

I shook my head. "No, too many carbs will make me sleepy this afternoon."

"I don't want Mr. Carpenter finding you asleep in the library."

THE FOLLOWING MONDAY Fred Godwin brought me a project. The tall, slender attorney was a new partner and walked around the office with a studious expression on his face. His car was often in the parking lot when I arrived for work and usually there when I left in the afternoon.

"He looks like secret information is going to grow out of his forehead at any minute," Julie observed after he'd stopped by the library to talk with me.

"That's bizarre."

"Myra Dean once told me he cozies up to juries and goes for the professorial approach. Once they're listening, he educates the other side out of court."

The file he'd given me was a business dispute. It contained nothing that could be used to manufacture courtroom fireworks. The attorney best able to simplify the complex facts would likely win. That kind of litigation appealed to me. After eight hours of work, I turned in a long memo with the satisfaction that I was serving justice without compromising my conscience.

Toward the end of the week, I received an interoffice e-mail that the motion for summary judgment in *Paulding v. Dabney* had been scheduled. I printed it out, and Julie saw it lying on the worktable.

"Mr. Carpenter wants you at the hearing?" she asked.

"Yes."

"What about me? I did most of the work on the deposition questions."

Julie sat down at her computer and quickly typed an e-mail. "He needs to know I'm just as much a tiger or leopard or jaguar or whatever it is as you are."

"With a crocodile thrown in for good measure."

THE HEARING ON THE MOTION was set for Tuesday afternoon at four o'clock. I'd already decided I didn't like later afternoon courtroom appearances. Better to go to battle early than have to wait in nervous anticipation. Even though I'd been busy, Sister Dabney's dilemma was always lurking at the back of my mind.

Mr. Carpenter gave Julie permission to attend the hearing but excused Zach. Vince came by the library as we were preparing to leave for the courthouse.

"Ready?" he asked.

"You better believe it," Julie answered. "Tami has been having all the fun while I've done the slave labor here in the library. It's time I get to see this woman in action. She may be a religious nut, but you have to admire her guts. There's more than one kind of feminist."

"How do you feel?" Vince asked me.

I looked at him with silent thanks because he and Zach had been praying.

"I'll be okay. I keep reminding myself what Sister Dabney told me at the deposition about walking in the fire and not being burned."

"I hope that's a metaphor," Julie said.

MR. CARPENTER WAS at Paulding Development preparing Jason Paulding for the hearing and left word for Julie and me to meet him at the courthouse. Our only assignment was to show up on time with the file. He would do all the talking.

"If Dabney is there, I don't want to get too close to her," Julie said as we drove down Montgomery Street. "It would creep me out if she told me that I ought to marry Joel or get back together with Biff Levinson."

"Biff Levinson?"

"I haven't told you about him?"

"No."

"That will take an entire lunch."

The hearing was in the same courtroom where I'd appeared on behalf of Moses Jones. It was empty.

"That's where the plaintiff's lawyers sit," Julie said, pointing to the table nearest the jury box.

We opened the low gate in the bar and passed into the area reserved for lawyers and their clients. Butterflies began to swirl around in my stomach. It was different from the Moses Jones case when responsibility for the case had rested on my shoulders, but there was still anticipation anxiety. Lawsuits were a lot like basketball games in high school. Somebody was going to win; another would lose. Waiting for the tip-off was the worst part.

The rear door of the courtroom opened. Julie and I turned around. It wasn't Mr. Carpenter with our client or Sister Dabney. A woman in her early thirties with short blonde hair, stylish glasses, and wearing a dark suit entered.

"Is this where *Paulding v. Dabney* is going to be heard?" she asked.

"Yes," Julie answered.

The woman walked down the aisle to the bar.

"I'm Brenda Abernathy from the paper."

The reporter could have passed for a female attorney. Julie and I introduced ourselves.

"Is this going to be open to the public?" Abernathy asked.

"Unless the judge decides it isn't," Julie replied.

"Anything dramatic expected to happen?" Abernathy continued, looking around the room. "I saw on the docket in the clerk's office that it was a hearing on a motion for summary judgment. What's that?"

Julie gave a good definition of the purpose of the proceeding and, to my relief, didn't mention the specific facts of the case. I stood poised to interrupt if she got out of line. Abernathy made notes with a PDA.

"Court is usually boring except to the lawyers and parties," Julie said.

"Have you been involved in a lot of trials?" Abernathy asked.

"No, but that's what everyone tells me. Are you going to put my name in the paper?"

The reporter smiled. "Maybe. Let me make sure about the spelling."

Julie gave her the information and added my name, too.

"Her real name is Tammy Lynn," Julie said, lowering her voice, "but when she came to work in Savannah for the summer she changed it to Tami. There's probably a human-interest story buried in that someplace. If you decide to write an article about Tami, I can be your primary source. We work together in the same room every day. She's kind of a younger version of Reverend Dabney, but without—"

"I'm not interested in having my name or life story in the paper," I interrupted.

The back door opened again. This time it was Sister Dabney. She was wearing a yellow dress I'd seen when I visited the church. Her face was flushed and red, making me wonder how she'd gotten to the courthouse. I hoped the overweight woman hadn't walked a long distance in the heat. She looked in our direction and squinted slightly.

"Reverend Dabney?" Abernathy asked.

"Yes." Sister Dabney nodded.

The reporter faced the older woman in the middle of the aisle.

"I'm Brenda Abernathy, the reporter you contacted about Mr. Paulding. We talked on the phone a couple of months ago."

"I remember," Sister Dabney replied. "You didn't believe me."

"Could I ask you a few questions?"

Sister Dabney glanced past Abernathy toward Julie and me. When her eyes met mine, the butterflies in my stomach died. Cold fire danced across the preacher's face.

"No," Sister Dabney said.

"You made some serious allegations about Mr. Paulding," Abernathy continued, "and I want to make sure I fairly report your side of this dispute. I can't do that unless you talk to me."

"You're interested in sensationalism, not facts," Sister Dabney answered. "I've seen your kind in other places. It's wrong to handle holy things in an unholy way."

I wanted to escape to the restroom and not be around for what happened next. The door behind the bench opened. A bailiff and the court reporter entered, followed by Judge Cannon.

"All rise," the bailiff said.

Julie whispered to me, "Where is Mr. Carpenter?"

31

The judge sat and looked around the courtroom.

"I call the case of *Paulding v. Dabney*, hearing on plaintiff's motion for summary judgment."

Julie nudged me in the ribs and gestured toward the judge.

"Say something."

"Uh, I'm Tami Taylor, a summer clerk with Braddock, Appleby, and Carpenter. We expect Mr. Carpenter any moment. He was coming to the courthouse from our client's office and must have been delayed."

"Didn't you appear before me a few weeks ago?" the judge asked, looking at me over his glasses.

"Yes, sir. You gave me leave of court to represent a man named Moses Jones in a misdemeanor criminal matter."

"That's right. I rejected a plea agreement. Then you went judge-shopping and entered a plea in front of Judge Howell."

My face flushed. "Other facts came out in the investigation, and Ms. Smith in the district attorney's office spoke with Judge Howell about a plea. I think all sides were satisfied with the result."

The judge waved his hand. "Judges talk, Ms. Taylor. We find out when lawyers manipulate the calendar."

"Yes, sir." I rested my hands on the table in front of me to keep myself steady.

"Where was Mr. Carpenter coming from?" the judge asked.

Julie quickly opened the file and slid it in front of me. I gave the judge the address.

"We'll give him a few more minutes. Is the defendant in the courtroom?"

"I am," Sister Dabney answered in a loud voice.

"Do you have a lawyer?"

"The best."

"Who is it?"

"The Lord Jesus Christ."

Julie stifled a laugh. I didn't turn around, but I knew Brenda Abernathy was furiously scribbling on her PDA.

"I've heard that before," Judge Cannon replied dryly. "The last person who made a statement like that is in the Georgia State Penitentiary. If you're ready to proceed, come forward to the other table."

I could see Sister Dabney out of the corner of my eye as she lowered herself slowly into one of the chairs. I expected her to have notes or papers with her, but the table was bare. She didn't even have a Bible.

"And who else is present?" the judge asked.

"Brenda Abernathy from the newspaper," the reporter answered.

"Is there any legal reason why the press should be excluded from this hearing?" the judge asked.

I leaned over to Julie. "What are the legal grounds to keep her out?"

"I don't know."

"Could we wait for Mr. Carpenter to address that issue on behalf of the plaintiff, Your Honor?" I asked. "Ms. Feldman and I are primarily here to observe."

"Very well." The judge turned to Sister Dabney. "Ms. Dabney, do you have any objection to Ms. Abernathy's presence?"

"It's what she does when she leaves that may be the greater sin."

"I'll take that as a no."

In my mind I could see every word spoken by Sister Dabney repeated in an article in the newspaper. The back door of the courtroom opened. It was Mr. Carpenter and Jason Paulding. Mr. Carpenter's face was as flushed as Sister Dabney's when she arrived.

"Sorry, Your Honor," the senior partner said as he walked up the aisle. "My car blew a water hose a few blocks from the courthouse."

"Do you need a few minutes to prepare or are you ready to proceed?" the judge asked.

"Just a moment to get situated. Our proof is attached to the motion for summary judgment."

"I reviewed the motion in chambers before coming into the courtroom. While you get organized, I have some questions for the defendant. Ms. Dabney, did you receive a copy of the motion?"

"Yes."

"Under the law you have a right to file a written response. Do you want to do so?"

"I can speak about it today."

"Does that mean you waive or give up your right to delay the hearing to a later date so you can file something in writing?"

"The truth won't change with the passing of time."

"Are you ready to proceed today on the issues presented in the motion?"

"I don't see any reason to put it off. Justice should be done speedily."

"I wish more lawyers agreed with you," the judge replied wryly. "Given your statement, I'll allow Mr. Carpenter to go forward with his motion. After he presents his case, you can offer your evidence and any argument you deem appropriate."

"Will I be able to question Mr. Paulding?" Sister Dabney asked.

The judge turned toward us. "Is this your client?"

"Yes, sir," Mr. Carpenter answered. "A comprehensive affidavit by Mr. Paulding is attached to the motion. I didn't intend to offer any testimony from him."

"I'll allow the defendant to question him. Also, there is a member of the press present. Is there any reason why this hearing should not be open to the public?"

Mr. Carpenter glanced over his shoulder. I leaned closer to him.

"It's Brenda Abernathy, the one who is writing an article about Sister Dabney."

"No objection on behalf of the plaintiff," Mr. Carpenter said.

"Ms. Abernathy may remain in the courtroom. You're the moving party, Mr. Carpenter. I'll hear from you first."

Julie and I sat at one end of the counsel table. The senior partner stood and positioned his body so the judge didn't have Sister Dabney in his line of sight. It was a subtle move consistent with Mr. Carpenter's attention to every detail. Since no jury was present, he spoke in a conversational tone. I'd heard it all before in bits and pieces, but having it laid out like a story was effective. I found myself wondering why on earth, or in heaven, Sister Dabney would speak ill of Jason Paulding. Not only was it unreasonable, it was a malicious verbal assault on another human being.

"Ms. Dabney is the minister of a church," Mr. Carpenter said, gesturing toward her for the first time. "She, above most people in society, should consider the effect of her words and actions. There is a responsibility that comes with a position of influence. This woman has abused that responsibility to an extreme degree, and we're asking the court to hold her responsible for her actions."

Mr. Carpenter then laid out the factual and legal basis supporting the motion for summary judgment. I knew this part of his presentation would be strong. As he went through the deposition testimony,

I pretended to be Sister Dabney's lawyer and tried to figure out a way she could wiggle out of the multiple admissions of liability. I considered several possibilities, but nothing workable came to mind.

"Judge, you also have the affidavit of Mr. Paulding, prepared by Ms. Taylor, one of our summer clerks."

I blushed, embarrassed that Sister Dabney knew I'd played an active role in the attack against her. Julie gently nudged me with her toe under the table and curled her hand up like a cat's paw. Mr. Carpenter didn't read the entire affidavit, only the parts that addressed the issue of damages. As I listened, I realized Sister Dabney could still attack the damages model Mr. Carpenter was presenting. The money Mr. Paulding claimed he'd lost because of her actions was speculative. I quickly formed several questions in my mind that would undermine our case. I was in the midst of my imaginary cross-examination of our client when Mr. Carpenter finished and sat down. The judge finished taking a few notes and turned toward Sister Dabney.

"The defendant may proceed."

Sister Dabney braced herself against the arms of the chair and pushed herself to her feet.

"Judge, do you know the story of David and Uriah the Hittite?"

"No," the judge said.

Sister Dabney faced the judge. "Then I'll tell you. Uriah was one of King David's mighty men. While Uriah was off fighting, David seduced Uriah's wife, then arranged for Uriah to be put in the worst part of a battle where he was killed. David thought he'd gotten away with adultery and murder, but a prophet named Nathan came to David. The prophet told King David a story about a rich man who was having a meal with friends. The rich man owned a large herd of sheep, but instead of cooking one of his own, he took a poor man's only sheep and fed it to his guests. Nathan used that story to confront David about what he'd done to Uriah. What do you think about that?"

"Ms. Dabney, the purpose of this hearing is not to tell me a Bible

story or ask me questions. This is your opportunity to respond to the
motion for summary judgment."

"That's what I'm doing."

"Do you know the legal significance of the motion?"

Sister Dabney squinted her eyes slightly. "If you grant the motion,
then I might owe Mr. Paulding a lot of money."

"That's correct."

"Would that be just? Isn't Mr. Paulding like the man in the story?
He owns property all over Chatham County, yet he's trying to take
the parcel of land I've dedicated to the Lord and his work. He's trying
to take the only little sheep I have. I want to give him a chance to
repent and stop what he's trying to do."

"I'll treat that as a motion to dismiss." The judge turned to us.
"Mr. Carpenter, having heard from the defendant, are you prepared
to voluntarily withdraw the motion?"

"No, sir. We believe the motion is both just and supported by the
law and the facts."

The judge looked at Sister Dabney. I could see Brenda Abernathy
furiously making notes.

"Is there anything else you want to offer by way of defense?"

"I want to ask Jason Paulding some questions."

"Very well. The witness will come forward and be sworn."

Mr. Carpenter leaned over to Paulding and gave him last-minute
instructions that I couldn't hear.

The judge spoke. "Ms. Dabney, I will give you latitude in your
questions, but I ask you to respect the dignity of the court."

"Paul respected the Sanhedrin. I can do the same."

Julie leaned over to me and whispered, "That's a Jewish council.
I learned about it at synagogue when I was a kid."

"It's in the New Testament, too."

"Really?"

The judge administered the oath, and Paulding sat in the witness chair. He tried to look relaxed and confident, but I knew he had to be nervous. I would have been terrified.

"Please state your name for the record," the judge said.

"Jason Paulding, president and CEO of Paulding Development Corporation."

"Ms. Dabney, you may proceed."

My chair was positioned so that I had a clear view of Sister Dabney. She was staring straight at Paulding, who shifted in his chair.

"Did you know the truth can either set you free or condemn you forever?" Sister Dabney asked.

The witness glanced at Mr. Carpenter, whose face didn't move a muscle.

"I'm not sure what you're asking me," Mr. Paulding answered.

"If you confess your sins and admit the truth, there is hope you might find mercy."

Mr. Carpenter stood. "Objection, Your Honor. That was a statement, not a question."

"He's right," the judge said to Sister Dabney. "You have to ask questions."

"Have you talked to your pastor about this court hearing?"

"No."

"Did you talk to your wife about it?"

"Yes. She knows I'm here."

"Did she know where you were and who you were with in Las Vegas last July?"

"I was on a business trip with two members of the board of directors of my company."

I held my breath, waiting for Sister Dabney to list specific details that would cause Mr. Paulding's face to turn ashen. The woman preacher stared hard at the witness for a few moments.

"Even if I don't know everything, you can't hide from the Lord," she said.

"Objection," Mr. Carpenter said.

"Sustained. Ms. Dabney, remember to ask questions."

"What about the man from Miami who loaned you money after you came back from Las Vegas?"

"I don't know what you're talking about."

"He met you at the airport in Savannah and gave you a brown briefcase filled with one-hundred-dollar bills."

Mr. Paulding's mouth dropped open. Mr. Carpenter stood.

"I know," the judge said before the lawyer could state his objection. "It's not a question. Sustained."

"What did you do with that money?" Sister Dabney asked.

"I don't know what you're talking about."

"Did you leave the airport with a man in a red car?"

"I know a lot of people with red cars."

"And did he take you to a meeting where the money was divided up with other people?"

"Since I don't know what you're talking about, I can't answer."

"Was there a man from Chicago at that meeting?"

"I know several people from Chicago."

Mr. Paulding shifted in his chair and looked up at the judge. "May I speak with Mr. Carpenter?"

"I know the man's last name," Sister Dabney continued. "It's Laramie."

The judge ignored Sister Dabney and spoke to the witness. "Unless legal grounds exist, your attorney is not allowed to advise you while you are subject to cross-examination."

"Your Honor, if you could grant some leeway," Mr. Carpenter interjected. "This is not a typical proceeding. I won't overstep the proper bounds in advising my client."

The judge looked at Sister Dabney. "Do you object to Mr. Carpenter speaking with his client?"

"They can talk, but it won't change the truth."

The judge stood. "Court will be in recess for five minutes. After that, I'll expect both parties to move forward expeditiously."

Mr. Carpenter met Mr. Paulding halfway between the witness stand and the table where Julie and I sat. The two men stepped to the side and put their heads together.

"What do you think Paulding did with the money in the briefcase?" Julie asked. "Do you think it was marked by the FBI in advance?"

"What?"

"Use your imagination. That's what the crazy woman at the other table is doing."

Sister Dabney was sitting with her eyes closed. Mr. Carpenter listened to Mr. Paulding, who was talking rapidly. I glanced back at Brenda Abernathy. She had a smile on her face. Whoever lost at the hearing, the reporter won.

"Something's going on," I said to Julie, gesturing toward Mr. Carpenter and our client.

"Yeah, he wants to know how long the judge is going to let her do this. I think she's just getting warmed up. Once she gets really delusional, this could go on for hours."

Mr. Paulding rubbed his forehead while he listened to Mr. Carpenter. The judge returned to the courtroom.

"Return to the witness stand," the judge said.

Mr. Carpenter stepped between Mr. Paulding and the judge.

"Your Honor, at this time we withdraw our motion for summary judgment."

Julie gasped.

"Does this mean I can't ask any more questions?" Sister Dabney said.

"Correct," the judge answered crisply. "The moving party has the right to withdraw the motion prior to entry of an order. The case will be placed on the civil trial calendar. This hearing is adjourned."

Judge Cannon left the courtroom. Mr. Carpenter came over to the table. Mr. Paulding walked briskly past us toward the back door.

"Mr. Paulding, I have a few questions," Brenda Abernathy called out.

"No questions," Mr. Carpenter said, holding up his hand.

Mr. Paulding kept going without looking back. Sister Dabney pushed herself up out of the chair. Her expression didn't reveal triumph.

"Take the file back to the office," Mr. Carpenter said.

"Should we wait for you?" I asked. "Your water hose broke."

Mr. Carpenter looked at me as if seeing me for the first time.

"Right. Jason is calling someone to pick him up."

Sister Dabney approached our table. Brenda Abernathy positioned herself directly across the bar from us. Sister Dabney stopped and instead of looking at Mr. Carpenter, directed her attention at me. I swallowed.

"It wasn't revelation," she said. "Don't ever claim God is speaking when the information comes from a natural source."

"Yes, ma'am," I answered, my mouth dry.

"Do you know what I mean?"

"I think so."

Sister Dabney sniffed the air. "You still don't smell like smoke. His hand is on you."

She continued past us. Brenda Abernathy blocked her way.

"Reverend Dabney, tell me more about the suitcase of money at the airport and the name of the man from Chicago."

"You have to know the right person and ask the right question."

"Who is that person?"

"Not me. Out of my way. I've got the Lord's work to do."

The old woman brushed aside the reporter and walked slowly from the courtroom.

"I'm going to run an article," the reporter said, stepping closer to us. "If you want a chance for your side of this to be heard, now is the time to make a statement."

Mr. Carpenter looked at her with steely eyes. "Ms. Abernathy, my client isn't a public figure. Unless you want to take Ms. Dabney's place as the defendant in a libel case, don't print anything you can't prove is true."

32

JULIE AND I LEFT THE COURTHOUSE WITH MR. CARPENTER, WHO didn't say a word until we were outside.

"Courthouse hallways have hidden ears," he said. "We'll debrief at the office."

No one spoke during the short ride back to the office.

"Meet me in the main conference room in five minutes," the senior partner said.

Julie and I went to the library.

"What just happened?" Julie asked. "You're the expert. Enlighten me."

"Mr. Carpenter dismissed the motion for summary judgment."

"You know what I mean."

"Mr. Carpenter was the one who talked to the client. He'll tell us if he wants to."

"Maybe, but Dabney was giving you the winks and nods, and spouting secret religious lingo that has to mean something."

I didn't want to speculate with Julie. "Sister Dabney is like anyone. There are layers to her."

Julie sniffed. "And all of them are filled with fruits and nuts."

WE WAITED IN THE CONFERENCE ROOM for Mr. Carpenter. It was the place I'd first met Jason Paulding. The painting of the antebellum Savannah waterfront hadn't changed during the past few weeks, but Paulding's dispute with Ramona Dabney had morphed several times. Vince opened the door and stuck his head inside.

"I saw you come in the building."

"Mr. Carpenter dismissed the motion," Julie answered. "We're waiting for him now."

"Why would he do that?"

Mr. Carpenter appeared at Vince's shoulder, brushed past him, and closed the door in his face.

"What did Dabney mean by her comment to you?" he asked me before sitting down.

"Which one?"

"About her source of information."

I'd had time to think about Sister Dabney's words while in the car. I spoke deliberately. "I'm not one-hundred-percent sure, but I don't think God supernaturally told her in a dream or vision about Paulding getting a suitcase of money at the airport. Someone she knows provided that information."

"Do you think you could find out who it is?"

"The only way would be to ask Sister Dabney."

"Is it true about the money?" Julie asked.

Mr. Carpenter made eye contact with each of us. "That's not the right question. Being a summer clerk is less formal than working as an attorney, but the rules of confidentiality and attorney-client privilege apply with as much force to you as they do to me. I'll be contacted by the state bar association before you take the exam next year. I want to be able to give you a positive reference. Is that clear?"

"Yes, sir," we both said.

"Our representation of Jason Paulding has taken a new turn. Tami, your job is to find out what Dabney knows. Then, if she agrees to keep quiet, we'll dismiss the lawsuit against her with prejudice. The newspaper reporter doesn't know anything more than what she heard in the courtroom. That's not enough to print a story."

"How am I supposed to convince her to keep quiet? Filing a lawsuit didn't do it. And is it ethical to protect a client who's committed a crime?"

"No crime was committed," Mr. Carpenter answered, his jaw set. "But the circumstances of the transaction would be embarrassing to Paulding and his business partners."

"I'm not sure I can do this."

Mr. Carpenter put his hands together in front of him. His face remained stern.

"Tami, I'm asking, not ordering. Let me know in the morning."

Mr. Carpenter left the conference room. Julie turned to me.

"Talk about a mission impossible. You know how at the beginning of the movies they ask the main character if he wants to accept—"

My blank expression about movie trivia must have stopped her. "Anyway, it's a long shot, but I'm sure you'll give it a try."

"How can you be so sure?" I asked.

"I don't understand Dabney, but I know you."

We returned to the library where Vince and Zach were waiting for us. Julie downloaded her pent-up energy telling them about the hearing and our return to the office.

"So, it's up to Tami to save the day," Julie concluded. "Didn't you just know that's where this case was going to end up? Of course, she has to pray about it."

"How can you be so flippant?" I asked. "These are real people whose lives are affected."

"Because you already take yourself too seriously and will get even more morose if you believe the future of humankind and civilization and the price of oil all depend on whether you do the right thing. All you can do is your best with God's help. How people respond is up to them. That's true in a lawsuit and in life."

"Julie," Vince said, "you're a philosopher, psychologist, and theologian all wrapped up into one."

"Are you serious?" she asked.

"As serious as you are."

Zach turned to me. "If you decide to talk to Dabney, maybe I should go along."

"Thanks," I said gratefully. "I might need the moral support."

I WARMED UP THE SUPPER prepared by Gracie while Mrs. Fairmont napped in the den.

"Did you have a nice day at work?" she asked when we sat down at the dining room table.

"It was interesting," I answered with a sigh.

"So many people don't really enjoy what they do for a living. They think a job is a way to collect a paycheck and good fringe benefits. Harry loved architecture because he could create something that would last. I got a sad call today. One of the first houses he designed in Savannah is going to be torn down to expand a parking lot for an office park. Can you imagine? We ought to drive over to the house so you can see it before it's gone. Would you like to do that?"

"Yes, ma'am."

Mrs. Fairmont was having a good day and kept me entertained with stories from the past during the meal. She didn't mention seeing the condemned house again until I finished putting the dishes in the washer.

"Are you ready to see the house?" she asked.

"Yes, ma'am. Do you want me to drive?"

"I think that would be safer," she answered with a smile. "My independence probably stops at the street."

She gave directions as we left the historic district.

"It was an innovative bungalow," she said, telling me to turn at the next traffic light. "So many houses built for middle-class families in Savannah after World War II had no flair, but Harry studied what was being done with smaller homes in California and brought some of it here. I wish I could remember the name of the first couple that owned the house. I can see the wife's face in my mind. Her husband had been an officer in the army."

We turned down a street that had gone through the transition from residential to commercial. At the end of the street was a single-story brick building that contained the offices of an insurance agency, a CPA firm, and two lawyers. A bulldozer was parked at the edge of the paved area. Orange ribbons marked the perimeter of another building.

"This is it," Mrs. Fairmont said.

We turned into the parking lot. There was an architectural rendering of a building identical to the present one with a notice across the bottom that spaces would be available for lease in six months. Behind the sign were three houses, two that needed to be torn down and a third that wasn't in as bad shape. Mrs. Fairmont pointed to the third house.

"It's run-down now, but it was very cute when it was owned by people who cared."

The house had an interesting roofline and a pop-out dormer on the second story. The bushes and landscaping had already been scooped from the earth. The lot was totally flat, but the house might as well have rested on the edge of a precipice.

"Do you want to get out?" I asked.

"No, and I'm not sure it was a good idea to come. It makes me sad. Change doesn't always consider feelings. Let's go."

I put the car in reverse. At the end of the road, Mrs. Fairmont told me to turn a different direction. A few blocks down the road I saw a sign for Gillespie Street. We were at the opposite end of the street from the first time Julie and I drove down it.

"Can we turn here?" I asked.

Mrs. Fairmont glanced up. "I wasn't paying attention. We're going the wrong way, but this will work if we circle around."

It was only a few hundred yards to the Southside Church. I slowed down and saw Sister Dabney sitting on the front porch of her house.

"That's the church I've been attending," I said, peering out the window. "And there's the minister's house. She's on the front porch."

Mrs. Fairmont looked out the window. "Let's stop and say hello."

"No, ma'am. You need to get home."

"Where I don't have anything to do except go to bed. You can turn around there," Mrs. Fairmont said, pointing at a pharmacy parking lot.

"Why?"

"So we can be courteous to your minister. What's her name?"

"Reverend Dabney, but everyone calls her Sister Dabney. But I don't think you want to—"

"You're sounding like Christine."

"She's not a typical minister."

"All the more reason to say hello. I like to meet interesting people. And we've gone to all this trouble to leave the house for a ride."

Mrs. Fairmont's jaw was set.

"Okay, but only for a minute."

I pulled to a stop along the curb. Mrs. Fairmont's shiny car looked out of place in the neighborhood. It was dusk and the streetlights were just coming on. When I got out of the car, I glanced toward the porch. Sister Dabney stopped rocking and leaned forward. I looked away and opened the door for Mrs. Fairmont. The old woman got out of the car and held my arm as we walked up the sidewalk to the house. Sister Dabney resumed rocking while we approached.

"Good evening," I said when we reached the front steps. "This is Mrs. Margaret Fairmont, the lady I live with. We were in the neighborhood and—"

"Come join me," Sister Dabney said, standing up.

Mrs. Fairmont leaned on my arm as we climbed the three wooden steps to the narrow porch. She extended a jeweled hand to Sister Dabney, who took it in her plain rough one. Sister Dabney offered her rocking chair to Mrs. Fairmont.

"My aunt Abigail had a porch full of rockers like this," Mrs. Fairmont said when she sat down. "The whole family would sit and rock on evenings like this. Sometimes we ate homemade ice cream."

"I'll get two chairs from the house," Sister Dabney said.

"May I do it?" I asked.

Sister Dabney eyed me suspiciously for a moment, then opened the door.

"Bring out the rocker in the living room and one of the ladder-back chairs."

I entered a small, simply furnished room. There was an old worn rug on the floor without a hint of an antique pedigree. I picked up a red rocking chair and carried it to the porch for Sister Dabney, then returned to get a simple wooden chair for myself. I sat so Mrs. Fairmont was in the middle. She was finishing her story about Aunt Abigail.

"She eventually sold the house in Vernonburg and moved to a retirement community in Florida. The buyer wanted to keep the rockers. Every time I went by the house it made me want a bowl of ice cream."

"I hope we're not intruding," I said.

"You're here because of hope," Sister Dabney answered cryptically.

And with her words the same sensation I'd felt in Mr. Callahan's kitchen suddenly permeated the front porch. I froze in my seat, not wanting to move.

"You know, don't you?" Sister Dabney asked, her eyes meeting mine.

"Yes, ma'am. The same thing happened in Oscar Callahan's kitchen—"

"This isn't a reminder of the past; it's the presence for now," she said, motioning toward Mrs. Fairmont. "For you and for her."

My mouth went dry at the thought that this might be Mrs. Fairmont's time to die. I'd been anxious about the number of her days on earth since arriving in Savannah. God was good, but there were gaps in my trust. Mrs. Fairmont, not listening, was staring off into the shrinking distance.

"What are you afraid of?" Sister Dabney asked me.

"A lot of things," I admitted. "And I have worries, too."

"All that is sin."

"I know."

"But honest confession is the door to forgiveness and freedom. The other day you helped me find the way out of a very dark place."

I started to say something self-deprecating but stopped.

"God used me."

"And he's used you to bless Mrs. Fairmont."

"That's true," Mrs. Fairmont said, coming back from wherever her mind had wandered and turning toward me. "I'm not sure what memories we take with us when we leave this life, but you'll be part of the ones I keep."

"Did you hear that?" Sister Dabney asked me.

"Yes, ma'am."

Mrs. Fairmont folded her hands in her lap, closed her eyes, and rocked slowly.

"There's truth greater than your fears and worries," Sister Dabney continued. "One of those truths is higher hope. Do you know what I mean?"

"No, ma'am."

"It's hope that can't be destroyed by what happens on earth. Circumstances of life will challenge it, voices will deny it, but its walls can't be breached unless we open the gate. It's one of the three things that endure."

"Faith, hope, and love."

"That's right. And you have to see it as a fortress, not a feeling; a place of security in heaven where the devil's arrows can't reach. The enemy has his strongholds. But God has prepared greater ones for his children. There's where your mind has to dwell."

I'd always considered myself a determined person. Sister Dabney's words challenged me.

"I want to live in that place," I said.

"You can."

I glanced at Mrs. Fairmont, whose eyes remained closed.

"And her?"

"You've been part of bringing her to a higher hope, not so much for this life as the one to come."

"How much time does she have?"

Sister Dabney smiled. "If I knew, I wouldn't tell you. It's not my place to issue that decree."

"Is this what you were going to tell me on the day of your deposition?"

"That's still rolling around inside. Do you want to know what I've heard so far?"

"No, I'll wait."

We sat in silence as a chorus of crickets welcomed the darkening sky. A few cars passed in the street. One, with its windows down, slowed. A young man yelled out the window, "The bulldozers will be here tomorrow to tear you down!"

Sister Dabney kept rocking.

"What's going to happen to the church?" I asked.

"That's none of your business," she answered.

"Sorry, I wasn't asking because of the case—"

"But you can tell your boss I've washed my hands of Mr. Paulding and shaken the dust of his sin from my feet. The man who told me about your client's shady business dealings won't be giving any interviews with the newspaper. He's just grateful for the help I gave in healing his relationship with a runaway daughter."

"You're not going to talk to anyone?"

Sister Dabney pointed up. "Except to him."

"Where's Flip?" Mrs. Fairmont asked.

"He's at your house."

"I want to see him," she answered, pushing herself up from the rocker.

I quickly reached out and steadied her.

"Flip is her dog. He's a Chihuahua."

"You'd better get back to him," Sister Dabney said. "I'm glad you stopped by."

I helped Mrs. Fairmont down the steps. At the bottom she turned around.

"I enjoyed your rocking chair. It's so peaceful here."

I'd never associated Sister Dabney with peace.

"Tell Oscar Callahan about our talk," Sister Dabney said to me. "He may not know it, but the gift of God multiplied in my life when his father laid hands on me many years ago."

JULIE, VINCE, AND I sat in the waiting area for Mr. Braddock's office. The partners were all assembled in the main conference room. It was the last day of our summer at the firm.

"Is this what it's like waiting on a jury?" I asked.

"Not really, because our future probably wouldn't be on the line," Julie answered. "Do you think if they don't want to offer a clerk a job, one of them drops a black ball in a little bag?"

"They had a special meeting on Wednesday," Vince replied.

"And I bet Mr. Braddock showed you the minutes," Julie shot back.

Fred Godwin came to the doorway. Since the young partner always looked serious, there was no way to interpret the expression on his face.

"Vince, we're ready to meet with you," he said.

"Good luck," Julie whispered. "You don't need it."

Vince smiled awkwardly and looked at me as he left the room.

"Vinny has a job sewn up," Julie said. "Do you know what he's really worried about?"

"No."

"Whether you're going to blackball him instead of Zach. I know they're praying for you and each other and the rest of the universe, but deep down inside, each of them wants God to send an e-mail awarding him the grand prize as your potential soul mate."

"I'd like to get a message about that, too."

"Which means you're going to have to come back to Savannah after graduation."

"God can speak to me anywhere."

"But there will be clearer reception when you're in the right place."

"That's true," I admitted.

"Yes!" Julie pumped her fist in the air. "It took all summer, but you finally agreed with me."

"Shut up." I smiled. "Are you going to tell the partners you've decided to work with Maggie?"

Julie shrugged. "In the one-in-a-million chance they offer me a job, I'll let them know in writing later. I think it would be more professional to graciously thank them for the offer and promise to get back promptly. In my rejection letter, I may ask Mr. Carpenter to refer Jason Paulding to Maggie, since no one here specializes in criminal cases."

The dispute with Carl McKenzie's company was only one of the problems faced by the developer. Since the motion hearing in front of Judge Cannon, the Dabney case had faded into the background after Paulding was sued by two different companies claiming he owed them money. And there were rumors the U.S. Attorney's office considered him a "party of interest" in an investigation into illegally imported goods from South America.

"Of course, the federal authorities would have to wait until she leaves the district attorney's office," Julie added. "If Maggie ends up with the case, it would be a bonus for you."

"How?"

"You wouldn't have to leave Mr. Paulding behind. Whether you work here or with us, he would be a client."

"That's one very good reason not to return to Savannah."

"The Jason Pauldings of the world are everywhere."

"Yeah."

Julie pumped her fist again. "That's two in a row."

I checked my watch.

"What do you think they did with Vinny?"

"Probably made him partner on the spot."

Fred Godwin appeared in the doorway. "Tami, we're ready for you."

The lawyer left without waiting. Julie grabbed me by the arm.

"If you don't come back in thirty minutes, I'm going to call the police."

"No, call Sister Dabney."

I caught up with Godwin, who didn't speak. When we reached the hallway for the conference room, I saw Mr. Braddock talking to Vince, who had a big smile on his face. The senior partner put his arm around Vince and led him a few steps down the hall. Seeing Vince happy made me feel good. He deserved every opportunity that came his way.

The conference door opened and Zach came out. Since he wasn't a partner, I looked at him in surprise. He saw me and pulled his ponytail.

"What are you doing here?" I whispered, holding back for a moment.

"Answering a few personal questions."

"Are we in trouble?"

"Nothing you can't handle."

Before I could ask anything else, Godwin opened the door and cleared his throat.

"There's a seat for you across from Mr. Carpenter," he said.

I entered a room of men whose staring faces were all focused on me. The next step of my future would be determined by what lay behind those stares. I tried to smile but worried it came out crooked. Mr. Carpenter glanced down at a stack of papers on the table in front of him. I assumed those must be the evaluation forms and memos about me from the other lawyers in the firm.

"Tami," he said, "a lot of clerks have worked here during the thirty-eight years I've been practicing law. But I must say you're one of the most unusual who has ever spent the summer with us."

Being called unusual was nothing new to me.

"It's fortunate that you came along now instead of ten or fifteen years ago. You have an aggressive, independent streak that probably would have led to your firing if I didn't have the experience that enabled me to look beyond your insubordination and see a piece of coal with potential."

Being called a piece of coal was new. I liked jaguar better. Mr. Carpenter continued.

"What happens to a piece of coal if it's placed under intense heat and pressure?"

I knew it either burned up or became a diamond.

"It becomes a diamond?" I responded hopefully.

"Exactly." Mr. Carpenter beamed like a professor who'd helped a dense student understand a new legal principle. "And we believe you have that kind of potential as an attorney. Assuming you complete your third year of law school and successfully pass the bar exam, we would like to offer you a position as an associate here at the firm. The terms of our offer are summarized in this memo. Vince just accepted a position so the two of you would have to fight over the two empty offices upstairs."

My mouth dropped open slightly. I remembered Maggie Smith's words that no female clerk had ever parlayed a summer job at Braddock, Appleby, and Carpenter into a permanent position. My mind sent an instant message to my mouth to accept immediately. I glanced down at the sheet and saw a salary for more money than Daddy made in three years as a supervisor at the chicken plant. And that was just the starting point for the future.

"Thank you very much," I said, making sure I made quick eye contact with all the partners. "I'll take your offer under consideration. When do I need to let you know?"

The surprise on Mr. Carpenter's face likely mirrored the shock on my own. I'd not been able to say yes to the job. I put my hand to my mouth. Mr. Carpenter turned to Mr. Appleby.

"December 1 would be fine," Mr. Appleby replied.

"I agree," Mr. Carpenter replied, regaining his composure. "There's no rush for an answer. Have a good year at school. That's all for now."

I folded the offer sheet in half and stood.

"Thank you for everything," I said, not sure if I was making sense or not.

I stumbled from the room. I met Julie in the hallway as she was being led toward the conference room by one of the other partners. We couldn't speak to each other, but I could see from the puzzled look on her face that she couldn't tell from my expression what had just happened to me. I slipped into the library. Zach was standing near one of the research terminals.

"Well?" he asked.

I held up the sheet of paper.

Zach nodded. "You've got a job."

"Not really," I said, collapsing into the nearest chair. "I didn't accept, at least not on the spot. I asked for more time, and they agreed to give me until December 1."

Zach grinned. "You're giving Mr. Carpenter fits."

"He mentioned that right before he offered me the position. What did they ask you?"

"Background information about your family. Apparently there was concern you might be a religious fanatic."

"I am."

"True, but I reassured them your beliefs and convictions would make you a better employee because you're honest, a hard worker, and very loyal."

"That's nice." I tried to give Zach a look of appreciation.

"And true," he added. "What kept you from accepting?"

"I couldn't say the words. It was strange. My head had one idea, my mouth another."

"And your heart?"

"Yes, it was my heart that hesitated." I put my hand on my chest. "I have to know in here that this is the right thing to do."

"I'd not expect anything less." Zach grinned. "It would be worth being a partner to see Mr. Carpenter's reaction. Did he tell you which area of the firm you'd be assigned to?"

"No."

"They'd probably move you around for a while to see what worked best."

"So I might work with you and Mr. Appleby?"

"Or with Mr. Carpenter."

I sighed. "I need to talk to my parents."

"Yes, but you know what?"

I saw the answer in his eyes. "I'm going to have to pray and decide this myself?"

"Yep."

The door opened. It was Julie. She drew her finger across her throat.

"They let me down easy with a bunch of compliments, but rejection is a cousin to death. What about you?"

I held up the offer sheet again. "They want me."

"I'm not surprised," Julie responded. "Everybody does, including some people who aren't in this room."

IT WAS MY LAST SUNDAY in Savannah. I left Mrs. Fairmont watching the white-haired TV preacher with the colorful choir and drove to Sister Dabney's church. On the way, I passed an office building Julie and Maggie Smith were considering for their new practice. Maggie had confirmed her offer of a job to me in an e-mail I printed out and immediately deleted from the computer before leaving Braddock, Appleby, and Carpenter. The two sheets of paper summarizing the terms of the two jobs were stuck inside my Bible where I wished God would miraculously stamp one "Yes" and the other "No."

I slipped into one of the pews to the rear of the church. The music had already started. They were singing their anthem. Sister Dabney was in her usual place, sitting in the purple rocker on the platform with her eyes closed. When the music faded, I streamed forward with the rest of the congregation for prayer. I didn't try to attract Sister Dabney's attention; however, the thought crossed my mind that she might be God's messenger delivering direction for my future. It would be an efficient way to handle my dilemma. God could use Sister Dabney to tell me where I should work and whom I should marry. But nothing happened. The preacher called out two other people and prayed over them. I remained invisible. But I told myself not to get frustrated. I'd come to hear the message of the morning, and I knew a sermon that changes the heart can be more valuable than specific instructions for the next stop on life's journey.

After the offering was collected, Sister Dabney rose to her feet. She looked directly at me. For once, I didn't feel fear.

"I usually preach to save you from your sins," she said. "Today will be different. I'm going to tell you what God has done for me. Open your Bibles and turn to John chapter eleven, the story of Jesus raising Lazarus from the dead." She directed her gaze away from me while the pages of Bibles rustled across the room. "How many of you believe Jesus' words are as powerful today as when he first spoke them and called Lazarus forth from the grave?"

There was a smattering of agreement across the room. Chills ran across my arms.

"How many of you believe those words can set *you* free from the tombs of this world?" she said, her voice rising.

The ripple of assent increased in volume. I sat up straighter.

"How many of you want to get rid of the grave clothes that bind your hearts, choke your faith, and suffocate your hope?"

Several people shouted. Sister Dabney's eyes flashed with fire.

"He's done great things for me! He can do great things for you! Get ready to hear the Word of the Lord!"

Acknowledgments

I received unwavering encouragement and practical help in writing this novel from Ami McConnell, Allen Arnold, and Deborah Wiseman. Special thanks to my wife, Kathy, a wonderful source of hope in my life.

Reading Group Guide Questions

1. When Tami brings Zach home with her to meet her parents, he's not what they expected or had wished for their daughter. In what ways does he overcome their first impressions? Do you think he is able to stay true to himself in order to convince her parents that he is worthy to court Tami? How or how not? Have you ever found yourself in similar situations where you didn't meet someone's expectations? How did you overcome their first impression?

2. Although Zach does gain permission to court Tami, he still encourages her to find her own path away from her parents'. Do you think that Tami should stay true to her upbringing or should she follow his advice and break away a bit? In your opinion, would Tami be dishonoring her parents should she break away from their faith? Could she still honor them and break away from them? Have you had to make some of the same decisions as Tami?

3. Tami's mother tends to lead with her head whereas Zach tends to lead with his heart. What are some examples of how they do this? What are some examples when they don't? What are the advantages and disadvantages of leading with one's heart and one's head? How do you lead, with your head or your heart?

4. Tami's mother describes Tami as a sum of her parents' parts. What characteristics has she inherited from her mother? From her father? Who else has had an influence on who she is? What characters is Tami helping to shape? Whose parts would you say you are a sum of?

5. Sister Dabney has a unique way of ministering to the needs of her church. What are the different ways she provides for those in need in her community? Do you think that she is effective as the head of a church? How do most people view her—in a positive or negative way? How does Tami feel about her at the end of the book? Is it what you expected?

6. It is obvious from the glimpses we see into Sister Dabney that she does have a gift for knowing the sins and troubles at the heart of those around her. Why do you think she couldn't see the sins of her husband? Do you think she is able to see her own sins? How would you react to someone who listed the sins in your past? This is a pretty powerful ability. How does she handle the power that comes along with the ability? How would you handle it?

7. Julie and Tami come from very different backgrounds. How are they able to strengthen each other (professionally, spiritually, socially)? Do they ever weaken each other; if so, how? Why does Tami come to rely on Julie for this case? What does Tami hope to gain from this friendship? Have you had friendships similar to theirs? What have you gained from those friendships?

8. Describe the character of Mrs. Fairmont. How does she change throughout this novel? What does Tami learn from her? Do you have someone like Mrs. Fairmont in your life? Describe her/him and what you have learned from that person.

9. Tami witnesses Mrs. Fairmont's and Mr. Callahan's glimpses of God. Describe both of those experiences. How are they similar and how do they differ? Why was Zach hesitant to tell anyone about his part in Mr. Callahan's experience? What does Tami learn about herself and her faith from these moments? Have you ever had one of those glimpses of God or witnessed someone having one? How did you react?

10. Tami finds herself in tense situations, both personally and professionally, throughout this novel. What hope does she receive in the midst of those situations? Where does that hope come from? Does she always recognize it for what it is?

Enjoy the best-selling first book in
the TIDES OF TRUTH series.

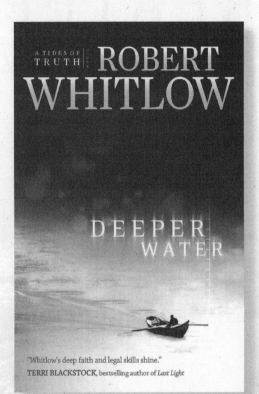

*A complex mix of betrayal and deception quickly
weaves its way through Tami's life—and the case she's
working on—as she uncovers dark secrets about the man
she's defending . . . and the senior partners of the firm.*

GREATER LOVE

Book 3 in the TIDES OF TRUTH series

COMING SPRING 2010

THOMAS NELSON
Since 1798

A poignant tale of
innocence and courage
in the tradition of
Huckleberry Finn and
To Kill a Mockingbird.
Experience *Jimmy,*
a story that will leave you
forever changed.

Can he trust his client's
dreams and
visions—even if
they threaten to destroy
his future?

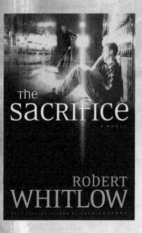

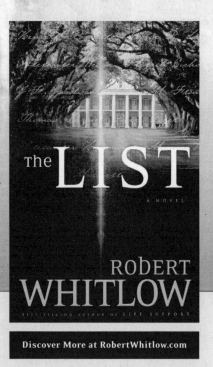